Malevolent Monarch

by

Alexandria Ausman

This book is a work of fiction. Any references to historical events, real people, or real places, are used fictitiously. Other names, characters, places, and events are products of the author's imagination, and any resemblance to actual events or persons, living or dead, is entirely coincidental.

Book cover illustration by Alexandria May Ausman
Editor: Jon M. Ausman

Library of Congress Control Number: 2026902462

ISBN: 978-1-963335-61-3 (ebook)
ISBN: 978-1-963335-60-6 (paperback)

Published By:
Ausman & Cousins LLC
1700 North Monroe Street
Suite 11, Box 284
Tallahassee, Florida 32303-0501

Das Kaiser Haus Series (8 books)

The Rise of the Priceless (Chapters 1 to 10)
Metal Illness (Chapters 11 to 19)
Jonas the Vampire (Chapters 20 to 29)
Prince of the Elders (Chapters 30 to 40)
Leo's Lamb (Chapters 41 to 50)
Mastermind Malfred (Chapters 51 to 58)
Priceless Lost (Chapters 59 to 67)
Broken Silver (Chapters 68 to 74)

The Collar King Series (13 books)

Return to Das Kaiser Haus (Chapters 1 to 7)
Felicity's Child (Chapters 8 to 14)
Tears of the Violin (Chapters 15 to 22)
The Golden Collar (Chapters 23 to 30)
Rise of the Mortar King (Chapters 31 to 38)
Prisoner of the Stone Palace (Chapters 39 to 46)
Mortar Transformation (Chapters 47 to 54)
Taube Returns (Chapters 55 to 62)
Chocolate Dreams (Chapters 63 to 70)
Pocket Soup (Chapters 71 to 78)
Lucus's Revenge (Chapters 79 to 86)
Night of the Stasi (Chapter 87 to 94)
Revenge of the Mortar King (Chapter 95 to 102)

The Most Brutal Man in Europe Series (4 books)

Claus's Revelations (Chapters 1 to 8)
Priceless Changes (Chapters 9 to 17)
Silver Well (Chapters 18 to 25)
Malevolent Monarch (Chapters 26 to 33)
Mortar Combat (coming soon).

The Psycho Series (7 books)

Cemetery Kid Redux (Chapters 1 to 20)
Stop Calling Me Psycho (Chapters 21 to 33)
Motor-Psycho (Chapters 34 to 44)
Delusion of the Collar and the Key (Chapters 45 to 53)
Brutality's Prisoner (Chapters 54 to 64)
Aesthetic Akathisia (Chapters 65 to 74)
Metallic Burden (Chapters 75 to 83)

27 Masters Series (12)

Anita the Benevolent (Chapters 1 to 7)
The Beast and the Witch (Chapters 8 to 16)
High Priestess of Schizophrenia (Chapters 17 to 24)
The Professional Dominatrix (Chapters 25 to 33)
Triangle of Trust (Chapters 34 to 41)
Minute Mistresses (Chapters 42 to 49)

A Secret 28th Master (Chapters 50 to 57)
A Touch Too Much (Chapters 58 to 65)
Bugs in the Wall, Turkeys in the Ditch (Chapters 66 to 73)
Death of a Psycho (Chapters 74 to 81)
A Harbor with a View (Chapters 82 to 89)
The Pig Masters (Chapter 90 to 97)

Stand Alone Books (1 book)

The Grannybat's Weird Tales & Gothic Stories Volume One

Book 4 Characters: Malevolent Monarch

Ada, Lady: a long deceased FemDom entombed in Haus walls
Agnette Krause: the mother of Christian Axel, daughter of Gregor and Ingrid
Alexi: a deceased FemDom
Almut: a former Torture Master who serves Valintin
Amanda: a Haus Torture Mistress
Anna Altergott: a Haus FemDom, member Vampire cult
Attila, Doctor: the Haus physician
Audry Baus: a Haus FemDom, spouse of Fritz
Bartram: a disgraced Dominant,
Birgit: a deceased black collar, lover of Xavier, sister of Viviana
Blum: spouse of Almut
Byron Schmidt: a Haus Dominant, a Voting Council member, son of Xavier and Birgit
Cary: the Shadow King, 1973 to 2024
Christian: the anger and lust shard
Christian Axel Schmidt: a Haus Dominant, the Priceless, son of Xavier
Claus Albrecht: an Elder of the Haus
Cora Reinherz: a Haus Fur Queen
Dämonen: the Demon sharing the shard Maximillian

Der Goldene Hund: the Voice or the Boss shard; the Conscious shard
Der Makellose: Leo's German Shepherd named 'the unblemished'
Die Brutale: three shards melded together; Mad Max, Max, and Christian
Drexel: a deceased Elder
Eric: a Haus Dominant, co-founder of FBL
Evelyn: Noah's deceased mother, a black collar
Felicity: the Mother Lamb, a shard
Florian Schmidt: the first Priceless, deceased
Freidrick Schmidt: a Haus Voter, son of Bernt
Fritz Finck: a Haus Dominant
Geraldine: a lamb that prepares Christian Axel's meals
Gerald: an Albrecht kidnapper of Christian Axel
Gretta Albrecht: a Haus FemDom, the Silk Queen
Grisham Krause: a deceased Dominant
Gustov Krause: a deceased Dominant
Heidi: the deceased Mortar Queen
Helmut: son of Sigrid
Hemmel Krause: a deceased Dungeon Headmaster
Henner: Gretta's deceased German Shepherd
Henri: the deceased Mortar Prince
Hubertus: a former Torture Master who serves Magnus
Ingrid: friend of Sigrid

Ingrid Reinhardt: spouse of Xavier, ally of Claus, sister of Keifer
Ivan: retired captain of the Russian Guard
Jacob Wagner: a Haus Dominant
Jaeger: Jacob Wagner's partner
Jaison: a Black collar Torture Master
Jonas Weiss: an Elder of the Haus. Spouse of Christian Axel
Jon M. Ausman: current Keyholder, Shadow King 2024 to present
Julian Krause: a deceased Dominant
Justus Schmidt: son of Bernt and Ingrid, half-brother to Christian Axel
Karl Krause: deceased elder brother of Malfred
Karstin Baus: a Head Dungeon Mistress
Kilian Altergott: a future Haus Fur King
Lenius: a Haus Dominant, member of Vampire cult
Leo Albrecht: an Elder of the Haus, cousin of Claus
Lucus: a Haus Dominant, a royal
Mad Max: the sadistic shard of Maximillian, aka the Heart and Judgment
Mad Maxx: husband of Meine Liebe; a Haus Dominant
Mad Maxx: the masochistic shard, also the Brain and Guilt
Mad Maxximillian die Brutal: the most brutal man in Europe

Magnus: a Haus Dominant, member of the Wolf Pack
Malfred Krause: a Haus Elder
Malte: a black collar Haus guard
Matz: a Haus Dominant, a pimp and manager
Max: the Soul shard
Maximillian: the seductive shard, the Libido
Maxximillian: the shard controlling the wheel
Meine Liebe: submissive and spouse of Mad Maxx
Mercy: see Snot
Milo: a deceased Haus black collar Torture Master
Nicholas: a black collar head waiter, married to Karstin
Noah: a Dungeon Master, son of Bladrick Reinhardt
Noathen: an executed Haus physician, a sadist
Peter Schmidt: a Dominant of Der Kaiser Haus; uncle of Christian Axel, son of Bernt
Rachel Krause: an American, known as Meine Liebe, designated wife of Christian Axel
Reece Altergott: a deceased clinical psychiatrist
Rolf Schmidt: a Haus voter, son of Derbeck
Roselina: a Haus black collar, spouse of Cary, Dark Bonded to Rolf
Sasha: a Russian Guard
Sebastian: an executed Palace Dungeon Master
Sigrid: a Haus FemDom, candidate to be Christian Axel's Regent
Snot: a dwarf silver collar, later known as Mercy

Superman: a person who lives between the walls of the Haus, the DJ

Taube: a Ram, Taube in German is "Dove"

Valitin: a Haus dominant, a member of the Wolf Pack

Vogal: spouse of Hubertus

Volf: a deceased Dominant, ally of Karl

Vivianna: a deceased Haus FemDom, sister of Birgit

Xavier Schmidt: deceased Fur King, father of Justus, Byron and Christian, brother of Derbeck and Bernt, known as the "Child Killer"

Preface

Christian Axel, also known as Mad Maxximillian, is the Mortar King. It is 1975 and he also holds the title of Collar King and Dungeon Master Supreme. He wears the triple crown. He is approaching his eighteenth birthday as this book begins. He is both an epileptic and a disorganized schizophrenic. He is also the Lord and Master of the Haus. Though the powers of such are often disputed by the Elders occupying the Fur Thrones.

The Haus he lives in is seven stories tall with the Fur King living on the seventh floor, his Five Fur Princes are on the sixth floor. The Silk Queen normally resides on the fifth floor along with her Five Silk Throne occupants. The Mortar King has imposed a death sentence on the Silk Queen. As long as she is pregnant the death sentence cannot be imposed. Her husband is Mad Maxximillian's half-brother.

There are three royal positions in the Haus. Sometimes they work together. Most times they oppose the other two.

Mad Maxximillian assassinated his father, Xavier, who was also known as The Child Killer. In turn, the five Elders took turns using Maxximillian as a sexual plaything. On the first Throne and temporarily acting as the Fur King since the Fur Queen is imprisoned in the Pit, is Claus who has a regularly schedule sexual session with Maxximillian on each Thursday at one in the afternoon.

Occupying the next Fur Throne is Jonas, a former agent with the Soviet military intelligence agency, who assumed his position at the end of World War Two. He married Mad Maxximillian in order to control his money and destiny. He has also adopted Maxximillian as his son. He regularly and forcibly sexually abuses Maxx.

The third Throne is held by Leo. This Prince loves Maxximillian. He is prone to play a waiting game in his disputes with Jonas. It makes him appear weak but some know there is steel in his spine.

Mastermind Malfred holds the fourth Throne. He escaped the Nazis while on a train to a concentration camp. He then expended numerous family members in his effort to gain power within the Haus. He recently discovered the Maxx was a cousin and has lost all interest in pursuing a sexual relationship with Maxx since Maxx is family.

The fifth Throne is held by Justus, the son of Bernt, Xavier's brother. Justus knows the history of the Haus and used Maxximillian to get to the fifth Throne. However, loyalty is not his strong point.

There are more persons than those listed above who are fighting for power within the Haus. Byron, a steroid loaded sexual sadist, is the half-brother of Mad Maxx. He wants to own Maxx. Sigrid, a woman of beauty who does the dirty work for the House leadership. Lucus, a relative of British royalty who is determined to be named Mad Maxx's Regent. Peter, the deposed Fur King who wants to return to power. Ivan, the 'retired' captain of the Russian Guard that prevents unapproved people from entering and leaving the Haus.

Finally, there is the top leadership of the Stasi who want their annual payment from the Haus full of war criminals. They also want each year for two promising submissives to be sacrificed to middle rank and rising Stasi officers as a reward at their annual December winter holiday event. Unknown to these Stasi officers is that the top leadership films the slaughter.

Finally, there is Meine Liebe who twice before was brought to the Haus as an infant. She is now a three year old living in the United States. The Haus Elders have approved of her since she met all the Legends of the Haus that prophesied about the rise of the Mortar Queen. There will be future battles over her. There're a multitude of powerful opponents who if they cannot cause the demise of the Mortar King have a backup plan to stop the rise of the Mortar Queen.

This is the fourth book of Mad Maxximillian's story recorded in "The Most Brutal Man in Europe" series. The tale of the Mortar Queen is told in the "Psycho" series and "27 Masters" series.

Language in Italics is the Mortar King, Mad Maxximillian, talking to his future candidate to be his

Mortar Queen, Meine Liebe. A question the two wonder about is will it ever be safe, once she hits eighteen, to bring her to Das Kaiser Haus.

Chapter 26: Crypt Keeper

I glared at Superman with fury as I bellowed, "How dare you mock the honorable Jacob, rapist scum. If I were you, I'd pray I don't recover my strength. Because if I do, I intend to send you to the bottom of these stairs."

The DJ chuckled deeply then replied, "You keep forgetting that I have the superhuman power of flight, ja? I also think at this moment you're in no condition to be threatening anyone other than the weakest of mice."

It took all I had to but I managed to stand up to full height as I responded angrily, "If that's so, then I demand you fight with me like the man. Or are you too much the coward to spar with the Mortar King while he's conscious and capable of proper defense, hmm?"

He shook his disheveled head slowly. "I don't understand why you so pissy with me, Robin. I'm not responsible for the cruelty shown to you by Batman and his vampire crooks. You should've learned by now that his superpowers are nothing more than slights of the hand. He uses his vast wealth and lies to fool the people of Gotham City into believing him the truthful hero."

My jaw nearly hit the floor as I stared at him in full shock. "What the holy fuck are you talking about, you idiot? There isn't anybody in the Haus named Batman, and I'm sure as shit not this Robin guy you seem to think I am. Maybe I go find him and ask him if you're drugging and raping him too. I bet he'd be more than happy join me in my quest to see you burned at the stake for jour crimes against the King."

Superman's expression appeared confused as he replied in the near whisper, "You really think Robin will be interested in helping you set more fires than you already have? Ah, well I'm kind of surprised to hear this about him. I'd always believed him to be the soft hearted. Guess, I'd better watch my back anytime he comes around. Thanks for the warning. You're the good friend." He shot me a relieved smile.

"What the fuck is wrong with you? You're not making a damned bit of sense. Oh, never mind. I suppose this is what I get for attempting the rational conversation with the madman. Look Superman, I know I agreed to provide you with special services upon your request, but since we made that agreement, things have happened that have impaired my skills. The problem is fixed and I require only the temporary reprieve from seeing your desires compensated. However, until Doctor Attila grants me medical release, I must insist you ask me before taking your sport. Say that you understand, and your past rude manners shall be forgiven." I held out my bandaged hand to shaken on it.

He backed away from my offer of peace and stuttered out, "Wait, you mean you think that I've, you know, lain with you? Nein, I've done no such the thing. Not yet, and not ever. Robin, you call me the madman but it's obvious you're the crazy one between us if you mistake me for the stud taking mount with you. Or maybe you're more in need of glasses than the break from special services."

I snorted loudly then replied in the sharp tone, "Fine, deny it if it pleases you. I need not hear your confession to sooth my troubled soul. The damage has already done anyway. It's merely enough to hear you say that you'll keep your bloody hands off me until I say it's safe to see our agreement fulfilled."

Superman shook his head wildly as he responded, "As you say Robin. I'm the patient man. I'm in no hurry to taste your skills. I would prefer that you move faster in getting me that mouse and the partridge in the pear tree."

My eyes rolled as I replied, "The mouse, well I can get one of those for you by tomorrow. As for that partridge, I'll get that beast too. Soon as you tell me what the hell it is and where one of them can be found."

His irritation was apparent as he said, "Are you deaf too? I already told you they live in the pear tree, you fucking fool."

I sucked in my breath doing the best I could to ignore the horrific pain in my hindside as I responded in the growl. "Fair enough. I'll hunt in the orchards over the next few days. Now that we've gotten that out of the way. I politely request that you give me something of worth in equal service for the ones you already have taken without asking."

Superman's seemed to regain his composure as he replied, "Ah, okay. what favor do you want?"

A gasp escaped my throat as I said angrily, "Not the favor that I'm asking for dammit. I desire the payback only. Give me the instructions on the best way to leave the house without having to exit through the guarded doors."

He stared at me for the moment with what I thought was humor in his expression before he answered in the whisper, "That's an easy answer, Robin. To do that, you just go out one of the windows. This is the fun game you've designed. Now, it's my turn to give the riddle for solving, ja?"

"God dammit superman. This is not the fucking game. I want to know how you manage to get out of the house without being seen by anyone." I roared both in pain and total frustration.

Superman took off down the dungeon staircase with silent speed as he called back, "I wait till everyone is busy having their breakfast in the Great Hall, Robin. See you tomorrow. Don't forget to bring that mouse you promised me."

And just like that he seemed to evaporate into the darkness like the otherworldly vampire I was beginning to believe him to be.

I knew that Noah was in need of being relieved of his duty as the temporary dungeon mistress, but at that moment, I knew traveling down the steps could prove deadly. The pain was near paralyzing levels. It also occurred to me that Lucus wasn't going to be thrilled over my arriving back to his care late. So, with a great deal of regret I abandoned my plans to retrieve him.

However, it didn't take but the few staggering steps for me to figure out that making it to the fourth floor apartment was likely impossible too. With the groan of misery, I used the wall for support and redirected my journey in the direction of Doctor Attila's office.

When I arrived the good doctor was just locking up his clinic door. He saw me approaching slowly, in obvious agony.

"Your Majesty, don't attempt to move another step. I'm coming to assist you."

I nodded and whimpered in the weak response, "I thank you for the mercy of it, doctor." With those words I collapsed to my knees.

The sweat was pouring from my forehead as the kind physician approached. He didn't take the time to ask any questions but instead gently wrapped his arms around me to aid me in regaining my footing.

In the anxious mumble I blurted out, "Please don't tell Lucus about the condition you find me in. He's sure to offer argument in allowing me to enjoy my daily freedom from his disgusting grips if he knew this accident has happened."

Doctor Attila groaned under the addition of my near dead weight as he replied, “Let me guess. Superman fed you drugged chocolate, then raped you while unconscious yet again.”

I couldn’t hide the surprise in my tone as I responded, “Ja, exactly. I know you warned me to stop eating the found sweets, but I swear I forgot your good advice, doctor.”

He nodded with the snort. “Ah, well thankfully I kept you safe from your shoddy memory long enough that this time, a little painkiller will likely be all that’s required to fix the damage.”

I moaned out in relief upon hearing this good news and with all my remaining strength did my best to help him help me to the clinic examination room of his choice.

Without hesitation he quickly assessed the, uhm, damage. He shook his head and uttered several curses under his breath but to his credit he made sure his accusations weren’t directly leveled at me.

I licked my lips in eager anticipation as I watched him fill one of his needles with the glorious pain killing tonic. He didn’t have to asking me twice to see that I offered up the willing hip for his stick of the medication.

While the magical liquid caressed my veins with the relief I desired with all my being, I decided to asking the doctor about something that had been bothering me for quite some time.

"Excuse me, heir doctor. It's come to my attention that for some this anal sex business doesn't seem to cause them much trauma. I've even heard it said that the pain that's common in the beginning of the act is usually calmed over time, and with practice. This isn't the experience I've encountered over my long experience with it. I there say it's never gotten easier nor less painful. Is this rumor I've heard around the halls only the myth or is there perhaps something wrong with me?"

Doctor Attila withdrew his empty sharp and sighed loudly before staring directly into my eyes to say, "I thought that one of the horrible men that misuses you had explained to you that for some anal sex is always torment without any improvement. In fact, for many both male and female this is the reality. For some there are psychological reasons this kind of sexual act is unpleasant. For others there are physical anomalies that are responsible for the intense pain of it. As I've already explained to Lucus, Jonas, and that so called Doctor Peter several times already, you'll always suffer worse than almost anyone else because you're plagued by both issues. However, I fear that my insistence that day to prevent your engaging in this kind of sex has fallen upon deaf ears."

I glared at him feeling the fury rising from deep within as I replied, "You told them several times, you say. Am I hearing you correctly that despite learning this information about my desperation they cause over there chronic enforcement of this hideous and unwanted act they decided to ignore your medical advice?"

He nodded and cleared his throat seeming to become anxious suddenly as he responded, "Ja, I believe that's what I just said."

I sat up with speed, which caused the doctor to flinch as I growled out, "And does this condition you say I suffer have the name? Or is this something exclusive to me only?"

Doctor Attila stammered, "Uhm, nein. This disease is well known to those men that find sexual interest in anal sex. It's called anodyspareunia. This basically means there is no pleasure nor improvement in the pain during the penetration action."

The fires of hell surely showed in my gaze as I bellowed at the doctor with fury. "Are you telling me they all knew about this condition and that I had it all this time but they never bothered to tell me about it? Those fucking motherfuckers."

I jumped from the exam table and motioned the now trembling doctor to assist me in pulling my breeches up. He moved with stealthy quickness but his demonstration of anxiety remained observable the entire time that it took him to return me to the condition of dress he'd found me in.

Neither of us shared another word, until I made the move to storm angrily from his office.

"Your Majesty, I don't assume you'd be interested to know this. However, you should be aware that attempting to confront men that we already know care nothing for the cruelty they inflict isn't likely to bode well for the continuation of either my employment as your doctor or for the future of my fine health, ja?"

I turned to look upon this fellow that had done nothing but show me extreme kindness since his arrival in my dark world. His slight frame was demonstrating the mildest of tremors. In that moment, I thought of how difficult it must be for this merciful man to stomach watching his hard labors fail to reach there zenith due to no fault of his own. The foul grunting, taunts then agonized screams of his foul predecessor Noathen echoed in the wheel room.

Like it or not, I decided it was best to heed his wise words and keep my new awareness of my unfortunate affliction to my own counsel. If for no other reason than that if I hoped to survive long enough to attempt to escaping the Haus, having the finest medical staff available was the must. Ha.

"I'd wish you the peaceful night, heir doctor. But, since I've not seen you this day such pleasantries would be impossible to offer you, ja?"

Doctor Attila smiled slightly as he nodded and replied, “Indeed it would, your majesty. I’d thank you for the mercy of it if I’d seen you, of course.”

With the nod of understanding, I returned to the journey that was already overdue by many minutes. I swallowed back the feelings of dread as I hauled serious ass towards the main staircase. I knew it was going to take one hell of the perfect acting job and the most clever lie to prevent Lucus from discovering that I had become enlightened to the degree of torture he and the others had so brutally enforced upon me for years.

Keeping my violent son Maxximillian Der Dameon from destroying each of them over this injustice was going to prove harder than I’d ever imagined it could be. Truth is that this indignity wasn’t really the worse thing any of them had done to us. Maxximillian didn’t believe we should allow it to continue without punishment.

Thanks to Doctor Attila’s wonderful pain killers I was capable of moving with easy once again. I managed to make back up to the apartment of Mad Lucus from my starting point of the clinic very quickly. I snuck a glance at the Haus clock and the groan of irritation escaped me immediately. I was more than forty-five minutes late. Lucus was sure to be pissy over my tardy return.

I stashed the cane Jonas had returned to me into the back of my breeches. then after taking a deep breath to steady my nerves I knocked lightly on the door with the head of that fancy walking stick Fritz had gifted to me. Within I could hear Lucus's footsteps and the sounds of his cursing my name. He swung open the wooden entry with the expression of fury on his face. "Well, well, seems you've managed to find your way home at long last Christian Victor. I was about to call on the Guard to see if perhaps it was necessary I come identify your dead body. Because surely you must have been killed if you'd not managed to keeping your word to your master, ja?"

I glared at him with anger in my gaze equal to that of his own as I replied in the low growl, "I hadn't heard the rumor that you possessed the submissive, Lucus. Where is that poor wretch that's you've purchased while I've been away attending to my kingly duties? I wish to caste my eyes upon the creature that's become the most unfortunate bastard that ever set foot in this Haus to offer my honest pity to him."

Lucus snorted and moved aside to allow me to come in unencumbered as he responded, "Do you believe insulting me is the smart thing to do, Christian Victor? I suppose this fantasy near brush with death that you're going to try to claim kept you from meeting your curfew wasn't enough thrill to see your death wish quenched. If this is the truth of it, then by all means do everything possible to increase my fury with you. Otherwise, I suggest you keep your cruel words to yourself. Beware, boy, I'm more than interested in finding reason to kick your ass tonight. Especially after the nasty way you addressed me this morning."

Without much effort I knocked him into the door jamb while I rushed past him into the living area. "Aw, my poor little lamb, did telling you the truth hurt your tender heart? I'd apologize to you for that, but honestly, I could care less if you find it distasteful that you're not the only one playing games in this Haus. Best that you remember that you're not the only man in this apartment capable of mindless brutality. Let's be honest with each other Lucus, I'm far more experienced in torture then you'll ever be in your most fevered dreams."

Lucus maintained his place at the door glaring at me while I quickly and quietly took a seat on his fine leather sofa.

Once I appeared comfortable he cleared his throat then said in the voice tone strained with underlying fury, "This you say about your champion ability to be cruel I don't dispute. Not too many souls are left in this Haus that haven't either tasted your shit fits or at the very least been witness to them. However, this fact should be of no consequence in the relationship between the malicious Mortar Monarch and his soon to be regent. Must I remind you nightly of the agreement you have sworn to me? The moment the clock strikes nine in the evening your powers and will belong to me, the Mad Lucus."

I snorted loudly then replied in a voice dripping with mocking humor. “The Mad Lucus, you say? Ah, so the rumor that my affliction is of the contagious sort are the truth of it, ja? Well, well, I offer my sincerest condolences for your misfortunes, my poor little lamb. Guess you shouldn’t have impulsively been sticking your cock where it does not belong. Nor ignore warnings of the bad things that become of those that think they know better on how to avoid the punishing flames than the King of Hell, himself.”

Lucus frowned deeply then with suddenness rushed toward my place on the couch. I flinched and coward involuntarily with the speed equal to that of his movement. He stood there in front of me, his lips curling upward in the condescending grin watching without blinking as I did my best to recover from that momentary panic attack he’d caused me.

The Dominant crossed his arms and chuckled under his breath as he said, “Funny that you bring up that devastating element, Christian Victor. Seems your obsession with fire has once again devoured the population of your own people. Tell me, with so much innocent blood on your hands how do you even sleep at night? Are the screams the I often hear you making during your slumbering about the abominable things done to you since your childhood or the horrible things you’ve inflicted upon others in response to that trauma?”

“Shut your fucking mouth, Doctor Freud. If I wished to receive the healing counselor, you’d sure as shit be the last man on earth I’d consider for the job. Now, I’m hungry. Why don’t you give me reason to believe you’re not completely worthless? Call down to the Haus kitchen and order me some wurst and kraut. Then get out of my sight before I resolve that one of the many, many others in this hell hole would be the better choice to speaking as my tongue.” I leaned back into the overstuffed cushion doing my best to appear confident.

Lucus’s stance of arrogance seemed to become less sure. He shifted slightly and dropped his folded arms. I didn’t break from his gaze. I was honestly hoping to see fear creeping into his consciousness that I may indeed utter another name during my interment ritual (that was now only a few months away). To my dismay, this pervert didn’t show any symptoms of anxiety in the least. He is either the finest of actors or the professional gambler.

Instead of the trembling and begging me to forget these unnamed competitors, his smile grew in size, and underlying cruel thrill, as he replied, “I am also the famished fellow, you know. If your stomach aches for filling, I’ve just the thing to sate us both. Get your useless ass up and head for the bedroom. As your faithful servant, I’m happy to fetch your supper for you, your Majesty.”

Without a second of hesitation I leaned forward and growled out, “Fuck you, Lucus.”

He laughed loudly then replied, “Stop flirting, Christian Victor. I’m the honorable Dominant and won’t do as you ask until the doctor says you’re healed properly. I only intend to gain the taste of your skill set that’s not forbidden at this moment. This stalling tactic, hasn’t worked in the past nor will it tonight.” He pointed in the direction of his bedroom.

I leaned even closer to him and in a deadly serious sounding tone said, “I think you misunderstanding me. I don’t offer to play your mare, fool. I intend to retire to that nasty cock bed of yours directly. But once there, it will be you on your knees tolerating my mount until I reach apex. Though I’d thought of having a bit of food to aid in my ability to ride you in the manner you’ve earned. So, I can eat first, or you kin. Up to you Lucus. Afterall, I never wish it said that I’m not the fair lover.”

That response wasn’t one Lucus expected. His eyes vent wide and his smile melted while his jaw fell slightly agape. For several minutes, silence filled the air. then at last he found his words.

“You surely don’t really expect that I’m going to let you force me into the position of submission in my own bed. That’s not how our relationship works.”

With the snicker I replied, “It doesn’t? Ah, I seem to recall you’ve sworn to me that we are the perfect team. Two sides of the same coin, you said. I’m your Majesty and you are my Lord. This you said, ja? Well, if this is the truth of it I must say that I don't recall Doctor Attila giving instructions that you can't endure penetration. Ah, but I suddenly understand why you're upset. You think I'm being unequal in my service demands of you. Well, I can assure you that I'm the fairest of Monarchs in the land. I'll see that your baser needs are met in the service you've made clear you desire after I've found my own are satisfied. You've no further arguments to refuse me, ja? Unless that is, that you're a dirty, rotten, lying, bastard with no honor When it comes to fulfilling his contracts with his partner I am the Mortar King and Master of this fucking Haus." I glared at him willing all the hate possible to seep from my gaze into his own.

Lucus stammered, "W, w, wait. I don't recall any details or discussions about our positions in the bedroom when we redefined our agreement. You only requested to be left to your own devices from the hours of nine to nine. After that you return to this apartment and resume your services to me as I request them. If this is the fact, then be aware that enduring your penetration isn't my pleasure. I've already told you I don't enjoy that kind of sex act. Before you argue with me over it, I can say with certainty I hate it. I politely ask that you do recall I've become the very experienced man at it thanks to your harshly sentencing me to be misused by the Guard."

I stood up with suddenness and Lucus backed away appearing fearful at last as I yelled, "End this noise and get to the bedroom lover. I care not to hear this grumbling about what bothers you. By your own admission you've become accustomed to unwanted, painful sex. That's lucky for you because I intend to rape you soundly and often, my pet. Why are you still refusing to obey? Move it or I'll break it." I pulled Milo's cane from its hiding place in my breeches and swiped the air just inches from his nose.

Lucus responded by jumping backward away from me as he shouted, "Nein, nein. Jonas has returned Milo's cane to you? Why the fuck would he be this stupid? Surely, he understands you cannot be trusted with the weapon of any kind."

The most maniacal laughter erupted from me while I pulled the cane up where we both could view it with ease as I replied, "The Vampire knows how to honor contracts unlike you, my pet. Long ago he swore he'd return my things to me after I'd broken my metal. I did, and so he did as he said he would. I'm not surprised to discover that the bastard that mislead me into false servitude doesn't possess the understanding of the meaning of keeping one's promises. It must be embarrassing to realize that even the foul Bat is the more honest man between the two of you. Screw this. I withdraw my interest in demonstrating my true affection for you, Lucus. I think I'll go to one of the others and find out if they are willing to see me pleased to completion." I started to limp toward the apartment door.

The pervert didn't attempt to prevent my trip until I was already at the entry trying to figure out how to unlock it with my useless fingers.

"Hold on a moment, Christian Victor. Perhaps you'd be agreeable to adding a few codicils to our original contract. Ones that will outline our roles within this partnership in the way that could bring us both a bit of peace, ja," he called out from behind me in the near whisper.

I continued to fumble at his locks and without looking back snorted, "You ignored my demands to leave me alone, then steal my apartment, put me into this blasted piece of yellow metal, sold me out to that bitch Gretta, left me to rot in the palace for months, and continue to fuck me over in ways too disgusting to speak aloud, and you desire to continue that rude behavior without any hope of even the most minor service return that offers me any amount of comfort. Yet, without any sense of remorse you still think to request I work out with you details on the contract you've already signed in your own blood willingly? Forget it Lucus. You're not worthy of my tongue. Not to use for speaking for me nor for your own pleasures. Now, open this fucking door and I will take my leave of you. Without the goodbyes and without any nasty kissing."

I felt Lucus's hand fall gently onto my shoulder just as he mumbled, "Please, Christian Victor. I beg you to stay. If only long enough to hear what I offer in exchange for the honor of serving as your humble regent."

I shrugged off his grip with violence and spun around. Lucus's face took on the expression of extreme stun but his legs held him to his spot within my striking distance. You could hear the pop of my cane on his cloth clad thigh for many seconds before the pain of it overtook the pervert's consciousness. He led out the wail of agony while his hands rushed to sooth the sting of my direct hit.

"Get your filthy hands off me, worm. You beg as poorly as you fuck. On your knees if you desire my ears entertain your worthless pleas for mercy." I pointed at my boots.

The shady Dominant fell to his knees with grace akin to that of the lame Billy goat. I towered above him glaring down upon this idiot trying to decide if killing him was worth the punishment I would surely get for it.

He didn't give me much time to consider my options.

"Your Majesty, I beg of you to grant mercy to this most unworthy of your servants. If you're the great monarch that all believe you to be, you'll grant my petition to add the minor stipulations to the contract we share. I don't expect to gain something at your expense exclusively. I know you are seeking relief in our partnership and I'm prepared to sacrifice something that can do this for my King."

My brows raised in mild surprise as I replied, "Oh you are? Normally I would crush you without care, but I must admit Lucus. You have awakened my curiosity. However, before you speak another word to piss me off further, I must warn you there isn't anything that can bring me comfort when soon I will be forever buried and forgotten in the bowels of this Haus. Tell me. what is it you think you could possibly offer the dead man that would quicken his cold, lifeless heart? Do you really expect me to believe you are willing to submit without argument to my perverted affections? Nein, you've made that very clear because you are on the floor and not the bed. Perhaps now that you finally recognize I'm no longer the psychotic that's easily fooled you've decided to remove your metal trash from around my throat, ja?"

Lucus groaned loudly, "Even if I want to you know damned well I cannot remove the gold collar, Christian Victor. The moment you step foot out of my care with the bare neck, the Silk Queen has the right to retaliate before her death sentence is carried out. Like it or not, that agreement I made with her to see you free of the palace until you're eighteen is still valid. No matter her transgressions against you or me, the Haus law is on her side in this situation."

With the nod I replied, "You always have the answer that works in your favor for everything, don't you? Never mind. It's things like contracts you make behind my back with my enemies that add weight to my thinking you're not the correct choice for Mortar

Regent. Now unlock the door or I will murder you and figure out how to hide your body where no one finds it." I pushed him backward with my foot.

"Re-negotiate our contract, and I will purchase the finest lambs available in Eastern Germany. Enough to fill the Mortar King's stables to bursting. You can visit them every day while free of the palace and I swear that after the interment I will sneak you out to see them even at the risk of my death." His desperate words flew from his lips while he attempted to regain his balance from my boot clad assault.

That caused me to pause, momentarily.

Then with the foulest of sneers I responded, "You going to have to do better than that, Lucus. Petting the soft lambs won't make the rough sex you force on me any easier to suffer. Nor will the hope of a daily visit with them bring me much peace while I waste away in the stoney hell below."

An audible gulp escaped him as he nodded frantically and replied, "This you say is the truth. I'd not expect you to settle this dispute so easily because as you say you're not the psychotic fool. So, I maintain my offer of the lambs, my promise to see you visit them even after you return to your palace and I will give you the answer to one of the questions you've been denied. Nein, I will do better than that. I will take you to view the horror they have hidden away from you with your own eyes, your Majesty." He bowed his head low as he said that.

I narrowed my eyes and knelt down to his level as I said, "You have gone mad. Do you honestly think taking me to see more horrors than I've already been cursed to view would be something of interest to gain the upper hand on me, Lucus? Try harder or shut the fuck up and leave me alone for good."

The pervert shot me the glance tinged with pure terror as he whispered, "But you say you desire balance if your fate is to bear the pain of the palace and your place of submission to me in our bed. This answer I offer you can do this for you. It's the equal sacrifice for me because I risk my life to give it to you. I swear it on the grave of my own beloved mother."

I scoffed then backhanded him with my bandaged hand as I screamed out, "If you desired to share secrets you should have told me the one about the fucking Mortar Palace before I found it out the hard way, asshole."

My blow opened up Lucus's bottom lip. Blood flowed from the split flesh while he tried in vain to stanch the flood with his right hand. To my shock he refused to flee from my obvious rage.

He glared at me with what seemed to be the pitiful expression as he replied softly, "I cannot turn back time, but if I could that mistake is the only one I'd fix. Since this is only the fantasy, I instead offer you the opportunity to do what I cannot for you or for them. You've voiced it many times that you suspect there are others that are condemned to far worse than what is in your future, your Majesty."

I was dumbfounded by his words as I stammered out, "Huh? What do you mean I merely suspect others are condemned to horrible futures? Do you think I am a total idiot? Nein, you think I am blind. Look around you, Lucus. There is tragedy in every fucking corner of this nightmare Haus. Not even the grounds are free of the bones of despair. I care nothing for the secrets to more of it that you wish to unburden from your soul. If you really wish to gain my ultimate loyalty and honest affections then tell me you will take me with you away from this dreadful place. Will you do this, Lucus? Save me and I swear on my life I give you my loyalty, my heart, my body, and my soul till the day the earth claims me for her own." I pushed his hand away from his bloody lip and put my hands around his face to force him to look at me.

Lucus's eyes began to fill with tears as he said through trembling lips, "Do you know how badly I wish I could do as you ask me, Christian? To hear you say this to me is making my heart break in the way I never knew was possible."

My gaze soften to that of pure adoration as I responded, "But you can do this, Lucus. And I can do it too if you take me away from here. I will even prove it by being everything you desire while you making the arrangements to make this happen. What do you say? We have the agreement, ja?"

He shook his head and pulled my hands off his face as he said in the bitter tone, "Christian, I'm as much the prisoner as you are to this Haus of horror. I thought after the truth of our situation was proven to you by Gretta's betrayal of you to become the plaything of our real oppressors you'd figured that out. I suppose you think if given the choice I'd choose to live among the monsters that call this place home. Well, you're mistaken my love. What I wouldn't do to go home to England or hell for that matter anywhere else in the wide world but here." Tears broke from his eyes and streamed down his checks as he said this.

I sat there staring at him unsure if I should believe what he was saying or call him on his attempt to bluff. Then with suddenness I recalled something that made me sure he was lying.

"You managed to see that Reece was fired from Heslach, Lucus. I've heard you threaten many that with only a word you could see them destroyed by the powerful royal bloodlines you share with others outside this Haus. Do you expect me to believe that given the evidence I've been witness to, you're incapable of gaining favor that would see you out the front door? I call bullshit."

Lucus dropped his eyes to the floor appearing shameful as he replied, "I didn't get Reece fired. Okay, that's not completely accurate. I did, but not directly. You see, when we went to the stables I told Gretta that Reece was giving you medication that was creating a dangerous psychotic symptom. I lied and told her that Reece was taking advantage of this and purposely making you think she was the enemy. I reported that I had it on the best authority that Reece intended to use your weakened state to see her assassinated, so Kilian could take her throne. She went to the Elders and reported this. It was that bastard Jonas that pulled the strings to see Reece fired. He's the only one in the Haus with such ability to leave as he pleases. Plus he has connections and money to make sure this was done without even Killian being aware of the identity of the man that made it happen. As for the other threats you've heard me voice, well since no one really knows the nature of my relationships outside of the Haus I'm able to bluff with ease. There, now you know that I'm the Dominant with the big bark but with no teeth to back it up, ja? Is this humiliation enough to gain your interest in renegotiation with me or does it end my chances to be your champion?"

I rolled my eyes then took back to standing. "Open this fucking door before the realization of just how much damage you have done to me sinks into my soft brain. I'd hurry if I were you. I surely will kill you if that happens. As it is, I'm done with this conversation, Lucus. More than that I'm done with you."

Lucus stood up with speed and wailed out, "Wait, okay, I see you're very angry with me over this latest information I've shared, and that's expected. I'm going to do as you ask me and let you leave this moment. But before you go, I insist on giving you the directions to locate that answer I've offered in return for renegotiation of our contract. I know you are the honest man and no matter what you say, you're heart isn't cold nor dead to the pain of others. If you do seek this answer to the question you've asked and find it, then I'm more than sure you'll return to me ready to make the additions I've requested."

Without waiting for my response he rushed off into the bedroom leaving me there to fume over this latest confession of his and stalling me from getting my supper.

To my relief he wasn't gone very long. The pervert returned with the small piece of paper in his hand.

He pushed it at me while he said, "These directions are correct, but be sure to memorize them before you head into the darkness. One wrong step and you'll need not worry about the palace nor who you name the regent. There are things in the dark capable of sending you to the devil before you even know you're gone. Don't stray from the path, ja?" With those words he began to hurriedly undo his many locks on the door to see me released from his hold.

Curiosity overtook me. Before I thought better of it I glanced at this 'makeshift map' he'd given to me. A gasp of horror escaped me which caused Lucus to halt his hasty unbuckling of the door.

He smiled as he said in the calm tone, “I don’t ask you how you come by it, but I already aware you have snagged the spare key to the Mortar Palace. Wherever you’ve stashed it, I suggest you retrieve it. This trip to find your answer can’t be granted otherwise.”

Lucus opened the wooden entry and stepped aside. He bowed low while I pushed past him still feeling the hot pricking of fury within my veins. I limped as quickly as possible down the fourth floor hallway determined to ignore this strange map that Lucus said held the answer to one of the questions I’d asked in the past. I suppose it’d been the wise thing to demand he remind me of which of the many, many questions I’d asked but as usual I’d been too disinterested in anything he had to say to think of that.

Once I’d traveled down the staircase to the first floor I turned off into the deserted hallway. Though I said I wasn’t interested in learning this answer Lucus was offering, I wasn’t the fool anymore. If I’d ever asked the question, it surely was important for my survival. With some difficulty thanks to my wrapped hands I got that paper maneuvered to the place I could examine it closely.

My heartbeat sped up as my eyes traveled the path Lucus made with the red pen. According to him I was to travel to the dungeon, go through the palace door under the stairs, then past the coronation chamber, the silver gate, the palace throne room itself, and take the left off the path that led to secret staircase that went back up to the physician's office on the first floor.

I had seen that there where many alternate paths that led in many directions when Peter first slipped me to see the dentist during my summer visit to the Mortar Palace. I just assumed these were old pathways that led to the tombs of the ancient dead. During my incarceration, and Noah had noticed it too, I'd often smelled the faint whiff of the long ago deceased.

Because of this undeniable odor, I'd decided that at one time the Mortar Palace had been the burial grounds. Then over the centuries the Haus had expended until it eventually overtook these old crypts, cemetery and likely the church that stood above it.

Then eventually the residents had carved out the Mortar Palace there because by then it was at the center of the Haus foundation and also the only part that was completely original and untouched by time. Including the coffins and bodies of their founders, you know, like the catacombs of Paris, ja?

Maxximillian shook his pretty head as he said, "Pops, I don't know what kind of answer can be found in the graveyard other than the evidence that life is the fleeting bitch. I say we toss this worthless piece of paper and go visit with that foxy Sigrid. Let's see if blessing her with the grace of our tongue is returned in equal service, ja?" His evil sounding laughter over his lusty inuendo filled the wheel room.

With the shudder of anxiety rolling down my hairy spine I replied, "You thinking with the wrong head, son. That woman is more likely to fuck us harder than Lucus in more ways than she already has done. Besides, she's too weak to be our regent. Gretta would see her pitched over the railing the second we named her as the one. Sigrid couldn't even protect her fancy hairdo from the voters Byron, Friedrick and Rolf, remember? Nein. If we choose from the three offering, it cannot be her."

Maxximillian pouted as he said in the whiny voice, "You deny my choice only because you are interested in playing mare to the stallion. This isn't fair to the rest of us. Die Brutale, don't you agree with me that the vixen Sigrid should be the one that speaks for us? Or are you like Mad Maxx in your taste for the man's cuddling?"

Die Brutale growled out angrily, "Nein. we don't enjoy Lucus's nasty touching nor that of any man in this Haus. However, Mad Maxx tells the truth of it. Sigrid has betrayed us once before and likely plans to make a habit of it. We'll never approve her as the regent. There isn't any good reasons to trust the other two either. Fritz is a sadistic freak and the Vampire would eat Eric for the late night snack. Maybe, if we wait a bit, someone that we can make the fair deal with will request we consider them, ja? I vote we refrain from the hasty promises to anyone, but I see no cause to refuse any gifts or pleasures offered in return for our consideration."

Maxximillian grinned with glee, "I agree with that last statement, brothers. So, you're out voted Pops. Drop this wild ghost chasing and head for Sigrid's. If we are lucky she's still up. Then we demonstrate to her that we are too." He grabbed at his crotch in the crass display of male prowess.

The sudden roar of fury emanated from my monstrous mouth. This frightening sound sent Maxximillian to his knees in the reflex reaction. Before he could recover his place of control over the wheel, I spun the boy towards the hallway exit. I limped faster than I believed possible (or natural) headed for the dungeon room entry. I'd decided that no matter what Die Brutale or my misguided son said, I wanted to know this answer to the question I'd apparently asked Lucus.

Both Maxximillian and Die Brutale argued with me the entire way, not even relenting there bitching as I carefully traveled down the dark, dank stone steps towards my creepy destination. Nothing they said could've persuaded me to end this journey of discovery. I didn't stop until I reached the worm eaten wooden door that led to my palace prison. It was then I recalled, with a loud groan of dismay, that my spare key was wrapped around the neck of my faithful lover, Noah.

Maxximillian smiled sweetly as he said, "Well, guess that settles this. Whatever it is that is hidden away in the dark is going to stay that way. Unless of course, you intend to drag that poor idiot along with us on this fool's errand."

I snorted in response, "Noah's assistance isn't necessary for this task. I was going to relieve him of his duty earlier until that madman DJ interrupted me. This problem can be solved by hitting two birds with one stone." I resumed my quick pace headed in the direction of the Dungeon Mistress's quarters.

Maxximillian cooed out in the tone dripping with menace, "As you say Pops. Go ahead and fetch your butt buddy all you wish. I won't complain about that, but I will say this. Since you find yourself hell bent to seek out this trouble Lucus is causing, rather than enjoying the fine solution Sigrid offers, do remember that there are two locks that key must open before you can send us off to our sure doom. I do believe the boy's hands are still broken, ja? How do you plan to see this trip to completion without the aid of Noah's nimble fingers? Is it safe to assume you are happy to risk his life along with our own?"

This caused me to pause for the briefest moment while I considered Maxximillian's statements. Then before he had the chance to further weaken my resolve, I decided to ask Noah to aid me in gaining entry through the barriers but to demand he halt at the palace gate. His safety would be assured if he were ordered to wait for my return instead of following me into the unknown dangers awaiting me in the darkness."

Maxximillian snorted loudly. "Good idea, Pops. Well, unless there turns out to be more barricades along the way, ja?"

I glared at my handsome son as I replied angrily, "If you'd paid as much attention to that map Lucus gave us as you did Sigrid's tits. you'd know there wasn't any sign of such impediments after we pass the Mortar Palace."

Die Brutale grumbled out, "Ja, and of course Lucus is the man we should believe in without question."

I was so busy arguing with my son and brothers that I nearly collided with Noah that had been rushing toward me in the opposite direction.

His face wore the sheepish grin of the young lover while he halted his mad dash and dropped to the graceful kneel. I approached him with quickness in my step but kept my eyes scanning the horizon seeking out the prospect of unwanted voyeurs to our private discussion.

"Why are you in the hallway instead of back at the Mistress barracks, Noah? Who is watching the silvers? How dare you insult your Lord and Master by leaving those helpless babes open for attacks on their dignity." I came toward him readying myself to backhand him with force.

Noah didn't even look up from the floor as he replied in the even tone, "The honorable Karsten arrived to assume her job as the new Headmistress about one hour ago. She continually insisted that I return to my post and allow her to take her own. I must beg your forgiveness for disobeying you by giving in to her demands but I realized that the hour of nine had come and gone. I stupidly thought that contract you have with the honorable Lucus would prevent you from setting me free of my duties until tomorrow morning. Believe me when I say to you, your Majesty, Karsten wasn't going to allow me to ignore her commands much longer. She may look sweet but that angel face hides the demon behind her eyes. Please punish me as you see fit, Sire. I surely deserve far worse than you about to give me."

I sighed loudly with both relief and resignation in the sound as said, "Get up off the floor, Noah. There is no reason to punish the man that grants the proper respect to the Haus Headmistress. Demanding you remove yourself from the girls' quarters is within her power and also her sacred duty. After all she was just doing her job of protecting the little females from the unbridled lusts of the nasty males to perfection, ja?"

Noah stood up rapidly and with that same sheepish smile on his pretty lips replied, "Ja, she was indeed, Mad Maxx. In only a short time I was witness to her skills with the silvers in her care. I could see with clearness that the abuses leveled on them in the past will not be repeated by the Honorable Karsten. She attended them all with the loving heart usually seen only in the most patient of mothers. There were as usual many tears among those little girls but the ones shed were not of the kind they've come to expect. First, all were grieving heavily over the news of their beloved Birgit's death. Then after Karsten arrived, the flood was caused by relief and gratitude for their continued good fortune despite their cursed existence in this Haus."

I cast my eyes to my boots as I responded in the bitter tone, "I suppose any kindness or time free from the abuses of their betters is the blessing to the silver females, no matter how fleeting it may be."

Noah nodded and his smile faded as he said, "That is the way of things in this Haus, Mad Maxx. This you know personally. Now, you are here and I am here asking if I may be of some service to you?"

With mild hesitation I replied, "You read my mind, Noah. Ja, I require that you come with me this moment. Do you still have the key to the palace on that chain your useless mother Evelyn gave to you?"

He nodded while pulling the metal item from its hiding spot under the collar of his shirt. "I do. Are we going to visit the Mortar Palace tonight?" His questioning gaze captured my own.

"Noah, I politely ask you to obey my commands to the letter. I forgive you for this business with Headmistress Karsten, but if you repeat such insolence. Well, I promise you that my wrath will be severe and possibly deadly. Say that you understand."

Noah blew out his breath and responded, "I understand, Mad Maxx. You've generously grant me mercy this one time and I swear I won't expect it ever again."

I motioned him to follow me, then without saying another thing I resumed my track toward the palace entry. He loyally trailed behind quiet as the mouse. Whatever deviltry he may have believed me to be up to that night or concerns he may have harbored in his heart for my safety he wisely didn't voice out loud.

That's Noah for you. The more trustworthy man simply doesn't exist. As I watched him unlock the silver gates to the Mortar Palace walkway. I silently thanked the lucky stars that I'd listened to my instincts and stopped him from jumping into the silver well. With him as the ally, friend and lover I was honestly starting to believed I might still have the chance of finding happiness. Though I hadn't gone completely stupid, I still expect that my odds of such a thing were miniscule at best.

Noah handed me the torch he'd retrieved from the coronation area and lit it while I bid him to remain vigilant at the silver gate. I could tell in his expression that he desired to be asked to follow me into the inky darkness that yawned ahead. However, he kept his word to obey without questioning my orders. I looked back only once to assure myself he had stayed behind.

I'd spent many moments memorizing that map as Lucus had told me to do. That didn't mean there wasn't the growing feeling of dread within. I was almost certain by then that I'd ignorantly stray off the path without being aware of it. Then only the Gods knew what hellish fate would greet me with open arms. This terror, along with the lack of adequate light being granted by the small fire on my torch, kept my steps slow and methodical after I took the first left turn on the path that boasted too many alternate routes to count with ease.

As with most stressful trips into the unknown, this one seemed to go on for the eternity. It didn't help that I had no idea of how to determine I'd reached my destination. I dare say the red X Lucus drew on his map wasn't likely to be the valid marker in reality and so I traveled on and on nearly at the pace of the crawl down the winding, narrow path in that pitch black void of untold perils.

Then just as I was about to give up this seemingly never-ending journey, my ears picked up the faintest of sounds not much further ahead of me. I halted my steps immediately and strained as best I could in the attempt to discern the identity of this noise. Before I could take the wild guess, there was the piercing scream that cut through the darkness coming from the direction I was headed. My heart beat frozen within my chest as this unworldly racket rang out in the repeat.

Maxximillian shot me the glance with the expression of terror written all over his face.

I swallowed hard and whispered to him, "That's not human, whatever it is."

He nodded slowly then as the color drained from his cheeks he replied thru trembling lips, "Maybe this is where the vampire people live. Think on it, Pops. This is the perfect hide out for those bats. The sun never rises here, and the crypt is there favorite place to party, ja?"

Terror had griped me with fullness as I suddenly realized I had indeed asked almost everyone at one time or another, including Lucus, where the hell Jonas had come from. I figured that as usual, curiosity was about to kill another cat.

Just as I was about to turn around and haul ass the direction I'd come, I heard another sound. This one I recognized as the baby crying for his mother. Once again, I stopped dead in my tracks. This baby's call of despair was quickly followed by the wailing of simple words that is common in the very young child.

I shot the terrified look at Maxximillian as I yelled out, "Oh my God, the vampires have kidnapped some of the Haus children. We must save them or those monsters are going to eat them for dinner." Without waiting for his response I took off through the darkness blindly following the sounds of those little ones agonized cries for help.

In only the shortest of distances ahead I spotted the unmistakable outline of a door. Maxximillian's warnings that Noah's aid might be required past the palace gate briefly crossed my mind. However, as I got close enough to view it more fully I determined to my relief, or dismay as it would come to pass, this entry neither appear to be locked nor even fully shut.

With ease I slipped inside this odd space. Given the urgency I heard in the cries of now what seemed to be many children being held hostage. I didn't believe I couldn't spare the time to snoop around and make sure I could enter with an assurance of safety. All I could do is to hope that no vampires were waiting to pounce on anyone attempting to interrupt their feast of young flesh.

You can only imagine my complete shock when instead of finding the horrific hoard of blood suckers chomping down on the Haus children I found myself in the empty room that was only slightly less dark than the tombs that surrounded it. That momentary startle to stillness was harshly ended by the ear shattering scream of infants in pain.

This time the location of the noise was easily identified by the appearance of a dim light down what I now could tell was the long corridor carved into the stone enclosure. I recognized the structure around me indicated at one time this had been the crypt of some important person. Perhaps it belonged to one of the ancient Kings or Queens of the Haus or even one of the founders themselves.

I can only say with certainty that whoever had been placed in that tomb clearly had spent the princely fortune to claim this much real estate for all eternity. Well, obviously there was no time for me to do the searching for epitaphs dedicated to one no longer in need of aid from their Mortar King.

I quickly doused the near useless torch and stealthily snuck down that rocky hallway toward the light that was barely visible within the murky gloom.

My nose was assaulted by the heavy stench of old rot before I was halfway to my final destination. Though by this time I'd unfortunately become very accustomed to the revolting smell of decay. This stink was so foul it sent me right to my knees. I gagged for several moments doing all I could to hold back the coming tide of stomach bile, but as you may guess. This was useless. Even with adrenaline driving my blood to the maddening levels, I was helpless to halt the onslaught of regurgitation that emptied my gut of its precious treasures.

I was terrified that the loud noises I was making during that barfing fit had alerted the vampires of their uninvited guest. However, to my relief, none stepped out of the shadows to subdue me during the entire embarrassing action. Nor, to my complete surprise, did any show up to take me there prisoner before I could reach the source of illumination at the end of the hall.

Remember I told you Meine Liebe that there are no such things as real vampires. Well, no matter what Jonas tells you, I swear there aren't. But that night, I discovered there are far worse monsters in the world than any mythical ones made up by mothers trying to scare their children into behaving themselves. The things out there that should make every child shake in their shoes, and every mother fear for their safety don't return from the dead, nor do they fear crosses or turn into bats. Nein, they walk around in the daylight and wear the finest suits that money can buy.

When I burst into the dimly lit room which was unencumbered by any door, I was ready to fight with the vampires of lore. That's not what happened though. My eyes instead were greeted by the sights more horrific than any gothic novelist could imagine in their worst nightmares. This open area was not much larger than the fine basement apartment Debbie has constructed for you, Meine Liebe. Though unlike your mother, the fiends that utilized this space didn't wish to grant the mercy of leaving it mostly empty of inhabitants.

The walls on three sides were piled high with the corpses of children. The ages and stages of decay appeared to vary from those of the freshly dead infant to the near skeletal remains of the young toddler. They were all heaped upon each other, naked and with the more recent deceased it was evident their end had been created by great violence upon them. The lifeless faces, gapping mouths and wide staring eyes of those that still maintained their flesh were frozen in the expressions of terror. To my absolute horror, I witnessed that some of them at the top of these piles had cheeks still wet with their tears of despair and pain. They surely had been breathing only a few hours or mere moments before I laid my eyes upon them.

I fell to my knees in the center of that sickening scene unable to pull myself together enough to have any coherent dots. My lungs refused to taking in the putrefied air as the pain of this tragedy tugged and ripped at my very soul. I opened my mouth to release the wailing of misery. But my anguish was so deep that no sound could escape my throat. My bandage clad hands did their best to block out the visions of the bloody broken little dolls all around. Try as I might there was nothing I could be done to erase the ghastly things I'd seen.

Then, in a moment of complete mental breakdown, I realized that Lucus had honorably kept his promised to answer one of the questions I'd been seeking the answer to. Like it or not, I could no longer say he wasn't the man of his word after all, I had been demanding to know where they kept the three year olds and the babies the Haus perverts were abusing since the day I'd broken free of my bat collar.

Well, it'd taken years, but at last I'd finally found out where they were hiding them. Sadly, for too many I'd not discovered them in time to end their suffering. Worst of all, they'd been there all this time waiting for help, not very far from the source of my own torturing. The sticks and pricks of intense guilt over my failure to these innocent souls was suddenly burned away by the sudden understanding that Lucus had known of this abomination all along.

I took to my boots with the strength of growing rage within as I yelled out in fury to my audience of dead babies, “If Lucus knew where you all were, how many others also been keeping this secret from the Lord and Master of this fucking Haus? I swear to you my children, your King shall see that every villain is tortured most foul, the burned at the stake for the crimes they have committed against you. You can now dry your eyes and sleep in peace knowing that never again will such vile practices be permitted to occur.”

“Please help me, father. Is that you? I’m here, I’m your Helmut,” a weak voice called out.

A tinge of fear ran through me as I caste my eyes over the piles of corpses seeking out the one among them who had been mistaken for dead.

Then Helmut cried out again, “Father, are you there? Where is mother? Please help me. I cannot see you. The bad men stole my eyes.”

I trembled with horror as I replied in the friendliest tone possible given this horrific situation, “Ja, Helmut it’s me, your father. I am here to take you home. But my son, I need you to keep speaking so I can find you.”

Helmut whimpered then wailed out, “Please help me, Papa. They hurt me and the bad men will come back soon. I cannot see you, are you there?”

This time I was able to pinpoint the direction of his pleas for mercy. His voice was coming from behind the furthest wall in that room. It was the only one free of corpses. With some tiny bit of hope filling my psyche I rushed toward the sounds of his cries. There was nothing I could do for the children already gone, but I could at least save this one poor baby from the horror that awaited him.

But as I'd most painfully learned through my experiences with Elke, Henri and Heidi. There is no bargaining with fate and she is the cruelest bitch in the universe.

Chapter 27: Blind Justice

When I reached the wall that was void of the corpses of the broken kinder, I was stopped with the sudden stillness of shock. I'd assumed that this injured boy calling himself Helmut was trapped behind it. Discovering the way to break through it to reach him was the only thing on my mind.

Yet, as luck would have it the vision of the third wall was merely an illusion all along. Due to the dimness of the lighting in the room it was impossible to notice, until you were nearly nose to nose with it, that there was a narrow opening into another area on the right side. It didn't help that the stone of the wall and the opening space entry were so closely color coordinated it created the perfect camouflaging effect.

It was then I realized the source of the weak light was coming from whatever was at the end of that hidden stoney corridor. I managed to regain my bearings rather quickly and without thinking better of it I rushed into this cramped empty space hoping to find Helmut at the end. Then somehow save him before it was too late.

In only the few steps I reached the exit of this room and like the clumsy fool, I nearly fell face first into the rocky floor of the huge room it spilled into. *This was nearly the end of your Master, Meine Liebe. There's no doubt I'd have busted my skull to terminal had I not managed to regain my footing at the last second. Yikes!*

This near accident happened because the ancient miners that created this tomb had either by design or mistake, not chipped away the stone of the entry evenly with the path into it.

While I did my best to recover my balance and nerves, my eyes took a few moments to adjust to the increased brightness of this hellish space. Once they did I can say with true honesty, Meine Liebe. I immediately wished I'd listened to my brothers and gone to visit with that shady bitch Sigrid instead of behaving the curious idiot.

In the corner of the room was a large cage made of heavy wire. It was perhaps twelve by twelve feet in size and the top of it reached clear to the ceiling. Though that sight was disturbing enough, it was the contents of this containment contraption that was the horror I wish to God I could erase from my memory.

Inside there were seven small kinder that appeared to range in age from twelve months to perhaps four years old. All of them were naked. I determined with rapidness that four were probably the females and three of them likely the males.

Is that confusion that I see in your eyes, Meine Liebe? Ah, you maybe heard me using the words probably and likely when discussing the trapped children's genders, ja? Well, this was the trouble, my demonseed frau. the sexual organs of all them poor little creatures were, uhm, mutilated to unrecognizable. The only thing that offered any clue to the boys from the girls was three of them still possessed the tiniest lumps on their pubis that was all that was left of their immature penises.

The females, most unfortunately, were the bit easier to determine. Each one lay in the pooling puddles of blood flowing from the massive gash between their baby legs. Though the three I thought male also swam in the pools of red. Their injuries seemed to be isolated to their tiny bottoms.

Ja, your pained expression tells me I need not explain what caused these injuries these poor little ones suffered. You are correct, Meine Liebe, I didn't need to speak to any of them to know each had endured violent sexual assaults in the repeat. Not to mention, obvious genital mutilations that had caused extreme and permanent damage to their sexual identities.

Do remember I said to you, none of these kinder were over the age of four. Most of them didn't seem to be older than two. It didn't matter what had been used to penetrate these children. Anything more than the temperature thermometer would have severely injured there little parts. Well, the villains that did this horror no doubt used far worse than their manhood. Cocks would rip the girls open, but the boys severed penises demonstrated the crooks used the knife too. No doubt, these ruthless bastards didn't spare the girls from the cruelty of their blade.

This traumatic scene of rape of the worst type doesn't even indicate the truthful nightmare that lay barely breathing before my disgusted eyes. They heard, and sum could see me standing there, my arrival. Each began to tremble and wail wildly while attempting best as they could to drag themselves to the back of that pen of pain.

But that was difficult to do, even if there had been anywhere for them to go. This is because every one of the toddlers had been relieved of more than just there sex organs.

Of the ones I thought female, two were without their arms. One was missing both her feet. Another suffered amputation of all her fingers and based on her sounds, her tongue. To my great misery I understood this girl's disabled cries were the sound I'd heard and thought wasn't human when first I approached this place of torture.

All three boys had sockets emptied of their eyes. And two of them were missing their hands and one leg.

To say this was the ghastliest thing I'd ever been witness to (and that's saying something given my history up till that time) would be the understatement. My knees felt like they'd filled with the water flowing from those tortured babies eyes. Wooziness overtook me and the room started spinning. Reflexively I leaned my sagging weight into the wire cage. The frightened kinder responded to this with increased terror. No doubt they believed I was attempting to enter there cage and hurt them some more.

Their screams of torment filled the air to eardrum shattering levels and there struggling to get away from me more frantic. This panic response was contagious. My own sense of danger was set off to full alert.

Before I could get ahold of my good sense I opened my mouth and wailed out, "Please God, make this nightmare stop. This cannot be real. Help, I beg mercy. I cannot take anymore. Please someone, burn this motherfucking Haus down. I will do anything for anyone if only they could end this pain. I swear it on all that is unholy." With that I let my knees buckle and took to the kneel before my audience of the seven soon to be dead kinder.

You see, I didn't require the medical license to know there was nothing that could be done to save them. Even without proper training I recognized the meaning of the black and green mottled flesh around many of their numerous wounds. Not to mention, the unmistakable smell of the gangrene that foul sight indicated.

This next thing I say to you, Meine Liebe, I don't say with ease or without much consideration. It didn't take the numbing of the trauma that comes with time for me to think death was the mercy for these violated kinder. What kind of life of worth could any of them hope for if they survived there grievous injuries? The disability of missing limbs, eyes or the lack of sexual ability was the least of the struggles they would face, ja? Even me with my long history of being tortured, couldn't imagine trying to exist among my fellow humans haunted by the visions these kids had endured.

Nein. Though I didn't dare to ask any of them, I believed – and still do – that the mercy of death was something each had more than earned. With all the strength I could gather I pulled myself together. Acting the crybaby over something that I couldn't change, and didn't cause, wasn't helpful to these the smallest of all my subjects. They were depending on me to do what was right, to end their suffering, ja?

The only decision left for me to make was of the quickest and least painful way I could give them the reward of eternal peace. So, with a deep breath I began to search the room for something that could aid me in my dark task.

However, this room was empty of anything other than the cage that held them except for one strange item. In the farthest corner, across from the innocent victims cell, was a small pile of straw with a moth-eaten old blanket covering it. It looked very similar to the shoddy sleeping accommodations provided to me during my stay in the Mortar Palace. I briefly wondered about the reason there would be this makeshift bed located in the place of no use to any of the tiny prisoners held here.

I sighed with frustration and deep anguish over my lack of discovering anything that could offer a gentle end to their suffering.

Then suddenly Helmut called out from within the squirming, wailing mass of injured babies, "Papa, hurry. the bad men are here. Help me Papa."

I spun around and looked upon the kinder just in time to spot the one calling for his father. It was of course one of the eyeless victims I'd thought was likely male. Helmut turned out to be the oldest appearing toddler. He was at least four years old but not likely much more than that. His elder status compared to his cellmates explained why he was capable of the speech that alerted me to their presence. The bastards that did this to him and the others hadn't removed his tongue as they had the much younger appearing female. Which suggested to me whomever did these abominations were doing the violence for sick thrills and not to merely disable there victims.

I sucked in my air and doing my best to hide the sound of sorrow in my tone I replied, "Helmut, my son, be calm. I've killed the bad men and they are never coming back to hurt you anymore. It's me, your papa, you are hearing in the room with you. You are safe now because I've come to take you home with me."

The mangled child's tear strewn face suddenly took on the grimace of misery as he wailed in response, "Oh papa, I knew you would come save me. It hursts so bad. Can you make it stop?"

Slowly I approached the wire door of their cell and examined the small padlock that kept me out and them in as I said, "Ja, my son. I can, but first I need you to tell your papa if you know of the place these bad men kept there keys." I silently damned myself for having Noah stay behind.

Once again I was sorry I didn't heed Mad Maxximillian's good advice.

Helmut groaned loudly as he replied, "Nein. There are no keys. Papa, please. Help me."

Keeping the trembling from my voice I said, "It's okay, Helmut. I managed to open the door just now. Can you come to your papa? Follow my voice, my Taube." I dropped down to the kneel and reached my arms through the holes in the wires ready to receive my 'son' into them.

The poor little thing began the agonizing process of dragging his broken flesh toward the direction he'd heard me call him to. I very softly began to sing to Helmut and the other frightened kinder the nursery rhymes I'd somehow learned but had no memory of where or how.

As my singing filled the air, the terrified shrieks of the babies began to calm. Before Helmut could reach me, their noise had quieted to the sounds of soft sobs and wet sniffling. Then at last, the blind boy was within my grasp.

Of those that still had eyes, they kept them on me with fear in there expressions. For the two, that like Helmut, were without sight I saw that they had begun to follow their brother's actions. I continued my songs designed to bring joy to the ears of the innocent while pulling Helmut to the wire. I did my best to cuddle the mangled little one while he struggled hard to get as close to me as the wire would allow.

I suppose I expected him to ask me why I wasn't removing him from that cage. However, he never spoke a word. His only interest appeared to be in that of the loving caresses of someone he believed loved him and had come to protect him from the fiends that didn't.

Soon I had two more babies blindly trying to receive the affection denied them in trade for abuses most foul. I was fair in giving them equal attention. I stroked there tiny heads and cheeks while pulling them to the wire next to Helmut.

The females weren't as forgiving as their brothers were. No matter how sweetly I called out to them nor how much I petted the males, they refused to come any closer. Much time had passed since I'd discovered this secret hell on earth. I didn't know how much longer I had before the ones that caused this carnage would return. Without the way to defend myself adequately and stupidly telling no one of where I'd gone other than that rat Lucus, I knew I couldn't waste too much time trying to give these babies release without traumatizing them more than they already were.

Mad Maxximillian shot the look filled with pity at me as he said, "Pops, best get on with it. Stalling isn't helping them or you. What is done is done, ja? Just remember this pain you must cause them will be the last of it for them forever. Then they sleep in peace too far for anyone to hurt them ever again."

I dropped my eyes and stared at my cloven hooves while I replied, "The little girls will be witness to my brutality on their brothers. This isn't something I wish them to take to the grave. They've suffered enough fear from men without me adding to it."

Die Brutale called out from behind me in the unusually gentle tone, "Mad Maxx, this isn't the time to be selfish. Your reputation among the traumatized toddlers won't matter once they are far from their pain. They won't be capable of telling anyone of your sin against them. Give them the mercy we've been denied and are too weak to take for ourselves."

I nodded then growled in response through my tears, "I will do as I must, and as you say brothers. But I demand the equal service return for the guilt I must accept in the crime I'm about to commit against those that never deserved this. We will hunt down and destroy every motherfucker that ever touched a single hair on these sweet children's heads."

Mad Maxximillian and Die Brutale said in unison, "Your will is our own, Mad Maxx."

Without any further hesitation I put my bandaged hands around Helmut's little head. It took almost no effort to twist it violently too far to the left. His tiny neck broke so quickly not even the smallest whimper escaping with his last breath.

I didn't even allow his battered and lifeless flesh hit the floor before I repeated this move on the boy next to him. Then for the third time in seconds I gave the only cure for their pain possible. All three boys slumped to the floor there cooling flesh blocking the only way into that damned cage.

One of the females watching uttered the tiny whimpering over what she'd seen. However, the other three merely stared at me with terrified wide eyes. I expected them to return to wailing but all four remained as silent as there fallen brothers.

"Now what do I do brothers? I cannot just leave these girls to die slow of infection. What if the criminals come back and continue their perverted games with them before that even happens?" I flashed the pained glance at Mad Maxximillian as I said this.

My handsome son pursed his lips as if deep in thought then replied flatly, "This wire appears flimsy, Pops. I don't think it would injure the boy too badly if we forced our way through it. Once inside, you know what to do."

I pulled my arms back through the wire and took back to standing. The females didn't break there anxious gaze from my own as I took several steps backward. Then I braced as I ran directly into the side of the wire cage. The flimsy metal squealed for a brief second before it tore free of the weak metal frame that had held it in place. This thing looked similar to the large wire chicken coop or kennel for the pet dog.

This first attempt to breaking through the wire was only partially successful at gaining me entry. However, it was completely successful at sending the watching females into absolute panic. They started screaming and doing their best to retreat from my direct path.

Their calls of distress helped to strengthen my resolve that I needed to speed this tragedy along. That wire didn't stand the chance at holding me back when I rushed it the second time. I crashed through so harshly that both the side I was attacking and the one next to it ripped free of their frame.

Had the little girls been capable of running away like any normal toddler, my horrific deeds would have been more difficult to accomplish. But there missing limbs prevented them from escaping from their cell and their murderous Mortar King. I ignored the pains of my breaking heart and their cries of terror as I rapidly approached each one and snapped their tiny necks. If anyone other than the ones I'd quieted for eternity had been there to see this nightmare I'm sure they'd have thought the whole scene resembled the cruel wolf breaking into the cage of innocent defenseless lambs to kill for merely the thrill of it.

The carnage was over in mere seconds, though the sounds of their screams seemed to continue for many minutes beyond the silencing of their tiny owners. When the last one had been dispatched to the green fields, I fell to my backside in the center of the freshly created corpses. There was this awful numbness that overtook me while I sat there blankly looking upon the bloody scene around. I'd happily stayed there until I found my own release from my wretched existence if given the choice. I didn't think I could live with myself after what I'd just done. How could I? They were helpless little babies without any chance to defend themselves or even have the capacity to understand why I'd done this to them.

For the first time since I'd taken on the form of Der Dameon I truly felt like that heartless demon. I didn't believe I deserve to live. But if I continued to exist after all the crimes I'm honestly guilty of then locking me away in the Mortar Palace hell was far kinder than I'd earned, ja?

Before I could sink any further into the mire of despairing, the sounds of the loud gasping caught my attention. I cast the anxious glances at the dishonored lumps of flesh laying all around me in that half destroyed cage. I suppose for the brief moment, I feared somehow one of them had survived my actions of their mercy killings.

However, to my relief, all of them were quite dead and therefore free of their hellish pain. Then it occurred to me, 'if not the mangled babies making that sound. who did make it?'

The slight stirring within the darkness of the narrow entry of the room caught my peripheral vision. I hurriedly got off that floor and stood tall as I could with my chest puffed out far as it could go.

"Show yourself, villain. You've been judged guilty of crimes against the Master of this Haus, the Mortar King. Prepare to die like the scum you are," I growled out in the authoritative tone-tinged with fury.

Then another surprise among those I'd already suffered stepped out into the light. The man of barely four foot six, with the observably crooked spine stood there staring back at me. Though he was slight in size, he was an obvious adult because he sported the long, unkempt facial hair.

You see, I quickly realized that this fellow was suffering from the affliction of Dwarfism. This was something that until that moment I'd never seen in person. I'd only known of this conditions existence from the medical books Peter had given me to studying for my pre-med testing.

This little fellow's locks and beard seemed to be dark brown but thanks to the layers of filth clinging to him, I couldn't even be certain of the true color of his flesh. His clothing was tattered and his feet bare. The thin material he wore was in such bad shape that it barely covered his near skeletal frame.

While his physical appearance was shocking it was the dull silver collar that decorated his abnormally short neck that really blew my troubled mind. This simply couldn't be possible. The silver collars are chosen for their close proximity to physical perfection. Nein, the dungeon masters tasked with sorting the submissive recruits would've rejected him. One with this fellow's disability wouldn't even have been viewed as capable of serving as the Haus submissive. It's unfortunately the truth that he should have been sold off to the circuit without a second thought.

So, thanks to that silver collar, I couldn't decide if this tiny man was the stress driven hallucination, or if some clever villain had sent him to distract me while his henchmen surrounded me.

The little man was shaking with heavy anxiety as he dropped to the graceful kneel and whispered in the terrified sounding voice, "I thank you for the mercy of relieving me of my burden as was promised me."

He dropped his light colored eyes to gaze at the floor after he said this but didn't attempt to move another inch.

His response wasn't the one I'd expected. I stood there unsure what to do or say next. This entire experience was beyond anything I'd ever imagined in my worst nightmares. Just when I was about to fall into another mental breakdown, my son Maxximillian pushed me off the wheel and took control of the boy.

Maxximillian glared at the dwarf fellow without expression as he loudly said, “I know nothing of mercy, worm. You think I promised you such fantasy? I think not. Who the fuck are you? More importantly, who sent you? Answer me with honestly, or I’ll do things to you so ghastly you’ll think the devil is the sweetheart in comparison to your Mortar King.”

His shaking got more pronounced as he replied quickly, “I beg your forgiveness, your majesty. I’m the useless pleasure submissive called Snot. It’s true you are speaking of the promised mercy that was given to me by the honored Fur King Xavier. His majesty placed me in the honored position of ‘used product removal’ from this sacred room. I’ve been waiting many years for him to return for me. He swore that after he’d decided I’d served my purpose to completion, he’d joyfully use great cruelty to retire me from my important duty to the leaders of Das Kaiser Haus. It was insolence to assume you’ve come here to send me to the yard at long last. My fate is yours to do with as you please, your majesty. I thank you for the mercy, oh, uhm, consideration because I’m surely unworthy of it.”

Maxximillian stood there stunned to stupid with his mouth hanging open unable to wrap his mind around the things Snot confessed to him. I quickly pushed my confused boy off the wheel and resumed the position of control.

"Xavier has been dead for many years now, Snot. I suppose no one thought to come inform you of this news, ja? Or perhaps you attempt to deceive me of your truthful purpose of being found in the vicinity of illegal and unholy crimes against babies," I said in a stern but cautious tone.

He looked up from the floor appearing confused as he muttered, "Honorable Xavier has died? Nein. this cannot be true."

I shook my head ja, and responded in the humored tone, "Ah, it can be and it is. I know this because I'm the man that killed that child murdering bastard. How dare you call me the liar? I should have you skinned alive for even thinking such a foul thing of your Lord and Master, much less daring to speaking it aloud."

Snot's trembling became so strong he could barely hold his spot in the kneeling as he replied, "This dishonor you say I committed against you, for that I beg your forgiveness. I didn't think before I spoke to one that commands my total devotion. Again, I say, I'm yours to do with as you please, Sire."

My brows raised with curiosity as I said, "You speaking pretty like the true pleasure submissive. Yet I cannot believe what my eyes say they seeing. You claim the name of no worth and wear the color of one of those creatures that bring lust to all that view them. But I don't feel shame to say you're not even close to quality flesh. Tell me, Snot, where did you get that silver collar you wear? Did you steal it from one of the unfortunate broken dolls that you claim you've been responsible to remove from this cage?"

He shook his head and with the small sigh replied, "I wish I'd committed the crime of thievery to come by this metal burden, your majesty. If I had, then I could expect to be punished, but after that I'd die the man free of the memories locked within the minds of all that are selected to serve as the playthings of the Masters. This collar is true and my submissive name chosen honestly. It was locked by the shedding of my virgin blood and my services claimed to be of the sublime nature notorious for one of my kind."

A gasp escaped me as I said in the near whisper, "Holy hell. Who the fuck purchased then locked your collar, Snot?"

He replied flatly, "I beg your forgiveness, your Majesty but I already tell you this. Xavier is my Master. His will is my own."

The shock of his confessions made it difficult to think clearly. Yet after a few moments of watching his body language it slowly dawned on me, Snot was being truthful. My brutal father had most cruelly selected him to wear the silver collar *(likely as the crude joke, like your own Master, Meine Liebe, ja?).* Then he'd doubled down on that distasteful action by buying this poor fellow and no doubt soundly raping him into submission. Yuck, yuck and what the holy fuck. This guy wasn't that much larger in stature than the healthy ten year old. I knew Xavier was one depraved motherfucker (pun intended), but using this poor man as the butt of his jokes (pun intended, yet again), that was beyond twisted.

Given this latest disgusting discovery. It wasn't that farfetched to believe Snot's accusation that Xavier was the man behind the deplorable things done to these babies as truthful also. However….

I was also telling the truth that Xavier was by that time long the rotting corpse himself. So, that meant that even if Xavier had been involved, or maybe started, this brutality against young children, someone had continued to engage in these criminal actions since his demise. Or perhaps, no longer had to share it with him.

Learning the name or names of those guilty of this shit was important. But it was also important to discover where these kinder had come from and why no one seemed to be missing them.

You see, Meine Liebe, it occurred to me that the Haus is many foul things but wasteful isn't one of them. Every child purchased from the traffickers resulted in loss from the Haus coffer. Claus had informed me that after the Stasi take over, the Haus residents were sentenced to pay 10,000 dollars per member annually for good.

This meant that not a single penny earned by the Haus activities could be squandered. Since I'd never been witness to the sudden mass executions of Dominants, I knew somehow the Elders had managed to pay all their bills every year, especially the restitution to their Stasi captors.

Claus's telling me about these heavy fines explained the reasons kinder rejected during collar selection, or found guilty of various crimes, were sold away to the Russian labor camps rather than murdered outright. Well unless, like Ryker, they were accused of something very serious.

Yet it was Ryker's fate that reminded me that when the collared, black or silver, are executed they were sent to the yard. I dare say the Haus orchard grows tall and strong from all the metal in its diet. Yikes!

But only a few feet away I could smell the evidence that children brought to this place weren't being buried. Though their flesh was still not treated with honor, I must say they didn't suffer becoming the lonely inhabitants of the unmarked, hastily dug graves.

This could only mean that whoever was responsible for this horror was attempting to hide the 'evidence' of these babies fate or existence or both. With that in mind, I realized that as I suspected this entire situation was illegal even in this Haus of abuses most foul. I'd been informed many times that sexually assaulting the child under the age of fifteen carries the severest of punishments. The person or persons behind all this was sure to be fearful of suffering the burning at the stake for the abomination they had done.

Even if Xavier and obviously another or others had managed to keep this the deepest of secrets. I had to wonder where the hell did these children come from? How did they get them here without anyone seeing them do it? Even if Xavier did have the key to my palace, babies cry loudly, ja?

More than that, how did this person or persons manage to keeping the loss of the income caused by not selling these rejected candidates onto the circuit off the radar of the Elders and Voters? Assuming that not every Elder or Voter (I thought better not be any of them) was aware of this disgusting and illegal misuse of babies. why wasn't anyone noticing these kids were missing?

My spine tingled with terror at the possibility that this shameful practice was some kind of holdover of ancient beliefs still held by the Haus people. Was this the place they sent select young ones to be sacrificed to the nefarious old God of legend? I couldn't put anything past these insane residents of the Haus, ja?

Or maybe that hideous Doctor Mengele (that fellow they called the Angel of Death), the one they never found after Hitler fell, what if he hadn't escaped to Argentina as so many rumored him to have. I suddenly began to worry, based on these children's injuries, that this fiend was lurking around in the darkness of the Haus tombs making demands none of the Haus leaders could refuse. Perhaps that Nazi bastard was using untold blackmail means to force the Elders to turn over the culled baby from the traffickers so he could sate his twisted desires.

All this guessing was starting to give me a huge headache. Okay maybe the stress of all this was causing that problem. There wasn't any reason to theorize when the answers to all my questions likely knelt right in front of me.

"Snot, you must accept that Xavier isn't ever coming back to fetch you. I'm the Mortar King, which means I'm also am the Priceless Collar King of the legends. Which means, I'm your Master now."

The tiny silver sucked in his air abruptly then fell onto his face in the prostrated position as he said loudly, "Long live the King. It's my pleasure to serve you, your majesty, though I'm unworthy of it."

I snorted then looked down my nose as if disgusted as I replied, "Well, thus far you are speaking the truth. You aren't worthy for even the honor of becoming the fuel to light the dark night. That will be corrected immediately. I command you to tell me where all these children come from. Who brings them here and who causes them such grievous injury? Do this and I swear to give you the peace you say you desire."

Snot didn't lift his face as he replied, "I don't know the answers to the questions you ask, your Majesty. I'm not permitted to be in this sacred room when the kinder arrive. I never see anyone when I drop them off in the playroom and I'm not allowed to stay there after I've delivered them. When I return they are in need of the mercy you've so graciously granted these lucky ones. I'm also forbidden to go to the selection rooms except to collect my daily meal left there for my substance. When I do this the holding room is always empty. I swear to you, Sire. I have never seen another soul except the cursed children since the day Xavier condemned me to this hellish task of watching children die, then removing there corpses to the pile outside this sacred space."

I growled out angrily, "Do you really think I believe you don't know anything about any of this? You say you been doing this dark task for years. Since Xavier sups with the worms for almost six years now, I believe this to be the only truth in your claims. However, even if I think you speaking with honesty, and I don't, some of these kinder seemed old enough to have the gift of speech. You say you sit here and see them dying. They surely speak to you of the ones that brought them to their brutal destruction. At least some of them have over time, ja? What have they told you? Speak up quickly, Snot, or I'll keep my promise to see you die in ways fouler than those babies you stack as if they nothing more than rotting wood."

Snot whimpered then replied, "Ja, your Majesty. some can speak, but they say nothing about the ones that damage them. Most call for their mothers or fathers. Others wail that bad men hurt them. This and begging for help is the only things I ever heard from any. Please, I beg of you, Sire, to find my words true. I'm telling you all that I know in the perfect service owed to my Master and King."

I rolled my eyes and sighed loudly then with the sudden idea said, "Okay, I'll be the patient monarch and may even offer that most rare thing know as mercy. If you are able to prove the things you claiming. I'm not denying there is a pile of corpses you confess you created and I stand in the demolished cage that housed the soiled innocents. I see the foul bed that you use for slumbering while ignoring the cries of the damned. So? Prove to me this playroom and selection room are not merely fantasies you make up. I think maybe you're attempting to shields yourself from my discovering you're the villain that commits these horrific crimes against babies, ja?"

Snot pulled himself up to his knees with suddenness.

With the look of utter disgust in his expression he replied, "Nein, this evidence of abuse done to these little babies makes me sick. I wished for death too many times to count, and if I wouldn't be discovered I'd do as you did to give them the merciful death before they were dismantled. I say this with respect, your Majesty. Even at the risk of your wrath. I also wish to say that if it's your intentions to see the monsters guilty of these unmentionable things to the helpless punished, Snot is the man more than willing to be of aid to you in any way you believe me useful.

I stepped carefully over the heaps of broken babies and exited the ruined wire cage. Snot held his spot as I slowly approached him.

"Then, my pet. I'm ready to receive your proof of this tale you telling me. Get off that floor and lead the way. Hurry the fuck up. You wasting my time." I used my left foot to tap his outer thigh softly.

Snot grunted then took to his feet with speed. I followed behind the surprisingly nimble little man while he took off down that narrow opening. Once we were back in that stinking room full of baby bodies, he stopped briefly to dig out the small flashlight hidden among the dead. He shot me the bitter smile then clicked on this source of manmade light.

"My Lord, the path is treacherous with broken stones and crumbling mortar. I beg of you to stay close that you may avoid the injurious fall," he said while gracefully bowing to me.

I nodded then said, "As you say, Snot. Now, stop stalling. I've more important things to do than to have my ears assaulted with shoddy fantasy stories. Prove yourself truthful and don't attempt any trickery. I won't warn you again. I mean it."

The short silver tore off into the darkness that pressed all around the tomb. It was more difficult to keep proper pace with this speedy little fellow than I'd anticipated. It didn't help matters that instead of rushing onto the path I'd followed to get there, he took a sharp right turn away from it. Lucus had warned me to stick to his directions or I risked death from unknown terrors.

Well as usual, Lucus was proven to be the dirty, rotten, lying bastard he truthfully is. It turned out that he was attempting to keep me from discovering more secrets than he was willing to share. Like the existence of the places Snot was taking me to visit.

We arrived to investigate his claims of the place he referred to as the 'playroom' first. Snot had taken me on several winding paths through what seemed like miles of ancient underground tunnels. The smell of mildew, wet rock and centuries of undisturbed filth filled my lungs to near choking while I limped at a near breakneck pace to keeping up with my swift little guide.

Then when I was sure he was leading me on the wild goose chase, his light illuminated the unmistakable evidence of yet another long buried crypt door entryway. He didn't slow his fast steps for even a second's hesitation. The moment we traveled up the three shallow steps in front of its arched door, he pushed it open with almost no effort. I took notice that all along our trip spider webs of alarming size dotted the dank landscape (what I could see of it that is). However, the outside of this tomb was strangely free of the evidence of arachnid activity.

In fact, it appeared to me that someone was spending a great deal of time and energy making sure the stone of this Haus of the honored dead was scrubbed to sparkling. I took a deep breath and braced myself. I was sure whatever I was about to find inside this place was going to haunt me from that moment until I became the permanent resident of the grave like this one.

Ah, Meine Liebe, I must tell you. As usual, the Haus didn't make my beliefs that of the false kind. I swear to you, a more horrific piece of real estate doesn't exist this far north of Hell. Whomever told Snot this place was to be called the playroom sure has the fucked up definition of playing.

He shut the power down on his flashlight and flipped the light switch located just within the entry. Immediately the huge room was illuminated by the glow of many fancy lamps. Right away I noticed three things.

First, this at one time must have been the final resting place of a family of vast wealth. It was huge even when compared to the most modern mausoleums.

Second, unlike the tomb that housed the cursed little babies, there was only this one large open area without hidden passages nor, that I could find, more than the single entryway.

The last thing was the most important discovery of this entire expedition. From front to back, wall to wall, implements and furniture used in torturing was scattered about. There wasn't a single thing the cruelest of sadist would require not stored in there. I don't care to get into too much description of the awful tools that I saw. I think it's enough to say that Snot proved to be the honest man when he said this was the place the villains were using to foully assault the babies.

Many of the blades, numerous chains, leather straps, manacles, restraining tables and thudding apparatuses were sporting blood stains. More gruesome than that fact, where the sight of several jars filled with yellowish liquid. Floating inside them were some of the missing parts of the little ones that I'd put to their eternal slumbering not far from that spot. I don't wish to say which parts.

The visions of intense pain and terrible humiliation made my stomach lurch violently. I fought the urge to purge yet again. Snot stood at the door with his eyes to the floor saying nothing while I belched, gagged and did my best to remain calm.

Then I spotted the item I recognized as the super eight movie projector. Everything in my soul told me to ignore that thing. Whatever film the fiends liked to enjoy surely were something I wouldn't appreciate seeing. But, as I tended to do back then, I ignored my better judgement.

Without saying anything to Snot, I walked over to it and though it took the minute to work it I managed to get it to share its preloaded flick. Snot led out the scream of anguish and ran out the door just as the first frame flashed upon the stoney wall.

Your Master is not the genius that Snot is, Meine Liebe. I stood there paralyzed to full on idiot status while those vile scenes played out before my shocked eyes. Things that no one should ever see, think, imagine, speak of, or do were burned into my memory forever before I could regain my mentality enough to shut that fucking horror flick off.

I realize you are curious to know what those villains' thought good entertainment. Well, Meine Liebe, that baby without the tongue, you recall her, ja? She was the star of the movie. I wanted to turn it off but I kept watching in the hopes that I'd see the identity of the creeps doing this. Unfortunately, they'd managed to keep the spotlight on their tiny actress, without giving away the director. I never saw any faces other than hers, and God knows I wish I didn't. And that's all I will ever say about this so don't you ever ask me about it. I'm taking that nightmare to hell with me, where it fucking belongs.

My poor attempt to contain my stomach fluids failed most miserably the second the projector stopped it's whirling noises. I went to my knees and dry heaved for several minutes. I hoped I would upchuck my guts or at the very least my eyes. Both of these organs hurt only slightly less than my heart. This was something I'd not been prepared to witness, nor do I think I ever could've or should've been.

They call this depraved kind of thing the snuff film. I've heard it said since my arrival in the United States that such things are the myth, mere rumors that there is no proof they exist. I can tell you with absolute certainty at least one does.

Okay, did.

After I managed to end my barfing, I grabbed that devil machine and smashed it into one of the stone walls. Then I ripped the film from it and yelled for Snot to find the match or lighter. He did as I commanded without any argument or hesitation.

While that piece of shit film burned, my eyes spotted the small notebook that was black in color laying on one of the torturing tables. It resembled that black book Voter Rolf gave to me. You recall the one filled with names of the FemDoms he'd conquered?

I rushed over and picked it up. In my haste I'd allowed the pages to flip. Several small slips of paper came free and fell to the floor. My hands were the useless bitches. Snot saw that I was interested in possessing these items. Without being told he came over and retrieved them for me. Grateful for the aid, I asked him to hold them up so that I could read the words on them.

In this case, there were not many words to view. It was mostly numbers. Big ones, nein, huge ones. It didn't take me long to realize these were paid receipts for purchases. It took even less time to figure out what those items bought had been. I'd accidently discovered the answer to how Xavier had managed to take the Haus broken to near splinters from the World War Two into the palace of depraved overindulgence and crass opulence with such speed. Even Claus couldn't figure out how he'd done it in less than five years.

It turned out he'd been filling the Haus busted bank by selling the flesh and blood of the babies to the rarest of perverts in existence. As I went over the many receipts with terror I started to understand that whoever was paying these obnoxious prices to destroy the innocent without interference or restraint had to be among the richest in the country, maybe the world.

This looking over numbers wasn't getting me the answers I needed. None of them recorded even the pseudonym of anyone. Only the price and the notice it'd been paid in full.

With growing frustration fueling my actions, I growled at Snot that he needed to help me examine the black book. I asked him to go through it and tell me the names he saw in there while I tried to locate other books or things that might give me some clue as to who was behind all this.

He frowned then said, "I cannot read nor write, your majesty."

I groaned loudly then pointed to the black book as I responded, "Of course you cannot. Xavier didn't bring you in his bed to read him stories till he fell asleep, ja?

Open that fucking thing, put it where I can see it with ease, and slowly turn the pages till I say to stop."

Snot's cheeks turned bright red over the cruel thing I'd said to him. However, he dutifully did as I commanded without rude commentary over it. That was the good thing for him. By that point, I was ready to blow and I was rapidly losing interest in who suffered from my growing rage.

Much to my relief and absolute disgust. That little book revealed the answers to the big secrets far too many had worked hard to keeping them that way. Names of those responsible filed before my bloodshot eyes. Each one that I recognized stoked the flames of pure fury within me. More than that, the sheer number of those both directly involved (and possibly indirectly) started to break down any hope I had of maintaining the shred of sympathy for anyone that called Das Kaiser Haus home. Many of those names honestly surprised the shit out of me. Others were people I'd suspected capable of heinous acts of any type, even this kind.

When Snot reached the final page I shot him the quick glance as I said, "Well my pet, seems you've managed to save your worthless life. Put that precious item into the back pocket of my trousers. But I'm warning you, you do it without touching me with your nasty hands more than necessary. Then we leave this rat hole and you take me to see this selection room. Though it does appear you're telling me the truth of your reluctant participation in these crimes, I must be witness to the evidence this book seems to claim of the origins of the kinder these foul beasts misuse in the most hideous ways."

Snot shuddered then said in the near whisper, "You learn all this just from looking at this book for the few minutes? They write down everything and leave it laying around so easily found?" His gaze ran across the dark cover with the expression of awe coming over his face.

I sneered at him, "Ah, are you disappointed that they have been this stupid? Or are you worried what happens when I track them all down. Maybe while I'm slowly torturing them to death they'll tell me incriminating tales about the submissive calling himself Snot? If you've been holding anything back, I suggest you unload that burden from your soul right this fucking minute. This is your last chance. If I hear another speak your name other than to beg you to stand downwind, oh my goodness, that will go very badly for you, my pet."

He shook his head, "Nein, Sire. None will claim I do anything other than I already say I do."

With the mild snort I replied, "Good to hear. Now, why you pissing me off by wasting my time? The book, do with it as you were told, fool."

Snot did as I commanded with perfection, but before he headed for the door to lead me to our next destination he dropped his gaze to his bare feet.

Then almost too quietly to be heard, he inquired, "I beg your forgiveness, Sire. But could you tell me of the method you employed to send Xavier to the devil's embrace? I thank you for the mercy of it."

The air filled with the sounds of my bitter chuckling as I replied, "Xavier was incapable of surviving my priceless pleasure submissive skills, my pet. His heart blew the gasket the moment he dared to partake of my potent ass-ets."

Snots face knotted into the expression of confusion as he responded, "Are you saying that you, uhm, your special services were deadly for him, Sire? This is why you warn me not to touch your, uhm royal highness? If so, then I thank you for the mercy of it." He shot the frightened glance in the direction of my backside.

My laughter grew louder and stronger as I replied, "You're the funny guy, Snot. Stop asking so many stupid questions and get going while you are ahead, ja?"

He nodded then practically flew out the door, once again forcing me to work hard to keep up with him.

We reached yet another large underground corpse chamber within only feet of this so-called playroom. This one was not too dissimilar to the first. The entry spilled into the large room but instead of piles of corpses there were long wooden benches on two sides. These simple seats were the length of the wall they hugged and across from each other.

Then in the back, like before, Snot demonstrated there was a secret passage. This one led to another room but there wasn't any wire cages. Instead, this one had been furnished to accommodate medical examination equipment. There was a single exam table with stirrups in the center, and several modern chairs place around the walls. On the furthest wall a large table with various devices required for the physical exam and the trash can sat quietly awaiting it's next unlucky customers.

The sound of disappointment escaped me after I'd quickly explored the area seeking further evidence and found none. I turned around and faced Snot. He stood there with his eyes glued to his crusty bare toes.

"Snot, you have demonstrated that you are the man of your word. But kin I trust you," I said in the gentle tone.

He didn't respond nor look up from his feet but merely nodded his head.

I sighed, "I've no choice but to hope I've correctly judge you the perfect pleasure submissive you appear to be. I know you've been promised the retirement from this accursed job assignment. I'm honestly upset to have to tell you this isn't going to happen. Not for a little bit longer anyway. I require some time to consider how to bring the end to this horrific practice. while I work on a difficult solution. Those involved must not discover there King has learned of their unnatural crimes against his youngest subjects. Ending your pain will alert them to this as would your speaking of my visiting with you. This you understand?"

Th little man nodded again but this time more slowly.

"I cannot hear you, Snot. Tell me that you will keep silent about everything until I return to give you the mercy you've more than earned. You do believe me when I say that I swear to come back and grant your release," I said in a sterner tone.

Snot sucked in his breath then lifted his eyes to meet my own as he softly replied, "You still believe that I agree with the terrible things I've had to witness in this hell don't you, Sire? You say that you swear to do what the Honorable Xavier said he would but never did. I say this with respect, your majesty. If you choose to leave me to rot for the rest of eternity, then I will do this without complaint. I even will sleep with a smile on my face if you never come back to end my pain. You need not swear to give me peace because this you already did. I saw what you did to those that I can clearly see you cared for more than yourself. I find comfort in knowing the ones that hurt all these babies will suffer far worse than I can imagine from this uncommon King of the common people. I swear my undying loyalty and adoration for you without quarrel. I thank him for the mercy he's so generously granted his most unworthy but most grateful servant." He fell to the graceful kneeling at my boots before bending down to place several soft kisses on the toes of my boots.

I reached down and petted the back of his head while I said in the pity filled tone, "Get off that floor, Snot. I know you say you no longer request nor expect me to keep my promise to you. But I believe me when I say that I will. Go back to your bed and resume your duties as they have always been. This time, I thank you for the mercy of it." Snot trembled slightly under my touching.

Then in silent suddenness he stood and hurried toward the exit. Moments before he'd gone too far to be heard he called out, "I left the flashlight on the benches for your use, Sire."

I briefly thought of how lucky I'd been Snot thought of the important tool that I hadn't. Without the strong light source there is no way I could've returned to Noah without likely falling down and breaking something important.

My return trip was slow and deliberate. I used Snot's lantern to get some vision of the sights hidden in the darkness around me. To my dismay, it's light uncovered at least the dozen more of these ancient stone mausoleums. I didn't have the time to investigate any more of them. To be honest, even if I'd had such leisure, I'd not done so. I simply couldn't stand the thought of discovering any more abominable practices that I'd never conceived could be the reality.

I'd decided the painful knowledge I'd acquired of the annual Stasi Night and now this latest nightmare were enough to fuel my high anxiety for, well, my lifetime.

By the time I'd found my way back to the palace gate. I'd calmed my guilty conscious about not investigating those other tombs immediately by reminding myself in only a few months I'd have plenty of time to get familiar with these dark markers of the long forgotten dead after I became the prisoner of that fucking Mortar Palace for life.

Noah saw my light cutting through the murky gloom before I spotted him.

"Mad Maxx? Is that you," he called to me in the loud whisper.

"Nein, it's the devil coming to steal your soul," I yelled back.

Noah nervously chuckled, "Ah, then I've nothing to fear Mister Lucifer. You're too late. That appendage already been taken by another. Maybe, you've heard of the fellow that holds it hostage? He's called Mad Maxx, the Mortar King."

I was making the final approach toward my anxious lover as I snorted then replied, "Heard of him? Why hell, that boy is practically my kinsmen. You in trouble now, Noah. I happen to know he'll trade me what I want for nothing more than the promise of release from his future as the King of fools. You better be ready to suffer my dark affections for the rest of eternity after I've successfully bargained with him."

Noah's grin was so large I could've seen it without the aid of that weak lantern when he said, "Well, if you swearing to have me for your pleasure forever, then I say go see him and make that deal. wrap my heart in your fiery grip and never let me go." He leaned in appearing wanton for the lip kissing.

I backed away from his eager attentions and said softly, "Nein, this isn't the good time for that, sweetheart. I'm embarrassed to say, my dentures are in need of the deep cleaning and my breath fouled by stomach discontent."

The burly dungeon master halted his affectionate actions, "Are you feeling okay, Mad Maxx? There is a rough stomach bug going around. Do you think you have fever?" He ran his eyes along my thin frame appearing to be seeking signs of illness in the dim light.

"Nein, Noah. It's not disease of my flesh that upset my gut. It's that of others. Never mind, listen lover, I've got some unfinished business that I thought could wait till another day. But things have changed and I need to attend to it with speed. It's not safe for you to travel unaccompanied through the Haus to your lodgings on the fifth floor. Since I'm headed that way already, I can drop you off at the apartment."

Noah's sappy smile melted to the concerned appearing frown as he replied, "I'm not sure I will feel comfortable in the apartment with Birgit and Vivianna gone, Mad Maxx. I mean I do as you tell me but is there any way I could stay with Matz and Cary. Just for a bit. Until I learn the rules of the Haus floors better?"

I shook my head nein, "I knew you'd find it bothersome to bunk alone up there, lover. Earlier today I moved Almut and Hubertus and their kinspeople into the honored Dungeon Mistresses apartment. They know to grant you the reverence that your status entitles you to have. Your room is to remain free of their interference but there are enough of them to keep loneliness at bay."

Noah's beautiful smile returned as he said happily, "Almut and Hubertus, you say? Ah, I know them well. You thought of everything, Mad Maxx. I'm the lucky bastard to bask in your generosity and affections."

"Are you, Noah? Ha-ha. Maybe I fucked your brain soft if you really think being ridden like the bitch by your lusty King is the lucky thing. Well, I might test that theory of yours sometime real soon. Until then though, I've got more important matters to attend. So move your pretty ass or I will move it for you in a way even your dementia cannot protect you from." I chuckled and swatted him playfully on the backside.

Despite the terrible feelings of dread plaguing my heart over what I'd seen and now knowing what will have to do, Noah's lighthearted banter managed to ease my growing tension ever so slightly.

We traveled the rest of the entire way back to the Silk Queen's old fifth floor apartment (that now belonged to Almut, Hubertus and their families) without incident. I stood there and watched Noah be welcomed into his temporary home by the smiling wives of the fallen torture masters.

Once I was certain my beloved headmaster was safe, I rushed next door. I stood there for the few moments doing all I could to calm my nerves. I hated dealing with my sadistic brother Byron. That was too bad for me.

The diagnosis Doctor Attila gave to me was devastating to hear. Without any hope that the torture I continued to suffer in my enforced place playing the bottom. His pain killing cures were the must. That is if I desired to end being the easy mark. I understood that as long as the penetration sex caused terrible torture, those bastards forcing it on me were able to maintain their strong hold over the behaviors of my they didn't like.

Then there was the hope that Byron was being serious in his promises to helping me escape the Haus. I no longer cared if I had to promise to service him on the outside as his masochistic lover. Nor did it bother me anymore that he was my half-brother. Believe me when I tell you the closer the date for my being sent back below for good, the less picky I was becoming about who fucked me over as long as they were going to be doing it far away from the Haus.

I knew that Byron was beyond pissed that I'd managed to wrangle myself out of the original contract we had. It was severely balanced in his direction and this wasn't the fair trade. This he was aware. That, however, wouldn't keep him from attempting to renegotiate another with me even more unreasonable than the last.

The death of his mother Birgit surely wasn't helpful to my desperate situation with him either. Going to him during this time of his deepest grieving with demands for contract on my mind, was no doubt going to have the appearance of insult.

I don't know how long I stalled there at his door, unable to talking myself into knocking on it. Then before I could think better of my actions and leave the wooden entry opened with suddenness.

My brute brother stood there in the middle of his doorway staring at me seeming to be confused by the sight that greeted him.

With the anxious clearing of my throat I bid him hello trying to appear solemn. "Honorable Byron, I offer my deepest condolences for your loss. Your mother, the honorable Birgit, was the headmistress of the highest caliber. She and her most honorably loyal sister will be greatly missed." I bowed low in reverence to him.

Byron scoffed then replied in tone seething with rage, "You dare to spill this bullshit from your mouth into my ears during this time of my grieving? You are the rudest sonofabitch I've ever met. Stop your fucking games, Maxx. What the hell are doing here?"

I feigned surprise, and wearing the expression of injured pride I replied, "I apologize honorable Voter for being misled into believing that offering honest sympathy to the bereft is bad manners. I honestly was never made aware of this. I beg your forgiveness for the poor training skills of my former Master, the Voter Peter. Apparently, his instructions on the polite way to offer solace after the loss of someone of immense worth were lacking. I bid you goodnight and will bother you no more." I quickly turned to flee the scene grateful that Byron's usual bitchy nature had given me the excuse to chicken out of dealing with him at that moment.

But I didn't get the single step of retreat made before he bellowed out, "Hold it, Maxx. You're not going to get out of your agreement to meet with me if you survived that beating you took from the Stasi scum so easily. Now I repeat myself. Why the fuck did you really come here? Am I to believe you're finally ready to negotiate the fresh agreement between us?"

I kept my back to him as I said softly, "Byron, it's no secret I adored your honorable mother as if she were my own. Speaking of such crass subjects when her beautiful soul hasn't had the time to settle in the peaceful void is something I refuse to do. No matter how much I wish to demonstrate that I am the man of his word. Birgit and your Aunt Vivianna more than earned the respect I'm showing them. Even if this means risking your accusations that I'm the untrustworthy asshole."

My brute brother snorted then replied, "Ah, you speak the truth of it. Mother and Aunt Vivianna returned your love with equal fervor. They said this to me enough times to be assured they meant it. With that in mind, do remember both them did all possible to bring you comfort. Since they have gone to the place they can no longer serve their King in the way that brought them happiness, I suppose that task falls upon their unworthy son and nephew, ja?"

His uncharacteristically honorable statement caused me to turn around to study him hard. I wasn't sure if this was the most cleverly delivered sarcasm, or if somehow the loss of his kindhearted mother had cooled the rage within his own.

Byron maintained his own gaze on mine while keeping his expression unreadable. Though I noticed his eyes didn't appear swollen nor red from the signs of deep grieving. That didn't really mean he wasn't very upset over losing his mother. Everyone demonstrates sorrow differently.

I broke the momentary uncomfortable silence between us first.

"Do you say that with honesty? Or are you the one truthfully playing the games."

"I ask you why I open the door to find you standing here in the hallway in front of it. You are my King, the man my late mother cleaved to her loving bosom, and I risk death by saying out loud my own close kinsmen. So, if you came here seeking comfort, then I say with honesty speak of it to me. I didn't claim that I am capable of seeing it granted to you right at this moment. Nor did I say that this is the proper time to offer it, Maxx," he responded flatly.

I shrugged my shoulders and said quietly enough that no other ears could hear it, "Fair enough, brother. If you reach into my back pocket you'll find a black book. I wish to ask you to take this inside your apartment with you. During your time of grief sequestering, I beg you to take the time to examine the contents carefully. I also beg your confidence in the things you find contained within. This odd request will become obvious once you do the first thing I've humbly asked of you. I seem to recall that the honorable Voter Rolf owes you a favor. The one he swore to you over your distracting that rat Killian long enough to allow him and the honorable Friedrick to making the honorable Jacob's complaint of injury from that shady fuck appear honest, ja? He also gained your silence in that matter that was essential in my bid to breaking my metal. So perhaps he still has two favors due to you. If Rolf still hasn't repaid these promises of aid over the things you've done to perfection: I wish you to transfer his owed favor to me. The other things I need to bargain with you to acquire you already are aware of. When your sorrow subsides,

I'm ready to seal the contract we both benefit from with blood."

It was Byron's turn to demonstrate the tiny bit of surprise as he said, "Your list of things necessary to provide you adequate comfort is the most expensive one, isn't it? I'm quite curious to know the level of desperation it would cause you if I cannot or refuse to do what you ask of me."

I grimaced, then shifted with observable unease as I replied, "If you refuse my requests, Byron, the results of it would be catastrophic for me and many others. Listen brother, I don't have the time nor the strength to argue with you about your place of advantage over me thanks to unfortunate circumstances. You name your price and I'll agree to pay it."

Byron shot me the cruel grin as he said, "Well, well, if it weren't for the untimely death of my beloved mother and favored Aunt. I'd say this has turned out to be one of the best days of my life. You do understand after those tricks you pulled on me during that pissy fit you threw in the Great Hall and your dishonorably forcing me to recant our original contract, I'm not going to just roll over with ease. I'm going to need some time to consider how much I wish to extract from you to calm my temper."

The anger shined from my eyes as I grumbled out, "Who is it that's playing games now? Fine, take all the time you like to come up with the most perverted, disgusting, horrid things you wish to enforce upon me. I already told you I won't deny you anything you demand. However, in the meantime, show me that you're the man worth selling what's left of my twisted soul to today. Do as I ask you in the first place, oh, and give me the small down payment tonight. The carton of cigarettes, the week and the half worth of painkiller pills and two sharps full of that miracle healing concoction. Ja, that should be enough to see me through till it's appropriate to seal our agreement in blood."

Byron dropped his head back to release the meanest sounding laugh I'd ever heard. Then without the slightest sign of shame he said, "Deal little brother, oh, and by the way, I happen to know that the period of grace you requested before we make this official is equal to the amount of time you have left as excused for being left unmolested. You should have asked me for enough of those comfort items to make your reintroduction into your life of enforced special services by the ruthless men dominating you perhaps the bit less brutal than it surely is going to be. But as usual, you're too stupid to consider important things like that. Too bad for you, but wonderful for Byron, ja? This way I can be assured your misery tonight isn't merely the momentary fleeting feeling. Ha-ha-ga. Hold on the moment. I have the requested items available inside. I give them to you right this minute, but once they are gone, well you will have to beg like the dog for more." He rushed off into his apartment without sticking around long enough for me to offer the snotty retort.

Once he'd disappeared from sight and earshot I covered my face with both bandaged hands. I used the ragged material to clear away the tears that were breaking free with vigor. I thought momentarily of just ending this torment by pitching myself off the banister.

But as usual, I had to do a few important things before I could even consider being so selfish. It was too late for Helmut and his poor little cell mates.

That black book told me very soon the bowels of Das Kaiser Haus would be attempting to mimic Hollywood. And no doubt, there were some in the halls searching for fresh new faces…

To star in their latest block busters, I mean kinder busters, I had to come up with a fail proof plan to stop there perverted movie productions. For now I need to spend a bit of time getting to know the three candidates for mortar regent bedder.

I decided to start with that foxy Sigrid and work my way down the short list in the hope of gaining strong allies while I dressed down the much longer one.

Das Kaiser Haus didn't know it, but her Mortar King was about to cut the high price of living within her walls.

Chapter 28: The Sacrificial Lamb

That last chapter was ugly, wasn't it? Well, I would apologize for that but sadly there is no way to sugar coat this latest of Mad Maxx's dilemmas. Though he couldn't save the innocent lambs, he sure as shit intends to make sure no more are slaughtered.

But the only way he can achieve vengeance and cease this horrible practice is to sacrifice himself.

So, hang on tight. This is going to be one rough ride The pun is intended.

Byron returned with the sundry items I'd demanded for the down payment to our future contract. He smiled with evil shining in his eyes while I did the poor job attempting to taking these necessary things from his meaty clutches. It was hard to do thanks to my fucking useless broken hands, ja?

After I'd dropped most of the pills, and sharps onto the floor he chuckled with menace then said, "Without fingers I wonder how you plan to enjoy these pleasures? It's humorous to imagine you trying to light the smoke but the idea of you getting those suppositories were they need to go, ah I thank you for the mercy of that comical vision."

I shot him the furious glance, "It's of no consequence to you how or even when I used the things, Byron. I thank you to mind your fucking own business.

I recall I've requested a steady supply of these for the foreseeable future. If I see them missing on the contract you compose, I will not sign it."

His smile faded to the deep frown as he replied, "Wait, how often do you think you going to asking for the pharmaceuticals?"

With the shrug I responded, "That remains to be determined, brother. Maybe daily. Perhaps hourly. Doesn't matter to you other than you will need to keep them on the ready at all times, ja?"

He shook his head roughly, "Nein, I refuse to bargain with you without the concrete amount known in advance. You have no idea how difficult it is to gain some of these things. If I were to be so stupid as to take on the open ended promises. No doubt, you'd be here so often with demands to see you compensated that I'd either go broke feeding the monster appetite or at the very least, come up short eventually. This would give you the right to claim I've breached yet another contract with you. Byron isn't the fool, little brother. You think you're clever, but you better think again. I want the amount expected settled before we finalize this between us."

I snorted loudly then replied, "So much for your lofty bragging that you're the man with proper manners. Did you not say to me this time of mourning isn't appropriate for haggling details over this disgusting contract between us? Fine, you can be the rude brute, and so can I. How many of these things can you manage on a weekly basis? And don't attempt to shortchange. I'm in no mood for your pathetic attempts at pulling the lamb's wool over my eyes. I've had one seriously bad night. Getting on my last nerve wouldn't be healthy, I think, for either of us." I caught his hateful gaze and maintained eye contact without blinking.

He refused to break from our stare down as he said in the low growl, "It's unsafe to taking the painkiller cure more than four times the day, so that's twenty eight the week. The sharps you shouldn't take more than once a day. As for the smokes, I think one carton a week is plenty,. Though I expect that soon enough you'll be begging me to give you more of each thing because you're nothing but that wanton little bitch in all things of the sinful nature."

"Go fuck yourself, Byron," I sneered.

His laughter rang out loudly as he replied, "Ah, don't be offended by the truth little brother. It's not the insult I give to you anyway. It's one of the qualities about you that I love the best. If you'd been of the moderate nature I'd have tired of your skills already. I'm the man that's easily bored or have you forgotten that? I suppose it's possible that despite the sublime pain I've inflicted upon you in these past years, I've been too gentle with you to peek your full interest. Don't you fret your pretty head over it. The moment I've honored this silly request you've made to read the bedtime story in this tiny book, and informed Rolf he owes the favor to you instead of me. Well, let's just say I intend to add fuel to your nightmares. I've been holding back but not anymore. I'm going to hurt you in ways you never thought possible and make you beg me for more of the torturing because I know how much you truly love it, slut."

I opened my mouth to say something crass in response, but to my dishonor instead of the words of defiance coming out the pathetic whimper escaping me. This sound of fear incited the beast within Byron to thrill. His face lit up with cruel joy and his smile nearly broken his jaw in half.

"What's this you say? Is that the sound of excitement I hear? Ah, I bet you can hardly wait to swing in my chains, ja? Save it, little bitch. For the moment, I cannot attend your needs thanks to the necessary somber mood expected of me. Go back to that freak, Lucus. Maybe he'd be happy to slap you around until I can demonstrate to you what a real man can do. I'm finished with this conversation. I'm not worried you'll not be back to sign the contract mere seconds after my sequestering period is finished. By that time you're going to be on my leash more tightly than the yard dog is to his hairy Russian master. There isn't anyone capable, nor anywhere else in this Haus, to gain the vices that offer you the tiny mercy from the tormented existence you've stupidly gotten yourself into."

He turned his gaze to the cigarettes that I'd finally managed to tuck under my arm for a brief moment. Then with the low chuckling he went into his apartment and slammed his door shut leaving me standing there near ready to have the crying jag.

I did think that just before he disappeared inside I saw the slightest glimpse of what I thought might be fear come over his expression. This might have been the stress driven hallucination on my part. But I definitely observed the shift in his mood, I think.

Likely, not long after I'd left and that brute went about satisfying his curiosity to read what he had ignorantly referred to as 'the bedtime story.' He realized too late that he should've known me better. He called me the stupid one between us. Ha. Only the total idiot would assume the overly experience Mortar King would come to offer to enslave himself to anyone without expecting the expensive price for the pleasure, uhm, displeasure of it. But that hubris of my brute brother was the thing I was counting on when I decided Byron was the best candidate to see my plan to save the babies succeed.

Though I confess, the tears and whimpering were not the play acting I was doing. This horror I'd sworn to end wasn't going to be stopped easily. The only hope I had to end it required that I give to others all the hard won dignity I'd achieved since that damned Stasi party.

And the worst part, not that being forced to play Byron's willing bitch wasn't bad enough, was that this tortuous deal with my older brother wasn't going to be the only unfair contract I'd have to sign. I'd captured the brawn. Now, it was time to gain the allegiance of the brains.

It was this heavy weight that made my chest hurt to near bursting. I turned and practically fled to the fifth floor staircase platform. Everything around me was blurred by the haze of tears of the deep sorrow pouring out of my eyes. My vision was so severely impaired by the well-earned waterworks that I didn't see Roland until it was too late to avoid the most unwelcome greeting from the wolf.

He stopped two steps below the one I claimed. I quickly used the sleeve of my vampire jacket to wipe away the signs of my salty despairing. But it was too late. That fucker saw that I was weeping hard.

The violinist appeared unsure as he said, "Your Majesty? Is everything alright? Is someone bothering you? Should I call on the Wolf Pack to set some villain on their ear for daring to fool with the Lord and Master of the Haus? Say the word, and see it done with perfection."

By then I'd managed to clear my vision a bit. I immediately noticed that he was holding a large bunch of roses like the ones he brought to that bullshit loss of his penetration virginity, ja?. He was also dressed in his finest outfit and smelling to high heaven of the stinky perfume.

With the bitter sounding tone I growled in reply, "So, you use threats first and romance second to try to woe Matz into taking your sorry ass back? What the fucking bastard you've turned out to be, Roland. To think, I even gave you the beautiful memory and called you the gifted artist. Seems that the rumor that I'm the monarch with the cracked crown has some validity to it, ja? Because I must have been crazy to ever believe you're the honorable man worthy of anything but my foot up your ass."

Roland shifted nervously on his step and looked to the floor as he responded, "I don't know what lies Matz has told you about our relationship. But I can assure you, your Majesty. whatever he said is an exaggeration. Matz is high strung with the tendency to drama. I thought you'd know this after living with him yourself for months. It's truth that I've lost my temper to the point of some mild violence in the past with him. I swear he gives as good as he gets. I sport bruises from his pissy fits many more times than he has from my retaliation over them."

I glared at him with barely veiled disgust in my expression as I said, "This shit between the two of you isn't of importance to me at this moment. Though I'm not the fool to believe Matz will stand firm against your dishonest efforts to gain his forgiveness. Your relentless courting will likely result in him allowing you to return to his bed in the much improved surroundings. I'll not try to stop you this time. But if I'm correct and you're able to talk him into giving you another chance, I ever find out you are using your fists on him again, do I really need to tell you what I'll do to you? Matz is the only thing standing in the way of my life in the palace being slightly less traumatic than the last time. I'm the grateful man for any mercy, even the smallest, that I can get these days. I won't permit you or anyone to do anything that put him in danger. Oh, and as for Cary. If my Shadow King ever tells me you touched a hair on his head for any reason, Roland, I'll make sure you damn your mother for giving birth to you. Do we understand each other?"

He kept his face turned downward and nodded his head in silence. I came toward him with suddenness. Then I used my shoulders to aggressively push him into the stairwell wall while I passed by. This was not necessary because there was plenty of room for me to move without touching him. The path wasn't that crowded. I did this because I needed him to understand, I was serious about the things I said to him. He already proved to me numerous times that his ears hear much better if you use your hands when speaking to him.

Roland smartly kept any complaining about my rough behavior to himself. *I swear to you Meine Liebe, had he uttered another word to me, I'd have happily pitched his skinny thug ass right over the railing. Believe me when I say that I was ready to blow my last gasket that night. Besides, I'd already put the innocent baby lambs to their rest. It seemed only fair to destroy their natural enemy, the crafty wolf as well, ja?*

Though I can blame that horrific scene in the palace tunnels for part of my edginess, that shady situation with my brother compounded my psychic pain further. It was the next move I had to make that was putting that final nail in the coffin of my ability to maintain my sanity.

Lucus was the instigator of this my final downfall. Like it or not, I understood he was the only man capable of guaranteeing that the work to save the babies didn't get undone. Or perhaps I should say he was, without any doubt, the man willing to put his life on the line to end this carnage.

I see that look of confusion in your eyes Meine Liebe. Are you wondering how I could believe that about Lucus after you already know he withheld this important information from me all that time? Well, I don't really know how or when he came about discovering the dark truth of this mess. But I did realize that night that he wasn't telling false tales when he said he was risking his life to share this grievous secret with me.

There were many in the Haus that would think nothing of destroying him for daring to reveal this situation to their murderous Mortar King. They actually would have to kill him and then me too. Once I had named my regent, and assuming that this was the person that spoke my words with honesty, making the law to stop the baby killing and seeing those responsible punished severely was within my power and my alone. Do remember, Meine Liebe. My words are the law.

Well, my words on the tongue of my regent are the law anyway. As you are probably guessing. Lucus obviously wasn't happy about these gross abuses of the babies being permitted to happen. His name also wasn't on the list. Oh and if I forgot to tell you, neither was Byrons.

It's the sad they in hell when two of the biggest perverts that ever walked the Earth are truly innocent. And some of the greatest hearts I'd ever known were the guilty, ja? But this was the truth that I had to face without flinching or showing weakness.

Despite all the nasty shit Lucus had pulled on me, including that neutering business. He does possess one quality of worth. That is to say he is honestly interested in ending the brutality leveled at the collared population of the Haus.

Three other souls had made the bid to coax me into naming them instead, ja? There was the possibility that soon many more would do the same. I could take the chance that someone with interests similar to my own, besides Lucus, would come along. That was the treacherous game to be playing. I didn't have much time left above the ground. Proper investigation of any potential candidate to make sure they were trustworthy wasn't possible. And the little ones that soon would be selected for the next slaughter were depending on their King to save them.

So, with the heavy heart I returned to the fourth floor apartment that fucker stole from me and after doing all I could to calm down. I knocked on the door with the head of my walking cane. *I must tell you, Meine Liebe. I'd not felt this beaten since the days I'd suffered in Xavier's chains. It was truly soul crushing to see the look of satisfaction on that rat bastard's face when he opened it and to find me standing there.*

He smiled slightly then said, "Are you here to stay or to pack your bags?"

"You already know the answer to your stupid question asshole," I grumbled out in reply.

He stepped aside and waved me to enter. I did this in total silence. Seething with rage at his cruelly trapping me back into his nasty grips.

Once I was far enough inside that I couldn't easily retreat he slammed the door shut and quickly secured all the locks on it. I ignored this rude behavior by moving swiftly towards his fancy overstuffed recliner chair.

Lucus turned around just as I started to drop into it and yelled out, "What the hell are you doing, Christian Victor? You know better. That's the Masters' chair."

I maintained my place in front of his "special seat" and replied in the snotty tone, "You are the Master of shit, Lucus. And you've not managed to conquer anything else that I'm aware of. No power, no wealth. Even your own kinsmen are ashamed of you. No one in the world wishes to see your ugly face. In fact, they hate you so much they pay the big bucks to keep themselves from having to gaze upon it even if only for the seasonal holidays. That's why you love to wallow in the cack, ja? You have affinity with it because that's what you are. And of course, the sewer is the place that the nobody like yourself can call himself king."

Lucus's smugness quickly reverted to the expression of rage as he yelled out, "I've had enough of you insults, God dammit. You've no right to be pointing out the flaws of others when you've so many to choose from yourself, ja? Perhaps I am the Master of Shit. However, you are the King of Nothing. So, I suggest you lower your voice and demonstrate manners appropriate for someone that's not in the position to behave like the wretched creature he truly is."

I chuckled bitterly then said, "I'm the wretched creature, you say? Ah, but at last, the truth rolls off the tongue of the professional liar. I think that hell must have just frozen over. Or maybe, the monkeys have sprouted wings and began to fly. I must be having the auditory hallucinations because this simply cannot be reality."

His glare was so vicious I swear if he'd had knives in his eyes they'd have cut me to ribbons as he replied, "You cannot be hearing voices, because apparently you've gone deaf, Christian Victor. You clearly didn't hear me tell you to end the insults. Now, if you've something of worth to say, pray tell share it. Otherwise pack your bags and get the fuck out of my Haus you ingrate."

My mirth ended with abruptness then I growled angrily, "Your Haus? You are the thief, the criminal and the pervert. Those are not insults, Lucus, they are the truth. If you think you're big enough to remove me from my Haus, then I dare you to try motherfucker."

Lucus's fury over my defiance caused the momentary lapse in his good senses. Before he realized that I'm far bigger and stronger than him he rushed at me with his teeth gnashing and fists flying.

That is what I was hoping he would do. Soon as he was within striking distance I used all the power of hate within me to lodge the well-aimed kick right into his hoddensack. That perverted Dominant fell faster than the stock market did on Black Tuesday. His hands clutched desperately at his injured manhood while he flopped and thrashed about on the floor in front of my boots. I didn't feel this had adequately gained his attention. Without hesitation I kicked him in the stomach even harder than my first blow.

While the man tried in vain to suck in air. I leaned down close to his writhing frame and whispered, "How many have died the worst of deaths while you wasted time playing games with my head? Did you not think even once to asking me if I'd comply with your plans to end this cruelty without all this brutality you've put me through? You wish me to trust you with my power, but you clearly have never trusted the man you manipulated into taking the Mortar Throne." Without saying anything more I sat down in his chair and watched him struggle in his agony.

It took maybe half an hour for Lucus to find relief from my attack. Slowly he lifted himself from his prone position to sitting upright. He didn't bother to look my direction for many more minutes. We just sat there quiet as a mouse.

Then at last Lucus spoke, "You are correct that I didn't trust you to do what must be done without using nefarious means, Christian Victor. Am I to assume you're saying this to me, means I was in error? Before you answer that do remember the cost of interference. Hell, even knowing what you now know is quite possibly a death sentence."

I rolled my eyes then with the sigh replied, "Stop calling me that, Lucus. I'm the Mad Maxximillian. This is the name that I earned through blood, sweat, and many tears. You had no right to taken that single honor I've earned the hard way."

Lucus shot the surprised glance my direction as he mumbled, "I suppose I hadn't considered that. I apologize for being non-empathetic about this. I will address you as Maxximillian if this would be suitable but I don't agree with the addition of the word Mad.

That was given to you as an insult. Surely, I don't need to tell you that."

"Ja, I do understand this was meant to be the insult. Yet I hear you call yourself Mad Lucus. This didn't bother you to do, so it shouldn't be the issue to show me the respect of calling me by the proper name," I replied flatly.

He nodded then said, "Okay, fair enough I suppose. I will call you Mad Maxximillian and you will never be permitted to top me in the bedroom during our lovemaking."

With the sigh of resignation I replied, "I don't request to fuck your ass, but you cannot demand I do anything that involves scat or breath play ever again."

Lucus groaned loudly then said, "I agree to end the scat play but I will not accept the sanction on the breath play once in a while when the mood strikes me. Nor will I withdraw my bid to the right to maintain your personal grooming with my own hands before you bring that up because I know you will. But if you are willing to soften your hard limit in these areas that bring me pleasure then I'm open to trading something for the rights to engage with you in them."

"Nein, after my hands heal, I don't want you ever wiping my ass, nor plucking my body hairs out ever again, dammit. No deal," I said with force.

He glared at me sternly then said, "You are often plagued with mental instability, Chris, uhm, Mad Maxximillian. The hygiene rituals you practice are too extreme and eventually will destroy what's left of your flesh below the waist. Not to mention your addiction to the enema nearly cost you your bowels. This isn't something I'm going to take off our bargaining table. So, pick something of equal value to trade or I think you will need to find another willing to help you clean up the atrocities you've discovered tonight."

I rolled my eyes and blew out my breath in pure frustration then said, "I hate you, Lucus. I will always hate you. I want you to know if I ever have the chance I'm going to murder you with calloused brutality."

The small chuckle erupted from him as he replied, "No doubt, you speak from the heart, and maybe you will indeed do as you say. Be that as it may, I don't scare that easily. And I don't revoke my demands. So? Pick something or say we are through in more ways than one. It's up to you."

I snuck the quick glance at the carton of cigarettes I'd rested on the arm of his chair before I responded, "And if I agree to these things you will speak my words with honesty? Even to that bitch Gretta? No matter what she threatens to do to you or me?"

"You realize already giving you the answer to your question tonight assures that Gretta's threats are the least of my worries, ja," he replied with some anxiety noted in his tone.

With the nod I said, "If I didn't, would I have returned to you?"

Lucus sighed as he replied, "Nein, you most likely wouldn't. I suppose you are willing to take the word of the man you keep claiming is nothing but the liar. If not, then what the hell do you wish me to say? I tell you, no matter how much you hate me for manipulating you as I have I did this because of my desire end the immorality in this Haus was of more value to me than any discomfort it may cause either of us. Please try to understand, Mad Maxximillian. There are so many suffering terrible things all around us. It can be fixed, but likely it will destroy us both to see it accomplished to perfection. Perhaps it was wrong of me to keep the truth of your birthright from you, the power that it brings, and the horror that comes with it. But imagine what would have happened if I had told you. Can you honestly tell me, you'd have still demanded the crown? Even if you agreed to be coronated, how could I be sure you'd willingly give up your freedom, and your life outside of that palace hell to save countless others in far worse situations?"

I gasped in shock as I replied, "There are not so many in the Haus suffering worse situations than being repeatedly raped while rotting away isolated in the cage underground."

Lucus focused on my gaze then said coldly, "You met some of them tonight, ja?"

With a shudder I replied, "Our original contract arrangement is to remain valid plus I will agree to all that you requested. But I want to add that until Doctor Attila grants me full medical release, you keep your filthy hands off me. I provide you with no services of any kind. I take the bedroom for my sanctuary. You will not enter it unless I ask you to come in. Furthermore, I demand that until my hands heal, you will aid me in lighting my cigarettes and putting my important medications where they need to go whenever I ask for the assistance. You will do only what is necessary to get the pills into me, but neither linger nor enjoy it. I also want the lambs you were willing to give to me with the visits to them as you promised. You put all of this in writing, then I will sign it in blood. You will file it with honor in the Hall of Records this time, Lucus. No more secrets between us and no more backstabbing. I fucking mean it. Take this deal or you can pack your shit and get the hell out of my life. This is my Haus not yours."

He sat there glaring at me for the brief moment then replied slowly, "You are asking for more than you're giving, Mad Maxximillian. And for the record, I'm paying the rent of this apartment. That makes me the owner not you."

I stood up abruptly. This sent Lucus into the cower with equal speed as I yelled out, "Lucus, I'm tired and want to go to bed. You take it or leave. I'm warning you.

I no longer give two shits about pretty much anything. I'm never going to be a father thanks to your stupidity. I'm never going to see the green fields nor feel the soft caresses of the Frau of my dreams either. I ask you for almost nothing from you and in return you take everything from me. This apartment was earned by my dignity and you stole both without shame nor regret. So, stop trying to treat me like the idiot fool. Go this minute and get your motherfucking contract written. While you are at it, find the flame source. I need a smoke before I lose it and kill you right where you sit."

Well, Meine Liebe, Lucus finally realized this was as far as I was willing to be pushed. He got his ass in gear and did as I told him to do. While I sat there in his favorite chair, he took the seat on his fancy sofa. Before I had finished my first cigarette smoked to the filter, he handed it to me for my approval and, of course, signature. There was nothing more to haggle out of this unfair arrangement with him. Thanks to my unfortunate role as the Mortar King it is required by Haus Law to name the regent to speak for me. I needed him far more than he needed me if you don't count his perverted interests in my skills that is.

The moment I signed away my last shred of dignity that night I retreated to the bedroom with the horrid cock bed. It took me a bit to gain the courage to call Lucus in there to prove he was honorable about our contract agreement. That pain killer Doctor Attila had given me was wearing off and things were getting uncomfortable.

Lucus followed my instructions to the letter. Though I could hear his breathing becoming excited while he undid my trousers then placed Byron's suppository in me. What a fucking sicko, ja? My disgust with him was evident but he pretended not to notice. After that I threw him the fuck out of the room.

I couldn't bring myself to get into the nasty bed of his. The floor was the poor alternative for that feather mattress but the trauma of seeing the things done to that little baby. Oh, Meine Liebe, I just couldn't get the scenes of that tragedy out of the wheel room. The babies screaming in pain over there horrific injuries, and terror over my giving them mercy rang out in the repeat so loud. I wished I'd go stone deaf.

Byron's painkiller brought relief to my physical pain but also helped to numb some of my inner turmoil. Any amount of mercy was the blessing during that traumatic wait before I could do anything to stop the baby killing. I decided until my brute brother came out of his grieving. It was best to lay low.

I had no way to know if Snot had kept his word to not alert anyone I'd been there. There was also that DJ sneaking around the halls, looking to taking advantage of my love for the chocolate to consider. Doctor Attila said that I'd healed enough that severe damage hadn't been done during his last attack on me. That didn't mean the injuries couldn't be reopened by more of this violence. I knew my disappearance would worry Noah. This was solved by sending Lucus to the fifth floor to tell the dungeon master to stay put till I came to retrieve him.

Ja, I couldn't even find the will to do that simple task. The fight had gone right out of me and as I lay on that bedroom floor, half out of my mind and high as a kite from powerful pain killers. I could feel the heavy burden of my triple crowns crushing my head into the carpet. Even though in reality my noggin was bare. I didn't have to put them on to suffer the discomfort of their immense weight.

Lucus kept his end of our arrangement for that entire week and four days with honor. I could sense he wanted to argue with me about the quantity of cigarettes and yellow pills I was consuming. It was the good thing for him, he wisely kept his concerns about it silent.

However, looking back on it, this was one time he maybe should've put his big nose into my private business. Because after laying on the floor doing nothing but weeping, flash backing, smoking, and pill popping for ten days, you could officially label me as the full blown drug addict. Yikes! As if I didn't already have enough drama without adding this latest problem to my huge list of them.

On the tenth day the honorable Birgit and Vivianna were finally put to rest. Lucus returned to the apartment after attending there funeral. He told me that it was done with great dignity. Many in the Haus thought it was far more than any of Xavier's old conquests had deserved.

That wasn't very nice of the fools that said that, but most of them never really knew those fine ladies. Or at least didn't know the torment they endured under their old Master Xavier. Anything of worth they got from him for what was forced out of them wasn't even close to balanced.

I didn't want to return to Byron's apartment to finish the contract agreement with him, not ever. But by the eleventh day, I'd exhausted my cigarette and drug supply. As I said, I was no longer able to function without them by then. If it had not been for that sad fact, I'd have stayed on that floor for maybe the remainder of my time left before I was to be put to the palace.

But to my displeasure Byron's prediction that I'd have to return to him crawling was on the nose. And so was Lucus's that I'd not be capable of ignoring the gruesome secret he'd shared with me.

With all my remaining inner strength, on the eleventh day, I managed to pull myself out of that abyss of paralyzing despair. Lucus helped me to shower, shave and do all things I'd been neglecting. Interestingly, not once during that time did the vampire come knocking to demand I hold up my end of our arrangement.

His lack of demonstrating irritation over such a serious slight wasn't usual for him. This made me worry that somehow he'd figured out that I'd been visiting the palace tombs. If this were the case, I knew I had a lot more to stress about then the simple beating from him. It was pretty obvious that Jonas's fangs were deeply buried in the illegal operations below. He'd already sold me out to the Altergotts several times for crimes he had been guilty of doing. I'd nearly been killed by their twisted fun with me before Byron finally put the end to them both. And Jonas sat by and let it happen without even trying to help. All because he wanted to avoid being sent to the dungeon for mild punishment.

There was no telling how far he'd allow others to go to force me to remain silent this time. If this secret got out, his ass was grass. Well, it was going to be feeding the grass. So, I won't lie and say that I wasn't scared enough to piss my trousers over the idea the Vampire was waiting to get me the second I left the apartment.

This anxiety that Jonas knew was actually the thing that calmed my nerves enough to aid me in doing what had to be done. The way I saw it back then, if he did come to destroy me to make sure the secret didn't get out then, on the bright side, I'd not have to deal with his gross fetish, nor my brothers unnatural interests in me anymore. After all the dead are grated the mercy of shedding all there burdens and pain.

Unfortunately for me but fortunately for many, including you Meine Liebe though you may not always agree, Jonas wasn't waiting outside the apartment ready to pounce. I hurried to the fifth floor while keeping the baleful eye peeled for the signs of any assassination attempts. There of course, weren't any. That didn't make me feel any better as I approached Byron's door.

I took a deep breath, braced and then very gently began to knock on the wood. Before my cane barely made contact for the first time the door suddenly flew open. Byron grabbed me by the gold collar and roughly dragged me inside with him, slamming his door behind us.

My senses were unable to grasp the meaning of his aggressive welcome. That was compounded when with suddenness he began to shake me like the rag doll in his grips.

In the terrified sounding tone he whispered loudly into my stunned face, "You little bastard. Where did you come by that book you gave to me? For God's sake this had better be your stupid attempt at the practical joke. Listen here idiot slut, I don't find this funny. I ought to bash in your brains for even coming up with such disgusting props and cruel lies."

His harsh treatment had addled my nerves a little bit which made it difficult for several minutes to understand what he was asking me. Plus I was starting to feel the jonesing and was in need of more of his drugs. It didn't help he was rambling nearly incoherently.

"Let me go, Byron. That isn't the forgery and based on your anxiety I think you already know that to be the truth of it. Stop behaving like the frightened nincompoop this minute. Get ahold of yourself brother," I breathed out excitedly.

He pulled me close to his face and through clenched teeth replied, "I asked you where it came from, but I also wish to know who gave it to you? If anyone else knows you have this and now me, we are so fucked."

I growled back in the low voice tone, "No one knows that I have that book. Well that either of us have seen it, Byron. Save one, and he's sworn to secrecy."

Byron's eyes went wide, and his brow broke into the stress sweating, "And you let this man live? You are not stupid, you are a fucking moron. Maybe he already betrayed you and the minute you leave they will kill you, and then me too."

The sarcastic chuckling erupted from my throat that he was squeezing hard, "Brother, did I not make it up here from the fourth floor alive and well? No one knows about this, and this man is honorable, that I can swear to you. Now again, I asking you politely to put me down, dammit." *Why you look at me like that Meine Liebe? That was polite of me to ask him rather than make him. Hahaha.*

Instead of releasing me from his brutal hold his expression went from that of fear to one of desperation as he said, "Okay, okay. Let's just all calm down. Maybe this man hasn't blabbed to anyone yet. But he will trust me on this. So, all we must do is return this book wherever you found it. Then we kill this fellow and hide the body. Then we will be home free and neither of us need be executed, ja?"

I glared at him as I replied, "It's too late to take it back. There is evidence that someone has taken this. It won't be too difficult to figure out I'm the thief that took it. You will help me fix this like we agreed or I'll be all too happy to claim you as my accomplice to whoever comes to silence my tongue. We survive together or we die together. Up to you, brother."

His mouth nearly fell to his apartment floor before he gained his composure and said in the breathy voice, "Why would it be easy to know this was you? Where the fuck did you even get this? From that man you say is honorable? Did he see you take it? Ja, he did. that's why you say they would find you."

"I already told you this man won't tell a soul I took it. But that won't matter because I'm the only one besides two others that hold the key to the Mortar Palace. They'll know it wasn't Claus."

Byron put his hand over my mouth to muffle my sound then leaned into my face as he said in the whisper, "And Jonas is the one keeping this going. Don't say another fucking thing about this. I mean it. Okay, let me think. Ja, okay. Me and you will go to the palace together. Once there you will put this back where you found it. Maybe once they see you returned it but didn't breathe a word of its contents, they'll let us live."

The sounds of mocking mirth filled the room as I laughingly replied, "You know I never found you sexy till just this moment. That's not surprising because I've always had the incredible weakness for pussy." He backhanded the hell out of my head for voicing that insult. It was worth it.

"This isn't the time for sarcasm, Maxx. You cannot be this damned cavalier about the possibility of the kind of execution they will level on us for this. What the hell are we going to do? Fuck. We are doomed." He dropped me with such suddenness I was unable to catch myself before hitting the floor with the loud and painful thud.

I didn't attempt to get back to my feet while I watched the big brute begin to pace back and forth in his living area. He was mumbling to himself about the suffering we were going to do while the Haus executors skinned us alive. Then make us watch as they feed our freed parts to the yard dogs."

This would have been great comedy had he not been speaking the truth of our predicament. If I couldn't plug up the hole I was planning to make in the Haus wallet being slowly cut to pieces was the penalty by law. Not Haus law, Stasi decree.

You see, when the Stasi placed that punishment on the Haus for her residents' part in the disgusting things Germany did to people during the World War Two, there was only fifty of the Haus families left alive.

That's because Xavier knew the Stasi were going to fine the Haus ten thousand per resident in advance.

Therefore he ordered the Russian guard to murder everyone under three. Then more of the Haus population was shot while trying to save their babies from this mass execution. Xavier planned that would happen. He was the evil genius to realize less people when the Stasi came to record names and the surviving numbers was equal to less he'd have to pay annually in that fine.

You see, the actual wording of the sentence passed on the Haus was most cruel indeed. The Stasi demanded that the surviving Haus members pay 10k per person for fifty of them in all. This equals 500k per year the Haus owes the GDR and her Stasi pigs. This applied to the Dominants only, the collars were viewed as innocent because they were basically slaves, ja?

Furthermore, no matter if any of them died after that original fifty were recorded as guilty. That 500k would never decrease. That is until the final member of the fifty was officially recorded as deceased. That means the more of them that passed away, the more of a financial burden on those left behind, ja?

Worse, this 500k had to paid in the lump sum. Meaning, if even the single penny wasn't paid on time, the Stasi would come and carry out the punishment on every single one of the war survivors. That was equal to the torturing they did to their victims during that war. You need not know much about the camps and what happened in them to understand the Haus residents would be subjected to the most horrific executions imaginable.

If you recall, Claus told me that at the time of the Stasi take over the youngest member of the survivors was the Honorable Jacob. This means every Elder, and Voter except Gretta and Byron were among the fifty from Peter to Malfred to my Leo. Jonas wasn't counted as the Haus member because, well no one has ever figured out why. Nevertheless he wasn't included as one of the survivors. Gretta came to the Haus after the war as did Lucus. Byron was born to the black collared Sarah (who was uncollared and renamed Birgit after the Stasi takeover).

Even in the seventies 500k per year was a fortune few possessed. When this sentence was passed in the forties, it may as well have been one million. There was no way the battered, beaten survivors of starvation, raping, and rampant pillaging by the Russians could come up with that kind of cash. Not in one year. Probably not for many years if ever.

Xavier put every survivor to work selling there flesh to the highest bidders in the attempt to get this fine covered. This of course didn't get close to meeting their needs. Those not able to work as the prostitutes were tasked with cultivating wealthy cliental willing to pay the big money for the thrill the Haus of the forbidden pleasure could offer them.

According to that book I found in that so called playroom, one of these survivors, it didn't record who (but I suspect it was that old devil Xavier himself) made contact with someone or more than one eager to pay the minor fortune to enjoy the biggest taboo of sexual thrills.

I already told you what that thing these fiends desired. This service request was provided for the price of the Haus annual fine. But at the cost of dozens of innocents yearly. You see that book also reported that this 'abominable' service was provided four times a year and as many as twelve little ones and at times as few as five were sacrificed to these monsters. The secret place assured they would never be discovered or disturbed. The torture tools they requested was provided by the Haus for an extra minimal cost. That old mausoleum was converted into the abomination called the playroom in the effort to coax these most hideous clients to return, year after year, to enjoy there foul delights.

Just so you know. That book also reported the annual Stasi night was another of Xavier's systems developed to bring in money for the Haus restitution payments. Two more young kids were handed over annually to be destroyed in the worst of ways and the Great Hall provided for them to do this in total secret from the laws outside the Haus.

Byron knew damned well that any, and maybe every, remaining war survivor would do whatever necessary to keep this deplorable act the unspoken secret. The Haus would continue to collect the cash without interference from morally minded Mortar Kings, ja?

Ah, are you feeling upset to learn that on that list of survivors that might be involved are the names of Leo, Jacob, Rolf, Friedrick, Malfred, Claus, Justus, your father Karl and of course that bitch mother of mine too. Well, so were several others that we'll discuss shortly. If you are saddened to hear this tragic truth. Just imagine how much this information broke your Master's heart.

I'd ignored that Leo, Jacob, Rolf, and Friedrick never bothered to tell me about the Stasi Night nightmare before it was too late. I'd overlooked that all them wandered around in the Haus everyday doing nothing of worth to stop the abuses of the silver and black collared people. None of them seemed willing to speak against the purchasing children like the livestock to be abused to uselessness, then sold off to suffer even worse. I knew in my heart this spoke poorly of their honest characters. I mean, after all, all but Jacob had used me, at least once, as nothing more than the sexual plaything before I was even thirteen years old. I was the child too, ja? If you have eyes it's impossible to ignore that my flesh tells the tale I'd already had enough long before they took advantage of the boy that was helpless to stop them.

This you surely realized already, ja? Perhaps, like your Master, you kept making excuses for them because they give me the lambs or give me the pretty pup? Or maybe because they finally think to stand up for one of us that never had the choice and do the right thing by seeing him freed of his bondage that was merely the illusion all along. I know, you forgive them for their chronic neglect of the basic humanity towards the collared children because they refuse to beat the fuck out of the same one not long before they pretended to be helping get free of their grips.

Stop that grieving Meine Liebe. There is no place in our world for fantasy friends or false love. You will always be capable of knowing the true emotions from the fake because you've suffered at the hands of those without any.

Understand this, it takes true loneliness to recognize true love when and if your blessed with it, and severe hunger to know when you're getting enough to eat, ja? Well it also requires you endure terrible pain to appreciate honest comfort. Once you cease the natural tendency to minimize, exaggerate or offer unrealistic excuse to things we experience in this life, we lose the ability to fall for the bullshit we feed ourselves. But more importantly, once we find the inability to tell ourselves lies, we can clearly see it when others are still doing it both to themselves and to us.

We all make choices in this life, Meine Liebe. Every choice is made in the hope we reach the desired outcome. And every choice also had the price you must pay. No one has the right to misuse another to pay their personal debts, nor should they be permitted any excuse to do this, no matter how much we may think we love them or them us.

Dis you understand, Meine Liebe, ja?

I nodded my head, but honestly I didn't agree that Leo and Jacob deserved to be killed over this. It just didn't seem possible they would let those people do the bad things to the Haus babies if they had known it was happening. I guess I wasn't ready to truly hear the lesson he was teaching me. Because as he rightly pointed out. Even if they didn't know about the babies. They did know about the bad things happening to my Master and all the children wearing collars. It just seemed to me that there wasn't anything the few of them could do about it against the many without getting themselves killed.

But you see that was my problem. The man telling me these stories was willing to give his life – and had given his potential life - and his comfort to do what none of them would. He didn't give up by just ignoring the bad things happening around him. Not even after he had thought himself free of it. Master Maxx didn't always win, but he never stopped fighting. No matter what it cost him.

I didn't say anything to Byron for a while. It seemed to me it was necessary for him to get this shit fit of his out of his system. Better he release this pent up doubt before he took his place next to me as my partner in gaining justice for the Haus babies.

But eventually his acting the fraidy cat got on my last nerve. And as I said, I really needed that next pain killer.

"Are you going to give me the pain killer now? You're wasting time we don't have brother. If you don't pull yourself together than we certainly are in real danger of becoming the dinner for the dogs," I said with the bored sounding sigh.

Byron halted his pacing and turned to look at me with the nervous expression as he replied, "Ja, ja. I go get one right after you give me one of your smokes and the fire to light it with." He held out his hand toward me.

I startled then said, "Wait, I didn't know you smoked the cigarettes."

He shook his head. "I don't. But it's the tradition to give the man about to be executed the mercy of the cigarette and blindfold."

With the sarcastic chuckle I handed him one of the cancer sticks. "You act like you don't trust the good judgement of your Mortar King, Byron. Do you really think I live this long without being the cleverest fucker in the land?"

He snort laughed then said, "I agree that you fuck cleverly, but as for your unexpected length of survival.

I think that was probably dumb luck more than anything."

He took the lighter from me and after firing it up took the long drag of it. Byron then promptly attempted to cough up one of his lungs.

With the eye roll I said, "Choking to death is surely the way to get out of meeting your end of our bargain. So, do you have that contract ready? If so, let's get this over with. I sign it, then you get me that pill I've asked you for multiple times. After that, I've got someone I need to meet with right this minute. But while I deal with this appointment, you go fetch Friedrick, Rolf and some other burly bastard you think you can trust or bribe easily. Meet me at that hellish storage closet I still have nightmares about in about thirty minutes, ja?"

Byron choked even louder then rasped in response, "You intend to begin this plan of yours this quickly then? Oh fuck me. Wait, are you not going to at least tell me who we intend to take down first off that list?"

My eyes twinkled with mischief as I replied, "You forget that contract I'm going to make with you states that I get my requested favor before you have free reign to play head games with me, brother. You know damned well who we take down first. You've known since the moment you read that book. Go get that pill you owe me. I'm going to be late if you keep fucking around acting the dumbass you honestly are."

Byron growled in response, "I'm going to enjoy beating you into submission smart mouth. If I were you I'd be praying they do kill us both. What they are going to do will be more merciful than what I have in mind to make you suffer."

He took off into his bedroom to get the item I'd requested. I shook my head and then yelled after him, "On second thought Byron, bring the pill with you. I will take it after we set the first of many head rolling. I think I may need to keep the sharp mind to assure nothing goes wrong."

He stuck his head back into the room and with the nervousness returning to his expression replied, "Nothing better go wrong. What about that contract? You wish me to bring that with me too? Not sure that's the wise ting. Do you even have time to read it at this moment? I wouldn't want you accusing me of sneaking anything in there we didn't discuss."

I groaned loudly then replied, "Bring the lancet and hurry up about it. I don't give the flying fuck what deviltry you've put in there that I must endure for your pleasures. As long as you help me save the babies, give me the number of pills and smokes I asking for, and find the way to get us the fuck out of this motherfucking hell hole before I'm sent to the palace, I'll do whatever, whenever and however you like. I'll be yours, flesh, and soul for good. But this time you going to file that contract in the Hall of Records. Don't argue. No one need ever see it as long as you keep up your end of our arrangement. I will check that you filed it so don't even think to try to fib about it. I mean it. Hurry the fuck up. I'm going to be late."

That sinister smile of his that I hate so much crept across his face when he cut my finger for me, broken hands, and I signed his contract. Without so much as glancing at the words on it. I think he honestly thought I was kidding that I was done trying to play the cat and mouse game with him. As I told you. I really wasn't concerned who was fucking me nor how rough it was going to be now that the palace was the only future that was certain if I didn't soon escape.

I suppose, I was hoping one of them would accidently and finally kill me during their overzealous attempts to make me scream out in agony. It made them feel like the big man to dominate me the way they did. My self-esteem, if I ever had any, had run away long ago by then. Byron didn't realize he was making the deal with the frozen heart of the corpse.

Thankfully, I would have his magic pain killers and miracle sharps to numb the worst of it. Or so I hoped anyway.

It took a few more moments I didn't have to give him some sketchy details of my plan. His initial anxiety seemed to calm substantially upon his hearing that I wasn't the idiot he convinced himself I was. Before I left he did say that if any plan could work to end this nightmare baby killing this would be the one to do it.

Well of course it would. It was the Master of the Haus that come up with it, ja? Everyone knows that brutal bastard always gets what he wants. If he doesn't, he'll murder your ass.

Though I'd healed as nearly as much as I ever was going to from that nasty Stasi night business. It still took me another five minutes to reach Sigrid's apartment on the first floor. This problem with choosing the proper regent had definitely attracted the sexiest of contestants. I had to work hard to restrain Maxximillian from taking the wheel hostage during this interview visit with her.

The foxy FemDom answered my attempt to hail her with promptness. She practically purred with thrill upon finding that her visitor was the one she desired the most. *Well, honestly, Meine Liebe the feeling was mutual. Seeing her standing there in the tight fitting, short cut, fashionable dress practically bursting at the seam's with female allure. It was indeed the breathtaking scene.*

She smiled wantonly at me as she cooed out, "Why, Your Majesty. to what do I owe this most unexpected pleasure? How can this your unworthy servant be of assistance to you?"

For that moment, her charms nearly stole my good senses. I quickly shook the rising lust from my consciousness. Then I bowed low to her as I replied, "Honorable Sigrid, your beauty is truly the stuff poets pine to possess for their muse. Would you do me the honor of being my escort to the Great Hall for breakfast?

I do believe you voiced the desire to be considered for the position of my regent, ja? Well, before I can dare to choose you for this lofty task, I would like to get to know you better. You know, see if we are the best match." I snuck the hungry glance at one of her perfectly shaped legs.

She caught my glance of desire. With the catlike grin she giggled then covered her mouth while cutting her eyes at me coyly.

I shrugged, then feigned embarrassment as I said, "I beg you forgive my bad manners, honorable Sigrid. Even your King isn't immune to your radiant beauty. I confess I'm the powerful monarch but am helpless at your pretty feet."

Sigrid swooned slightly then while twirling the small ringlet of her blond hair while licking her lower lip suggestively she replied, "You keep flattering me like this Your Majesty, I'll forget that I'm the honest lady. If that happens I fear you'll never be capable of thinking of me in the same way ever again."

With the gentle movement I put out my arm and invited her to take it, "My Lady, there isn't any chance I can think of you the same way I've done in the past. Come with me this minute, and I'll prove that my affections for you have indeed been reformed. And if you are willing to allow me this honor I swear you'll find that your status has also evolved thanks to my change of heart for your company."

Her smile was beyond heavenly to see while she put her arm through my own. We took off together down the crowded hallway doing our best to prevent the other travelers from breaking our bond of limbs.

We hadn't gone far in the direction of the Great Hall before Sigrid leaned into my ear and whispered, "Let's take the cut off and bypass this clogged passage, Your Majesty. It's so loud in here I can barely hear my thoughts of affection for you."

I lightly squeezed her arm with mine as I whispered back into her ear, "I happily do anything to you, oops, uhm, I mean your wish is my command my Lady." I blushed over my accidental slip of that sexual inuendo.

Sigrid giggled and appeared to blush while we broke free of the crowed. We took off down the path that was often nearly void of travelers. To this day I'm unsure why so many avoid that hallway. It leads to the Great Hall, and no matter the time day or night there never seems to be anyone there. Well, except the random black collar headed for the huge supply closet that is there.

We traveled that quiet route in silence until that closet from hell was within our sight. I suppose Sigrid felt the slight trembling I always do anytime I see that accursed place. Too many bad things happened to me in there. Of course she was one of the ones that give me the PTSD for it in the first place, ja?

She stopped walking abruptly which forced me to follow suit or lose my arm for it.

"Listen Mad Maxx, I forgot about this being down this way. It was ignorant of me to assume you wouldn't find discomfort at going by there in the arm of one of the women who stupidly hurt you so long ago. You know what they say. The folly of youth is the regret of old age, ja?"

With the nervous sounding chuckle I replied, "You are many things my beauty, but old isn't one of them. Never mind this silly conditioned response I'm demonstrating. You are correct. That bad business is history. And you've been punished for it, already. It's rude to discuss past offenses once the culprit has served there sentence. We should keep going. Just ignore that shaking crap. Maybe one they I'll stop having the trauma feelings every time I walk by it, ja?"

Sigrid furrowed her perfectly plucked brow then with force pulled on my arm as she said, "Wait, I think there is the way to solve your panicking over that closet, Mad Maxx. Come with me. I can fix this with ease." I felt that I was going to faint the entire way while she dragged me to its door.

She opened it, then flipped on the lights and pulled me inside with her. The smell of chemicals filled my nostrils to sickness. That table that the voters had assaulted me on still sat silently in the same place it always had been. It's rusting frame was the cruel reminder of my disgrace. For the brief moment I thought I was going to barf all over this luscious female.

What a romantic fool I am, ja? Talk about knowing all the right moves to capture the heart of the ladies. Hahaha.

She saw my distress. To her credit she backed away and gave me a bit of space.

It took several moments to calm my lurching stomach but eventually I managed to croak out to her, "I apologize my lady but I don't understand how you think watching me barf is the way to curb the anxiety attack."

Sigrid's expression took on that of concern, "Well, to be honest I intended to allow you to have your way with me in here on that table, the one that, never mind. Maybe if you have a wonderful experience in here with me, you'll stop fearing being anywhere near here. I really do think this could cure you. Please Mad Maxx, I say to you I grant you consent to make love to me. Right here, and right now." She came closer to me and brushed some of my hair from my eyes as she said this.

I snatched her hand from my face and pulled her knuckles to my lips to kiss as I replied, "But beloved sister, if I did that it would be the crime more foul than the big sister that rapes her helpless little brother with sex toys. I realize that extreme perversion runs in our family. But hell, even the Mad Maxx isn't that fucked up. Ah, speaking of family. Where is that son of yours?

What was his name again? Seems someone told me it was Helmut."

Sigrid pulled her hand from me with the expression of terror overcoming her face as she yelled out, "You call me your sister? Why are you asking about some child you hallucinate that I have? You truly are insane aren't you? I change my mind. You can consider my bid to serve as your regent immediately withdrawn." She rushed for the door of the closet opened it and attempted to run.

But before she could escape, Byron blocked her from the exit.

He was chuckling in his menacing tone as he pushed her back into the storage space. Then he closed the door trapping her inside with the only other living direct descendants of that demonic Child Killer, Xavier, besides of course the daughter of the late great Vivianna. Sigrid was Xavier's secret love child and keeper of his legacy both above and below. Of the three of us fucked up siblings she somehow managed to inherit the capacity for perversion that rivals his.

Byron shot me the smile of dark humor as he chimed out happily, "Well hell, if I'd known there was going to be the Schmidt family reunion in here, I'd have worn my best. Hey, little brother, did you share the good news with this beautiful sister we never knew that we had?"

Sigrid's eyes grew even wider with obvious fear as she shuddered then whispered, "How did you and Byron find out about me, Maxx? Mother and father never told a soul. He arranged that I was raised in the proper Dominant household. How did you know that I have the secret son named Helmut?"

I glared at her with hate filling my every molecule as I growled out, "You mean you had the secret son named Helmut, you sick bitch."

Byron put his finger to his lips shushing us then chuckled hard as he said, "Now, now you two. Barely known you were the secret siblings for two seconds and already you're fighting like you've been brother and sister all your lives. Now, Maxx, did you give sis the good news? Or did I miss it?"

I snickered at Byron's attempt at cruel humor, which was pretty clever I hate to admit. "Oh shit, leave it to the oldest to ruin every fucking surprise. Nein, Byron. I was just getting around to it when you arrive for the party."

She glared at us both defiantly and said in the haughty tone, "I've the surprise for you two brothers. You dare to touch a hair on my head, you're dead men. So go ahead. Try to scare me with your threats of death. They won't work."

Byron made the gleeful sounds, just as he opened the closet door to then invited Rolf, Friedrick and Fritz inside with us. Ah, looks like the gang is all here. Let the games begin.

Chapter 29: Little Mercy

No matter how loud our Mad Maxximillian has screamed, nor how hard he has fought the Haus, nothing has ever really changed. Not for him, and not for those cursed to wear metal around their necks. Every tiny victory has cost him far more than he has ever won.

The Vampire Jonas has managed to get his fangs back into him, too deep to remove this time.

Perverted Lucus tricked him into another situation that promises Mad Maxx will suffer more than those that are truly guilty of the crimes.

His twisted half-brother Byron once again has him backed into a corner without any hope of escape.

Ending up right back where he started has been the story of his life up until now. Of course, that is because finally Mad Maxximillian will get what he's been begging for right from the start. All it took to reignite his ebbing will to survive was a little mercy.

Rolf, Friedrick and Fritz, who I assumed Byron thought could be trusted or bribed with ease, came inside the closet at Byron's bequest. Each of them had an expression of utter confusion on their faces. I rightly assumed that my brute brother hadn't bothered to give away the secret as to the reason we'd hailed them to our aid.

This was a good thing for us, but very bad for them. Well, two of them anyway or should I say three.

Sigrid shot a hate filled glance at me and then Byron. Then that dark heart harpy whipped up the crocodile tears with speed.

She practically flew into the completely shocked Voter Rolf's arms sobbing loudly as she said, "Thank God you have come honorable Voter. I demand these men be arrested immediately. They have kidnapped me and I dare not even speak of the things they said they were planning to do to me. That is before you honorable Princes of the Silk come along to save me from there cruelty." Sigrid pressed her face into Rolf's chest while pointing back at me and Byron.

Rolf's expression of surprise deepened into that of irritation while he growled out, "Maxx, this kind of harassment I'd expect of Byron. But you? I thought you were of the better morals than to attempt to taking anyone by force. Especially after enduring so much of this kind of foul abuse yourself and in this very room too. Shame on you."

Before I could reply to that most unnecessary calling out of my shady past. Byron let out the angered snort. "Asshole, you dare to claim that I have the reputation of the rapist that goes around pulling people into closets to fuck? Take it back Rolf. While you still have moments left of your life to beg my forgiveness."

I shook my head and rolled my eyes then said in the bored sounding tone, “Let it go, Byron. You are the fucking brute that Rolf accuses you of being. Where he’s made his mistake is in thinking it’d be the females you’re brutalizing against their wills. Your preference for victim is the male creatures that can offer you the challenge. Friedrick, my old buddy. wouldn’t you agree that this is the truth?”

Friedrick snuck the anxious glance at the fuming Byron and then said softly, “That’s been my experience with him, Mad Maxx. Though I know he does fuck the girls sometimes too. I’ve seen it.” He quickly dropped his eyes to the floor appearing overcome with shame.

Rolf took on the grin of gloating as he said loudly, “There you have it, Byron. I don’t make false claims. Now, will one of you tell me what the hell you were thinking? Sigrid, sweetheart, calm yourself. I swear we going to get to the bottom of this. I promise you’ll see them both punished for their rude behavior.” I put up my hand and Rolf halted his words mid-sentence.

Then I glowered as I bellowed out in the wicked tone, “Ah, promises, promises. You make many of those, don’t you, Rolf? I wonder if any of us be in this situation this morning had you always been so keen to keeping your word instead of paying them lip service only. However, I must say dearest Sigrid, this time Rolf tells you no charming lies to gain your affection. Because criminals are about to be punished for their crimes. And you Mein Schatz (pet name that translates to My darling, treasure, or precious) will be the witness up close and personal to his sudden reformation of speaking truthfully. Byron, restrain that bitch and grab her too. Hahahaha."

Byron rushed the Voter Rolf that was slightly smaller than himself. Rolf pushed Sigrid aside safely out of the line of attack. She started to flee for the door again, but Friedrick ended her flight by snatching her by the long flowing locks of her hair.

She punched at the simple minded Voter while screaming, "Unhand me this minute you retarded bastard."

Friedrick endured her blows without so much as flinching as he replied, "Nein, there must be the good reason Maxx pulls you in here. I know he doesn't like this place very much. Until this is settled. You're staying put."

You know, Friedrick isn't the brightest bulb, but sometimes. He has the honest stroke of brilliance.

That battling between Rolf and Byron didn't last long enough to bother discussing. I'd assumed if those two ever sparred it would be the battle royal. Well, I was wrong to think it. Within seconds Rolf was angrily cursing Byron while being held his prisoner in the bear hug.

Fritz had, smartly, kept his mouth shut, and place holding up the corner of that room through all this drama. He strangely didn't seem to appear anxious in the least either. I suppose I thought at the time this made sense. Fritz is the honest sadist at heart. Likely the rough play of these brute Voters was the unexpected pleasure for him, ja?

Though I did make a mental note to asking him about the reasons he was oddly present twice during my business of setting the Haus on her ear. Remember he was there with Jonas when I send that fake silver and the false black collar to their deaths on the sixth floor, ja?"

Rolf groaned from Byron's tight hold around his chest then said, "Morter King or nein, this is the severest of crimes you're committing Maxx. If you release me this moment and leave. I'll pretend none of this happened, because I always have called you my friend. Had you been anyone else in this world I'd laugh while you burn at the stake."

Byron feigned the pout while pretending to be about to cry, "You think only to forgive Maxx, old buddy? What about me? I thought we were the best of comrades. I suppose all this time, you've been giving me the line of fake intent. You know, like the ones you used for years on the silly women you've targeted for bedding?"

Rolf growled out, "I'm going to do more than chuckle when they punish you, you bastard. I'm going to light the pole you're tied to, Byron."

Byron snickered with glee then replied in the humored tone, "Big talk for a man that hasn't killed anyone that can defend themself. You going to discover it's more difficult to murder men bigger than you than it is the innocent babies."

Rolf's face fell into the expression of pure stun. "What? You think I've killed babies? Maxx? What the fuck is Byron talking about," he said in the near whisper.

With the sneer I glared at the sulking Sigrid then turned my attention back to Rolf as I said hatefully, "Are you going to deny the existence of Helmut as this bitch of yours has done? Before you open that lying mouth of yours Rolf, do understand I know for the fact you are, were, the papa of that poor little baby boy Helmut that may have had your eyes. Of course, now the perverts do."

The burly Voter sucked in the air appearing very startled. "Maxx I swear on my life I have no fucking idea who the hell this Helmut is, nor will I admit that I am the father, jet. Rosalina isn't due for many months with my first." I interrupted him again…

"Nearly four years ago, in this very spot. I was the sad recipient of your callused sport with me. After you finished your fun at my expense. You were witness to the dishonorable pegging I suffered at the hands, uhm, strapons of the women you were dating at that moment. You'd been sporting Sigrid and Ingrid on your arm for weeks prior to your cruelly using the little boy to impress the bitches you already had conquered. Ah, but you've had so many minute lovers, maybe you forgot that old flame of yours, ja? Wish I could. But the nightmares are always there to remind me of you both. Ah, but I digress, ja? Rolf, don't make this worse by trying to deny this union with Sigrid resulted in the unplanned pregnancy. If you there to try and say you were unaware of this, I'll kill you where you stand without hesitation. Like I did your beautifully mangled baby boy."

Sigrid gasped then whispered out, "Nein, this is a lie. Rolf, don't you listen to him. We never had a son together. He's insane and having a schizophrenic fit. Everyone knows the Priceless is mad as the hatter."

The cold sounding chuckle erupted from my throat as I replied, "Oh, okay so then she kept the pregnancy from you, did she? Come on Rolf. Fess up. Tell me the truth. Not that I don't already have the proof of it. So, lie to me if you dare, old buddy."

Rolf cast an anxious eye toward the equally nervous appearing Sigrid, then look down his gaze down as he said, "She was supposed to get rid of it. I mean the pregnancy, Maxx. She didn't wish to marry me nor me her. Not after that bad business with you. We broke up. I thought she had ended it, like we agreed." He led out his breath slowly as if in pain over his words.

With the nod I replied, “Ah, but don’t look so sad there papa. Sigrid did as you told her to do. She did get rid of it. Well, she certainly did her damnest to. But as usual, I took it up the ass because you think with your cock instead of your head. Now, that sweet little boy is food for the worms and I’ve the dilemma of deciding how best to make his uncaring parents pay. One of you for not accepting responsibility for his actions. And the other for squandering the life gifted to her by the fickle lover.”

Sigrid growled out with suddenness, “I don’t know who the fuck told you. Nor do I give two shits. But you must realize that you cannot kill either of us Maxx. In fact, I’m the only one these very special clients trust to supply them with the quality product. Even if you did manage to keep our bodies hidden, someone very important going to notice we are gone with promptness. That’s because there coffer will be missing the most important money that I collect for them. You don’t understand anything about any of this, you idiot. This business I run must run smoothly. If not, then the Haus will come up short for the Stasi payment. Are you listening to me, fool? These Stasi officer’s will kill everyone in this Haus, even your crazy ass. I was short by one male this cycle. Thankfully, I knew where to get the extra, since no one else had any at the right age ready for reaping.”

Rolf’s eyes went wide with sudden horror as he wailed out, “Nein, Sigrid you didn’t. Not Helmut! Why?

Nein, nein, nein. Oh my God, nein." Tears flowed down his cheeks in the cold rain of despairing.

Sigrid hissed back at him, "So now you think to care about the son you never bothered to visit nor claim as your own. Where the fuck were you all those years? Off sleeping with every bitch that spreads her legs for you is where. Well, it costs money to raise the baby, Rolf. I cannot afford to live in this God forsaken Haus and be the mother without any means of worth. You never even sent a single penny for him, did you? Too bad for me and too bad for Helmut. It's my job to protect the Haus from the Stasi scum. I do what I must to see it is done. I needed the male and that was that. Better Helmut than everyone we know, including us."

Friedrick frowned then shook her harshly as he growled out, "Shut up. I don't know what this is all about but I think you are confessing that you killed Rolf's baby for money. What kind of mother does such evil to her children? Maxx, say the word and I will murder this one without any feelings of fear for the stake. I gladly burn to be the hero that ends the mother that murders her own babies."

Byron, who had been uncharacteristically silent through this, said with the harsh tone, "Moron, if we wished to hear your voice we'd beat it out of you. Hold your stupid tongue still and let the men handle this."

Friedrick shook his head then replied, "I'm not afraid of you anymore Byron. You wish to do this beating. Then better come try it. See what happens to you this time."

Byron smiled with evil contentment as he said, "Lather up bitch. Right now I've no time for foreplay with you. But no doubt, I'll be the happy man to fuck you over once more after we finished here."

I put up my hands then said in the mocking tone, "Boys, please. We can measure our cock size anytime. Let's get back to the situation at hand first, if that's alright with everyone. Fritz? Did you bring that little pen knife you like to carry?" I glanced at the Dominant that seemed to be intently studying the unfolding scene in silence.

He nodded, "I did. You already know I never go anywhere without it. Why?"

With the snort of frustration I replied, "Oh I don't know. I was just standing here wondering what you carry in your pants besides that huge ego of yours. I asked because I wish to borrow it."

Fritz jumped as if startled then while mumbling apologies for asking dumb questions. He dug it out and tried to hand it to me. I lifted one bandaged hand with the loud sound of irritation escaping me.

"Hold on to it asshole. Now, where were we? Ah, ja. So first let's deal with this deadbeat dad. Rolf, I know Byron has requested you grant to me that favor you owe to him. This is true, ja?"

Rolf continued to weep quietly but nodded his head as he replied, "It is. Though if you planning to kill me and Sigrid I don't think it matters much if I refuse to grant it to you. Reputation doesn't matter much to the dead. Course, she's right you know. If you murder her this Haus will burn before the summer is upon us brother. Her deplorable job is all that stands between us and total destruction. I don't agree with it but you must understand, Maxx, we are all prisoners here. Everyone in the GDR is."

Byron's brutal smile faded slightly as he said, "Maxx, Rolf is right you know. We kill Sigrid, and that money stream ends. The Stasi won't hesitate to destroy this Haus. I say we end him but get what we can by making the deal with Sigrid. I bet she has the ear of one that can see us both free of this nightmare hellhole. Isn't that right sister? Hurry up and save your life while you can. Tell Maxx, you can make his wish to be the free man happen, ja?"

Sigrid rolled her eyes then glowered as she replied, "Byron, if you want to feel the grass on the other side of the wall, that can be arranged with ease. This idiot though. Nein. He's stupidly accepted the crown of the Foundation. Plus, you already know that the only man capable of greasing the right palms to see him out of this country has personal reasons to never set him free. So, tell you what. Tell this simpleton to let me go. Unhand Rolf and we gang up on dipshit here. Once we have him, we lock him in his palace where he fucking belongs.

Then I make sure you're headed west by sunset tomorrow. Deal?"

I shot the glare of hate at Byron as I said, "Don't you believe a fucking word she says. She's the lying baby killer."

Byron shifted nervously and pulled his gaze from my as he replied, "Fuck, Maxx. I honestly don't know what to do. I do as you want, maybe we all die. I listen to Sigrid, I'm the free man at last. Decisions, decisions, how can I be sure you're able to stop this baby killing without getting us all murdered?"

My dentures gnashed as I responded, "You can be sure I kill at least you if you dare to consider betraying your oath to me. Stop listening to that soon to be dead sister of ours."

Rolf gasped then looked at me with sudden returned surprise, "Sister? Are you shitting me? Ah fuck me. Yet another of Xavier's devil children. This Haus is lousy with the lot of you."

I snickered. "Does that bother you that you fucked your first cousin Maxx and his sister too. Oh, hey, brother Byron. Did he fuck you too? Maybe he wished to collect the whole set of Xavier hell spawn, ja? How about you cousin Friedrick? Ever sleep with Cousin Rolf?"

Fritz's sound of his air being drawn in sharply filled the room then he whispered, "Holy hell. You're the son of Xavier Schmidt too, Maxx? Nein, that's too fucking good to be true."

I glared at him angrily. "Calm down there lover boy. Keep it in your pants. I'm certain we'll be discussing this thing you shouldn't have been made aware of soon enough. Now, Rolf how about that favor you owe me?"

Rolf nodded slowly, "Okay, name the favor and I swear to see it done in front of all these witnesses. At least the ones you intend to let live. I suppose you wish me to commit suicide. So, you can be cleared of any suspiciousness over my death, ja?"

With the glimmer in my eyes I replied, "Gosh Rolf, I thought you said you are the straight man. If only you'd speak dirty like that to me all those years ago when you took advantage of me. I'd think more fondly of that sex with you. Tempting as your offer is, nein. As it is, I seem to recall you owed Byron two favors, not only just one. He has granted them both to me. So, first, you are going to join with your two brothers here and give to my pretty sister everything you did to me and so much more roughly. Friedrick, bring that bitch and hold her to that table I hate so fucking much."

Rolf gasped while Sigrid began to struggled in Friedrick's strong hold with all her might while wailing for help that wasn't coming.

The big voter watched seeming to be in a trance while Byron hauled his ex-lover and ex-mother of his son over to the table.

Then just as Byron threw her on it like the sack of potatoes as he whispered to me, "You saying you want me to rape Sigrid as the favor repayment? Up the, uhm, in the unnatural way?"

I laughed with much humor as I replied, "And I thought Friedrick the slow one. Fritz, get your ass over here. You are the only man in this group that honestly has no business being here. That means you have plenty of reason to go telling tales about us. To assure your hands are too dirty to claim clean of guilt. You're going first. Ah, no lube allowed fellas. I want this bitch to bleed from her ass like her poor little baby did. Don't skimp on the roughness and for God's sake make it hurt like hell. I'm personally aware that each of you are more than capable of that. Oh, and let's make it more fun. The one that can hold off his orgasm the longest, I let live for sure. The two losers, I'll consider it, maybe. Ha-ha-ha!"

Fritz wore that sadistic smile on his face that I hate so much as he approached me and said, "What about this pen knife you asking about? Do you wish me to cut her hole up with it?"

I glared at him with barely veiled fury as I replied, "Sicko to the bone, aren't you? No wonder the Stasi wish to kill everyone in this Haus. Surely would be the favor to God or the devil if they did. Hand that to Byron, motherfucker. Then get over there and prepare yourself to mount that lump of nothing. I'm already tired of looking at you." His grin didn't wane even as he gave the sharp to Byron and walked over to where the squirming, squealing piggy was being held to the spot.

With the grimace I glanced at Byron. "Let Rolf go, brother. I think he won't attempt to flee now that he realizes the error of his ways. Rolf, get in line to repay that favor you owe me. You're up next. Byron, you know what to do."

The brute released his hold and Rolf walked over to take his place for the gang raping with his head hung low. But he said nothing while doing this.

Byron opened Fritz's small blade then approached the now sobbing and pleading Sigrid. He put up his hand in the gesture to halt Fritz from beginning his act of sodomy on her. She saw this and wrongly thought that Bryon had come to save her from this assault on her dignity.

He leaned down close to her face then said so we all could hear him, which was loudly since Sigrid was really bawling by this time.

"Well sister, I'm afraid you've brought this on yourself. Normally, it's the job of the men in the family to look after the best interests of their women. But since you deny us that privilege to know you exist until we find out by accident I don't feel any obligation to stop these fiends from fucking you to severe injury. Maxx and I discussed how best to avoid hearing you bitching to us later about our lack of honor with regard to your own. We decided that because we never heard any complaints from you before this moment why end the good thing? Open your pretty mouth sis. Helmut doesn't bother you with his crying anymore, and in the moment, you cannot annoy your brothers with the sounds of yours either."

Sigrid clenched her jaw shut with all her strength. That did nothing to slow down Byron's work. She screamed the last words she'd ever be capable, 'It was nein, you cannot do this,' just as the brute used that dull knife to separate her from her tongue.

Blood spewed from her mouth while she emitted the gurgling screaming sounds. For a brief moment I felt the swoon come over me. That baby girl in the film's noises echoed within the wheelroom. Thankfully, I'd held off that pain killer of Byron's or surely I'd have fainted right there over that flashbacking I was doing.

Byron laughed while watching Friedrick flip her to her face on the table. "Guess as usual you go last, brother." He glanced at the huge Voter to see if this mild insult got to him.

Friedrick frowned then replied, "Are you and Maxx going to fuck her too?"

Byron snorted and took on the expression of disgust as he yelled out, "Hell nein. You always been the dumbass. This is our sister, fool. That is an insult to even suggest such perversion."

The slow minded giant shot the surprised look at me. "But you fuck your brother without care, Byron. If Sigrid is your sister and his, then Maxx is your brother, ja?"

Byron rolled his eyes then said with the snort, "You're just now catching up are you? Ah, I apologize for saying you're stupid. We have the fucking genius in our midst brother Maxx. Look here, Friedrick, I didn't know he was my brother back when we had our fun with him. This was a long time ago and it'll never happen again. The honest mistake, ja? Maxx isn't complaining about it. Besides, he cannot get pregnant with the inbred baby, but Sigrid can. This finally clear to you, professor dummkopf?"

Friedrick shook his head slowly, "But what if she gets pregnant by one of us today? If you planning to kill her after we are done, that's true murder because the baby didn't do anything."

Byron started laughing hard and was going to say something mean to the dimwitted fellow but I put up my hand to silence him.

"Friedrick, how is that lovely lady you been courting. Are there wedding bells coming in the future for you? Is this why you seem hesitant to get your rocks off? You're afraid she'll find out you been fucking around behind her back, ja," I said flatly.

Sigrid, that's wet sounds of pain had lowered suddenly led out the unearthly sounding wail. Fritz had taken that opportunity to plunge into her hindside with force. He didn't allow her the moments peace from his brutal thrusting appearing oblivious to our discussion going on around the scene of his vicious assault.

Byron that had been focused on Friedrick turned his attention to the more taboo action. His grin was huge and the front of his pants tightened. What the pervert. He admired Fritz's sadistic attack on Sigrid's most personal space.

I shook off the feeling of disgust for my brother's noticeable excitement and returned my attention to Friedrick.

"Well? You going to ask me for the mercy to excuse you from this task I've assigned you Dungeon Master?"

Friedrick's big shoulders slumped as he replied softly, "She dumped me, Maxx. There will be no wedding for the big dummy Friedrick. The Frau doesn't like it when her man has been the plaything of another man. They really hate it when that man isn't that smart either. I think I'll never know the joy of the baby feet that this mean woman has stupidly thrown away. There is no future for the man without the children to love him. So, you can kill me too whenever you done murdering Rolf. That is if you have the time."

Byron chuckled then shot me a glance full of menace as he said, “You hear that brother? Friedrick realizes that he’s worthless as I always told him he is. Finally he says something intelligent. Please brother, let me be the one to send him off. I will trade something for it, even agree in the blood contract to get this pleasure.”

I clicked my tongue then said in the bitter tone, “Shut up Byron. Friedrick, hold that bitch dammit. When Fritz finishes, he can switch with you. Taken your turn after Rolf. And you better not go easy on her. Not that you ever did on me.”

Fritz finished his mount with the loud moan of satisfaction mere seconds after I said that. He remained inside that uncaring bitch for the few moments appearing glassy eyed and spent. I had to yell at him to withdraw and take Friedrick’s spot so that Sigrid couldn’t gain the mercy of rest.

Rolf moved into position while Fritz did as I told him. He grabbed her by one of her butt cheeks, digging in his nails till she squealed in pain as he said angrily, “You never asked me for the money for that boy, you cunt. I’d have given it to you. You should’ve ended that pregnancy when I said to and none of this would’ve happened. Now I’m going to repay this favor to Maxx. I want you to know I do it happily for Helmut.” With that he entered her with the single move causing her to scream out in agony.

His thrusting was wild, strong and fueled with intense fury. Even Byron seemed a bit worried the way he was slamming into her that she might not survive it. I thought of demanding Rolf take his severe aggression down a notch, but hell, Sigrid earned this. Honestly, even if he had killed her with his cock, it was too merciful of a death for her after what she'd done to countless babies over the years.

When at last Rolf reached his apex and could do no more damage. It was Friedrick's turn to bat. I blocked the suddenly overeager Voter, he always gets stupid whenever excited, from taking his turn.

He stood there with the hard dick in his hand and expression of confusion on his face as he said, "I thought I was supposed to fuck her Maxx. Did Rolf kill her? I lost my chance to fuck this beautiful woman because she died, ja?"

Byron snorted then rolled his eyes while I shot my brute brother the glance of caution.

Then I motioned Byron to approach Friedrick while I said loudly, "Friedrick, you live because many others more innocent than you have died in your place. You of all the guilty are the one of the least of them. You already paid the heavy price of brain damage and of suffering the pain of being forced to serve as Byron's plaything for years. I have considered these facts before deciding your sentence for the crimes committed in your name. However, much I believe you mostly innocent, I cannot allow you to live, at least not in the eyes of the Stasi.

I hereby condemn you to the long drawn out death of lifetime service to the Palace of the Morter king. You shall leave the world above and be recorded as dead to all. No one shall ever see your face above ground again. Sigrid, my dear sweet sister, you have instigated the most heinous acts that can be done to another. You have forfeited your right to life, but because I know your father too well, I understand the violence, hate, and lack of empathy is the only things you been taught since you were born. You cannot understand the errors of your ways. To be honest a quick death is too good for you. I know you sacrificed Helmut but I also am aware you send two others before him to suffer the pain that I ended for your son and my precious nephew. These babies you sent to slaughter because you don't wish to marry but love to use your charms to gain favors. This ladder climbing did you no good. The first floor is where you lived because the ones above you made sure you never rise. They don't wish to lose their connection to their cash flow, that you exclusively were trained to do. This is the reason you wish to destroy Gretta. You know she has blocked you from the fourth floor luxury you think you are owed. You owe the Haus three souls for the ones you have wasted. Friedrick, come here and allow Bryon to cut your schwanse. This worthless woman is to be your blood bonded. I condemn her to serve her Mann and return to the Haus the property she has destroyed. She will remain below in the dungeon cell, locked away, for all of her remaining days, forgotten, and isolated save for the conjugal visits from her husband. Friedrick, you shall raise your children and be financially responsible for them. Once they are of age, they shall climb the dungeon steps and take their rightful places denied to their siblings. Now, fuck your wife Friedrick and then you take her to her new home and you pack your shit and get below to yours. Do it now or I forget myself and fucking kill you both anyway."

Friedrick's eyes teared up and the quivering smile erupted as he whispered, "Danke Maxx. I will serve Your Majesty with gladness in my hertz." With that Friedrick took his mount and with the overly harsh thrusting became my brother-in-law.

Rolf sighed deeply but kept his eyes to his boots as he said softly, "So, you intend to have big men assault me, after cutting out my tongue. Then send met to rot in the dungeon cell next to Sigrid?"

With the chuckle I replied, "You think you getting off that easy Rolf? Nein. I've something special in mind for your punishment. But ja, I will watch you rot. Don't take it personally. I can send every motherfucker in this Haus to rot in the dungeon. It won't save me from that very same fate, ja? Last I checked, the Palace is the cold stone cell in the dungeon too."

He nodded, then said, "I know you intend to see your justice done to me, Maxx. But if you ever felt anything for me other than contempt, I would beg you to pass your sentence and get this over with. If you would be so kind as to show your old buddy any mercy, any small mercy that is."

My eyes rolled as I snorted in reply, "Since you in the hurry to get to dying. I'll give you the equal service return of mercy that is only really mercy for the one giving it. You know, like apartments you knew I couldn't have without the roommate, or refusing to beat me during the coronation but never telling me such the thing was my fate in the first place."

Rolf glared at me then said, "And Felicity? Is that the mercy I give to you or merely clearing my own guilty conscious as you accuse me of doing."

With the growl I replied, "You give me the toy that evil men used to hurt me worse than they already were. You never gave Felicity to me. The mother lamb has always been with me long before we met. Now, shut the fuck up. I'm ready to sentence you for your crimes against the innocent. Rolf, I hereby remove you as the Silk Prince. You are dark bonded to the frau of the Shadow King that has borne the rival to my own throne of Morter. This woman you call the future mother of your own children. You owe the Haus the price of the son that's been lost due to your chronic neglect of family duty in the pursuit of carnal pleasure. No one can be sure that you don't have other kinder that suffered sacrifice or exist awaiting there turn in this Haus thanks to your lack of proper restraint. Therefore, it's my judgement that you shall be removed from the Haus walls and relocated out in the black collar cottage. You will be taking that worthless frau with you and all your kinder but the little ones of royal blood shall remain in the care of Hubertus and his wife on the fifth floor. You are banished to remain in the yard cottages for all your days and as far as the Haus is concerned Rolf is dead."

Rolf gasped then blurted out in the pleading voice tone. "Nein, you cannot do this to me, Maxx. I'm the honorable Voter that's done much to help improve the lives of your collared subjects. You know this dammit. Plus, I've done nothing illegal in the eyes of the Haus Law. I didn't know Helmut was sent for sacrifice but you must realize that every one of us Dominants is expected to give up one of our kinder to be sacrificed or we are fined more than we can pay. Unpaid fines as you know result in severe punishment and even sometimes death. How do you think your ruling will sit when the Silk Queen hears that you dare to put one of her princes to pasture."

His words of arrogance caused me to laugh with the hearty sound as I replied, "That bitch Gretta doesn't dare to bother with me now that she's in indebted to me with the overdue bill herself. As for your doing things to aid the suffering in this Haus. Look around you, fool. nothing has changed because you bastards are afraid to stand up to the big, mouthed bitch Queen. The tiny changes to anything have been brought about by the sacrificial blood of their Collar and Mortar King. Besides you, by your own words, have breached the law. You say you never give Sigrid permission to hand over the baby you claim all Dominants must pay to the Haus, ja? Or do you wish to change your story about your involvement with Helmut's destruction? Which is it? You complied with the Law or you were the unwilling participant in this murder of your son?"

The soon to be ex-Voter's eyes glistened with wrath, "You twist my words to suit your desires, Maxx. Whatever, this doesn't even matter anyway. No Dominant is permitted to lodge with the black collars. This is also the strict Haus Law. I seem to recall if you attempt to use your words to change it, you have broken that contract your champion Lucus holds with Gretta. In other words, you cannot impose banishment upon one of my rank and status. Guess you better try to kill me, ja?" He shot me the rage filled smile.

My eyebrows raised in the feigned expression of surprise as I replied, "Oh my Gott. What was I thinking? You are correct Rolf. thank you for correcting my error before I fucked myself up worse than I already am. Hahaha. This sentence I hand down on you is banishment to the yard. As the fully coronated Mortar King, I don't need to amend the existing law to do so. I merely need to make your status in the Haus equal the specifications of your punishment. I think you forgotten that Gretta stupidly overlooked neutering the power of my throne to raise or lower any resident's level I wish to. Lucky for you she did make this honest error of judgment in her haste to negotiate that unfair contract with Lucus. Otherwise I'd have to murder you, then stack your decaying flesh on top of the pathetic remains of your poor boy Helmut. And the way I see it, you aren't worthy of the honor of sharing the mass grave with that sweet child. Byron brother, you did remember to bring that black collar with you? Be sure that the lock is tightly secured around his neck, before you send it, oh I meant to say, this freshly acquired Haus submissive to the Black Collar Mistress. Inform her that he is be assigned groundskeeping duties as is the proper place for all the yard black collars."

Rolf's mouth dropped open and his expression became fraught with fear.

"Maxx, please don't do this. I've made mistakes, this I can clearly see that is true, but nein. Mercy please," he said with his words breaking with hoarseness from the rising terror of his understanding of the seriousness of his punishment.

I padded him on the shoulder and feigned the pout as I replied, "Ah, now please don't be upset with me old buddy. Look at it this way. You can fuck all the Haus submissives you wish. Seems to me that you've always had that dangerous habit. And this way you need not worry about accidentally siring Kinder with any FemDom's since the unions with the black collars are illegal. No more of your offspring will be candidates marked as sacrifice to pay the fines to the Stasi. Do recall that the silver and black collars are not subject to that sentence since the Stasi don't view them as human. The Dominant Rolf, found guilty of the war crimes, is officially dead and the Haus servant that stands before me is invisible to them. Why do look so sad to hear this good news? I was sure you'd be thrilled to hear that for the rest of your life you'll be toiling in the soil up to your ankles in the lovely Haus gardens. The ones that you've spent so many days and nights balls deep within your numerous minute lovers."

Rolf's shoulders slumped and he dropped to his knees at my boots. He finally realized, this was the honest mercy I granted him even if at that moment he didn't see it that way. Ha!

Byron chuckled menacingly under his breath while quickly producing the collar of the black metal. Rolf didn't flinch while his onetime buddy and fighting partner sealed the lock that ended his freedom of choice.

During Rolf's collaring, Friedrick had been very gently readjusting his blushing, well bleeding, bride's disheveled clothing. Then he lifted the nearly unconscious woman to her feet and held her up by wrapping one of her limp arms around his shoulders and taking her by the waist with one of his own. Fritz stood there watching the entire scene in silence with the expression of humor on his face.

He set his eyes on her mouth that was still seeping blood as he said, "Maxx, can I take my Frau to see the doctor? I'm thinking she's in need of stitches or maybe the heavy bandages. I think if we don't stop her from bleeding maybe I be the widower soon." I groaned upon realizing he was likely correct.

With the nod towards Fritz I said, "Help Friedrick haul that bag of flesh down to the dungeons please. Byron, take Rolf this minute and do as I told you to. I'll go alert Doctor Attila of the client the requires his services down below."

Byron shot me the worried glance, "Wait, you shouldn't be traveling around without escort. There are far too many around the Haus that may be seeking to prevent your taking your rightful place on the throne soon."

I rolled my eyes and with the snort replied, "Fine, then you get this Haus property handed off, and you fetch the doctor, Byron. I'll go with Fritz and Friedrick to make sure my command is followed to the letter. No one stupid enough to ambush three of us, ja? Once you've finished your tasks come down to the dungeons. I should be finished by then. If I do before you get there I'll be waiting at that wooden door under the stairs. We have another in need of rapid sentencing and I don't desire to waste too much more time getting him marked off my to do list. Does this plan calm your jittery nerves, mother hen?"

Byron growled in response, "Ja, it does, Your Majesty. Just make damned sure you go nowhere else before I can get there to watch your back." I waved my mildly irritated brother off, then motioned the other three to follow me.

With as much speed possible given the dead weight being carried by Fritz and Friedrick we traveled down that empty hallway. Luckily, this pathway had the cut off that lead to the dungeons as well as to the Great Hall as I told you earlier. This meant we were able to move the damaged Sigrid through the Haus without too many eyes seeing the show. That was useful in that I needed the news that the Mortar King was on the war path to remain a secret for as long as possible. I didn't wish to start the panic among the residents. You know it is easier to be the victorious hunter if the prey is unaware you're on the prowl, ja?

We made good time to reach our destination thanks to the reasons I already give you. Once below, I instructed Friedrick and Fritz to place Sigrid in the stone cell adjacent to Friedrick's own palace master barracks room. This was once the home for the late Sebastion, remember that bastard, ja?

Then I had the simple minded newlywedded husband place the heavy metal manacle around her neck and chain her to the floor in the center of that cell. Friedrick, and the man standing in for Noah as the Dungeon Master (one of the Finck family, Fritz's uncle to be exact), listened intently while I give them instructions,

"This fool is to never be spoken to by anyone except her Mann the honorable palace master Friedrick from this day till she is no more. If you must feed her due to her Mann's duties keeping him from it, you throw it on the floor. She has behaved as the animal and the animal is how she will live for the remainder of her days. The Haus doctor shall be permitted to visit with her only for the checkups, necessary medical treatment, and if attending any birthing she may do. Friedrick is solely responsible for any care or mercy she receives of worth. He shall also be financially responsible for her upkeep because this thing and her husband are henceforth the property of the Mortar Thrones. Friedrick may do with her as he pleases, but to everyone else in this hellhole dungeon or above it, they are forbidden to touch, speak, or even to view her forever. I set the penalty for anyone caught messing with this, the Mortar King's property, as death by fire. I do not grant Friedrick the power to override my final judgments on this even in the event of my or his death. Are we clear fellas?"

The Dungeon Master glanced down at the pathetic remains of Bartram (Das Haus bitch remember him? Hahaha.) on his leash while he nodded, "Your will be done, Your Majesty. This sentence of being the Untouchable, we know the details of well, sire."

His mention of the curse suffered by my beloved Noah briefly made me shudder but I quickly shook this off and replied in the stern tone, "Do you understand what I've commanded Friedrick?"

The brute nodded slowly while never taking his eyes off his groaning bride. “I do, Your Majesty. I thank you for the mercy of it. I will serve you to perfection.”

I glared at him angrily. “Ah, well if this were the truth of it, Friedrick, then I must wonder why you are still lingering here when I’ve ordered you to empty out your apartment above and notify the Silk Queen of your departure for your lifelong assignment down here as my Palace Master.”

Friedrick frowned then replied, “I will go right this minute if you think my wife will be okay till the doctor comes. But, uhm, jour majesty, I don’t dare to question your good judgement but I wonder if I could request you grant Rolf the relief to remain in his apartment even if wearing the black collar I’m sure he’s earned.”

My eyes went wide in furious shock as I yelled out, “You dare to ask me for anything more for yourself or that idiot cousin of ours. I’ll kill you where you stand, Friedrick. Get your big ass up to the fifth floor and do as I command before I fucking change my mind about letting you live, dammit.”

Friedrick nodded then hauled serious ass out of that cell to mind my orders. The temporary Head dungeon master got the message that I was not the man to mess with too. He quickly and silently returned to his duties, dragging that mess Haus bitch along behind him.

Only Fritz had the balls to remain behind while all the others fled the scene. He stood there next to me, staring at the writhing Sigrid with that same humored expression from the closet earlier on his face.

I shot the glance at him, then said, “So, you managed to get your big nose into my business too deep to extricate it easily or cheaply, ja? What is it that you want to keep your tongue still with regard to the secrets you learned today, Fritz? To name you regent no doubt.”

He chuckled low and responded, “Nein, though that is the tempting thought. Your Mann Jonas seems to think I can persuade you to do that without the need to resorting to blackmail to gain it. My true interest to see me the amply compensated man is the one I already voiced to you when I gave you that lovely cane gift.”

“Ah, I see. You thinking to make the move to climb higher than merely voice of the Mortar King are you? You’re interested in one day sitting on the fancy chair covered in fur I suppose.” I said softly to assure no one other than Fritz could hear me.

He nodded with a wicked grin. “Ja, that would be nice, hahaha. But I am asking you to do this for me for a more pressing reason. If I’m to ever hold that lofty throne, I must first prevent the rise of someone to the Silk. I think you’d agree that after Gretta’s death sentence is carried out neither of us wish for that one I wish to erase to be named queen in her place, ja? So? Do we have an accord or nein?”

I narrowed my brows leaned in close and replied, “Meet me with the future silk queen at the back door of the Haus later tonight, say around midnight. I leave it to you to come up with the excuse to get that bitch to accompany you there. I'll provide you the muscle to see she doesn't flee, and the hiding spot to assure no one find any evidence of the crime. But this is your problem more than it is mine. I've got far too much on my plate of problems to be concerned about the future queen that may or may not be my enemy once she rises. And I've enough blood on my hands too. I vow to help you get this dark deed done smoothly but you're going to be the one guilty of this sin. So, you better bring whatever weapon you need with you, ja?"

Fritz's smile widened as he stuck out his hand, "Deal, Your Majesty. I thank you for the mercy of it. I've much to do and little time to do it. So, I beg your release and I bid you good day until we meet again at midnight." He bowed low after I allowed him to shake my bandaged hand in agreement.

I waved him away. Then he rushed off without another word between us.

I sighed loudly and took the final glance at Sigrid. She was laying on the floor on her side in the slowly enlarging puddle of her own blood, glaring back at me with heavy tears in her eyes.

"You're thinking that you've been treated unjustly, sister? It's okay if you wish to complain about this fine home and lovely new necklace with accessories I give you aren't up to your standards. Ah, what's that? I cannot hear you, hahaha. Without that tongue you can never make your husband feel like he's lesser than you nor can you tell him nein when he comes to take his rights with you either. Or for that matter outrun him. After this moment, I will neither speak nor look upon you again in this life. That's the mercy for you, sister. But thanks to your cruelty I will never stop seeing what was left of the face of that innocent baby boy you sent to the slaughter. I hope that Friedrick treats you like the monster you honestly are, but I know him too well, far too well. He will love you and treat you with affection despite your deplorable character. He's too kindhearted to understand the evil in yours. If I were you. I'd remember that and return his good favor with extreme gratitude. Even if it's always going to be the faking from the likes of you. Because if ever I hear he's dissatisfied with his bride, well sister, a divorce I will grant him without hesitation. The outcome will lead to you finding this harsh situation you in the more merciful lifestyle. I wish for you to live the long and tortuous life, bitch." Sigrid let out the mournful sounding wail as I turned my back on her and hurried off towards the Mortar Palace.

Intelligently, I'd had Noah leave that wooden door full of rot under the dungeon stairs unlocked and the gate to the palace too. After making sure no one was around to see it, I opened it up and slipped inside. With all the speed I could muster, I rushed to the Mortar Palace to collect that flashlight I'd stored there.

As I snatched it and worked my wrapped fingers to turn it on Florian cleared his throat and called to me in the mocking tone, “You leave me here among the lowly courtiers like I’m of the common blood. You are the rudest bastard that I’ve ever known.”

The lantern come alive with false light just as I replied to in the humored tone, “Perhaps you prefer I place you on the throne of the Queen mother, asshole. If I did that, then you can call me out for bad manners. You going to have to just live with it because for the moment, I’ve got better things to attend. You can bitch about your lodging all you like to me soon enough. That clock is ticking, ja?”

Florian’s evil sounding laughter echoed off the mortar walls, “Hahahaha, you cannot find the escape route, can you? The more you struggle. The more trapped you become. Is Doctor Attila coming down here to visit? Maybe you better go ask him if he has some good news to share with you about that bat, the nasty scat man or perhaps your sadistic brother? That doctor is going to be the busy man with his gossiping to so many fellas about the perfect health of their Mortar King. Oh I meant to say his majesty, the plaything. I think that your time has already run out, lover boy.”

I glared at the bone head with malice. “Shut up, motherfucker. I’m not listening to you.”

He began to singing with much cruel humor in his tone, “Run, little rabbit, Run. The wolves are coming for their tender dinner. They going to scratch and tear at that rabbit hole till he can take no more. Have you ever heard anything so pathetic as the rabbit screams?"

His taunting was getting to me more than it usually did. that's because, I knew he was speaking the truth of it. Normally he just tries to lie and get me to believe it. The amount of time Doctor Attila had reported was required for me to be left unmolested, errr, not penetrated had come to an end. There wasn't any doubt that Jonas, Lucus and Peter had started harassing him demanding he give me the full medical release.

He still hadn't done this. I knew that because, thus far, none of them had come seeking me out to call in their rights – they all had by contracts with me. But I knew there wasn't any hope that Doctor Attila could hold them off me much longer. It hadn't gone unnoticed by me, and likely the rest of them, that the good doctor had been purposely neglecting to give them the green light. Though I was grateful for this small mercy he'd granted, I knew this was all he could do. He and I both were aware there was no way to permanently stop them from sexually abusing me other than total destruction of my, uhm, personal space that is.

The ability to return to being used like their pincushion might have healed in the physical sense. My psychological capacity to manage enduring this deplorable act, however, wasn't even close. That business of the brutal multiple gang assaults the Stasi did to me had messed my head up worse than it had been prior to that night. I knew without the aid of Byron's pain killers there wasn't any hope I wouldn't lose my shit the second anyone tried to put anything inside me again.

I'd asked Byron to hold on to the pain killers he'd sworn to provide me per our agreement because of the fear that later that they I was going to be literally completely fucked.

With Florian's cruel song repeating in my ears, I tore out of the Palace with speed. I was halfway to the ancient tomb where I'd found the mangled baby bodies before his noises faded away. That bone head had been successful in upsetting me to the point of high anxiety. My heart felt like it may explode in my chest over the softest sounds of the rat's feet while they rushed away from my light. I must have damned him one thousand times before I finally reached the entry of that horrible place I was headed. I covered my nose with my blouse. Then took the deep breath of the musty air and went inside.

Despite holding the stench at bay, the sight of all the rotting corpses of the babies still caused my stomach to go sour. I rushed as fast as possible past them through the narrow passageway. I certainly wasn't in the hurry to linger anywhere near that gruesome scene. Yikes.

When I entered the hidden room I expected to find the busted cage empty. I unfortunately saw before I could look away that Snot had done his job to perfection. Ja, all the little ones I ended were on the pile.

To my surprise that's not the vision that greeted my eyes. Snot was nowhere to be seen but I immediately noticed that at some point he had repaired that wire cage. That little man had done this with such skill none would be capable of realizing it had ever been damaged. I was thankful that he'd worked this hard to assure no one discovered I'd found there dark secret out.

I spent the few moments investigating his craftsmanship and waiting in the hopes he'd return without having to go seeking him. However, after several minutes, I knew I couldn't delay any longer. Byron will finish his assigned task soon. Then if I weren't where I told him I'd be, no doubt that brute would be going nuts thinking someone ambushed me or worse that I'd betrayed him somehow. That's just the way that bastard thinks, you know.

Anyway, now with Sigrid out of the picture there was no one that even knew this dwarf man existed. She'd been the one bringing him the daily meal. Snot was already skin and bones. Without that measly amount of food she bothered to leave for him he was sure to starve very quickly. I could've just let that happen and pretend I never met this most rare pleasure submissive. But, I believed Snot had more than earned the mercy he'd asked me for.

Plus, I may be the mean bastard but leaving this poor fellow to die painfully of starvation, forgotten and all alone, well, I'm not totally heartless.

With the groan of dismay, I realized that Snot was probably at that disgusting ‘playroom’ trying to repair the super eight projector. This made sense he would do this, since he had fixed that cage, ja? So, begrudgingly but rapidly I rushed off into the darkness. While I moved with a quick pace I hardened my resolved to give Snot his release from this tormented life he’d suffered at long last. Even though I understood, it would be one of the most difficult things I would ever have to do.

I reached the horrid playroom quickly. The door was easy to push open as it had been before. I went inside calling out for him, but I found the place empty. Well except for all that gross stuff it had in it the last time I’d been in there. That movie projector I’d damaged had been cleaned up, and nothing else appeared to have been moved or changed.

Just as I was going to haul ass toward the only other place Snot could be, the examination tomb, I heard the door squeaking open behind me. I turned to give the silver collar the friendly greeting, but it wasn’t Snot standing there in the entry.

It was Byron. I sucked in my wind in the terrified gulp. My heart sunk in the sudden realization that the brute likely been followed me the whole time. I’d thought those noises were rats fleeing. Hiss eyes were wide with awe and his face wore the ecstatic grin as he said in the breathy tone, “Oh my Gott. I must have died and gone to heaven. Where has this wonderful place been all my life?”

I pointed at the door then said in the anxious tone, "We need to get the fuck out of here brother. You have no idea what you looking at here. This place it's not one we wish to be discovered as the trespassers, trust me on this."

He grinned even wider then crossed his arms as he replied, "Is that so? What kind of real estate is so sacred that even the Lord and Master of this Haus cannot tread upon it? I think you are telling me lies. Like you always do. Well it won't work this time. I can clearly see what this really is. This is where you come to get all your nasty habits fulfilled, you wanton slut. Isn't it?"

I shook my head nein violently, "Byron I swear to you, this isn't of my design nor pleasure. This is where I found that book you're afraid of. The people that come for the babies torture them here. Please, listen to me. We must leave immediately before they come and catch us snooping."

He nodded then turned around. I thought he was going leave, but instead he shut the door. Then he turned back to me and his smile faded to that of the angered snarl.

"The only one that could've caught us in here is rotting in the dungeons. You forget that I read that book too. These so called clients that use this place aren't due to return for a couple months and you know this. What I really wish to know is why you are so eager to halt my lingering the bit to enjoy the lovely décor it contains.

Perhaps that's not the reason you in a hurry for me to leave? Maybe, you're concerned that I may decide to borrow a few things and give the little bitch the thrashing he has coming. Tell me. Is that what you're really afraid of, Maxx?" He started walking toward me slowly while overtly flexing his huge muscles.

Unconsciously, I began to back away as I stammered out, "Nein, I'm not scared of you, Byron. I've done nothing to earn any fucking beatings. Besides, you signed that contract with me and filed it. You cannot put your hands on me until after you've completed your promise to help me end the baby killings. That task is far from finished so back off motherfucker. You've no cause to be acting like the asshole. Touching me, and that contract is busted. Worse, I swear I will take you down with me if I'm unsuccessful in my plan to stop this butchery."

The brute stopped his march of menace and glared at me hatefully as he replied, "Funny you mention taking me down with you just now. Because that's exactly what you have done isn't it, you fucking slut. While I was running those errands for you, I heard the most curious rumor. It's being said around the Haus that the Mortar King has coaxed the Fur King to empty the third silk throne of its prince. And had him thrown out of his fine apartment banished and condemned to live in the palace dungeon masters' barracks with the rats. Hmmm, which silk throne is it that I hold? I seem to recall that I am the Prince of the third Silk throne. Is this gossiping I'm hearing true? Are you going to admit that you've gone behind my back and plotted against me with Claus or you going to dare to try lie to my face about it, little bitch?"

An uncontrollable trembling overtook me with viciousness while the words he was saying sunk into my addled brain. I had indeed requested that Byron be removed from the Voters level when visiting with Claus. However, I'd not been made aware he'd granted it. This wasn't supposed to happen until I was officially confined in the Mortar Palace.

You see, I couldn't risk giving Byron two ways to taken advantage of me after I was rendered helpless below. As the Mortar Palace dungeon master, I could have him removed if he became the problem which I assumed he would. But if left as the Voter, he'd still have the rights to come visit me in the palace.

Making him angry by ordering his removal after he chronically mistreated me in my palace, which as I said was likely, surely doing that could be dangerous or even deadly the moment he was permitted to visit me as the vengeful Voter. He knew that was the serious threat that would prevent me from trying to block him from continuing to do as he pleased to me in the cell deep below where no one could hear me screaming for help. He'd already proven during my first trip to the palace, that he was more than willing to end my life if he thought he'd be blocked from getting to torment me at his leisure. Claus was well aware of this problem and also understood Byron would only need to make one visit as the pissed off Voter to make sure there was no more Mortar King to sit on the stony throne. Yikes.

This unexpected (okay, earlier than expected) move by the Fur King to give me the bit of protection from Byron had the most unfortunate timing.

He clenched his hands into fists after I maintained my silence for several moments then he yelled out, "I would kill you for this, but where is the fun in that? Instead, I think I will rip you apart slowly, very slowly. And make you fucking beg me to make it hurt more. That sound like the fair trade for the nightmare life you have condemned me ta, slut?"

I shrugged and did all I could to appear unruffled by his threats even though I couldn't stop that infernal shaking that I was doing.

"You are suffering nothing worse than I must if you are being untruthful about your promise to see us both free of this hellhole. Besides, I don't understand why you'd be the least bit upset by this bullshit of spending the hot minute in the dungeon barracks. That is, unless you are the one doing the lying. Can you get us out of this Haus or not?" I stood my ground and glared at him feigning confident defiance but in truth I was scared shitless of this monstrously huge and strong older brother of mine.

Byron's fury seemed to cool into the expression of barely veiled malice as he replied, "Oh, I intend to keep that promise to you, impatient little slut. But first, I'm going to punish you severely for being the duplicitous bitch that you honestly are." With that he struck out his right fist with force.

He made a direct connection to my jaw. I swooned for the briefest of moments. Then I fell like the ton of bricks right to the floor, knocked stupid by his sucker punching.

Before I could recover the ounce of my senses, Byron rushed over and flipped me to my face. I gasped and shook my head trying shoo off the brain fog and regain my bearings. The brute knew that he didn't have much time before I'd become capable of giving him the honest struggle.

I always assumed it's my fighting him that is the turn on for that brute. This incident proved me wrong. He managed to pull down my breeches in record time and unbutton the front of his own. By the time he'd positioned himself to penetrate me with his overly engorged member, that punch drunkenness had started to wear off.

The scream of hot white pain flew out of my throat as that bastard rammed himself into me with a single brutal stroke, and without the mercy of lube, that motherfucker. Once he was balls deep, he halted his assault and his laughter mingled with my screams of insult.

I struggled with all my might trying to buck him off me, but he successfully held me hostage with his immense weight. Well, pinned me to the spot to be gross about it.

He leaned down into my ear and whispered, "I've waited the long time to taking your virginity, little bitch. I know you think you're the overused slut, and that's right, you are. But I've heard another rumor in the halls. They say that fine doctor Attila gave you the new set of pipes after you managed to bust your old ones with your wanton behaviors. You know what? I'm glad you didn't take that pain killer earlier. It gave me this opportunity to break you in the way you honestly deserve to be, without any mercy. Ha! I finally beat Jonas, that fucker Lucus, and even Peter to taken my proper place as the first instead of suffering the sloppy seconds, or third, or millionth. So, fight all you want, cry and scream, or just lay there and suffer, you sonofabitch. I'm not stopping until I'm the satisfied man. Just know that no matter what you do, your ass is mine. And I'm never letting you free of my brutal attentions."

With that he began his thrusting action with intense vigor. This – along with the horrible things he said, and the vision of this similar situation being ordered by me on Sigrid only the short time before – sent me into the full on weeping, begging, mental melt down.

To think that I, the Priceless Collar Mortar King of nearly mythical sexual history could still be violated to the status of blithering idiot was pretty astounding. Yet Byron managed to do it. I suppose it didn't help that I couldn't get the vision of those monsters ripping babies apart in the very spot my own fucking brother was raping me. It wasn't one of my more dignified moments. Yikes!

If this weren't bad enough, it turned out that the so called new pipes Byron mentioned I'd gained were far from the stuff of idle gossiping. The pain prior to the repair job was really bad, almost too much to tolerate with any honor. But that day, I found out that sometimes fixing the problem can make it even worse. The torment was increased to excruciating levels.

Byron was drawing out his cruel pleasure as long as he could. All the while I writhed, sobbed, cursed, and wailed while begging him to just fucking cum already. Of course the more I plead with him to get to it the longer he purposely held it off.

Then just when I was sure I was going to lose my fucking mind for good, Byron suddenly stopped his pumping into me. My eyes had been forced closed tightly from that tormenting pain, so I hadn't seen what caused the big brute to halt before reaching apex.

But when I felt his huge frame go limp and then fall to the floor next to me, I opened them in pure shock. I thought, wished actually, for a brief moment he'd died from the heart attack like Xavier had. However, the small voice calling out to me brought me back to reality.

"Sire? Can you hear me? Did Byron hurt you severely? Do you need the doctor?" I recognized this voice belonged to the dwarf silver collared called Snot.

I winced against the residual pain and rolled to my back as I breathed out, “Nein, I’m okay. This happens all the time. What have you done to, wait…how did you know this man’s name?” I focused my vision that was foggy with tears upon the small mildly disfigured face of my savior.

Snot wore the expression of disgust while he spat out, “I spent many years in the presence of Xavier, sire. This bitch is one of his bastard half breed sons. I’ve always worried after he was banished by Queen Ingrid to the dungeons, with his black collared mother. That one they he’d find this place. He’s always been the brutal cunt. I’ve waited too long to knock his block off. Maybe if we are lucky. I’ve killed him, ja?” He shot the mischievous grin at me as he said that.

With the groan I sat up and turned my attention to the unconscious Byron. “You hit him then. With what?” I glanced back at Snot.

He held up the rubber mallet that I’d managed to miss he had in his tiny hand as he replied, “This. Sire, I beg your forgiveness for not discovering this crime being committed against you sooner.” He dropped with suddenness into the graceful kneel.

I snorted then said, “How do you know this is the crime you encountered? Maybe, I give consent. Are you forgetting that I am of the Priceless class, ja? My special services skills are of the legendary status.”

He kept his eyes to the floor as he replied, “Forgive me for saying this, Your Majesty. But I know that Byron is the offspring of my former Master Xavier. I also recall you told me that Xavier is your father as well. This makes him at least your brother by half. Taking of special services of the sibling is perverted and illegal. I know that you weren’t the willing participant in this assault because I could hear you begging from kilometers away. I certainly could tell those screams I hear from you weren’t of thrill. I believe you to be the true Mortar King and the proof is in that golden band of disability you sport around your neck. It’s the legend that such a thing would be necessary if the Foundation Monarch be the truthful one.” His response full of intelligent deductions surprised me to the near stun.

After regaining some composure I said, “I suppose that a hero such as yourself deserves a reward of equal value to his perfect valor in protection of his King. You tell me what it is that you desire, and I will see that you are fully compensated.”

Snot kept his eyes lowered and voice even as he replied, “I beg your forgiveness, Sire. I stupidly didn’t make it clear when I requested that you grant me the mercy Xavier promised me many years ago. This is the thing I wish for the most. I thank you for this mercy, though I’m certain I’ve done nothing of worth to earn it.”

With the shudder over his words, I snuck another quick glance at my brute brother. Byron was out cold, but alive and well. I could see that he was breathing, dammit. I returned my focus to Snot and studied the little man's features closely.

Then I said, "Did Xavier ever give you the details of this mercy he promised to you?"

Snot looked up at me with apparent startle in his expression as he replied, "Nein, Your Majesty. I just assumed he intended to murder me like he did all the other children he bought from the surrounding towns."

I sighed, "This is how you come to belong to the Fur King too, ja?"

He shook his head, "Nein, Sire. I was abandoned at the church in the town far away from here as a baby. They didn't want me because of, well, I'm different, ja? These church people sold me to the circus performers. When I was ten years old, these performers that owned me were hired by Xavier to perform for his wealthy benefactors. I was doing the juggling act, and Xavier decided he enjoyed the jeering and taunts that I drew from his guests. He bought me from the circus and forced me into his submission. The rest, I believe I told you already. I served his fetishes until he tired of my skills and put me down here to await the mercy of death."

With the confusion no doubt coming over my expression I asked, "But why do you choose this submissive name Snot? You misunderstand the meaning of this at that time, ja? and how did Xavier manage to keep your collar? The Elders are forbidden to own the silver."

Snot sniffed loudly then replied, "Xavier kept me hidden in his palace apartment from everyone but his family and the outsiders that come to see his taboo shows of public torturing of children. As for my name, I chose Snot because it was better than being known as Smegma. Xavier only give me the two choices."

I jumped with a startle when he said this. "Yikes, he offer you the names Snot and Dick Cheese? That's awful."

Snot chuckled bitterly, "It's not so bad, Sire. I didn't choose Smegma because I was the little snot anytime I could get away with it. But never could I claim any affinity with dick cheese."

His humor caused me to chuckle too despite his deplorable story and my unfortunate circumstances while hearing it.

With a quick motion I hand signaled him to aid me in returning my breeches to their rightful condition. He did the dressing service with speed and grace that was breathtaking to witness. I stood there admiring this tiny man with the huge brain and seemingly bigger balls then most fellas I'd been dishonored to meet. I don't tell lies when I say, I liked Snot immensely and not only because he hit Byron hard enough to nearly send him to oblivion. There was just something special about him. Though at that moment I couldn't put my finger on it.

After I was fully dressed, he dropped to the kneeling at my feet and patiently awaited me to grant him his reward request.

I pursed my lips then said, "I cannot officially own the silver collar, Snot. But if I could possess one, it'd certainly would be you. If I bring you above, you must have a master to protect you or you'll be sent to auction. I cannot paint you black because you're slight size makes you the target for assassination by those idiots that don't tolerate anyone that looks different than them. This is the painful lesson I learn with two little lambs I once tried to save this way. But I cannot send one that has earned his right to survival more than anyone else I've ever met to the grave either. You say that Xavier promised you mercy, and this is the thing you desire the most. Therefore, I hereby make you the property of the Mortar Throne and name myself as your honest champion. You shall serve as my court advisor and must have the name as honorable as your new position. I, the Lord and Master of this Haus, proclaim from this day till the earth claims your bones you are to be called Mercy. Because that is what you are."

Mercy looked up from the floor with suddenness. His eyes filled with tears and his lip quivered slightly as if he may cry. I couldn't tell if this was from joy or truthful despair.

Then suddenly he said in the wavering voice tone, "You do me great honor, Your Majesty, though I'm unworthy of your attention much less your affection. I swear to you on my life, I will serve your throne with loyalty and will willing give up my life to see that you're comforted in any way you command. Without hesitation, regret nor question I shall serve you." He fell to the prostrated position and kissed my boots softly three times, one for each of my crowns, ja?

I motioned him to return to his kneeling then said, "Well, I thank you for your vows, Mercy. However, I can assure you your dignity I'll never violate. I'd free you from this hellish metal curse if I could. That's not possible while we are condemned to reside in the walls, and then the bowels of this Hell Haus. For now, you will travel with me above wherever I go, but come June 2nd, you'll be stuck suffering in the Palace with me. I apologize to you for this horrible fate, but there isn't anything I can do to prevent it other than try to find the escape route out of here."

Mercy shot a quick glance at Byron seeming to be assuring himself the brute was still not awake. Upon finding him nonresponsive, he leaned in close and whispered, "Come with me, Your Majesty." Then he took to his feet, dropped that mallet, picked up his flashlight and rushed off toward the door.

I didn't understand where the hell he was going nor why I should follow but follow I did.

We wandered through several tunnel paths for what seemed like forever. I didn't say anything to him because I was concerned he wanted to show me more of the carnage going on that I honestly didn't wish to know about but then he stopped with suddenness and pointed to some old rock steps that led to the round door in the ceiling of the mortar.

"There, Your Majesty, is something that may bring you some comfort."

With the expression of confusion on my face, and fear in my heart for what I was about to discover this time. I went up the steps, blindly trusting that Mercy meant well but as usual I was shocked to realize just how stupid I still was despite falling into so many traps before this one. As I pushed on that round door it gave way with ease. Light poured through it that was so brilliant it blinded me. While shielding my eyes with one of my wrapped hands I climbed the final step and with the gasp of true terror found I just popped headfirst right up through a manhole in the middle of the street of the town I'd been trying to escape to for years. Mercy had been showing me the secret tunnel that leads out of the Haus.

Chapter 30: Loophole

I stood there unable to believe the sights of wonder before my eyes. The sound of my heart blood rushed loudly in my ears.

‘This can’t be happening,’ I thought.

I closed my eyes tightly and shook my head harshly, trying to break myself out of this strange delusion. It had to be fiction, ja? There was no way after all those years looking for this mythical escape route, I’d finally found it. After all, dreams never came true for the worthless catamite boy named Mad Maxximillian.

Yet when I opened them, the vision I’d begged for so many times I had long lost count, was still there. Running along both sides of the street was a sidewalk. I could clearly see the town’s people walking briskly by. They were in such a hurry to get wherever they were going. They didn’t even notice the appearance of the pale, scarred up Mortar King gawking at them in awe.

The sound of a small bell chiming tore my attention away from the eclectic group of traveling folk. A small gasp of thrill escaped me as I saw the object that had emitted that noise. A young man that didn’t appear much older than myself was riding a bicycle that flew pass me on the left.

Other than that time Rolf had taken me to town on that disastrous trip to chase after women. I'd never seen such a marvelous machine. Well, other than in Leo's magazines, whenever I was able to see them.

Since I had been a very small child I'd fantasized about the things I would do first, or the things I would say, once I had escaped the Haus. It's almost comical to admit that now that I'd accomplished my goal. I was too frightened to do anything but stand there frozen to the spot like a dummkopf.

Well, to be fair, it wasn't really stupidity that glued me to the spot half above the ground and half below. The skills and lessons I'd mastered weren't useful aids when it came to knowing how to navigate my way in the outside world. I was just a naïve teenager though I was far from innocent as you well know. I had no concept of how to do anything other than endure fierce brutality and struggle for survival.

Hell, I didn't know how to ride a bicycle, drive a car, or shop for groceries. I didn't even have any idea the name of the town I'd accidently stumbled into.

None of that mattered to your Master, Meine Liebe. I took a deep breath to calm my nerves, and with all the inner strength I could still muster. I climbed the final steps to freedom.

Ready or not, happy people. Here comes the Mad Maxximillian to join you, I thought with my chest feeling as if it may explode from the rising joy of this ultimate victory and perhaps terrified excitement too.

Just as my right boot took its first step onto the aging asphalt of the street, my left was snatched by someone below. I let out a yelp of surprise which appeared to catch the attention of a young woman that had stopped to light up a cigarette only a few feet to my left.

She halted her actions of flicking her lighter and her eyes focused on the tall stranger that had called out in distress.

The woman pointed at me then screamed out, "Oh Mein Gott, look everyone over there. Does anyone know why he dresses like that? Hurry, someone call on the Ministerium für Staatssicherheit immediately. This man is a criminal no doubt."

Extreme terror both from the woman alerting the Stasi and from the harsh tugging of my leg by the unseen assailant from the tunnel sent off a panic reaction within me.

I grabbed the leg being held hostage with both of my bandaged hands. Ignoring the pain that ripped through my healing fingers, I did all I could to free myself from the attacker. No matter how hard I struggled, I couldn't break free of his hold.

Several people had stopped their journeys to watch this weird show going on in the middle of the street. I noticed an audience I had collected, and like an idiot, I believed one would volunteer to be my savior. All I had to do was ask, ja?

"Help me, please, someone help me. I'm being held hostage in the Haus. They kill babies in that place and rape me daily. Listen to me, people. These men are evil and they will come for your children too," I pled in the high-pitched voice, losing all sense of decorum.

Yikes, even in this moment of pure desperation, I could feel the heat of shame color my cheeks over this most unmanly public admission of the indignity I had endured.

Instead of coming to my aid, most of them took on the expressions of disbelief. Then a light chuckling broke out in waves among the small throng of curious onlookers. What started as the mild rippling of this humored noise quickly became the roar of side-splitting laughter.

My begging became more frantic upon realizing these outsiders weren't taking me seriously. If I'd had any sense at all, I'd changed tactics or at the very least shut the fuck up.

However, as I said many times, Meine Liebe, your Master is not very intelligent and completely worthless.

I screamed out pathetically, "Nein, listen to me people. The Stasi are behind this criminality of the Haus. Stop laughing at me. I need help. Why don't you care? Do you think I'm lying? I'd never be so dishonorable. I swear to you all. Ask Felicity, she'll tell you I'm a man of my word. Gottverdammit, someone help me."

It was at that moment I heard the loud whining of a siren in the distance. I knew this sound meant trouble. I recalled hearing something like it the they the men in white coats hauled me away to Heslach.

Of course, I had no idea this time it wasn't a white padded cell and the Altergott brothers that siren signaled. This was the call of the Ministerium für Staatssicherheit. Ja, the Stasi police were coming. If they had gotten to me, they would've taken the undocumented Maxximillian to wherever those fiends take people that are never seen again. No questions asked and no evidence of the foul murdering would ever be found.

I am sitting here with you today, Meine Liebe. Therefore, it's obvious that the Stasi police didn't get me, but this was a very close call. Especially, since as far as the Stasi were concerned, I had been killed during that awful Stasi night at the Haus.

It's true I had no papers that the Stasi could use to identify me as a survivor of their brutal games. However, there is a strong possibility that one or more of the officers in that police vehicle would recall the teenager with the unusual scar running down his left cheek and everywhere else too.

Even if I had gotten lucky and none of the men coming had been at the Great Hall that night. Surely, once I was taken to one of their secret interrogation areas, someone there would remember their old buddy Puppers, ja? Yikes.

The siren in the distance had been effective in getting me to end my silly begging for help from the cruel town people. I became even more wild in my actions to free my caught foot. Everything within me wanted just wanted to run until I escaped this nightmare. Or expired from the total exhaustion of my flight to unknown destinations.

However, my attacker was simply too powerful for me to shake off. This struggling and yelling fit had worn me out. To my horror, I finally realized this person was successfully pulling me back down into the Haus tunnel. There was nothing I could do but give up.

Just moments before the sights of blue skies and smell of fresh air were stolen from me, I managed to wail miserably, "You are monsters, all of you. Don't ask Maxximillian for any mercy when they come for you. I won't hear you screaming for help either, you bastards."

Then just like that, I was sucked back into the nightmare that never seemed to end.

Just as the light in the world above had initially blinded me. The pressing darkness momentarily prevented me from identifying the sonofabitch I intended to murder most gruesomely. There had been few other moments in my life I could claim caused me more fury than that one. That intense anger over being prevented from escape was as useless as my begging had been. My hijacker had managed to gain a very tight hold around my waist.

With all the energy I had left I kicked wildly and blindly while screaming, "Let me go. You can bet I'm going to kill you, motherfucker. Do you know who you there to offend, worm? I am the Lord and Master of this Haus. My words are the Law."

Byron groaned loudly then replied, "Stop struggling you little shit. Do you have any idea what you have done? Fuck me this asshole is strong. Snot, this is all your fault. Help me. Grab his feet, God dammit."

The small form of the Dwarf pleasure submissive suddenly emerged from his place of hiding in the darkness.

Mercy snorted with irritation as he responded, "It's possible the Mortar King could've outrun the Stasi. If you'd have stayed out of this gift I'd offered his majesty, he might be in Dresden by now or even further. Your unwanted interference has put all of us in great danger, not mine."

Realizing that my brute brother was the man behind foiling my escape further fueled the rage within me. I yelled at the top of my lungs, "Why are you doing this? Do you not understand this is the way out of the Haus. If we hurry, we can still get away. I thought you wanted out of this hell hole as badly as I do. Are your actions because you have been lying as I have always suspected you to be doing? Let me go and I swear I will forgive you for rudely assaulting me. Are you listening? Unhand me this minute, Byron, or so help me I will kill you, you rapist bastard."

Byron's voice sound strained but menacing as he replied, "We can't get out of here through there, you idiot. The Stasi are aware of that hole and they use surveillance cameras to keep an eye on it. They are always waiting for dumbasses like you to try to break out of this fucking prison. Stop yelling and listen for a moment, will you? Do you hear it? That is the sound of our death coming. They have guns, brother. We will be assassinated without question."

I heard his words and amazingly, I actually calmed myself enough to mind him. Once I was silent the applause and fading laughter of the townspeople wafted down from above us. Initially the idea that those people were assuming what they saw was merely some street performer doing a comedy act, reinvigorated my anger.

Then I heard that siren getting louder until it finally drowned out everything else. Byron was telling the truth. The Stasi police vehicle had arrived. The faint reverberation of two car door slamming closed echoed through the air.

Mercy's expression was fearful as he whispered out, "Oh my Gott, the Stasi are here. Quickly, follow me. Run boys or we are done for." The little man took off with incredible speed into the darkness of the tunnel.

Byron snorted then gasped, "I'm letting you go, Maxx. I must trust you realize the seriousness of this situation. You haul ass behind me or brother let me say goodbye to you. You won't survive them this time, ja?" With those words he released me then fled chasing after Mercy.

I stood there watching the two of them disappear into the void of that dank passageway for a moment. Everything in me wanted nothing more than to rush back to that hole and take my chances that I could outrun the Stasi officers, but I knew better.

The injuries I had suffered, thanks to Gerard's cruelty towards me as the small boy trapped in his barn, had hampered my mobility without the use of a cane and a smooth surface or I wouldn't get anywhere very fast, ja?

The sudden appearance of a boot dropping down onto the steps that led up to the hole made up my mind. I didn't stick around to find out if it belonged to a curious townsperson or to a Stasi thug. I hobbled with all the speed I could possibly manage in hot pursuit of Byron and Mercy. I was no longer interested in taking a stroll along the streets of freedom.

All I could think was, 'Dear Gott, don't let them catch me. I can't go through that again.'

I'd barely managed to catch up with the pair before the harsh sound of an unknown man yelled out from behind me, "Halt. You there, I said stop this instant or I will shoot."

Well, Meine Liebe, that fellow could go fuck himself. The Mad Maxximillian wasn't going to obey his orders. The only thing the Stasi officer managed to do is get the lead out of my ass. And apparently that of Byron and Mercy's too. The three of us moved like the wind as we retreated the way we had come.

With suddenness Mercy took a sharp right turn. It happened so fast, Byron and I almost missed his clever attempt to shake off our pursuers. He called out to us in the harsh whisper, "We can hide here. Be careful, don't make a sound, ja?"

We joined the tiny submissive behind a crumbling stone wall that jutted out of the main pathway. Mercy put his finger to his lips motioning us to be quiet. Byron nodded his understanding at his warning, but I huddled there thinking concealment wasn't our best option.

I leaned in close to Byron and whispered, "When they've passed by us. I say we sneak up on them in ambush. Once we have their weapons, we kill them both and go back to that hole, ja?"

Byron's face wore the expression of disbelief as he whispered in reply, "Shut up and be still, fool."

I was going to say something insulting in response, but before I could. What appeared to be the form of two large men rushed by in the darkness.

I heard one of them say, "I'm certain I saw him go this way."

Then the other man replied, "Maybe he did, but if we don't find him soon. I think we will go back to the car and notify headquarters that one of these monsters tried to escape. I hate it down here. Too many places for someone to accomplish a blind attack, ja? Besides, these tunnels have always creeped me out."

His voice took on the echo that indicated the men had traveled far enough to be almost beyond ear shot.

Mercy gasped then whispered, "Do you think they will call for more of them to come looking for us?"

Byron growled out in reply, "We'd better hope not. As it is, if they don't get us. The elders may."

I snorted then whispered harshly, "See, we must destroy them before they can tell anyone about this. They've left us no choice."

The big brute ex-voter snatched me by Lucus's gold collar and shook me violently, "I've already told you, fool. They have guns. You of all of us should understand how deadly those weapons are. Maybe we could take one of them by surprise, but then his buddy is sure to kill us all. Now, again I tell you to be still dammit. Say another word and I will knock you the fuck out. I mean it, Maxx."

I glared at him seething with hate as I replied, "Another word, motherfucker."

Before my huge brother could carry out his threat to beat me to unconsciousness. We heard the voices of the Stasi Officers. They were returning and nearly right next to our hiding spot behind that wall. Byron halted his aggression towards me. All three of us held our breaths, frozen in fear like living statues.

The men didn't linger in their journey back the way they'd come. Lucky for us, they also didn't bother to take a quick peek around that wall either. The two of them were satisfied that whomever they'd been chasing had changed his mind about trying to leave the Haus. Or at least, that was our hopes that they did.

Several moments elapsed before any of the three of us decided the coast was clear. Collectively we let out the air we'd been holding and allowed our bodies to relax. No one said a word for many minutes more.

Then finally Byron broke the uneasy silence between us, "Snot, if those Stasi bastards notify the Elders about this I hope you know before I'm sent to the pit for a beating it is your name that I will give to them. What the hell were you thinking, giving this idiot directions to that Stasi trap? I always thought you were smart. You managed to outfox Xavier all those years, only to prove it wasn't intelligence but the old man's senility that kept you alive."

Mercy shook his head then spit out his words in response, "Stop calling me, Snot. I've already told you my name is Mercy."

Byron began to laugh, "Mercy is the one thing you will not get from the Elders, nor from me you little bastard."

He lunged at the little man ready to pound him into a pile of bones and bloody flesh.

However, not only was Mercy seemingly unafraid of my huge brother. His small stature allowed him to move much faster. The tiny submissive rapidly stepped aside, leaving the charging Byron without a target.

Byron realizing that he had been bested by the dwarf let out an angry roar, "Hold still damn you. I have waited for years to send you to hell."

Mercy chuckled then replied, "You're perverted father already beat you to that, half-breed."

Before Byron could make another strike against Mercy, I stepped between the feuding duo.

I put up my arms and yelled, "Stop this shit. We have more important people to kill than each other. That will simply have to wait, ja? Now Mercy, tell me something. Is what Byron is saying the truth of it? Is that escape route watched by the Stasi they and night?"

Mercy shook his head then replied, "I don't know about the surveillance of it during the day. I suppose that is likely. However, I happen to know it's not so closely guarded at night. I've slipped out of that hole and toured the town above hundreds of times since Xavier condemned me to this place. So far as I know. I've never been captured on their cameras or at least they never sent anyone after me for it."

I snuck a glance at the still fuming Byron as I said, "So, all I must do is wait until dark. Then I can return here and poof. No more fucking Mortar King, and no more goddamned Haus. Ja, this could work."

Byron growled in response, "Oh brother, even Friedrick has more brains than you do. Even if you managed to sneak through that hole without being spotted. Tell me, what will you say to that pervert roomie of yours when he asks you about the huge sack of clothing and snacks you surely intend to take. You know, in case you were successful in not getting yourself shot immediately. Maybe you think food is easily found lying around in the outside, ja? How do you plan to support yourself? Ah, I know. You intend to keep selling your ass to strangers, ja? Well, I hate to break it to you, little slut. People in the real world don't find used up boy whores as sexy as they do in the Haus."

"You need not concern yourself with my business any further, Byron. As it is, rudely attacking me earlier has officially broken the contract we had between us. I do believe you and I agreed you would keep your filthy hands off my royal person until after the sacrificing of the Haus babies had been stopped. I'm certain you think holding your promise to help me escape over my head will force me to forget this or bring me back for re-negotiation. Too bad for you, I've discovered the way to do this is without your aid. You are dismissed, worm. Be on your way before I decide to kill you just for the sheer thrill of watching you die," I said in an arrogant sounding tone while looking down my nose at the brute.

Byron grinned with menace as he replied, "As you wish, Your Majesty. I'll be happy to leave you losers here with the Stasi. Before I go, I'll go get the pain killers, cigarettes, and sharps I brought with me. I seem to recall these are the items we agreed I would provide weekly. No doubt when those officers catch you or the elders find out about this, you'll be grateful Byron is a man of his word. Ah, but wait a moment. If our contract isn't valid anymore. I no longer owe you those precious mercies, ja?"

My glare filled with hate while I responded, "It's your brutality that made such things necessary in the first place. As it is, I no longer require your assistance. You have no further excuse to treat me like your punching bag. So, keep your poison, you bastard. And if you know what is good for you, your distance too."

My brute brother bowed low in an act of feigned respect. Then he turned and retreated back towards the Palace at a brisk pace. The echo of his evil chuckling lingered long after he had disappeared into the dark tunnel.

I stood there staring after him seething with both hatred for that man and anxiety over having lost access to his quick fix cures. It is true by then I had acquired a physical addiction to his drugs, but I was completely unaware of it.

I had been studying the medical books Peter had given me for months. The concept of drug dependence was known to me at the academic level.

However, I was just a stupid boy without any real-world experience. It was my belief that if I could end the pain the brutal men forced upon me, then things like painkillers and cigarettes weren't necessary anymore.

Of course, those men weren't going to stop playing their ruthless games with me. Not if I remained hostage to the Haus that is. Now that I'd found the secret way out. All I had to do was hold it together until the sun set.

Mercy cleared his throat quietly. His polite attempt at hailing my attention managed to bring me back from that place of emotional upheaval inside my head. I shifted my sight from the empty tunnel Byron left in his wake back to that of the little man.

His expression was one of concern as he said, "Sire, is what that half breed scum said true, the truth of it? Did he promise to give you those dangerous things? I beg your forgiveness for daring to be so rude, but I feel

I must beg your punishment for it. Because anything Byron has offered you isn't anything you should ever take from him. Xavier taught him many tricks that he used to abuse the children unlucky enough to be in his possession. Byron was the perfect student for his cruel craft. I swear to you, that bastard is all the worst of Xavier. You could say perversion perfected."

With a loud snort, and light chuckling I replied, "Is that so? Well, my pet. If I am also the spawn of that demon Xavier how can you be so sure I'm not a far worse version of him than Byron could ever boast? Maybe you have forgotten what you saw the first time we met? That brute might be the perfect pervert, but the Mortar King Mad Maxximillian is the wraith in the flesh, ja?"

Mercy raised his brows and pursed his lips for a moment, then said, "This you say I believe to be the truth of it, Your Majesty. I confess that until that day I found you granting the cursed mercy, I'd not been aware a Priceless had been discovered. However, I've been in the Haus long enough to know most of the legends of her history. Any unfortunate wearing the silver of that level surely has suffered hell even I can't imagine, and I don't want to imagine. He surely would be full of demons seeking vengeance. Yet I cannot ignore what my eyes say to my heart. This King over all that suffering may represent obscene brutality, but it's directed only at those who have earned his wrath. It's my pleasure to serve you, Master. Wherever you go, whatever you do, whatever you need, Mercy will be there to satisfy your needs. Your will is my own. Long live the Mortar King." He fell to his knees gracefully, kneeling at my boots to await my command.

I motioned him to return to his feet in silence.

Then with a loud sigh I replied, "If you mean what you say, then I think I should warn you. The path we will travel will be fraught with perils. I intend to return here to this place tonight. But first, we must gather the things we'll require to ensure this time, our escape will be successful."

Mercy's face lit up with what appeared to be an expression of pure joy as he said, "Did you say our escape from the Haus, Your Majesty? Does this mean you intend to take me with you? Or am I merely hearing what I wish to hear."

I chuckled. "Nein, my pet. You heard your Master correctly. There are so many things I will need to survive out there in the unknown world. But the one thing I'd be a fool to leave here without is Mercy, ja?"

Ah, Meine Liebe, the smile that spread across his small, deformed face was a beautiful sight to behold. I know you are wondering why I would take this dwarf man with me in my bid for freedom from the Haus. It is likely you will realize that his obvious disabilities would cause too many eyes to focus upon us. Or at the very least, it may slow us down. This would surely increase the likelihood of discovery by the Stasi, ja?

Well, as I have said, I was just a stupid boy with big dreams and no sense. I thought I had the perfect plan of deception and Mercy's small size was essential to see it to fruition. And of course, I believed the poor fellow had suffered enough terror in his life to have earned this gift I was hellbent to give us, all of us.

But before I could do anything more it was important that I finished what I had started. The babies of the Haus would be vulnerable until or if I could find someone on the outside willing to end the evil of those monsters that call it home.

The pain from Byron's torturous assault was by this time causing me great distress.

Despite that unfortunate fact, for a change, I was grateful that he had done it. He couldn't have picked a better moment to behave in his usual rude, impulsive way. Thanks to his breach of contract, I was free to attend to the next person on my list without having to worry his temper would ruin my plans.

That was very important to me because this person, well persons really, were the most innocent of all the guilty, and that included Friedrick. More than that, though he and his partner were on the list of surviving war criminals. They were also recorded in that black book as owing massive fines for refusing to comply with Haus law. You know, the one that demanded each of the war survivors sacrifice a child for the annual payment to the Stasi, ja?

I must admit. I found it very comforting that both these fellows had been forced to pay huge amounts of income to the Elders over the last few years due to their noncompliance. If I had not discovered this awful secret of the Haus killing the kinder when I did it was likely these two were going to suffer far more than simply a big hole made in their wallets. Sigrid had written in the final pages that the next step for them if they continued this noncompliance was execution.

When I read that, Meine Liebe, I swear to you I nearly had a heart attack. I have often told you that I don't believe there is a God and that is the truth. How could someone like me have faith in a deity that cares little for his creations? That he allows places like the Haus and people like the Stasi or Xavier to exist, ja?

Well, this is the one time, besides finding you, that has led me to wonder about the existence of the almighty. Because whether it was God or fate, had I not stepped in to stop it, Jacob and Jager were slated to be burned at the stake.

Ja, I hear your gasp of surprise, Meine Liebe. I know you are aware of how much I honestly love Jacob for all the kindness he showed me. Well, after he had me kidnapped and then came to his good senses that is.

Of course I had forgiven his momentary lapse of good judgment long ago. He was the one man that had done more for me than anyone ever had and he never asked me for anything in return for it.

Ah, except for my honest affection and that he will always have in abundance.

However, like it or not, I had no choice but to make Jacob and his partner Jager disappear forever. How to make the Stasi believe they were both dead was the only decision regarding the fates of those on the list that I struggled with.

Banishment to the yard, as I had done to Rolf, wasn't a fair punishment for these two. They hadn't done a thing to earn living lives in squalor with their reputations in tatters.

Sending them to spend the rest of their days in the dungeon was also too cruel a sentence for these soft-hearted men. Jacob's heart is pure, and his colorful personality would wither away in the harsh coldness of that prison hell, ja?

Jager, well maybe he could handle it, but I wasn't willing to enact such evil on him either.

That left me with one option. Perhaps the worst punishment any person of the Haus could receive.

Banishment, Meine Liebe, was the thing I had learned that all the Haus residents feared the most. It was as good as condemning a person to death, but not just any death. It is one that may be quick from the bullet of a Stasi rifle or a slow, lingering demise from exposure and eventual starvation.

As you may recall, Meine Liebe. No one in the Haus had records to prove they existed. Without such important documentation, especially for those born within her walls like Jacob and Jager had been, there was no hope of gaining employment or housing.

That is if the person wasn't immediately accused of being a spy, arrested then executed.

It wasn't going to be easy to look my beloved Jacob in his eyes and pass that terrifying sentence on him, and on the man he loved as well. But I had to do it. Allowing them to remain as survivors on the Stasi list, assured that more innocent babies would pay the price in their place. Too many had already died, so that they could live.

I just had to believe in my heart that Jacob would realize he and Jager had taken enough already. No matter what the outcome, surely, they would see the wisdom in giving up their lives in exchange for those that deserved to live as much as they ever had, ja?

Mercy didn't require me to give him any further command to follow behind me as I turned and took off back towards the Palace. Time was no longer my friend. I had to hurry if I intended to get everything prepared for my great adventure later that night.

The journey out of the tunnels and out of the secret door located under the dungeon steps was uneventful. As was our trip up to the first floor.

Once we exited onto the main hallway of the Haus, however, things got a bit crazy.

Apparently, Mercy had been telling the truth about Xavier hiding his existence to all but close family and outsiders. The expression of shock on the faces of every resident, Dominant or submissive upon seeing the tiny man traveling behind me was, well, comical.

One would think none of them had ever seen such a thing as a little person before. Likely, few even knew such a condition as dwarfism could happen.

Needless to say, Mercy and I were the show all eyes wished to see. We hadn't managed to make it to the main staircase before the sounds of tongues wagging excitedly assaulted our ears.

Ah, what boring lives the Haus people live that they found the sight of Mercy such powerful fuel for their ceaseless gossiping.

I briefly glanced back at Mercy to assure myself that he wasn't taking the rude behaviors of these onlookers too seriously. He kept his eyes to the floor and his steps at a perfect three steps behind my own. He wore no observable signs on his face that the taunts and jeers were getting to him. My chest puffed up with pride. It was magnificent to witness Mercy adherence to the perfect protocol expected of his status despite the bad manners of everyone else around him. His calm demeanor, and courageous expression convinced me that he was the faithful companion I'd hoped him to be.

I have no idea if the cruel things being said around us honestly bothered him. If they did, he never complained to me about it. Nor did he let any of those vulgar assholes know it either. I admit Mercy is one of the bravest men I've ever met.

We reached the fourth floor with the loud murmurs and waves of chuckling still hanging in the air around us. As we started down the long hallway that led to our destination my heart began to pound wildly in my chest.

The noise of insults no longer had my attention. All I could think or feel was intense sorrow. I didn't want to reach Jacob's apartment door. For the first time since I'd met him, I didn't want to see his beautiful face or hear his comforting voice. *I wanted to run, Meine Liebe, as far as I could too forget everything I'd learned.*

I thought silently to myself, 'Oh my beloved, if only we could have met in another place, another time. I just can't do this to my dearest friend, nein, my only friend in the whole world.'

But this wasn't the fantasy world and Jacob never belonged in that horrible prison in the first place. It was far past time for him to go and Jager too. If I didn't send them away. Their lives were as good as over no matter what.

This is what I kept telling myself, while I took a deep breath then knocked on his door. Jacob answered immediately as if he'd been waiting for our visit.

His expression went from mild curiosity to extreme thrill as he popped his tongue then yelled out with a smile, "Ah Jager honey, you won't believe what gift has been delivered to us. Heat up the teapot and the sheets. The most gorgeous man, ah man and a half, are here to rock our world. Oh, I just knew it was going to be Jacob's lucky day. My horoscope said to expect the unexpected. Well color this girl impressed because this is truly a surprise. Come in Maxx, and uhm, bring your little friend too. It's such a pleasure to see you both or let me say it's going to be a pleasure very soon."

I took a deep breath.

Then in as stern a tone as I could I replied, "Jacob, this is not a social call. I'm afraid I've come to you as your Mortar King, the Lord and Master of this Haus. Call Jager here right this minute. I've business to discuss with you both.

Jacob's smile faded to that of a confused frown as he said, "Maxx honey? What is this all about? If someone has told you something vile about your Auntie Jacob or Uncle Jager. Let me assure you they are liars. Please tell me what is bothering you, Maxx. You are scaring me."

I nodded. "You should be frightened little rabbit. It appears the wolf has finally come to eat you for his dinner, ja?"

Jager came into the living area, his expression one of concern as he said, "Jacob? What is going on here?"

Jacob glanced at his lover and responded in the anxious tone, “I don’t know, baby. Maxx doesn’t seem to be himself today. Maybe you should go upstairs and fetch Leo. He’ll know how best to handle this, uhm, seizure fit our sweetheart is having, ja?”

Jager started to rush past me to mind Jacob’s request, but I blocked him from the door with my arm.

I growled out angrily, “Halt, you criminal. You’ll not escape so easily as that. Jacob, I’m not ill nor are my actions due to epilepsy. I’ve discovered the secrets you have tried to hide from your Lord and Master. My eyes are open and there is no way to put your King back to sleep. I find you Jacob and you Jager guilty of crimes against my smallest subjects. For this abomination I hereby sentence you both to Banishment from the Haus. You have till tomorrow night to leave her walls and property, and you are commanded to never to return. If you try to disobey my orders, I will have you arrested and taken to the hill for immediate execution. Are we clear?”

Tears welled up in Jacob’s eyes as he quickly glanced at the seemingly shocked Jager and said, “Oh my God Gott. Honey? Is this happening? Have I fainted and am having a nightmare? Please, hurry and wake me up.”

Jager’s brows furrowed as he replied, “This is a bad dream but in the flesh. Might I ask why you’ve barged in here calling us foul names, Maxx? Is this supposed to be your idea of a funny prank? Well, I must tell you if so, you have a very poor sense of humor. Just look at your Auntie. You've frightened her to death. I should thrash you for daring to upset her like you have. If it weren't for how much Jacob adores you, believe me. I'd wipe the floor with your face for daring such insult."

I snarled in reply, "You could certainly try and find out just how brutal a monarch I truly am. However, as it is, I've no need to pull a muscle teaching you any unnecessary lessons, brute. I also refuse to repeat myself. You are the condemned. There is no reason to argue with the dead. Get ahold of yourself Auntie Jacob. Pack your shit and leave. I have spoken. That is all I have to say to either of you."

With those horrible words I turned around and left their apartment at a brisk pace. I didn't hazard a glance behind me. Not because I wanted to appear uncaring for what I had just done to my beloved Jacob and Jager. Though it was important that I did the perfect cruel tyrant act.

But that was the problem. This wasn't an act at all. The sentence I passed on them was valid and I was ready to force them to obey it.

The truth is, Meine Liebe, I left with haste (and without explaining further) because my own eyes were filled with rain. My chest felt like it been hit by a Stasi bullet and was splitting into two. I hated hurting him more than words can convey. Having to see the injured expression on his face, his grasping at his chest and hyperventilating actions nearly killed me. Well it did kill a part of me. The best part that was left of the boy once called Christian Axel.

I intended to run away from the Haus myself that very night. I knew without the sweet sounds of his tongue pop and silly antics to look forward to I would be miserable. No matter if I was able to gain my freedom or if I was trapped forever. My world was about to become darker than ever before, perhaps unbearably so.

So, with a heaviness within me threatening to crush out my breath, I hurried down the fourth-floor hallway. I didn't need to look behind me to know that Mercy was trailing close on my heels. Ah, and with the next step I had to take to ensure my job of ending the Haus slaughtering completed. That was the only Mercy I was ever going to know for a very long time.

Lucus's expression of total surprise was almost comical when he opened the apartment door to find it was his wayward charge that'd hailed him. He stood there with his mouth open, seeming unable to come up with anything snotty to say to me.

Then his shocked gaze fell upon the small, dirty, barefoot silver kneeling in perfect grace behind me.

He looked at me with wonder in his eyes as he said, "Christian, I mean Mad Maxximillian? Where in the hell did he come from? Oh wait a moment. I mean to ask. Where the hell did you get him? Have you done something stupid and illegal? Take that back wherever it came from this instant."

I snorted then chuckled in barely veiled defiance as I replied, "It has a name, Lucus. This is Mercy. You should be thanking me for coming to see you bearing such a wonderous gift instead of behaving like the rude brute you truly are. It is interesting you assume that I've lost my mind, showing up at my own door in the middle of the they to make an offering of permanent peace between us. I suppose I shouldn't be too surprised you'd think this a joke. I've treated you poorly for so long, this is true. But, at last, I've come to full sanity. Let me in and speak with me for a bit, Lucus. I can swear to you for a change, you'll happily take my advice if you do."

He appeared to perk up as he stepped aside to usher us in and said, "Ah, well I would be a total idiot to refuse such an intriguing offer and no doubt entertaining story. Where are my manners? Welcome, come inside boys. Do tell Lucus all about this peace offering you've cleverly tempted me with."

I rushed past him and took a spot in the center of the living area. Mercy followed in perfect step. I quickly gave him the hand gesture that ordered him to move to the corner of the room and kneel quietly. This negotiation with Lucus wasn't one he should have endured at close proximity, ja?

Mercy minded my command in silence. Lucus walked over to his overstuffed easy chair. He maintained his gaze at me while he sat down then leaned in close as if waiting to hear a secret. His expression of arrogant humor was irritating but I managed to control my urge to lash out at him like I usually did.

When nothing was said between us for many minutes, he finally broke the silence.

"Okay, I'm listening Mad Maxximillian. What is it that you want so badly that you believe only I can give to you. I know you are desperate because I'm the last person on Earth you wish to bargain with, ja?"

I dropped my eyes to the floor and nodded, "You speak the truth of it, Lucus. However, if you agree to the things I ask you. I'm willing to give you the most coveted prize in return."

Lucus gasped and his face fell into that of sheer disbelief as he whispered out, "You go too far with your teasing, Your Majesty. You know better than to make promises you don't intend to keep."

I shook my head no. "I swear to you I'm deadly serious, Lucus. You give me the few things I ask of you and in return I give you possession of me in every and anyway you desire. No more complaints, no more refusals, no more fighting. I will be compliant and call you my tongue and Master. This vow I make to you I will sign in blood, but first you must pay my price. All of it."

He leaned back in his seat and narrowed his eyes as he responded, “This is quite a lucrative offer you are making. Freely of your own will, I must assume. But before I agree to any purchase of such rare quality, you must know I would like to know how much it will cost me.”

I glowered at him then angrily replied, “I wouldn’t there to approach you with this offer unless I knew you could afford it. Stop insulting me, dammit.”

He chuckled lightly then crossed his arms as he said, “Ah, so there is the vicious boy I’ve come to love. Okay, if you honestly think I’m capable of giving you your heart’s desire, who am I to disagree, ja? You have a deal, Christian Victor or perhaps you intend to demand I stop calling you that?”

Lucus’s smile turned bitter while he awaited my usual fit of rage over his disrespecting my legal name.

Of course, I didn’t take his bait. I held my spot without even so much as flinching.

If finding me at the door in the middle of the they was shocking to him. Watching my subdued behavior even after taunting me really astonished the perverted Dominant.

He took to his boots with speed and mumbled out, “Wait here. I’ll go get a pen, paper and lancet. Lucus isn’t the fool that turns down an unexpected treasure.”

I refused to budge an inch or protest even when he attempted to rub against me on his way to collect the necessary items to seal our contract. He realized, at last, that my actions weren't just lip service. My interest in giving him full reign over my royal person, my future, and my power was proven to be sincere.

This realization that I wasn't kidding hastened his journey toward the bedroom. I didn't look up from the tiny spot of lint between my boots that I had been focusing my attention on.

Though I demonstrated a stoic demeanor. Inside I was filled with dread. It was my secret hope that Lucus wouldn't be in a hurry to test out his new position over my will.

Well, I mean new in that before I had never pretended to be amenable to his nasty touching.

However, I was no longer a believer in luck or dreams coming true. I knew damned well the second my blood dried on his parchment. I was literally fucked. Lucus knew me better than most. There was absolutely no doubt in my mind that he was going to order me to provide him with the most profane special services that he could conceive. If for no other reason than to test my resolve to adhere to my side of our contract.

The knowledge that after this gross encounter with him, I'd finally be free of his foul hold and unwanted penetration sex from anyone else too, eased my disgust over what he was surely going to force me to endure.

But I'd be lying if I said, knowing it was going to be the last time, helped make it easy to brace for it. It didn't help that by that time the blessed effects of Byron's pain killers were long gone leaving the detox effects in their wake. Mild trembling, growing anxiety, and a killer headache has caused the irritation caused by Byron's assault. Feel far worse than it normally would.

Believe me, ouch doesn't get close to how bad my, uhm, money maker was burning.

Ah, but you look at me with that cute little expression of confusion on your face, Meine Liebe. What is that? Maybe you are wondering why if I believed I was that close to escaping from the Haus, and therefore Lucus. I would offer to willingly allow him to, well, shit on me one more time. Give me just a moment, yuck.

My apologies my little demonseed Frau, but that Lucus is one vulgar bastard, ja?

Anyway, perhaps it's important to remind you that your Master doesn't take on arrangements of any kind lightly. Obviously, the things I wished for Lucus to give me in return for tolerating his uncouth affections were very important to either my survival outside of the Haus or to the survival of someone else, someone I love more than I could ever love myself, ja?

So, Lucus returned to the living area in record time. His facial expressions betrayed his inner eagerness to see that I kept my promise to seal this bargain with him.

He sat down briefly and started to write down the demands from his side of the arrangement but stopped suddenly before getting much written down.

He thrust the paper and pen at me and said, "I have no idea how to construct this contract, Christian Victor. You are the man in charge here, at least until you put your blood to paper that is."

I rolled my eyes then snatched the articles from his hands as I replied, "It is simple Lucus. For the price of three non-negotiable items, you get everything you desire, no questions asked by either of us, ja?"

I rapidly scrawled my demands upon his paper.

Then before he could read it or object to the things I said. I motioned Mercy to approach. The tiny man moved smooth as silk, already sure of what my next command would be. He took the lancet from the place where it had dropped on the floor next to me.

Broken hands, stupid Lucus, ja?

He pierced the tip of my finger, and I signed the contract in blood. This happened so fast, Lucus sat there staring dumbly at Mercy that had knelt before him holding the drying agreement to take into his possession.

Finally, Lucus relieved Mercy of the paper. His eyes moved rapidly across the words written on it.

He gasped loudly then said, “Holy hell, Christian Victor. What you want is impossible I tell you. I mean, okay, I’ll agree to care for Mercy in our home and keep my hands off him until he is interred in the Palace with you. For what reason you wish to possess a dwarf’s silver I don’t even want to know. And this request to spend all night with your Mann Jonas tonight, isn’t too much a burden. But weird that you would give in to my desires in return for suffering his brutal assault even for one night. However, this last thing you want. That’s not within my power to give to you. I already confessed to you that I have no connections of worth, real wealth or power other than that you grant to me. Why the hell did you think I could get false papers and two one-way plane tickets to Tahiti? Is this your idea of a fucking joke? Even if I could get those, do you really believe the Haus leaders will let you and I use them? You must be insane, ja? That’s it. Well, dearest boy, Doctor. Attila is going to increase your anti-psychotics immediately. You’re going psychotic again.”

I glared at him angrily as I replied, “I told you already, I will not bargain with you over these items, none of them. You were able to get passports and plane tickets for Jacob and Jager in the past. You remember, ja? Funny that was when you were desirous of getting them out of the way so you could hijack my life, the impossible was suddenly possible. Well, Lucus. If you want my compliance with your disgusting fetishes and my vow to name you my regent, then you will find a way to do it again.”

He narrowed his eyes then whispered, "Wait a minute. You aren't selling yourself to me in the hopes of getting a vacation in the sun, are you? Ah, ja, I said it, but it didn't register. You want to give someone else their freedom, two persons. But maybe you are thinking of yourself and who? Leo, maybe? Certainly not me, I can be sure. Tell me right now, Christian Victor. Who are you intending to send away?"

Unable to control my DT driven mood any longer I yelled out, "I told you already, Lucus. You will get papers and two one-way plane tickets to Tahiti for Jacob and Jager by tomorrow morning or you can kiss my ass goodbye forever. I don't care who you have to kill to get it done. Just fucking do it already."

Lucus smiled and his form relaxed in the chair as he laughed then replied, "Ah, well, for those two men you are correct. I do have a solid connection that may be willing to see this silly request of yours fulfilled. However, if I do this for you, I must be assured you aren't merely stringing me along. This favor I must call in to get this done will cost me more than you can imagine. But I suppose it's worth it to gain your honest affection when my actions result in saving your precious Jacob and his man Jager's life. And what a waste it would be to stand aside while these fine men end up warming the Russian Guard during this harsh German winter, ja? I don't know how you found out he and his lover were slated for execution soon, but maybe the information came from the same place as this fine fellow who needs bath service immediately. Holy Christ does he ever stink. Anyway, so are you prepared to give me a taste of the sublime before I must devour the bitter to see you're amply satisfied that I'm a man of my word?"

I let out my breath in the mournful sounding sigh.

Then I replied, "I'm yours to do with as you please, Lucus. Before, I submit to your, uhm, desires. May I request to release our silver Mercy to his room. As you say, he needs to attend to his hygiene before his odor offends you. He offends you? I don't, ah, but never mind. I'm also a man of my word. You save Jacob and Jager as you say you can. Then I give you no further quarrels for the rest of the time we have together, ja?"

Lucus's smile widened as he quickly began to record on our contract his understanding of what I had promised him in return for giving me the things I had listed.

He was so deeply involved with this he didn't even glance up as I motioned Mercy to follow me through the apartment.

I led the little man to the door that once had been Matz's room.

With a pained expression on my face, I said, "Mercy, this is yours for the remainder of this time we are trapped in here with that fiend. If you know what is good for you, you'll get in the shower and run the water full blast. Not because I really mind your state of cleanliness, but because, well, Lucus isn't a gentle lover. It would injure my dignity to know the man I respect greatly might hear me."

Mercy put his tiny hand on one of my bandaged ones to interrupt my shameful confession.

With an expression of true concern, and empathy he replied softly, "Cry, all you wish and loudly as you need if it can get you through this terror. I won't think less of you for it. I'd beat any man to death that would there to insult you for suffering in the place of those you love. For what it is worth, Sire. Until this moment, I had lost all faith in humanity. But after seeing the amazing thing you have done I have found it again. I thank you for the, uhm, pleasure of serving you, Sire."

He bowed low in respect for me.

I shuttered from the rising sorrow as I motioned him to enter his room. "I thank you for being my Mercy. Now go and when I'm, when he's finished with me you will need to be ready to go. There are four more stops we must make before the glorious night arrives to end our nightmares, ja? There are some old clothes my ex-flat mate left behind in the closet. If you can find something that fits or able to alter any of it to your needs, then consider it my gift until we can buy you new outfits worthy of you."

Lucus called out from down the hallway. "Christian Victor, I'm waiting. You know I'm an impatient man. Hurry your pretty ass up. I seem to recall I promised to feed you dinner not long ago. I sure hope you are still hungry, because I'm fucking famished. Hahahahaha."

Mercy shot me a bitter smile and said, "Thank you, Sire. Do not worry about me. You may attend your duties, and I will be ready to go the moment you call."

I watched the tiny submissive retreating with rapidness behind the spare bedroom door.

Then I took a deep breath to calm my nerves and slowly walked back down the hallway towards the master bedroom. I found Lucus standing in the entry wearing nothing but a cruel smile waiting to pounce on me. Behind him, just visible in the shadows, that horrific cock bed sat, sheets turned down ready to receive its unwilling victim.

I wish I could tell you, Meine Liebe that the warning I had given Mercy was without warrant. However, that would be a shameful lie. That afternoon, Lucus reminded me of all the reasons I'd found the risk of death by Stasi rifle preferable than playing Lucus's vile little pony boy.

I swear to you, that man forced me to endure every nasty fetish he'd ever fantasized about in his twisted, sick brain. There is no doubt, Mercy would have had to be twelve feet under the water, and in the middle of the Atlantic Ocean to have avoided hearing my loud crying that day. Lucus's penetration and disgusting games were beyond painful to endure and far too perverted to repeat any of the details. Yikes and fucking yuck.

Once Lucus's greedy lust was sated, he added the indignity of tolerating his weird interest in attending to my personal hygiene with his own hands. By then, the nagging irritation of my drug withdrawal had become the raging fire of intolerance. It took all I had to not rip that pervert's head from his shoulders while he plucked and tweezed what seemed to be my every hair follicle.

Then, thankfully, he could find nothing more to demand from me for the moment. With observable disappointment he finally allowed me free of his gross attention.

He didn't have to give me permission to go twice. I rushed from that bedroom with the speed of a cheetah. Okay, a clumsy cheetah with a prominent limp.

Just as he promised, Mercy was at my side in mere seconds after he heard me call for him. Lucus came out of the room and watched us hauling ass towards the front door with the expression of suspiciousness on his face.

To his good fortune, he kept his thoughts about the reasons for our mad dashing like that to himself. I honest to God was ready to murder him and let the chips fall where they may. I never wanted to hear the name Lucus for the rest of my fucking life.

We made it to the staircase in record time, despite my limping being more severe than usual. God damn Lucus. Once we were where I was certain no one could hear our conversation.

I halted and said to Mercy in a whisper, "Stay close to me Mercy. We must go to the fifth floor and retrieve the Dungeon Headmaster Noah. He lives next door to that brute Byron. My ass can't take another assault today. Hopefully, it never has to, ja?"

Mercy nodded then replied, "I can understand that Sire. I must beg your punishment for asking, but why would you be seeking to fetch the headmaster, half-breed Noah from the Voters' floor? I thought queen Ingrid condemned him to the dungeon as untouchable."

I said with a small chuckle, "She did but I found the treasure she threw away. Seems Xavier and Ingrid had the same bad habit of tossing gems of rare quality, ja?"

Mercy blushed upon hearing my flattering remark about him.

Then he said in the whisper, "Okay, but Master. Why do we need him? Protection from Byron maybe? He is a strong fellow, but won't he tell on us if he figures out what we are planning to do?"

With a snort I replied, "Nein, my pet. In fact, he holds the key to our successful escape. Out there in the world there is only one thing that will bring a man respect and hopefully a pass to the free West."

Mercy frowned then said, "A man capable of breaking heads, ja? That is what Noah is going to do for us, Master?"

I laughed loudly then replied, “Ah, my sweet Mercy. Money is the correct answer. We need that, and lots of it. And thankfully, your Master just happens to be rich. Come, my pet. It’s starting to get late. Let’s go get the key to the Bank of Mad Maxximillian.”

Chapter 31: Needful Things

Mercy and I hurried up the staircase. We traveled quietly as possible, with our heads down but eyes open. The Voter's floor was devoid of traffic which is usual. This is because, you may recall, no one other than the men and women living on that level are permitted to be there. Except of course, the black collar staff that have been specially assigned to meet the needs of those holding the silk thrones.

While Byron had been officially de-throned and informed, he was to leave the fifth floor immediately. I wasn't dumb enough to believe my brute brother was going to obey that order until he was forced to do it.

Therefore, me and Mercy were in real danger of being caught out in the open by the very angry ex-voter. With Friedrick already moved down into the dungeon, Rolf off to take his place in the yard and Matz too small to be of any use. That left only Peter, Almut, and Hubertus to aid us if a fight with him broke out. I dare say, those three men had plenty of reasons to stand back and let Byron beat the stuffing out of me, and probably the tiny Mercy too.

It was possible that Noah could block the worst of Byron's fit of rage if he spotted us.

However, I wasn't willing to risk getting my new lover busted up over something that Byron had no right to complain about.

Afterall, being named my palace dungeon master was his idea. He had used his position of power over me during that awful night in the Great Hall to gain permanent access to continue his abuse, even during my lifetime interment in the Mortar Palace.

Well, he got what he wanted. I was going to be damned if I would allow him to bitch about it now. Or to be clear, make me his bitch over his mistake, that is.

We slipped past Byron's door without incident. I hand gestured Mercy to remain standing as I very lightly knocked to hail Almut or Hubertus. Neither man answered my call.

Instead Blume, the pretty wife of Almut and mother of Jaison, stood gaping in awe at the entry.

She dropped her gaze to her shoes and said softly, "Your Majesty. What a pleasant surprise. What is it that we can do for you, Sire?"

I growled back in the mildly irritated tone, "You can invite us inside, dear lady. Hurry up. You are wasting my time woman."

She gasped then without a moment more signaled for us to follow her. It wasn't nice of me to behave like an impatient brute, this I know. Blume had never done a thing to incite being treated with anything other than my total respect.

She had proven herself an excellent mother to my black collar children in her care. And to her biological son Jaison too. Almut was a lucky man to call her his Frau. Few women would still adore her Mann after my sentencing him to becoming the plaything for the Voter Valentin, ja?

Yet love him completely she still did. I've got to hand it to Blume. She is quite a magnificent woman.

In my defense, by that point. The rough sexual encounter with Byron, then Lucus, plus the detox effects of the drugs were making my life pure hell.

I honestly had not felt that bad since after the Stasi men finished tearing me apart only a few months before. It's truly a wonder that I didn't lose my shit and started tossing everyone in sight over the banister that afternoon. That's how thin my patience had become in response to this growing feeling of urgent needing within.

Of course, I wasn't sharing this most important information with anyone. As usual, I kept it all to myself, assuming that somehow, I could control it. Ha. What a damned fool I was, ja?

Blume led us into the large dining area of the apartment that once had been home to the Silk Queen. Sitting at the head of the table was Noah. He was happily stuffing his face with wurst from the plate piled high with fine foods in front of him. To his right Jaison the new head torture Master and next to him the head torture Mistress, and his lucky Frau, Amanda.

Five other small faces turned their eyes from their dinners to gaze upon the sudden appearance of their Mortar King, and benefactor. I recognized these kinder as the silvers I'd painted black. Each of them wore expression that seemed both grateful and curious. Obviously, no one in this home had been expecting my visit, ja? Hahaha.

The woman that called Hubertus her Mann, Vogal came out of the doorway that I assumed led to the kitchen. She was carrying a large dish that honestly smelled absolutely delicious. My stomach rumbled in wanton approval, but I ignored its interest in taking a moment to sample from this most appealing feast.

Vogal had initially missed my standing at the entry. When at last she noticed everyone at the table was focused on something other than her fine cooking, a gasp of surprise escaped her throat.

She dropped to her knees so gracefully she managed not to spill a drop from the bowl she held.

In a whispering tone she said. "Your Majesty. Willkommen in unserem Zuhause."

I glared at Noah while I growled out angrily.

"Was ist heir los? I work like a slave and come in here to find my servant enjoying an undeserved vacation? That is unacceptable. Noah, you lazy bastard. Get your ass up from that table and grab your shit. We have much work to do, ja?"

Ah, I apologize mein dameon seed Frau. You are still learning to speaking German. Was ist heir los means: What is happening here? This you understand, ja?

Anyway, Noah dropped his fork immediately and took to his boots. He was still chewing the mouthful of savory wurst while he hurried to take his place behind me, ready to serve his Master without question or hesitation.

This would've been the end of this lovely scene of a family enjoying a peaceful lunch together, if I had not been so full of drug withdrawal demons that afternoon.

However, just as Noah obediently came to my call. I noticed that unlike the joyful glances I was getting from everyone else sitting there. Amanda was glaring at me with a hateful expression on her face.

Normally, I would ignore this silly display of mild insolence from one without any power to act upon some unresolved quarrel they had with me.

But as I said, that was not the they for anyone, especially one that owed me her very life, to there to mess with the rage filled Mad Maxximillian.

With a slow, limping gait I approached the seemingly seething young woman. She refused to look away from this ‘stare down’ going on between us, despite the obvious menace in my behavior.

I took a place between her and her Mann Jaison then said in a sarcastic tone.

“So? Is there something you wish to say to me, little rabbit? If there is, then I bid you to voice it. If not, then I suggest you wipe that nasty look off your face. Before I decide to do it for you.”

Amanda snorted loudly then responded in an insolent tone. “You had no right to dishonor my father-in-law Almut and the great Hubertus as you have done. I would think you, of all people on earth realize the cruelty you have forced upon them, is disgusting. How there you treat men that loved you like they did, so poorly? No one else is brave enough to say it, but I am. You’re no better than any of these motherfuckers that pretend they have rights over us. They behave as if we are nothing to them. But it is you who is the nothing. Just a perverted useless bastard. Nein, you are worse than that. You’re a brutal catamite pretending to be a King. One that revels in the suffering of his people while he thrills at sucking wealthy cock and letting them ride him like the dog he truly is. There, I have said the truth of it. Kill me for it if you wish but I will die an honest woman among the liars that pretend that you are the Mortar Monarch of legend.”

Well, now those crude insults were uncalled for, ja? Even if I must admit, there was indeed some truth to the mean things Amanda said to me.

Ah, but honest or not, I couldn't allow such insolence to go unpunished. Nor should I have.

I glared at the fuming beauty, for a moment, my eyes blazing with the fires of hell within them.

Then with the suddenness of a cat, I turned and backhanded her Mann Jaison. He let out a yelp of pain followed by a heavy thud as he flew from his chair onto the floor. My blow was so vicious it nearly sent him into unconsciousness.

I limped over and took a place above him then spat out my warning to him.

"You should be ashamed of yourself. Are you even a man? Nein, you can't be. No real Mann would allow such dishonorable behavior from a woman under his own roof. If you know what is good for you, you'll start keeping your bitches under control, especially in the presence of guests to your haus. One day, this rude Frau of yours is going to cash a check your ass won't be capable of paying, little boy. Now, get up and attend your duty before I really lose my fucking temper. Come Noah, and you too Mercy, I've better things to do then teach proper manners to babies, ja?"

There was total silence in that room, while I limped rapidly back toward the apartment exit. No one dared to move a muscle nor did any of them attempt to stop my journey to leave. I'm sure each of them, even Amanda, was grateful to bid me goodbye, ja?

Noah pushed open the door and respectfully backed off to allow me to pass him unencumbered. Before I could do this, Blume came rushing into the living area, fell to a kneel then yelled out.

"I must beg your apologies, Your Majesty. Jaison's failure to attend his household properly is my fault. I swear on my life, I will correct this immediately. If you would be so generous as to grace us with your glorious presence again soon. You will be well satisfied Jaison has assumed his proper place as the man of this haus. I can assure you that Almut and I have been shamed by the dishonorable behavior he demonstrated today. I thank you for the mercy of your forgiveness and understanding, Sire."

I sighed loudly in frustration, then without turning around to look at her growled in reply.

"I've shown much mercy to this family already. Amanda forgets herself. I've taken a whore and turned her into a respectable wife. I gave her father-in-law the promise her children will have a choice. The ones she nor I ever had. She sleeps in a feather bed, in a beautiful palace with a full belly. This is so much more than her catamite king can boast, ja? You my beautiful lady, are forgiven the faulty lessons you've given your son about behaving as the proper German husband. This one time.

Next time I'm disrespected by any of your kinsmen, I won't remember kindness either. Good day to you."

I stepped into the hallway, and in perfect protocol, Mercy then Noah followed out behind me. Blume quickly closed the door behind us.

With a nervous shutter I glanced at Byron's apartment only mere feet away. I motioned Noah and Mercy to maintain silence as we began to move quickly towards the Voters' back staircase.

There was no need to tempt fate twice by passing by my brute brother's home just to take the heavily traveled main steps, ja?

However, apparently, Mercy and I were fools to believe we'd managed to stay off Byron's radar in our haste to fetch Noah. Our odd little group hadn't gone more than ten paces before the huge ex-Voter stepped out of one of the side hallways to block our retreat.

An unconscious gasp escaped me as I stuttered out.

"Ah. Fancy meeting you here Byron, uhm, is there something you want? If so, would you be so generous as to hurry up and tell me. I've, uhm, got to be somewhere this minute. I'm in a hurry."

Byron's face lit up with a most evil appearing smile as he replied.

"I wonder where you are going in such a rush. Perhaps you've got a hot date, ja? I bet your buns are tingling with anticipation of the pure delight awaiting you. Tell me, slut. Am I right? Is your ass tingling? Or maybe I've used a word not quite strong enough to describe that sensation you're feeling, ja?"

Byron took a step towards me and without being asked Noah moved out from behind me. He took a spot between us, shielding me from the chance that the brute could pull any more of his nasty sucker punches on my royal person.

Noah glared at the now furious ex-voter as he growled out.

"How dare you call the Lord and Master of this Haus such a foul name. Don't you come any closer or I'll make you sorry for it. Now, you owe his majesty an apology. You will give it to him, dog."

To my surprise, instead of appearing angered by the headmaster's aggressions, Byron seemed humored. He backed away a few steps while his nasty smile grew larger.

The trembling that had been plaguing me for the last several hours started to strengthen. I was doing my best to hide this unmanly action from all the men present, but my battle was suddenly lost. This was because, at that moment, I saw Byron was clutching a fresh pack of cigarettes in his meaty claws.

Eagerly I licked my lips and shook like a newborn lamb as I pushed Noah aside then said, "Wait. Let's not get too hasty, Noah. Allow Byron to answer my question before you start the fisticuffs, ja? So, uhm, what can we, I mean I, do for you honorable dungeon master?"

Byron chuckled and replied, "Ah, but you ask the wrong question, my little bitch. It is what I can do for you, ja? You know, lately I've been feeling a bit ill. It's likely that flu bug that's been floating around the Haus. They say it's very contagious. How have you been feeling lately, Your Majesty? I wonder because I can see the beads of sweat upon your royal brow. Maybe you've come down with a fever, ja? You know, I've heard it said that having a good smoke often will calm the anxiety one gets from suffering the pains of disease. I'm going to try out this rumored home remedy for myself. Perhaps, Your Majesty would like to join me in this experimentation?"

I nodded my head wildly and said, "Ja. I've heard smoking is wunderbar for illness. I think you may be right. I am feeling a bit under the weather."

I faked a cough to cover my obvious thrill over gaining the object of my truest desire from the brute.

Byron feigned the expression of concern while he lit up one of the cigarettes then replied, "Oh, my goodness. You poor thing. It does sound like you've come down with a bad case of something. Here, you can have this one. Consider it a gift, ja? After all, I've got plenty more where this came from."

He reached out and very gently placed the smoke in between my grateful lips. I took a deep drag of the calming vessel of nicotine.

Letting out a long sigh of relief I said, "Thank you, Byron, for this unexpected pleasure. If it wouldn't be too much imposition, could you, would you be willing to part with a few more of these curatives? I'm not sure one is enough to prove or disprove this theory it's helpful to calm symptoms of flu."

His smile faded to that of a concerned appearing frown as he replied, "Oh my God, no. Giving you this one is more than you should have. Hasn't anyone warned you that smoking is addictive? As it is, I'm already hearing in your tone that I've done you disservice. What the hell was I even thinking, courting such a dangerous dependence in a youth far too naïve to realize the difference between good and bad. Well, I beg you to accept my sincere apology, Your Majesty. I won't be making such a grievous mistake in the future. Next time we meet, I won't be so easily misled by the desires of a foolish boy."

I gave him a furious glance as I responded, "I'm many things honorable dungeon master, but a child is not one of them. Stop trying to play mind games with me. Name the price you are asking for that pack of cigarettes. Hurry up dammit. I already told you I'm going to be late to a prior engagement."

Byron glared back at me with a reptilian expression on his face as he replied, "Well, that all depends. Lately, every time I make a deal with someone. I keep my end of the bargain but then get the short end of the stick when it comes time to receive the payment."

I growled out angrily, "Nein. I seem to recall it is me that ends up getting the stick in these shady deals with you, Byron. I'm not kidding asshole. Tell me what you want. Give me the smokes. Then get as far from me as possible or else."

He chuckled. "Or else what, little bitch? You're going to throw one of your famous hissy fits, perhaps? Maybe you will call on your pathetic bodyguard to fight your battles for you, ja? I'm truly frightened that your so-called untouchable headmaster might try to slap me around. However, this time, I will offer him the honest battle. I'm not helplessly chained up, and this is not the pit. But luckily Noah. I'm in no mood to argue with you over something that you are begging me for. Tell you what, Mad Maxx. I have always been jealous of that fine apartment that Rolf greedily took for himself. Get Claus to authorize my moving into his old place, now that he has vacated it. And I'll give you this whole pack. No other strings attached."

Mercy, that till this point had been quietly kneeling behind me, called out in an anxious whisper, "Nein, Your Majesty, I must beg your punishment but the price he is asking for the prize the honorable dungeon master offers is unbalanced in his favor. You have named me the advisor to your glorious throne, Sire. It is my esteemed duty to caution you against agreeing to this arrangement with that dirty, rapist, lying, half-breed sonofabitch."

Byron focused his hate filled gaze upon the little man as he shouted out, "Shut up, Snot. If you say another word I will take you out to the ballcourt and hand you over to the black collar teens for use as their football."

Mercy jumped to his feet. His face was beet red with fury as he yelled back, "Come over here and try it motherfucker. I'm not afraid of you. You're nothing but a falsified Dominant. A half-breed bully whose brain is as filled with air as his false muscles are with steroids. You have no right to hold a Silk Throne, much less walk around this Haus without the black collar, that is your birthright. This man you dare to take advantage of had his metal tested and he broke it with honest might. I will be damned if I will stand here allowing a worthless piece of shit to manipulate him as you are trying to do."

Noah put up his arm to stave off the verbal assaults the men were hurling at each other as he said, "Both of you shut up right this minute. Sire, I must beg your punishment for daring to act in the manner that isn't within my power. However, I fear that if I stand here doing nothing these two are going to engage in a battle that is truly mismatched, ja? I must agree with Snot, eh, I mean Mercy. The honorable dungeon master does appear to be asking a price that is unequal to the item in question."

Without saying a word, I turned and backhanded Noah with a force that was so brutal I nearly broke my hand all over again.

He took the blow without flinching nor uttering even a slight gasp. I glared at him angrily as I said, "That will be enough out of you, worms. Your complaints are hurting my ears. I'm horrified at the insolent behaviors demonstrated by men that I've thought were respectable. Mercy, how dare you accuse your Lord and Master of being easily misled? And Noah, I can't believe you'd think yourself righteous in pretending you are in charge here. Well, I will properly punish the two of you in good time. But for the moment, Byron should be thanking you both for persuading me to agree to pay his price. You heard me, honorable dungeon master, ja? Give me the pack of cigarettes and you may consider Rolf's old home your new one."

I held out the bandage hand that was undamaged by my correction on the headmaster, ready to receive the most coveted prize. Byron's face wore a victorious grin while he placed the opened pack into my gauze covered palm.

He then snuck a quick glance at Mercy and Noah then leaned in close while he whispered, "It's always a pleasure to do business with you Maxx. I hope this makes your illness more tolerable. No doubt, they will be helpful. However, to find true relief I think you'll require something with more of a bite, ja? These Haus flus can be stubborn bitches."

Byron reached into the front pocket of his jeans. Then very briefly, a waxy yellow pill enclosed in a plastic wrapper was produced. Once he was certain I'd recognized the item, he just as quickly stuffed it back into its hiding place. I let out a gasp of excitement upon my realization he'd brough one of the coveted pain suppositories with him.

"Ah. I've heard the same. So, do you have any suggestions on where I may go to find this relief?"

His evil grin widened as he nodded and very softly replied, "I do indeed. This one is on me, little brother. When it wears off, and in six hours or less it will. I suggest you come to me on your knees begging like the good doggy. See you soon puppers, my boy."

He reached out and patted me on the head.

My fury at this most insulting display of mockery over my unfortunate situation with the Stasi night was set off instantly. I shook off his hand and growled out, "Leave the pill and then you can fuck off Byron. The only reason I'm not going to pitch you off the banister immediately is because I'm already late to be elsewhere. However, say another word to me and trust me, motherfucker, I'll make the time to do it, and deal with the consequences with a smile on my face from your screams of terror in my ears, ja?"

Byron chuckled low then bowed as he replied, “As you wish, Your Majesty.”

While he acted out this feigned move of respect, I saw him release the yellow pill from his pocket. I watched it fall to the floor with anxiety filling me to near madness. My fear was that my brute brother was going to pull a nasty trick such as stepping on it before he moved on.

However, to my extreme relief, Byron didn’t pull any cruel pranks. He merely shot an angry glance at my guardsmen. Then without any further arguing or banter took off in a rapid stride towards his apartment.

Byron had barely disappeared behind his door before I practically leapt upon the plastic baggie at my feet. Stinging sweat poured down my face in rivers, blocking my vision to near useless. I clawed blindly at the carpet with my damaged fingers trying to get possession of it.

When after a few moments I was unable to get a grip on the pill, I yelled out in full desperation, “Goddammit. Noah, you lazy bastard. Help me. Grab that bag and follow me into the hallway over there. Mercy, you stand guard and call out if you see anyone coming. Do it now, you motherfuckers or I’ll kill you both just for the hell of it.”

Noah moved with speed to answer my call. I didn’t wait for him to do as I had commanded. With the yearning pushing my every step I limped to the hallway opening to check to see if the coast was clear. I'd determined quickly that there weren't any prying eyes watching this pathetic scene just as the headmaster arrived to join me.

I glanced over at the entry to assure myself that Mercy had also obeyed my command. The loyal little man didn't disappoint me. I saw he'd taken a spot at the mouth of the hall with a clear vantage to easily view any unwelcome visitors.

Noah stood there in front of me, his expression that of total confusion as he whispered, "Mad Maxx, I have what you asked for, but I have no idea what it even is. What's going on? You told Byron you are ill and you certainly look it too. Your fever must be raging. I've never seen anyone sweating so badly and still able to walk. Should we make a trip down to the clinic? Surely, you'd rather trust Doctor Attila with your health than that shady sonofabitch, Byron, ja?"

I glared at him angrily as I replied, "Shut up and undo my breeches, Noah. I'll get prepared for this curative, and you will release that pill from its container. When I tell you, push it into me far as your finger will allow. Use only one digit to do this, I mean it. Hurry up before someone comes along and catches the untouchable finger fucking the Mortar King."

His face took on the expression of surprise as he whispered, "Are you tell me to stick my finger into your, Mad Maxx, are you sure we should be doing this, right here? Right now? But what about Snot, I mean Mercy. Aren't you afraid he might tell someone about us being lovers?"

I reached out and smacked the shit out of him with a rapid movement. He held his place despite the velocity of my blow. Before he could recover from the force, I grabbed him around his huge neck and pulled his face close to mine.

Then in a vicious tone I growled out, "I'm not ordering you to engage me in a kinky fetish, lover boy. That is a pain killer you hold in your hand. I need this more than you can ever imagine in your wildest nightmares. Unfortunately, it only comes in a suppository form. Have you ever heard of a suppository, Noah? If not, then allow me to school you in the function of such things. It cannot be taken orally nor can it be delivered by a needle. So, Einstein, if not by mouth or vein, how else could medication finds its way into the body?"

Noah blushed as he replied sheepishly, "Oh, my apologies Mad Maxx. I just thought when you said someone might think we were, you know, fucking. I just assumed that you intended to make good on your promise to allow me to play top in our intercourse."

I rolled my eyes and said in an irritated tone, "If you thought sticking your finger up my ass is me letting you play the stud this time. Oh brother, you really didn't learn a thing from Brigit. It's not your finger that you stick into a hole when having sex, Noah."

He chuckled lightly then said, "To be fair, Mad Maxx, I seem to recall you prepped me for your mount with a finger, ja?"

Despite my state of desperation, a giggling escaped my throat over Noah's most true response. "Okay, you've got me there, Noah. Now, stop playing and help me get that pill where it needs to be. After the calming effects have soothed my pain. We need to get moving. You will not believe the incredible news I've come to share with you. However, that will have to wait so hurry up."

Noah no longer hesitated in his actions. Within mere moments, my face was against the wall, grimacing in agony from the pain of his finger penetration. It took all I had to fight the urge to scream bloody murder it hurt so bad. Yikes!

However, it only took a few more minutes before that initial torturous discomfort began to melt away to the glorious sensation of numbness. I turned around and clumsily motioned Noah to cover up my naked lower half. He smiled with mischief as he joyfully obeyed that command.

With my eyes closed from the blissful relief I said, "Ah, now that is so much better. Noah, you are my angel fallen to earth, I swear it to you. Tell me something. Do you ever miss your home in Heaven?"

Noah startled then replied sounding a bit confused, "Uhm, I guess so? Or maybe nein? My apologies, Mad Maxx, but I don't understand the question."

A soft chuckling erupted from me as I slurred in response, "Mercy showed me the secret way out of this hell Haus, my Taube. Tonight, we will dance under the moonlight as freemen. You, me, and Mercy too. They won't be able to force you to eat shit, while suffering alone in a cold bed anymore. Mercy will be able to walk proudly without falling to his knees before men that aren't fit to shine his boots. And I, oh Noah, I won't have to take it up the ass ever, ever again. Though that bitch Lucus has stolen my ability to sire kinder, maybe I'll find a Frau willing to overlook my disability. Just think, baby. We are going to be free."

He gasped then reached out and grabbed me by my vampire jacket. He shook me gently, while staring into my face with an expression of terror on his as he said, "Mad Maxx. Are you okay? What was in that suppository? Oh, holy hell what am I going to do? Snot. Come here. Something is wrong with the Mortar King."

Mercy came running to Noah's anxious call. He stood there with terror in his expression as he replied, "What has happened? Did Byron give him poison?"

Noah shook his head then me again as he replied in a frightened tone, "I don't know, maybe? He's babbling, slurring, and not making any sense. It could be he is dying."

Mercy's face suddenly relaxed to that of relief as he said, "Oh, my God. You scared the hell out of me, Noah. He isn't in danger of death, fool. This behavior is normal when taking Byron's nasty pain killers."

The headmaster appeared even more confused than before as he responded, "What? Are you sure, Snot? I've never seen him act like this before. He's rambling about secret escape routes and not enduring special service requests. And his mood is pleasant which isn't normal for the king I tell you."

Mercy chuckled bitterly then replied, "Will you please listen to me, you idiot. The mortar king is high as a kite. Give him a few moments. The effects will settle down shortly. Then once his head clears a bit, he'll be back to himself, well for the most part."

Noah let me out of his grip. I promptly fell right to my backside on the floor at his feet. I didn't attempt to get up but instead sat there laughing like a hyena.

My humored gaze fell upon Mercy as I said a bit too loudly, "Ah, tell him Mercy. About the hole down in the tunnels, ja? We are going to be freemen. I can't wait to ride a bicycle, wear modern fashions and chase women. Ah, it will be fantastic. Can you believe it, Noah? Me, a real man. No more fucking pony boy for the Mad Maxximillian. Oh, but what time is it? There is still so much left to do."

Noah flashed a glance of surprise at Mercy then in an astounded sounding tone said, "Wait a minute. This what he says is the truth of it. You really did find the rumored secret way out of the Haus? Oh my God, and we are going to leave this horrible place tonight? Together? All of us?"

The little submissive chuckled lightly as he replied, "Just catching up, are you? Ah, and even the Mortar King drugged to the gills can process information faster than you, Noah. Ja, he may be a bit tipsy, but the king is speaking truth. We are planning an escape for later tonight. Well, we were planning it. Now that the Master is off in space, I have no idea what he was up to. Only that he said something about being rich and needing money to survive outside of the Haus."

I interrupted their conversation with a snort, "Excuse me fellows but I can hear you. Mercy tell Noah to go to the bat's Haus and make him turn down those fucking speakers of his. Goddammit. Hey, did you know that Jonas thinks he's a vampire? Tell Noah to watch out or that man will want to drink his blood."

Mercy shook his head then replied, "Oh boy. The king is really bugging. Byron must have given him a hit of his high-quality shit. I suppose we will just have to hope the worst of it wears off soon. Otherwise, it might be tomorrow night before we can break out of this hellhole, ja?"

Noah furrowed his brow then said with suddenness, "Nein, just a second, Snot. You said Mad Maxx was talking about being rich, and that we need money to be successful on the outside, ja? I think I know what he was talking about, but I'm not sure if I should say anything more about it."

The little man crossed his arms and started tapping his foot as if he were irritated as he replied, "Stop calling me Snot, Noah. Obviously, you've heard the Mortar King refer to me as the honorable Mercy. Start showing respect for this wonderful gift he's given to me or so help me I'll catch you sleeping and carve a fresh air hole in your throat. Whatever the king has shared with you in secret you can tell me. I've sworn that I'll serve his majesty with total and complete loyalty. Even upon the pain of torture or death."

Another loud bout of laughter burst forth from me as I shouted out gleefully, "Do you know my good friend Mercy, Noah? I was going to introduce you, but I think there is some history between you two that I'm unaware of, ja? You kept calling him Snot, but I don't remember telling you that used to be how he was known. It's the nasty name that dirty, rotten, kinder killing Xavier give to him a long time ago. Oh, and I noticed you are both around the same mature age of forty, ja? Hey, wait a minute. You two are brothers, aren't you? That's it, ja? Well, bet Olaf hated that, didn't he? Hey, has anyone seen that stupid bastard lately? Oh, ja. I forgot. He is dead."

Noah shook his head and with an expression of concern said, ""Nein, Mad Maxx. Mercy and I are not brothers. Not in the sense of blood, that is. Sometimes,

Evelyn, that useless mother of mine would take Olaf and me up to visit with our shady father Bladrick. You remember him, ja? Olaf would often bully Snot, eh, Mercy and I didn't like him doing that. I took a few beatings from Olaf trying to end his cruelty. Mercy was grateful and if we ever could sneak away from prying eyes we would play silly games of hide and seek or wrestle like little boys like to do. But then, Queen Ingrid sent me to the dungeon. I never saw anyone, but Olaf again. Olaf told me Xavier sold Mercy away to the camps. Until today, I thought, well I thought him long gone from the Haus. For what it is worth, Mercy. It's good to see you again my old friend. I'm happy the rumors I'd heard were untrue."

He glanced at the little man, and a beautiful smile crossed his face.

Mercy smiled back then replied, "I thought you had forgotten me, Noah. But I wish you to know, I've never forgotten your kindness during those dark days. It's my pleasure to see you thriving too despite that dreadful and unfair sentence Queen Ingrid imposed upon you. The Mortar King apparently has seen within you the goodness that even that bitch couldn't hide away in the darkness of the dungeon. His choice in allies is perfect. It only goes to prove, his majesty is truly the savior he was prophesied to be, ja?"

I sat there staring at the two of them, glassy eyed, out of my mind from Byrons' pain killers. My eyelids were becoming heavy. Extreme fatigue was starting to overpower my ability to stave off the need for sleep.

Just before I slipped away into a deep needful unconsciousness, I was sure I saw a scene unlike any other. The huge headmaster of towering strength, dropped to a kneel. He reached out and put his arms around Mercy. Then Noah gently hugged him. It may have been a drug driven hallucination, but I swear to you Meine Liebe, I thought I could see tears streaming down both men's cheeks while they did this.

In the Haus full of so many broken hearts, and shattered dreams. It was a most beautiful sight to see these two mismatched unfortunates had managed to forge a lifelong friendship from the tiniest of, well, mercies, ja?

My next memories of that afternoon are a little bit fuzzy.

Noah and Mercy told me later that I fell asleep there where I'd fallen in a nap that lasted for two hours. They said I snored so loudly they worried someone was going to be alerted to our hiding spot there in the shadows of the Voters' hallway. Hahahaha.

However, they also said I woke up several times and rambled about the things I wanted to do once we were safely free of the Haus. Both told me the conversations they had with your Master, were comical, good natured, and engaging. I've forgotten many things from my brutal past, and that is a blessing in most cases.

However, this is the one time I honestly wish I could remember the things we said to each other. Knowing Noah, and Mercy like I do. I'm certain it was something I would treasure still.

Especially when you realize that the rest of that day and night things happened that I only wish I could forget. Yikes!

When at last, the harsh side effects of Byron's curative suppository had worn off. I became alert enough to return to the plan of escape already in motion.

I returned to my boots, with Noah's help, and with a sigh of disappointment over my stupidly losing so much time. I motioned my companions to come in close so I could be sure no one heard what I told them.

"Noah, take Mercy with you down to your old barracks in the dungeon. Collect all the money you've hidden for me and put it in a carrying bag. If you don't have one large enough, go to the commissary and buy one. Oh, and while you are there. Buy something that fits Mercy perfectly but make sure it is an outfit a young child would wear, ja? You will also purchase clothing that the yard black collars would wear. Two outfits that will fit you and I. Make sure to buy a hat of modern tastes. I will need something to cover my scar if the Haus reports us missing that identifying mark will need to be hidden, ja? Now, Mercy, you will use some of the money to buy a good razor and scissors sharp enough for a quick haircut. Have Noah aid you in cutting your mane short and shave off your beard. I hate to insult you like this, my pet, but it would be better if we appeared to be two young men traveling with a child rather than, well you know. Before you remove your signs of maturity, Mercy, go with Noah back to the fourth-floor apartment. Bid Lucus to permit you to go into my closet in the master bedroom. Try to ignore that nasty bed in there. I apologize you must see that. Anyway, tell him I've soiled my clothing and I've sent you to get me a fresh outfit. In the very back you will find my heart lambs. Collect them in a bag and grab a pair of my breeches to cover them from view. Return to Noah's barracks and both of you work together to get Mercy prepared. After you finish, get some rest. At nine thirty on the dot, meet me at the back door of the Haus. Do your best to make sure no one sees that Mercy is clean shaven. I'll join you both around that time and fill you in on the rest as it happens. Are we clear?"

Noah frowned then whispered in reply, "We will of course obey your command, Your Majesty. Forgive me for saying this but is it wise to leave you without either of us around to protect you should there be trouble? Like say from someone like Byron?"

I shook my head and responded, "It is the danger you and Mercy will be in while we are parted that worries me, Noah. As for me, the terrors I will be facing are of the usual kinds. I'm due upstairs at Jonas's apartment in less than fifteen minutes. He's sure to be angry at me for not fulfilling my end of our contract over the last fortnight. There will be hell to pay, but thankfully the pain killer still seems to be working. Maybe, this visit with the vampire won't be as brutal as it normally is or I can hope, ja? I would have you fetch Friedrick to add eyes to watch your backs, but even though he is feeble minded. It's too risky to chance he might hear or see something that could be used to either stop us, or worse punish him for failing to alert anyone about what we're doing. So, like it or not. I must trust that you two will remain vigilant and look after the needs of the other. Why are you still here bothering me? Get going you two. You are wasting time we don't have."

I watched in mild humor as the huge Noah and tiny Mercy scrambled off down the hallway appearing frightened by my shouting at them like that. Hahahaha.

Then like a ton of bricks, the realization that it was time to take a trip upstairs hit me. *Oh, Meine Liebe, how I loathe dealing with Jonas. But you already know this, ja?*

That day as I hauled butt up the back staircase I thought to myself. 'I wonder why the vampire didn't raise hell over my absence these last few weeks? Oh, I bet he's going to be pissed. I hope the pain killer doesn't wear off. Please, dear God, permit me this one mercy, just this one time. I wish to leave this nightmare forever without suffering another moment of sheering agony from that man's horrific affections, or any other man.'

I approached Jonas's door slowly with heaviness in my heart. Taking a deep breath to brace my nerves I gently knocked on his door.

To my shock, there was no answer. I stood there for a moment, trying to comprehend this most unexpected situation. Then I knocked again, harder and louder this time. Still, no stirring came from within.

Since this had never happened before, I was befuddled about what to do. I thought to myself. 'Should I just leave? Is this good fortune or what?'

The confusion over my next move had me too deeply focused to notice the slight movement to my left. Had I been paying attention I'd have seen the shadow that was growing larger, moving toward me in a menacing fashion.

Meine Liebe, it's important that you remember it is far too easy for a vampire to slip up on a distracted victim, ja? Suddenly a pale, thickly clawed hand reached out from the darkness of that hallway and grabbed me by my shoulder. I let out a blood curdling scream.

Then fell to the floor, scratching and clawing the carpet in my terrified efforts to get away from what or whom I didn't care to know. The sound of Jonas's humored laughter brought me back from my place of terror.

He snorted then said, "Always a bit nervous aren't you, my beautiful boy? It's so good to see you. My bed has been cold as ice without you in it. Now, get off the floor and stop tempting me to take you out here in public. It's wonderful that you're offering me such a rare gift. It's the double treat to see that you recall it's a guilty pleasure of mine to fuck you where we could be viewed with ease. However, you also know better than to tease me unless you honestly mean it."

I halted my crazed behavior and rolled to my back to glare at the brutal man as I spat out in reply, "You scared the fuck out of me Jonas. What the hell are you doing slinking around in the hallway? Ah, never mind the question. Of course, this is what you do in your spare time. I wonder, does the black collar maid complain often about having to clean up all the bat shit out of the carpets up here on the Elders' floor?"

Jonas's smile faded and he turned up one of his hairy brows while he leaned down close to my face to reply, "Ah, now do you think it wise to demonstrate insolence towards your Mann, Christian? Especially after I've shown you such loving compassion during the last two weeks. You know, while you convalesced from that nasty business with the Stasi men. I should think you should be thanking me for permitting you to be free of my wanton affection, but here you are behaving in a manner that I've come to regretfully expect of you. Oh well, so much for romance. Now, I certainly hope that my little game hasn't honestly, as you say, scared out your fuck. But that's okay because I've got plenty to loan you if yours is in deficit."

With a snort I said, "Doctor Attila hasn't given me a medical release yet, Jonas. Looks like I'm still on light duty, ja? Too bad for you. I suppose you'll be one ancient bat before I'm ready to endure a special service request from you again."

The vampire's expression broke into a sinister smile as he replied, "Oh, my goodness. I guess you hadn't heard. That is not very professional of the doctor. You know, forgetting to notify everyone involved of the good news. Oh well, that's okay, well not for you but definitely for me. Christian, I spoke to Doctor Attila this morning. He told me, you're all healed up and just nearly brand new. It's been harder than you can know waiting for six o'clock to arrive. I'm so excited to take out my fresh plaything for a joy ride. Don't make me repeat myself twice, boy. You know damned well what happens when you make me angry."

He held out his claw in a polite bid to help me from my place on the floor at his feet. I groaned in dismay but wisely took his offered assistance. Once I was back to my boots, he ushered me inside his lair appearing more than a little eager to have me where escape wasn't possible. Nor where anyone could hear my screams for help, ja?

Anyway, he bolted all his locks then pointed at his hallway entrance as he said, "You know what to do. I won't hear any arguments about this. Say anything other than 'yes Master' from this point on, and Christian, I swear to the devil I will make you sorrier than you've ever been for it."

Well, he did make me sorry. Sorry that I was born, that is. I need not get into details about this first day back to my duties playing his so-called donor. Other than to say, it was a good, damned thing that Byron had given me such a high dose of his pain medication.

Jonas was like a man possessed. He didn't even allow me to provide him or myself with proper dressing services. The vampire, instead, practically ripped off my clothing, and his own not long after that. I was forced to endure his gross lip kissing, fondling and ja, eventual penetration.

This time, he chose my inner right thigh for his blood drinking fetish. I had assumed he'd want me to gain sexual heat before making me into his dinner. That was the usual way he said it had to be done for him to remain forever young, ja?

However, this time I think he believed I was anxious enough about returning to play mare to his stud to not need any further preparation. He didn't tell me that, but I'd been with the fiend long enough to have some idea of what he was expecting of me.

I asked him to use the chocolate when he demanded I give him oral services. He refused my request citing that it was better to keep things between us sterile as possible until he was sure my sensitive area wasn't going to tear too badly.

That was a smart move on his part. I did rip and I did bleed quite a bit despite the earlier attacks I'd already suffered.

Thankfully, I didn't feel the damage. Well, that's not completely true to my sheer disappointment before Jonas reached his screaming apex. The pain killer began to wear off. He hadn't even uncoupled before the shearing burning and sharp agonies, I'd grown far too accustomed to, began to alert me that this kind of sex wasn't fun for me.

It was even more unfortunate that Jonas was feeling particularly greedy that night. He went for seconds, ignoring the obvious torture his intercourse was causing me. Perhaps he was punishing me for minding the doctor's orders to the letter. I guess he thought the time I needed to heal was for everyone else, but not him, ja?

Well, whatever the reason for his rare second tapping of my royal highness. By the time he was sated to gluttony. I was a moaning, groaning lump of uselessness. The time I was stuck in his grips, as we'd agreed by contract, was nearly up. I knew I had to pull myself together or this nightmare existence of being used as a vampire's pincushion was never going to end.

With a shutter and plenty of yelps from the shooting pain, I rolled off his bed into the floor. I couldn't find the strength to limp over to my clothing scattered about the room. The only thing I could do was crawl slowly to them, hoping against hope that somehow the worst of his assault would calm before the clock struck nine.

Jonas lay in bed watching my creeping movements with an expression of humor on his face and satisfaction in his eyes. "What's the matter, Christian? Did you pull a muscle from your magnificent acrobatics, perhaps?"

I groaned out despite doing my best to appear unfazed by his cruelty as I replied, "That's likely, Master. Next time, maybe you'll remind me to do some stretching before engaging in such strenuous exercises. I thank you for the mercy of it."

He sat up in his bed with startling quickness as he said in a humored tone, "Ah, well if you are very sore, why not just come back to bed. We could call Lucus and give him the excuse that your old injuries are acting up. Come on, baby. Stay with me tonight. It could be like old times. What do you say to that, Christian?"

A shutter of disgust ran down my spine. Just thinking that my only choices, if I failed to escape that is, was to be condemned to being repeatedly attacked by the pervert extraordinaire Lucus or nighty suffering painful and bloody assaults in his hairy cuddles.

Well, there are no words strong enough to describe the horror of either bad scenario except maybe, yikes.

I glanced up from the floor into Jonas's eyes as I replied nervously, "I thank you for the mercy you most generously offer, master. However, if what you said about the doctor releasing me to full duties is the truth of it and I must assume you'd never lie about such important things, then I can't avoid returning to offer my services to my regent in training. To do so would be a breach of our contract. I'm a man of my word. This you know, ja? I beg your forgiveness, but could you release me so that I may clean up a bit before I go?"

Jonas's eyes turned stormy with poorly veiled rage as he responded cryptically, "You have always been a fool, boy. Yeah, you may go and take your shower. Make sure to scrub as hard as you can. Maybe if you scour deep enough, you'll cleanse me out of your soul, but I doubt it. Later tonight, while you are in dark despair. I hope you remember that I offered you sanctuary from your habit of making very bad decisions. This being the worst in fact. Oh well. I suppose you're always going to have to learn lessons the difficult way. Go on, get out of my sight. When you are finished. Leave immediately. I'll be seeing you tomorrow night. Yes, I think so."

The vampire didn't have to give me permission to leave twice. Ignoring the horrific discomfort, I crawled rapidly to collect my things. Jonas never took his beady eyes off me while I worked clumsily to cover myself. He also didn't bother to offer me any assistance in this nearly impossible task.

Fucking broken hands were just as much a pain in the ass as well, the pain in my ass. What's that look for

Meine Liebe? That's not funny? Where is your sense of humor, huh? Oh okay my sour little Frau. I'll stop the comedy. I suppose having fire in the hole isn't fun. This you know, ja? Ah, oops, I make another joke, ja? Hahahaha.

Okay now where were we? Oh ja. So, I somehow managed to get my clothing on. Well, mostly I did. I couldn't button my blouse or breeches but at least I wasn't rushing from the bat's apartment completely naked.

As you may have figured out, I skipped taking a shower. Though I really wanted and needed one badly after that blood sucker had finished making me his unlucky bitch. But I honestly was too afraid to linger in his Haus another moment.

Something about the way he spoke when he released me was troubling. I just couldn't quite put a finger on it. Though as usual it would've been wise to spend a bit trying to get him to say more.

I tore out of his lair limping at full speed as if my ass were on fire and it was. Oh okay, stop looking at me like that, Meine Liebe. I'll stop with the description of flames and my backside. Hahahaha.

Without any hesitation I rushed down the back stairwell all the way down to the first floor. If you recall that staircase is only for use by the Voters and Elders, ja? Well, you may also remember that it empties out at the back door of the Haus. This was the old station of my Shadow King, Cary. Though since I'd had Malfred buy out his collar, he was no longer employed by the Haus to stand guard at it.

Since Cary's upgrade to mercenary status, hahaha, before I threw a silver collar on that winey bitch. A black collar guard named Malte had taken the assignment. The tall, skinny man saw me rapidly descending the steps in a state of disheveled dress.

The expression of surprise on his face would have been comical, had I not been more than a bit irritated. I glared at the stunned black collar guard as I said in a harsh tone.

"Malte, I've a bone to pick with you. The bathroom down that hallway is often used by the silvers in training for practicing illegal sex actions. I've caught one or two of the little fuckers twice this week alone. Why are you not doing your job as you have been hired to do? Perhaps, it's time for King Claus to find someone more worthy of your position, ja?"

Malte's eyes went wide with an expression of fear as he replied, "Nein, Your Majesty. I swear to you I wasn't aware of this activity. There is no reason to notify King Claus of my honest mistake of forgetting to patrol the bathrooms. I beg your mercy and forgiveness for it. If you would be so generous as to allow me time for correction of my past failures, I'd be most grateful to you, Sire." He fell to a graceful kneel.

I nodded my head and pursed my lips then responded, "Alright Malte, I'll grant you mercy this one time. However, be warned. Those silvers usually gather around and watch for guardsmen around this time. In about fifteen minutes one or two will go in there and pretend to be using the facilities. If no trouble is spotted by their lookouts. By ten o'clock the place will be swinging from ceiling to floor with the little buggers. I think until you can discover the ring leaders of this gang of ruffians you may want to keep to the shadows and watch the doorway from afar, perhaps at the hallway exit on the far side of the Haus. I'm sure that after tonight, you'll have no reason to fear laws are being broken right under your big nose."

Malte smiled then suddenly appeared anxious as he replied, "Wait, Sire. I agree that I must put a stop to this illegality. However, I'll be sent to the pit if I dare to leave this door unguarded for more than a few moments at a time. Someone will notice I'm not at my post and report me, ja?"

With a bit of a sneer, I said, "You are a bother, Malte. Yet, I've always had a fondness for you. Ok, I will do you one more mercy this night, but don't you ever ask me for a God damned thing again. The headmaster will be here, oh there he is coming now. I will assign him to take your spot here at the door until eleven o'clock tonight. You go and get into your hiding spot this minute but I'm warning you, you'd better be back here at eleven on the dot. Not a moment sooner nor a second later, ja? If you do manage to catch those criminals. I suggest for now, just take down their names and give them to me. I'll help you out by arranging they all receive the punishment they deserve. This is a secret between you and I though. Say nothing to anyone, and I too will keep my lips sealed about your frightful performance as the honorable guardian of this Haus."

Malte nodded in agreement just before he took to his feet and rushed off to obey my command.

Noah and Mercy slowly approached, both keeping a baleful eye on the retreating black collar door guard. I glanced at the newly shorn Mercy and with a chuckle said, "Well, my pet. You turned out to be quite the handsome fellow underneath all that hair. The ladies out there in the world don't stand a chance against your charms. I think when I am out seeking a mate of my own, you'd better keep your distance. Otherwise, I may die a lonely man when every girl chooses to run away with you instead."

Mercy blushed and cast his eyes to the floor as he replied, "You truly have the silver tongue of a Priceless, Your Majesty. I thank you for the, uhm, kindness of your generous flattery. Though I'm unworthy of it."

I reached out and pulled his downcast face up by his chin and stared into his eyes as I responded, "After tonight, Mercy, things like Priceless and words like unworthy are never to be spoken between us again. This you understand, ja? Besides there is no flattery in the truth. Now, Noah, my beloved. Would you accompany me under the staircase for a moment? I'm in need of strong fingers, yet again. But before you get excited, lover boy. This is a call for dressing services only."

I motioned for Mercy to keep to the shadows, while the headmaster and I disappeared into the hidden spot under the stairs.

He quickly began his task of buttoning my breeches and blouse as he asked in a whisper, "You may wish to know, Mad Maxx. Mercy and I were successful in getting all that you told us to do without any signs of arousing suspiciousness. I hope to hear you have also managed to avoid severe pitfalls in your duties, but I know Jonas. He is a ruthless brute. I wonder, is there anything I can do to provide you comfort? That is assuming you need any?"

I shook my head then replied softly, "Ja, there is, Noah. Don't fail me tonight. We must get the fuck out of here. I just can't take it anymore. I think I will go insane if, oh never mind. We are leaving, my Taube. Only a few more hours, and poof, we will be ghosts, ja? Now, you stand guard at the door until Mercy and I return. When we do, I will have the honorable Fritz and his Frau Audrey with me. When I give the signal you will know what to do."

He finished pushing my last button into its hole as he asked, "And what about Mercy? Shouldn't he be hiding? Maybe under here?"

I chuckled lightly then replied, "Nein, Mercy is coming with me. After all to catch a woman, as I already said, he is the perfect bait, ja?"

Chapter 32: All is Well that Ends Well

Noah frowned as he said, "If, I mean, when we are out there in the world, Mad Maxx. Will this relationship between us change? Will we still be more than just friends?"

I chuckled low then leaned in and put my lips to his own. He initially stood there stiffly, appearing unreceptive to my attempts to woo him with my wiles.

However, I'm the Priceless of legendary sexual prowess. By that time in my young life, I'd become so talented at employing special services I'm certain if I'd wish to do it I could send a statue of stone into a frenzy of lust without breaking a sweat.

Well, if it was the male mannequin that is. When it came to the ladies, your master was severely lacking even the most basic skills.

Anyway, within only moments I felt Noah's body relax. He reached his arms around the back of my head and pulled my face into his wantonly. The heat between us had melted away his fear that Mercy or anyone else might happen upon this taboo scene. I permitted his tongue entry into my mouth and thrilled over the sensations of his tasting muscle explorations.

It wasn't that I was in a hurry or even interested in enduring yet another horrific penetration situation. Neither with Noah nor any man. His inexperienced eagerness, and honest affection were the true attention I was seeking.

He has always been able to make me feel loved. Noah never treats me like his plaything, or just a hole to release his tensions into. The headmaster's desire for my companionship often leads to a sexual romp, but not always. Sometimes, we can find complete satisfaction merely by the mildest touching, hugging or as in this case, passion fueled kissing.

I'm unsure how Noah can tell the difference in my tender actions being of the hunger for orgasm or of the mere yearning for comfort. But over the years, he has proven this is a gift he possesses in abundance.

Of course, Noah is still just a man. His desire to rut is perhaps far stronger than that of almost all my suitors. This is because, as you may recall, Meine Liebe, he's been forbidden to engage in intercourse. Well actually touch of any kind.

It's a sad fact that at the mature age of forty, the man could count his number of sexual encounters on one hand. And all of them were with me or two overly ripe women. That can warp a person's sense of self. Much less result in some rather odd attractions. *But I'm getting ahead of myself, Meine Liebe. We'll get back to Noah's strange fetish in good time.*

For now just try to recall that I told you Noah's fascination in the realm of sexual appeal is different.

You could say he has a fetish almost as rare as Drexel could ever boast.

Is that sour look on your face because I mention that nasty statue fucker or because you are worried about the creepy things I may tell you about Noah's carnal appetites? Ah, well my little demon seed frau. When I finally get to that part of my story, this time you will be laughing at the answer rather than anxious about Noah's continued appearance in our lives. Just be patient, this fact is worth the wait, ja?

So, anyway. While we were wildly embraced by mouth like this our bodies were brushing against the others. You could say Noah's natural responses were working overtime. I could feel his willing schwanz pressing into me through his jeans. That was my signal to end this momentary pause of reassurance of our connection.

I pulled away from the towering headmaster with some effort. He whimpered softly and started to try to regain his grip on my mane. A quick glance of caution from me made him retreat from his unwanted approach.

He dropped his eyes to gaze upon the floor then said softly, "I suppose that question I asked of you is an unfair one. Once we are freemen, you'll be in a hurry to take a wife, ja? I doubt the lady in question will be happy to share her bed with another man."

I reached out and very gently slapped his face as I replied while chuckling low, "You will remember that I told you already I don't share my things, Noah. None of them. Not with anyone else and certainly not with each other. Help me do what no other has been willing to do and I swear on my honor I'll never leave you wanting for anything. Any Frau that professes to love me, will learn to love you too, at least from afar. But if I ever catch either of you touching my things. Oh Noah. I wouldn't wish to be either of you."

He glanced up at me with mischief in his expression. "But for the first time in my life I'm grateful to be me, Mad Maxx. I have a beautiful lover and a future out there in the world. Ah, but everyone should be jealous of Noah, the richest man on Earth."

With evil in my tone, I replied, "Enjoy the delusion of that title while you can, my beloved. Because once we are out that hole, Mad Maxximillian is the man that will steal it from you. Ha. Now, hurry up and take your place at the back door. Try not to speak to anyone unless you must. Mercy and I are going to hurry as fast as possible. At any point you think there may be trouble, don't hesitate to get your sexy ass to the safety of Almut and Hubertus's apartment. That's a directive."

He nodded then moved with a brisk stride to do as I'd commanded. I took a deep breath and allowed a very soft groan of discomfort to escape my throat. Jonas had done a real number on my, uh, tail.

Oh, you don't know what Teil means, Meine Liebe, ja? Well, it translates exactly as it sounds. Hahahaha.

Okay, I must apologize because I'm making a crude joke again, Meine Dameon seed frau. It actually means part, like body part. Kind of the same thing it sounds like and that is comedy. Nein, you don't think so? Stop frowning. My cane says it was funny, ja? Hahahahaha.

Anyway, since I know you don't appreciate my attempts at comedy, we will continue this story without all the silly commentary, ja?

So, with Noah standing guard at the back door, and Malte off on a wild goose, eh, wild silver chase. I motioned the newly shorn Mercy to follow behind me in total silence. I couldn't make a visual on his location, but I knew he could see me.

I must say that little man was wonderful at staying hidden. No wonder Noah enjoyed playing hide and seek with him. *I tell you, Meine Liebe, only the shadows had knowledge of his place in them.*

He came barreling with speed to take his rightful spot trailing his master. I didn't halt my rapid limping. We were heading directly for the first-floor apartment that belonged to Fritz and Audrey.

If you recall I'd told Fritz to meet me at the back door of the Haus at midnight earlier when we were in the dungeon. Turned out my plans had changed drastically since making that arrangement. It'd also been made clear to him it was his responsibility to tempt Audrey to come with him.

However, that was no longer an important issue for me either. Though I was unsure if I'd be successful in getting the snotty Audrey interested in making a trip out to the yard. I was hopeful that she'd be unable to refuse the offer I was prepared to make to her to see she would be.

We reached their door pretty quickly. Before I knocked to hail the occupants, I knelt down and pretended to be lacing my boots.

That of course was impossible with those broken fingers of mine. But all the passing blacks, silvers and Dominants didn't know that, ja?

While playing I was attending my dressing I leaned over and whispered to Mercy.

"I must apologize to you my dearest friend for what I'm about to do. I beg you forgive me for saying the things I will say in my effort to use you as bait. Please know I mean none of it but this dishonorable situation can't be avoided. If you are willing to overlook the faults of your Mortar King I'm prepared to reward you greatly for the mercy of it."

Mercy looked up from the floor into my eyes as he replied, "You can never be faulted in my eyes, Sire. I'm at your pleasure, willingly, and happily. Nothing you say or do will ever be questioned by your most loyal servant. The grandest of prizes has already been granted to me, in abundance. It is I who thanks you for your, uhm, grace, Your Majesty."

I nodded and then said, “You’re a good man, Mercy. We can’t leave this end loose. If Fritz showed up at midnight for our meeting and we weren’t there, he’d be sure to alert someone to it. He knows me far too well. I’m a man of my word and only death would prevent me from keeping it, ja? Okay, if you are ready. Let’s get this over with.”

Mercy nodded back. “I agree, Your Majesty. There is no reason to risk it. I’m ready and will respectfully follow your lead.”

I took back to my boots and tapped on the door softly with the head of the fancy cane, Fritz had gifted to me. A stirring within let us know the Fincks were home. I did my best to stand up straight, despite my terrible aching. It was important that I appeared calm, confident, and of course, above all powerful.

Audrey opened the wooden slab and immediately her oversized eyes got bigger from obvious shock. She let out a little gasp then said excitedly. “Your Majesty, hat a wonderful surprise. Welcome to our home.”

She bowed low in a gesture of respect, but kept her gaze locked on my own.

I looked down my nose at her as I snorted then replied in an arrogant tone, “It was your honorable Mann I was seeking audience with Audrey. Is he here?”

The silk queen in waiting’s thin lips broke into a most unattractive grin as she responded, “He is, Sire. I bid you come in. I'll let him know of his fortune to be entertaining the pleasures of the Mortar King."

I limped into the apartment with Mercy following at three paces in my trail. Audrey had missed his tiny frame knelt behind me in the hallway. She let out a loud yip of surprise the moment she noticed my most unusual companion.

I glared at her attempting to appear impatient as I growled out, "Is there a problem, Frau? Do you believe my precious time is within your right to waste? Hail your Mann with haste or find out just how much I charge by the minute for abusing my resources."

Audrey nodded and hauled her skinny ass off into another room to do as I'd demanded. Mercy fell to his graceful kneel next to me there on the Finck's living area floor. I sighed deeply, feeling truly sick over the disgusting way this kind man was forced to behave.

Neither Fritz nor Audrey were good enough to even know his name, much less believe he wasn't worth being permitted to stand up in their presence. Oh well, that is the Haus for you. The useless rule and the decent must eat their shit.

Fritz emerged from the back of his apartment relatively quickly. He saw me standing there and his face lit up with thrill. "Ah, Your Majesty. So, Audrey hasn't become delusional. You are here to bless our humble home. How can I be of service, my Lord?" He bowed low just as Audrey had done moments before.

I snorted then scanned the room trying to discover the whereabouts of our target as I replied haughtily, “Fritz, you’ll never believe what happened to me today. I was out at the old playground, and I heard a strange noise. It was most odd because it sounded like many people speaking, but the voices were high pitched like those of children. I decided it is best to investigate this situation. To my absolute shock I discovered an entire village of elves living just beyond the tree line.”

Fritz chuckled then said, “Your Majesty, it’s not my place to question anything you say, but do you seriously think I’m going to buy such a tall tale? Elves aren’t real beings, and even if they were. What the hell would a village of them be doing anywhere near this Haus?”

My eyes blazed with evil as I growled in reply, “Oh, you think such things the fantasy of a mad man, do you? Well, for your information, Fritz. I have proof of it right here. See this little creature? Look upon him and tell me again how I come to visit you to share false stories.”

The shady Dominant startled upon realizing Mercy had been on his knees behind me the entire time.

“Holy shit, it is an elf. Audrey, come here woman and see what the Mortar King has with him. Oh, Mein Gott, and you say there is a whole village of these, uhm, tiny men in the yard? Fuck me.”

Audrey practically flew back into the room as she responded loudly, “See, I told you, Fritz. Have you ever seen anything like it? It’s the most amazing thing I’ve ever laid my eyes on. Oh, and you say there is a whole village of these elves, Sire? What I wouldn't give to witness that. Hey, Fritz. Do you think it's got everything a man does. I mean like is it built just like a man. Wait, it is male right? Did you check?"

I chuckled low with much malice in the sound as I said, "Oh, it's male alright, my Lady. Do you really think I'd bother with it had it not been? As it is, I recalled that your Mann Fritz was once interested in tasting my metal though he is obviously not into men. And why should he be, with a beautiful woman such as yourself on his arm?"

Audrey cut her eyes at me with a blush coloring her cheeks over my most untrue flattering remarks. She covered her mouth and giggled, then responded, "Why Your Majesty. You are too kind to say such lovely things. What a silver tongue you have."

I blew a kiss at her then said with a wanton sigh, "Be that as it may it occurred to me that Fritz was only seeking a thrill in the forbidden and never intended to insult me all those years ago when he tried to rape me in the hallway. This is the truth of it, ja Fritz?"

He nodded but never took his stunned eyes off Mercy nor showed any sign of remorse over my factual statement.

I glanced at the excited Audrey for a moment then said, "Anyway, I really wanted to share this most uncommon secret with someone that could appreciate the possibilities. All of them. Hahahaha. So, Fritz, what do you say? Would you come with me to take a walk on the wild side?"

Fritz looked at me with an expression of eagerness overtaking his shocked expression as he replied, "Hell ja. We can go right this minute. Let me grab my coat. Audrey, my dear, don't wait up."

Audrey's grin of thrill faded to the expression of disappointment as she whined out, "Huh? Wait. I want to go too, Fritz. This is not fair. I also tried to get a taste of the Priceless, remember Your Majesty. Why take Fritz to satisfy his craving for the forbidden but leave me with the ashes of only hearing what he is blessed to know?"

I shook my head nein as I replied.

"Ah, but can I trust you to keep this most sublime secret, my lady? I know nothing of the heart of a woman. Men, are my area of expertise, ja? I simply can't risk allowing too many to know about my new playthings. If everyone found out, they'd wear the little buggers out in no time. You are well aware of how greedy the Haus residents can be when it comes to sating their darkest desires. Plus, I'm the man of extreme hunger myself. It will take half the village to even come close to filling my twisted desires. I see no reason to share even one more of these things than I must. I merely wished to brag to one of my good fortune. So, Fritz, ready or not I'm heading out."

Fritz rushed off to get his wrappings against the cold winter air. I turned and started for the door with Mercy quietly taking to his feet to follow.

Audrey raced to block me from the exit. She stood there before me, her expression full of defiance on the surface. With sinful desire just below it. She did her best to cut her humongous eyes at me as she purred out coyly, “Your Majesty, what is the hurry? Those things aren’t going anywhere, ja? So, I’ve heard it said you’re a lover of superior quality, and of course that is the truth. Men of great prestige have been lain low trying to savor the taste of your charms. You’re the Priceless of legend and they should have been more careful. However, it’s also gossiped you’re most powerful weapon has been mostly untapped. There are whispers that any woman that becomes the victim of the Mortar Kings lustful touching is bound to be damaged or even killed by the blessing of it. I wonder if there is anything I could offer in trade to gain your dangerous affection. Please take mercy on me. Make me your victim, Sire. I beg of you.”

I glared at the ugly FemDom without any clues in my expression to suggest I was interested in her offer as I replied flatly, “Do you really seek to travel the road your competitor has already blazed, ja? It’s not a secret that Gretta claims to possess my penetration virginity, Audrey. When they pull the fur prince Justice’s baby from her loins, she’ll be lighting up the night for her crimes against the mortar crown. You’ll be sitting on a silk throne within the hour after that, ja? So, dear lady, why risk everything to take a bite of a cherry that’s already been chewed by a mouth you despise? There is no need to prematurely tempt the rumors of the dangers of my embrace. Even if my history with your rival isn't bothersome to your conscious, once I'm interred in the palace, I'm helpless to prevent the sitting Queen of the Silk from taking anything she wants from me."

Audrey grinned widely as she nodded then said, "Ah, but that is the truth of it, Your Majesty. However, I've always been a woman that finds the arcane more a thrill than the absolute. In the Mortar Palace you'll be shackled and subdued. Where is the thrill in a canned hunt, my Lord? I prefer to stalk prey that can fight back. Heeheehee."

I slowly ran my gaze over her skinny frame, appearing suddenly wanton as I replied, "Now you are speaking my language, my Lady. Perhaps, I've been too hasty in believing you an unworthy opponent. Okay, I will agree to take you to a place few can boast about having returned from but on one condition."

She nodded then purred out, "Anything, Your Majesty. Just say it and I will agree without hesitation or regret."

With a growl low in my throat, I said, "Say the words I want to die, Your Majesty. Because my Lady if you come with me this night, by dawn you'll be supping with the reaper. If you don't truly wish to leave this world, and the bright future you're assured then run away now. This is your last chance, Meine Schatz.

Tasting the Priceless silver is indeed deadly. That's not a rumor at all. It's the honest truth. Survival isn't possible once you've endured my vengeful cuddle."

The FemDom smiled then practically yelled out, "I want to die in your arms, Your Majesty. Take me to that place of dread and fill me with your righteous wrath till I drown in it."

I reached out and put one of my bandaged hands around her throat gently. Then I pushed her into her door as I leaned into her suddenly very frightened face. I growled low, "Your wish is my command, Meine little rabbit. Say goodbye. Tonight, you die."

Her smile suddenly returned as she replied in a breathy tone, "Oh, meine Gott. You're magnificent in making your seduction feel dangerous, Your Majesty. You're rough wooing is so sexy yet has me shaking in fear. I swear I've never been this turned on in my life. The legends of the Priceless are true indeed. Ah, I'll get my coat and be right back. Fritz can have the elves. I get to fuck the brutal Mortar King."

She pushed my hand from her neck and took off to get prepared to come with us right to her death.

Fritz returned to the living area before Audrey did. He snuck a quick glance at the door she'd disappeared behind. He then leaned in close and whispered, "This was quite the surprise, Your Majesty. Great job getting Audrey to agree to come along willingly. However, I must ask. Where the fuck did you get this dwarf? Very imaginative plan by the way."

My glare was full of hate as I whispered back, "Don't push your luck, Fritz. I agreed to offer you the muscle and the place to hide the evidence, but I refuse to do the evil deed you want done. Audrey may be a snotty bitch, but she's never done anything to me or anyone else to deserve such a fate. Her blood is exclusively on your hands. I've done all I can to offer her a reprieve, but the stupid woman thinks this is a kinky game I play with her. We do this and after that I never want to hear another word about it ever again. Oh, and this lovely man is called Mercy. You will respect him or I will send you to the place your wife will soon be. Are we clear?"

He laughed softly then narrowed his eyes while looking Mercy over. "Hahaha. Okay, I hear you, Your Majesty. I need not know the details of your mastery anyway. After tonight I'm finally free of this harpy and that is all I'm interested in. Oh, and speaking of being a widower, I spoke to Matz. He said you'll be back to work sometime in the coming week. Do you think you can fit me in as one of the first clients on the list?"

I shook my head then said bitterly. "You know better Fritz. Matz handles the schedule. You pay him and I will do whatever he says you pay for. Now, shut the fuck up before Audrey finds out the full extent of crimes her fucking snake husband has committed against her. Poor thing. I usually don't feel sorry for any of you shithead Dominants but this woman, well, I suppose too bad for her. Can we move this along? I have other pressing things to do."

Fritz's smile faded to an angry frown as he growled back, "You speak ignorantly because you don't know that bitch, Maxx. Well, no matter. I will attend this business as agreed. Audrey, hurry up love. We are going to leave without you woman."

The would-be silk queen came running still trying to zip up her heavy coat. The four of us left the moment she returned to join us. I took up the head of our group, with Mercy and the Fincks following closely behind.

We arrived at the back door to find Noah milling about playing guardsman. He saw us coming and took a place next to the heavy wooden exit trying to appear focused on a professional stance of menace.

I came forward and quickly gave him a hand motion where none of my companions could see. He nodded slightly then politely pushed the door wide and held it open waiting for us to pass.

However, when Audrey, trailing all the rest of us, walked by him he reared back his arm and punched her in the face. Noah's aggressive move was so sudden and strong that Audrey didn't see it coming. The fragile woman didn't even gasp as her unconscious body fell lifelessly to the floor.

Fritz, that was only a few paces ahead, heard the commotion behind him. He halted and turned to find his Frau laid out cold at the headmaster's feet.

He sounded completely bewildered as he whispered out to Noah, "What the hell man. Do you know who you just clocked, fool? I could see you whipped for this, you know."

I chuckled from just behind the shady Dominant as I said, "Shut up the dramatics Fritz. Noah has done us all a mercy, especially Audrey. Easier to end a life, when they don't struggle or scream, ja? Noah, pick her up and come along. We are headed to the silver well. Hurry up, dammit. The Russians will be scanning this area soon. Best they don't find us lingering around the playground with a half dead Mistress in tow, ja?"

Noah scooped up the felled silk princess like a groom carries a bride. I rushed into the darkness of the yard and motioned everyone else to hold their positions while I made sure the coast was clear. After several moments of silence, I gestured the group to follow but to move their butts while doing it. I knew Shasha and his yard dogs would be along shortly for their hourly patrol.

Obviously, Shasha didn't catch us sneaking out to the silver well that night. The entire trip to that dreadful place went smoothly. No one made a sound, and Audrey remained blissfully unaware of her impending doom.

I admit to you, Meine Liebe, I meant what I said to Fritz about that woman. Audrey wasn't a nice person to know. If you recall from back in the days when I wore the bat collar. I'd been most unfortunate to select her and Fritz to practice my conversation services on while trying to flee from an attack by Karl and Volf.

She was a well-known cruel gossip starter. She was hateful to almost anyone that she viewed as prettier, smarter, richer or better than her, which was almost everyone. Back then she and Fritz were engaged to be married, but Fritz never wanted to call her his wife.

You see Audrey was from the Baus clan and Fritz is a Finck. Those two founding families have been rivals since the beginning of the Haus like almost all the founding families are.

However, the rule of the Schmidts was due to come to an end or at least everyone hoped it would after Xavier fell.

As a rule or tradition, the next family in line for the silk thrones are the Baus, and after them the Finck. It's been that way since anyone can remember.

Well, Gretta isn't a Schmidt, a Baus or a Finck. She is an Albrecht like Claus and Leo.

Anyway, Gretta had manipulated her way onto a throne that was never supposed to be hers. She then ignored the proper protocol for assigning the founding families to serve on her thrones.

Gretta raised Peter Schmidt, and Peter raised all his cousins and my mother, but we know what happened to that Krause witch, ja? Hahahaha.

Anyway, this shitty move had put the Schmidts onto the Silk Thrones for a second time in a single generation. This had all but assured the Schmidts a double dip on the Fur Thrones once they'd come of elder age.

Now that really pissed off the Bauss and the Finck clans, and rightfully so too.

As you may recall, the families take turns. Well, plot and murder each other really while holding the Voters and the Elder thrones. They must do this because if they don't do it every couple of generations their kin go broke and living in the Haus is expensive, ja?

Anyway, Gretta's usurping the silk throne angered the Baus family so bad they choose their kinswoman Audrey as their Queen if only they could get Gretta's ass off Audrey's throne. The Finck clan cut a most uncommon deal with the Baus, their natural rivals, strength in unity, ja? Better to have a finger on the power of the Silk than to have no hold on it at all, ja?

So, Fritz was chosen to marry the Queen in waiting Audrey, but as I said, he didn't want to marry her. He was forced to do it by his family. His kinsmen understood with the untouchable Noah as headmaster down below, there was no chance any of their men would ever qualify for future Fur King.

Ah, you look confused, my Frau. You see, historically, after the Schmits are in the fur, which happens usually after the Krause hold the Silk, next in line are the Baus on the Silk and Finck on the Fur.

However, the Krause lost their places on the Voters' floor thanks to Malfred's little trick of gang blood bonding to me. Malfred tried to overtake the Fur thrones before finishing their terms on the Voters thrones.

Anyway, you remember how all that went. Julian, Alexi, Grisham, Gustov, and your father Karl were all thrown off of the Voters' thrones by the Elders as punishment for their part in Malfred's plot.

That is when Gretta raised the Schmidts instead of the Baus like she was supposed to do after the powerful Krause fell. That's because she feared Audrey and Karsten's rise. Yes, Karsten is Baus too. She was the second pick for Silk Queen should Audrey not survive to adulthood.

Both women were far more popular and had been raised from birth to assume the role at some point in their lives. Gretta was universally viewed as a poser. If either Audrey or Karsten got in the silk, no doubt the residents would have voted to remove Gretta in favor of one of them. Even the dour Audrey had more support than the flighty and neglectful Gretta Albrecht, who also wasn't born in the Haus. She is a transplant like Lucus, ja?

Just so we are clear, Audrey and Karsten are natives but neither of them were on the list as war criminals.

What had happened is when I raised Noah to serve me, I had to assign the eldest Finck temporary headmaster below. As I said already, the Baus should have been on the Voters' thrones, but the Fincks now had a real chance to take the fur as the Elders died out because of my move. This was an unintended consequence of my desire to have Noah at my side. Yikes.

Essentially, I'd signed Audrey's death warrant by this move.

Allow me to explain. Do recall that at this time in my story, the remaining Elders were a strange mix that included: Cora Reinherz, Malfred Krause, Justus Schmidt, Leo and Claus Albrecht, and Jonas Weis. The last of which isn't a member of one of the founding families.

This lack of family unity was the leftover chaos that Xavier had purposely created. It was actually a very clever ploy to prevent any single founding family from becoming a serious threat to his rule, ja?

To become a future Fur King or Queen or even hold one of the thrones of the Elders you must serve at least five years in the dungeon and be over fifty-five years old. As you may recall from Claus's story, attaining the title of headmaster or headmistress is the usual way to qualify for the highest throne, the Fur monarch.

However, Noah was raised to headmaster after Hemmel Krause, uhm, died suddenly. Hahaha. The problem here is that Noah is sentenced for life to the dungeon because he is a half breed. Half breeds, as you recall, unless they are claimed by the Dominant that broke the law and made a child with a black collar, are doomed to wear a black collar. Unless they're sent to serve as a master or mistress in the dungeon at age twelve.

In the dungeon they will be respected as full Dominants but they can't ever come out or they will be collared immediately.

So, Gretta had named Noah headmaster which officially blocked every Finck from the title until Noah was no more. Gretta and Cora were working together to keep the Baus and Finck families from ever becoming a real threat to either of their crowns, ja?

With Noah being a young man of forty and the most qualified serving Finck dungeon master nearly fifty-five. There was no way the Finck choice of future Fur King was going to outlive Noah or if he did, he would be ancient before any of the serving Fincks could obtain the title of headmaster.

Then I made Karsten head dungeon mistress, but she is a Baus. Ah, I see that light coming on in your eyes, Meine Liebe. You are starting to see how I'd accidentally foiled Gretta and Cora's plans to hold the Baus and Finck at bay, ja?

So, now the Baus had both a future silk Queen, Audrey, and a rising Baus headmistress in Karsten. I had sentenced Gretta to death, and Cora to the pit. The possibility of a total coup was very real. The Baus were now poised to take both sets of thrones in less than a decade.

The Fincks were not going to just sit there and let this happen. If they missed their ride to the thrones this time their family would be going to become hopelessly bankrupt.

This has happened to families of the Haus before, going broke I mean. When it does the entire family will be banished. We don't need to go over the danger in banishment do we?

So, while the Finck end up on the wrong side of a Stasi rifle, the Baus would become the richest and the most powerful ever seen in the whole history of the Haus.

When I assigned the oldest Finck headmaster during Noah's brief absence, well with this loophole the fellow had become a viable rival to Karsten for the fur monarch.

That is, if the Finck clan could somehow stop the Baus from rising to the silk before they had time to neutralize Cora and quite possibly eventually Karsten.

Hence, Audrey had to go, at least the way the Finck saw it.

But as I said already, Audrey wasn't a good person but she wasn't a criminal. I found no evidence she'd ever abused a silver, wasn't on either list, or other than starting vicious rumors was mostly harmless.

Truth is that she may have been a silk queen that I could've co-existed peacefully with but unfortunately I will never know. By the law of unintended consequences, a couple of my moves to neutralize the power of Gretta and Cora made Audrey a target for assassination.

Fritz had me in a corner and thanks to Byron's stupidity choosing him to help punish Sigrid with Rolf and Friedrick. I was stuck. If I refused to help Fritz neutralize the growing Baus threat, he would no doubt literally make sure I burned for it. Yikes!

As I've said countless times, I don't enjoy ending life. It's something that I've regretfully had to do too many times. Sometimes for mercy, and other times for my own survival. This time, neither motivation existed.

Fritz wanted Audrey removed for greedy reasons. He could've worked out a deal where she shared the profits of her Silk Throne with his kinsmen. But he didn't want to share with the Baus or his wife. He wanted it all for himself.

So, with a heavy heart I led our small party into the center of the woods. I thought several times that night of pitching Fritz into the well after Audrey. I wondered what kind of future the Haus could expect if a man like him were to ever take the mantel of fur into his sadistic grip.

Then it occurred to me that if I successfully escaped the Haus, I wouldn't stop until I found someone willing to listen. I'd assured myself I'd send help for the helpless of the Haus. Fritz couldn't hurt anyone while sitting in a jail cell, ja?

If I failed to escape, by death or other, well Fritz was definitely a worthy rival to Jonas. I already determined that soon enough the vampire would be wearing the silver crown of the fur thrones. That realization made shivers creep down my spine.

There are few in the Haus that don't fear that brutal bat. Fritz, however, is a rare exception. With that in mind, I'd finally determined this man was going to end his wife with or without my help. Better to hedge my bets and keep this sonofabitch on my side just in case everything I'd tried failed. Ah, of course you already know your master is a worthless bitch. Failure should be my middle name but it's Keifer or Axel depending on who you ask, ja?

Anyway, we arrived at the old well without any impediments to our journey. We had all traveled in revenant silence until Fritz saw the object of our destination. He let out a soft gasp then said, "Brilliant, Mad Maxx, absolutely perfect. No one will ever find the cunt at the bottom of that relic. I got to hand it to you. You're truly a man of surprisingly clever solutions."

I turned with suddenness and growled in response, "This is the completion of my so-called solutions when it comes to our arrangement, Fritz. What happens from this moment forward is your problem. Not mine or any of my men. Do as you will, and be assured, we've seen and heard nothing. But whatever you do, do it quickly dammit. I've got better shit to do than watch a man murder his wife over nothing more than her being a hen-pecking nag."

Fritz grinned evilly while he pulled several pieces of rope from his jacket. "You're always such a grouchy fella, aren't you? I would think a man with a twisted past as your own would be at least a little turned on over a scene of violence like this one."

He walked over to Noah and directed the headmaster to pass the unconscious Audrey into his arms. I watched the men make this exchange of flesh while I replied in a hateful tone, "I'm simply not as perverted as you are, Fritz. Make sure to clean up any mess you make. If anyone were to happen upon this spot. It wouldn't be a good thing for them to see blood, hair or tissue. They might decide to follow the trail of evidence, ja?"

He let Audrey drop to ground without any visible attempts to break her hard fall as he said, "The only weapon I've brought is the one I hold. I had intended to throttle her with my bare hands. However, I must assume this well is deep and that there likely is water at the bottom. I need not get my hands dirty when the rope can achieve the same outcome, ja?"

I shook my head with disbelief as I gasped then replied, "Surely, you don't intend to throw her in alive. She will drown Fritz. That is far too cruel a thing to do to someone that hasn't earned such a slow and horrible death."

He knelt next to the prone Audrey and began tying her limbs together in his elaborate knots as he said, "I seem to recall you said this is where your responsibility in this matter ends. Well, Mad Maxx, if this is the truth of it I suggest you butt out. Watch the show or turn away. However, do it quietly please. I wish to spend a few moments with my ex-wife without rude interruptions."

Noah slipped over to my left then leaned in close and whispered, "I brought a knife, Your Majesty. If you want, I could give her a quick release."

I shook my head then replied sourly, "Nein, Noah. This isn't your fight. You've done all possible to grant her mercy already. Maybe if we are lucky, she'll never regain her senses."

It is almost as if Audrey heard me say that because at that moment she began to stir. I groaned low as realized the woman was slowly returning from the void to this one last nightmare.

By that time, Fritz had completed his elaborate restraining of her limbs. He took back to his boots and stood there above his barely conscious victim to admire his cold-hearted handiwork.

Finally, Audrey opened her eyes and rasped out groggily, “Fritz? What’s happening? Did I fall?”

He didn’t bother to answer her but instead he quickly dragged her wriggling flesh to the mouth of the well. He laid her on her back upon the crumbling lip. He chuckled low while waiting for her to stop struggling long enough to look into his eyes.

By this time, Audrey was apparently starting to comprehend Fritz’s betrayal. She ended her attempts to escape his rope work and returned his humored glare with a hate filled one. Her fog of confusion appeared to clear as she sat up and yelled angrily into his face, “How dare you? I will see you hung by your toes for this, you asshole. Fritz Finck, I hope you realize you and me are through. You’ve always been a useless mother fucker anyway.”

Fritz laughed loudly then replied, “For the first time since we met, I agree with you. We are through. Consider this a formal announcement of divorce, but I must insist that I keep all our assets. Goodbye Audrey.”

He used both hands to push into her chest with all his strength.

She let out a yelp, then teetered for a mere second before falling backward into the hole. For several minutes we could hear the hapless woman's terrified wailing before finally the faint splash of water echoed on the stoney walls of the well.

I turned away and closed my eyes trying to erase the image of the poor woman's terrified face as she disappeared into the darkness. My stomach felt sick and for a moment I was fighting for air, likely as hard as Audrey only a few feet below us.

Fritz broke me from that weird place of empathy for the lost silk princess by letting out a gleeful sounding yippee.

Without bothering to face him I called out angrily, "Shut the fuck up fool. Do you want to alert the guard to our location? If you are satisfied, then I suggest we head back to the Haus. Lingering around the scene of the crime isn't wise."

Fritz chuckled wildly then replied, "No problem Mad Maxx. I'm more than happy to go home now that it's free of that trash. Hey, do any of you fellows want to join me in the Great Hall for a celebratory beer? My treat. Even you Mercy, the magic Elf are invited to be my honored guests."

I took off in a rapid stride heading in the direction of the Haus back door as I growled in response, "Don't be an idiot, Fritz. Tomorrow the residents will be wondering what happened to their silk princess. If any of them recall her drunken husband acting like he's won the lottery the night she went missing, you do the math, fool. Come on or stay out here and freeze. I honestly could care less. We are leaving."

Well, Fritz decided it was best to let me play his guide once more. The return to the back door was also uneventful and thankfully silence reigned between us. Once safely back inside, Fritz wisely broke from our little pack. He took off like a man running a race, in the direction of the apartment that was now exclusively his.

Mercy and Noah remained at my side quietly while all three of us watched Fritz rush off. When he was far enough away to be out of ear shot, Noah leaned close and whispered, "What next, Mad Maxx? You said we were going to try to escape as soon as it got dark. I dare say it's pretty dark out there."

I nodded then replied softly, "Yeah, no sense in waiting any longer. The sooner we go the more time we have before anyone realizes we are missing. You take Mercy and head for your barracks. Collect the money, clothing and heart lambs. Use the palace key to let yourselves in but make sure not to be spotted by anyone. Leave the door unlocked. I'll linger here for a few more minutes and join you at the palace throne room shortly. Best we aren't seen together just in case, you know."

Mercy moved in close to the two of us and spoke, "It's going to be fine, Your Majesty as soon as we will breathe the air as freemen, ja?"

I softened my gaze and looked upon the little man as I replied in a whisper, “Ja. Not much longer now. See you in about fifteen minutes. Remember, don’t let anyone see you. Get going you two.”

The burly headmaster and tiny submissive strode off as if they were headed to put out a fire. I stood there watching till I was certain they were safely to the dungeon stairwell.

Then I slowly began to limp down the hallway, doing my best to appear strolling without any destination in mind. The collars all fell to the kneel as I passed them. The Dominants and FemDoms bowed low then hurried off to avoid getting in my path.

Honestly, I was doing some reconnaissance. I confess at the very least, I was concerned that Byron may have alerted the Elders or Voters of my plans. The other danger that was provoking anxiety was that the Stasi officers had done that without his help.

Either possibility bothered me enough to keep me from making a mad dash for freedom. I needed to assure myself that everything and everyone in the Haus was behaving normally. My keen eyes focused on the details of the movements and actions around me that would be predictable while seeking any that were abnormal.

After at least twenty minutes of this voyage to nowhere, I’d decided nothing was amiss. There were no obvious signs that I was about to walk into a trap. I had to assume that by that time, Mercy and Noah had successfully gained entry to the palace. If they hadn't been stopped then it was clear that our plans hadn't been discovered.

At least not yet.

So, I took a very deep breath to calm my nerves and turned around in my tracks. I started the slow limp toward the mouth of the dungeon stairwell. I was nearly to my desired exit when I heard a familiar voice call out from behind me.

"Your Majesty, what a pleasure it is to run into you at this late hour."

I sucked in my air and turned to find myself face to face with the Fur King Claus. Standing next to the crossdressing monarch was his fourth prince of the fur Mastermind Malfred. Both were grinning ear to ear and looking me up and down as if I were a menu at the Great Hall.

With a feigned attitude of thrill, I replied, "Your Majesty, and honorable Prince. How can I be of service to you two fine gentlemen?"

Claus chuckled and shot a glance of mild humor at Malfred as he said, "Shouldn't you be home with Lucus, my boy? You know how dangerous it is for you to be wondering about unescorted. Especially with your interment ceremony so close at hand. There are many around here still seeking to cut their teeth to get their taste of the forbidden Priceless blood."

I nodded then replied calmly, "I was just about to head back to my apartment, Your Majesty. Lucus can be difficult at times. I just came out for a moment to get some fresh air is all. No harm done."

Malfred sighed then said, "Well, I can't say I blame the boy, Claus. Have you by any chance visited with Lucus since he moved into Maxximillian's Haus?"

Claus frowned then replied, "Nein, I must confess I've not been on the fourth floor since that idiot tricked our beloved Priceless into his gold collar. Why? What do you know that I don't?"

The elder Malfred groaned as he leaned in close to whisper into Claus's ear. I didn't need to hear his words to understand he was telling the Fur King about that horrible cock bed of Lucus's. Claus's eyes went wide as if in disbelief as he replied loudly, "You've got to be kidding. And you've seen this with your own eyes? It's not just a vicious rumor your repeating?"

Malfred shook his head then said softly, "Claus, I don't think anyone could make this up if they tried. Trust me, it's something you need to see to believe. But once you do, there is no unseeing it."

The elder chuckled bitterly under his breath. King Claus bit his lower lip then snuck a glance at me while he said, "Fair enough. I'll make a point of meeting with Lucus in the next week or so. However, that information my brother prince just shared doesn't give you good reason to be taking a risk of assault, Your Majesty.

Perhaps it's best if you allow me and the honorable Malfred to walk you back to where you belong, ja?"

A mild sweat broke out on my brow as I started to realize my serious predicament. If I allowed the Elders to take me back to Lucus. The pervert would know I lied to him about staying with Jonas that night. If I refused their offer, they might become suspicious I was up to something. This was a no win, all around bad situation either way I went.

Then suddenly, I came up with a plan to shake off these two old goats and keep them from talking to Lucus at the same time. I cast my eyes to the floor in a false display of submission as I said in a whimpering tone, "Okay, I can tell you two are on to me. I confess, I've lied to Lucus and told him that I'm staying at Jonas's tonight. However, I'm desperate to avoid my husband too. Both have returned to demanding I provide them with special services, but Doctor Attila hasn't officially granted a medical release. I just can't handle another request from either until I've had a little rest. They've been overly greedy. So, I was sneaking off to stay at Leo's tonight. Unlike those monsters, he respects a doctor's orders. He can be trusted to keep his paws to himself. Please, I beg of you. Don't tell Lucus of my deception. I honestly wouldn't have told such a fib if I wasn't fearful for my safety, ja?"

Claus and Malfred both let out a gasp. Then Claus clicked his tongue and said, "I've always been disgusted over the poor management of our beloved Priceless by our prince Jonas. As for Lucus, there are no words that can truly describe my abhorrence for that man. However, Your Majesty, be that as it may you simply can't be sneaking around in the Haus without a guardian. While normally, I would be willing to pretend we didn't have this conversation, nor discover you are not where you said you would be. But, if I did such, and something disastrous happened to you, I'd never be able to forgive myself."

I kept my eyes on my boots as I sucked in my breath then said in the barely audible whisper, "Ah, ja, I understand this is the bargaining we are doing. Okay, Your Majesty. If you would be willing to forget this situation and hold your silence in the matter. I'd be willing to offer you a second visit to add to the one you already enjoy with me. This would be provided to you at your request. As for you, honorable Malfred. I must assume you'd be amenable to receiving something in return for your confidence as well. Perhaps a single bath service to be provided at your discretion, ja? I will even do this in the nude as you prefer."

Claus chuckled low and shot the humored glance at the seemingly stunned Malfred as he replied, "What a good boy you are, Maxximillian. You've learned your lessons well I see. Alright, I'll agree to this fair offer you make to me, but I can't speak for my prince. What do you say, Malfred? Does what the Mortar King say stroke your interest?"

Malfred seemed to lose his expression of surprise as he responded in a cautious sounding tone, "I've no problem aiding the King in avoidance of further abuse at the hands of those two brutes. But I'm not interested in his offer as it stands. If, however, the honorable Maxximillian would be willing to exchange a single bath service for say a dip in the pool one afternoon with me, I'd happily agree to the trade."

I nodded my head slowly then replied, "The exchange for service request is one I'm grateful to make honorable Malfred."

Claus cleared his throat then said with suddenness, "Wait just a minute. I change my mind, Your Majesty. Instead of just an additional visit with me for special service besides the one I already claim. I desire to have what my prince so foolishly throws away. A bath service with you in the nude, sounds absolutely heavenly."

With a deep sigh I replied, "This can be arranged, Your Majesty. I thank you both for the mercy of it. Now, if you are well satisfied, could I beg you to release me. I need to be heading for the Elders' stairwell so I can get to the safety of Leo's apartment as soon as possible."

Claus narrowed his eyes and said, "How do you plan to get into Leo's apartment, Your Majesty? He is at the Great Hall already as are most of the Elders and that asshole Lucus. He is the one that called this meeting. He said he wishes to announce some important news. Since I honestly could care less about anything he says, I took my time getting there as did Malfred here. Oh, and Jonas too. He's still upstairs. We ran into him not too long ago. Our brother prince said he'd come but Lucus could wait till he felt like it."

I groaned then responded, "Fucking Lucus has called all of you to announce he's managed to force me into a contract that assures him named Regent to the Mortar Throne. The blood has barely dried on the page and already he seeks to boast about it. Typical. Anyway, Your Majesty, Leo gave me a key to his house. He told me anytime I needed sanctuary I was welcome to hide there. If tonight isn't one of those moments that I require such luxury, then I would never need it, ja?"

Malfred blew out his breath then said in the clipped tone, "Leave the boy alone, Your Majesty. He's been honest with us and we've become wealthier men for it, ja? I say we continue our journey to the Great Hall to listen to the hot air and let the Mortar King do what he must to find comfort."

Claus nodded while chuckling. "That is the truth of it. Okay, you're released, my beautiful boy. Oh, be careful though. The Elder Jonas will be heading this way shortly if he is not already on his way. If he were to catch you here as we have, well, I won't be enjoying the view as much when I get that bath service, you owe me. This you understand, ja?"

I nodded then replied, "I thank you for the mercy of your wise warning, Your Majesty. I will see you both, very soon. Good night to you."

I bowed low in a show of proper reverence as the Elders returned to their trip towards the Great Hall. I stood there watching them fade into the distance for only the briefest of moments.

Then like a mad man I took off in the opposite direction. Not only did I fear running into Jonas, as Claus had cautioned could happen if I stuck around, but I also realized that since all the Elders were meeting with Lucus in the Great Hall to hear his bullshit bragging, Byron had not alerted anyone about my plans to escape from the Haus that night.

If he had told on me that little unexpected conversation with King Claus, and the clever Mastermind Malfred would have gone a hell of a lot differently.

With my mind eased that no one was the wiser, I hauled serious ass down the stoney steps of the dungeon. I didn't fool around too long in the darkness after reaching the floor. The silence was nearly deafening. That lack of noise assured me that there wasn't anyone around to witness my slipping into the rotten secret door that led to the Mortar Palace and the escape tunnel.

I found Noah and Mercy quietly milling about around the palace silver bars. They saw me and both men’s faces lit up with what appeared to be happiness and relief.

Noah called out, “Thank God. We were really starting to worry something had happened to you, Your Majesty.”

With a light chuckle I replied while limping to join the headmaster and tiny submissive, “You’ll become the old man if you don’t stop stressing so much, Noah. As you can see, I’m here. I just needed to check out the territory and that took a minute. Better safe than sorry, ja?”

Mercy smiled as he said, “No need to explain, Your Majesty. We are ready to go if you are. More than ready in fact.”

I nodded then pointed towards our destination of dreams as I replied, “Lead the way to Freedom my good man. Noah, don’t forget to grab the bag of cash and lambs, my love.”

Mercy hit the switch of his flashlight and watched as the headmaster loaded our necessities upon his broad shoulders. Within only a few seconds the three of us started our trek with a bounce in our steps and joy in our heart. Our moods were as bright as the air around us was dark. We spoke in excited whispers to each other about all the things we hoped to be doing by morning. Mercy even made up a clever poem about a fast car and a faster woman that made us laugh till our sides felt like they might split.

He sang out softly from his place as our leader.

"I once had a fast car but the day came it wouldn't start.
I turned the key but the engine would only belch and fart.
A pretty girl happened by and said hey handsome boy.
My husband was a dud and I'm seeking a new toy.
I told her I would happily woo but my engine died.
She said forget that metal heap she could be my ride.
First, I jumped that fast car and then she jumped me.
My car is a fast fuck but nothing fucks as fast as Mercy."

Mercy is truly a clever fellow.

As with any trip to a place of great desire it seemed like an eternity before we were fast approaching the hole of escape. Though we were all still filled with thrill, a heavy silence was suddenly descending upon us.

I suppose, in those final steps, the gravity of the danger we were about to encounter hit us like a ton of bricks. While our plan of escape was a solid one. The reality was that our survival out there was unlikely. Each man understood that when he'd decided to go on this expedition.

However, I must assume that like me. Mercy and Noah had concluded that death by Stasi rifle in the fresh air under blue skies was better than a crushing one trapped forever in a world of darkness and stone.

Once we were under the hole covering, Mercy halted his march and turned to me and Noah. His face wore an anxious grin as he said softly, “Well, we are here. What now, Your Majesty? I suggest that one of us go and check to see if the coast is clear. You know, just in case the Stasi officers are still hanging around watching.”

I nodded then replied, “I agree that is a smart thing to do. I’ll go and if you two hear gun shots or voices other than my own. Run for your lives. Don’t try to be heroes. Better only one of us get blown away rather than all three, ja?”

Noah gasped then said in a frightened tone, “Nein, allow me to go Mad Maxx. I couldn’t take it if you were, I can’t even say it.”

I turned to face him and glared without any sign of the true fear that was gripping my soul as I said sternly, “Noah, you will do as I say. I outrank both of you. This moment is all I’ve dreamed of for as long as I can recall. No matter what is waiting for me up above, I’ll embrace it with no regret. You and Mercy are more precious to me than you can ever know. So, if no bullets ring out, I’m happy to call you my companions in the free world. But if I am to be killed, then I can die peacefully knowing at least two good hearts still beat in this Haus of demons.”

Mercy fell to a kneel as Noah dropped his face to look at his boots and whispered, “If you say I must obey then I do as you command, Mad Maxx. Just know and remember even if it's your last thought. I love you with all I am and all I will ever be. This will be the truth of it till the day I become dust."

I watched a tear leak from his eye down his cheek. With a soft sigh I approached the burly headmaster and pushed his face up to gaze into my own.

"I will always love you too Noah. Don't be afraid for me, meine Taube. There are far worse things than death. I've met them, all of them. Kiss me for luck, then get your asses into the shadows and wait till I give the all clear or, well, you know what to do if it goes the other way."

He nodded then leaned in and embraced my mouth with his warm lips. I could taste the salt from his tears of true love and concern.

Oh, Meine Liebe, did it feel good to be so adored even in that moment of uncertainty of having a future with him at my side or at all. Noah didn't even care that Mercy was there to witness this breaking of taboo between the infamous Priceless Mortar King and the legendary Untouchable Dungeon Headmaster.

That meant, he really meant everything he said. If we escaped, fine. The bullshit titles and sentences of the Haus wouldn't be held against us in the outside world.

However, if by any chance we were caught and returned. Mercy could use this infraction to leverage a lesser punishment if he desired to do it.

Of course, I trusted that Mercy would maintain his silence in this personal matter. I wasn't sure why I did, but deep in my heart I knew the little man was the most honorable kind of person in existence.

Noah must have sensed that in Mercy too, but as I said, I'm unsure why he didn't try to hide our relationship from him. He's never told me to this very day, and I've never asked. After a few moments of basking in the lippy adoration of my lover, I broke free of his charms. He dropped his face and tried unsuccessfully to wipe the rain away from his eyes. I patted his wide shoulder in a final act of reassurance.

Then I turned and motioned for the knelt Mercy to hand me his flashlight. He shook his head and said. "You'll need your damaged hands unencumbered to lift the lid, Your Majesty. Allow me to light your way from here. Oh, and no matter what, it's been a pleasure to serve you, Sire. A joy I shall treasure till my dying day. I thank you for the grace of it."

I chuckled and replied, "Good thinking, Mercy. Thank God I've brought only the most intelligent of men with me. How have I survived so long without you at my side, ja?"

He blushed then pointed the flashlight at the manhole cover. “Okay we are ready, Your Majesty. It’s now or never, ja?”

I nodded then headed up the crumbling steps that lead to the ceiling of that ancient tunnel.

Once I reached a perch close enough to move the lid with ease, I reached above my head and started pushing on it. But unlike earlier that day it wouldn’t budge. I used all my strength but couldn’t even get it to wiggle.

Panic started to fill my chest. Something was wrong, I didn’t recall that lid being that heavy. I reared back and like a bull rammed into it using my shoulders. Still, it held tight.

Mercy whispered out, “Sire? What is wrong?”

I replied in a harsh whisper, “I don’t know. The lid won’t open, Mercy. Noah, come here and lend me your strength. I’m too weak perhaps.”

Noah rushed up the steps and the two of us pushed and rammed at the lid with all our might. But the lid remained unfazed. We plowed into the damned thing until me and Noah were sweating and panting with fatigue.

Finally, after several moments watching our failure to move the lid Mercy dropped the flashlight onto the stoney floor as he said, “Give it up, Sire. The Stasi must have welded it shut. It would take more than any man possess to open it now. We are trapped and there is nothing we can do about it until we can find a tool capable of breaking a thick metal seal."

I shook my head wildly then yelled out in total terror, "Nein, nein. This cannot be happening. God dammit. Noah, put your back into it. We just aren't trying hard enough. It's going to open. It has to open. I cannot do this anymore. Can you hear me? I have to get out of here. Oh, Meine Gott. Get me the fuck out of here. Help me. Please someone help me."

With those words I began to bash my head into the metal lid, almost insane from the idea that my only hope of escape had been permanently blocked. Noah moved quickly to restrain me from severely injuring myself in this shit fit of frustration I was throwing. I kicked, writhed and cursed the headmaster while he calmly dragged me back down the steps to rejoin Mercy at the bottom.

Once safely back on solid ground, Noah allowed me out of his hold. I fell to my knees, put my head into my hands and wept loudly. I was so miserable I didn't even care that my most trusted men were witnesses to this most unmanly display of emotional breakdown.

Mercy and Noah stood guard while I emptied the contents of my troubled soul into my bandaged palms. Neither said a word nor did they grant me any room to try another run at that plugged hole.

For quite a while I sobbed like a baby, babbling things like: ‘That contract with Lucus. I just can’t, please nein. Don’t you understand? They won’t let me die. They won’t leave me alone. Its tearing me apart. Do you see the scars? Why me? I just want peace. I don’t want to be the king. I just want to be a man, a normal man, any man. Oh, what am I going to do? I’m so fucked. Help me Felicity. I tell you I can’t do this anymore.”

Then suddenly through the darkness I heard Florian singing out:

“Tick Tok, Tik Tock, goes Mad Maxx’s clock.
Tick Tok, Tik Tock, He cries but they don’t stop.
Tick Tok, Tick Tock, he is bottom not top.
Tick Tok, Tick Tock, he can hear the skull talk.”

I dropped my hands from my wet eyes and screamed out into the tunnel, “Shut up, Florian. I’m not going to listen to you anymore. You bastard, you’re dead. Stay dead, God dammit.”

Florian’s voice echoed off the walls as he called back, “Who is dead? Not me. But you certainly are. Look around you Mad Maxx. This is your tomb. Oh, my, do you hear it? They are coming for you, little Rabbit. Run, run, and run some more. Always chasing your tail, oops, I mean they are always chasing your tail. Hahaha. Face it. You’re trapped and never getting away. Hahaha.”

I covered my ears tightly and groaned against the painful sounds of his laughter at my failure to escape the Mortar Palace hell.

Noah put his hand onto my shoulder gently as his soothing voice cut through my agony, “Mad Maxx, it’s going to be alright. We still have each other. They can try to break us, but together we will stand, just as together we were willing to fall. Listen to me. You aren’t going to be alone in that horrible cell this time. Mercy and I will be there at your side to fight off the rats and the loneliness, ja?”

Then a tiny hand joined with Noah’s huge one as Mercy said, “Noah speaks the truth of it, Sire. Come what may, we will do it together. There was one way out through these tunnels. There must be another. If we can’t find it before the internment ceremony, then we will have all the time in the world to locate it after that. Hard to stop us from seeking it when we are permanent residents of this hellish place, ja?”

I shook my head slowly then sobbed in response, “You’re right. There must be another hole to the outside somewhere in this maze of stone. The ancients wouldn’t have just had one. I thank you both for the mercy of your concern and understanding. What would I do without either of you?”

Noah and Mercy chuckled bitterly as Noah said, “You’re never going to find out, Mad Maxx. Now can you stand or maybe you need me to carry you? If we are to have another shot at seeking a fresh way out it is best we don't linger here long enough to be discovered missing, ja?"

With a moan and shutter, I returned to my boots then while wiping my face with my sleeves.

"That's smart thinking, Noah. Alright, I suppose I've behaved like a little bitch long enough. Let's go, wait, better we don't leave together. Just in case anyone is loitering near the dungeon stairwell. I'll go first, while you and Mercy stash our getaway cargo in the Mortar Palace. Until I assign new palace mistresses, our stuff should be safe from prying eyes in there. Just make sure to ignore any nasty things Florian says to you. He's nothing but a stupid bone headed bastard."

Mercy gasped then said in a low whisper, "You spoke of Florian a few moments ago, Your Majesty. I've never heard of this guy before. You said he is in the Mortar Palace? Is he a palace dungeon master? Won't he tell someone about the things he sees us doing there?"

Noah put his hand up to silence the tiny submissive as he replied in a cautious tone, "Florian is not a threat to us, Mercy. He lives at the foot of the mortar throne along with all the other boney courtiers that are condemned to serve their Mortar King for eternity. I think it's best we just do as his Highness says and not ask him too many questions, ja? Perhaps you have forgotten that the mysterious voices that give the

Priceless his wisdom are not for us to understand or to hear. Greater men than us have found their graves for daring to seek those answers."

Mercy's eyes went wide and he seemed startled as he stammered in response, "Ah, okay, got it. Noah is correct to remind me of my place, Your Majesty. I beg your punishment for asking about the qualifications of any man or men you have deemed worthy of the Mortar Palace."

I waved Mercy off as I replied in the saddened tone, "Punishment denied, Mercy. You'll get to know Florian soon enough. For now, just remember you are the advisor to the Mortar King not him. He's sure to be jealous but if he gives you shit, I grant you permission to kick his. Well, just kick him. Alright, we'd better head back. As I said, once we reach the palace you two stay behind. Store the stuff, wait around fifteen minutes, then head out. Noah, take Mercy with you back to Almut and Hubertus's place for the night. I'll pick you both up in the morning."

Noah nodded then asked, "But what about you, Mad Maxx? Where will you stay? You can't go back to Jonas's and surely don't intend to return to Lucus."

I sniffed than said, "I'm going to see an old friend. I'm certain he won't ask too many questions if I show up unannounced. Enough of this, let's go."

We returned the way we'd come, but the atmosphere wasn't the happy one we'd enjoyed only a short time before. None of us spoke. The playful banter was replaced by deep despair and random sighs of disappointment.

I did my best to hold on to the hope that Mercy was right, and another hole existed somewhere in those tunnels. However, I couldn't shake the feeling that this was my last chance to escape on my own terms. From this moment on, a future as mad Mortar King, chained to the floor while enduring assaults too foul to contemplate was the most likely outcome for me. I had started to lose faith that I could do anything about it.

These dark thoughts were plaguing my troubled mind as I bid my loyal companions goodbye till the morning. Noah and Mercy broke away from our pack and into the Mortar Palace to do as I commanded. I kept going, limping briskly towards the exit of that stony hell.

I took one last deep breath to brace my nerves, repeating to myself that there was still hope. Then I pushed open that wooden door full of rot.

A gasp of terror rushed from my throat. There before my horrified eyes stood all the Elders, even my precious Leo. Each man stood shoulder to shoulder with Claus the Fur King in the center. Their faces wore cruel smiles while Jonas's chuckling matched their unified expressions of 'gotcha.'

Chapter 33: The Sweetest Goodbye

I whimpered and backed away slightly as I said, "Ah, to what do I owe the pleasure of this magnificent greeting? I was just checking on my palace affairs. So, I guess I'll be on my way."

Claus's wicked smile melted just as he shouted out, "Byron, Friedrick, arrest the Mortar King. Take him to the mortar receiving chamber immediately. Strip him and clip him into the chains. You will then await our arrival. We will be there shortly. We have a few questions we'd like to ask our beloved brother monarch of the mortar."

This frightening vision of the Elders had temporarily distracted me. I had not noticed the menacing sight of my two huge dungeon masters standing just behind them.

Before I could comprehend the seriousness of what Claus had said, the brute Byron and huge Friedrick rushed forward to subdue me. I wailed out in frustration the moment their meaty claws took my upper arms into their incredibly powerful grips.

There was no chance I could escape. These strong men didn't even break a sweat despite my furious efforts to struggle from their hold. Friedrick and Byron pulled me kicking and screaming bloody murder towards the rotten door that led to the Mortar Palace.

However, before they could drag me into that hellish place, Lucus came running down the stoney dungeon staircase. His voice cracked with the tone of underlying anxiety while he shouted, “Why are you manhandling my ward, honorable Elders? What has he done to warrant such ill treatment from his brother monarch and princes of the fur? Surely you all know that if you have some issue with the Mortar King, it’s proper protocol to take it up with his Regent. Unhand him this moment. If there is to be punishment, I’m the one responsible for enduring it. Though I do believe it’s my right to be told of the infraction I’m accused of committing first.”

Jonas snorted loudly then replied, “I agree with the honorable Lucus in one respect. He should also be punished. Unless there are any objections from my brother Elders, I believe Lucus should report to the Pit immediately.”

Every Elder, including my precious Leo, nodded their heads in agreement with the vampire. Lucus held his ground at the bottom of the stairwell while he did his best to appear defiant.

He replied, “As you wish honorable Elders. I will go without a fight nor need for restraint after, you let Christian Victor go.”

Jonas began to laugh, “Do you think your role as Regent to be to a throne of stone entitles you to give orders to the power of this Haus? You are more a fool than this idiot boy that calls himself Lord and Master. Oh, this is too much fun we are having here tonight. We have managed to capture two gnats with one swat. Friedrick, Byron? Why are you still here? Take his majesty to his precious palace reception room as King Claus commanded. Or perhaps you two are seeking a sample of what we are prepared to dish out?"

Byron and Friedrick nodded at the bat. Then they returned to their task of taking me through the palace door. Before they could drag me off into the darkness I screamed out, "Go to hell, motherfuckers. Go ahead and beat me all you like. I hope you beat me until I can't walk or even stand. Then after I'm a broken mass of mush all of you can go fuck yourselves. Because Mad Maxx won't be doing that for you anymore."

Jonas replied, "Ah, you're such a foolish boy. It's almost a crime to love you like we do. Christian, my beloved, you need not be capable of doing anything but laying there. In fact, we prefer you that way."

The brutes hauled me off, slamming the door behind us. The vampire's laughter echoed through the darkened narrow path for several minutes.

I ended my pathetic pleas for mercy. Our journey to the ancient palace reception area, a torture pit really, was relatively short. Once we had arrived in the circular room that had been crudely carved into the stone, Friedrick restrained me by my arms. While Byron began the task of removing my clothing with cruel efficiency.

My brutal brother threw the vampire jacket I was wearing onto the dusty floor. Suddenly, Taube's tiny voice called out to me from his hiding place in its pocket, "Mad Maxx, listen to me brother. You've forgotten about Noah and Mercy. If they are caught by these assholes or worse by the Elders, oh my God. Hurry, you must find a way to alert them. They are about to walk right into a trap like we did."

I realized the dirty ram was right. At any moment, my loyal men would be rushing through here totally unaware of the unexpected and dangerous developments since we'd last spoken. Then, the shrill voice of Florian screamed out from just behind the Mortar Palaces silver gate, "They got you Mad Maxx. Did you really think they wouldn't figure out your games? Ha. When the wolves hunt the fox, he isn't as clever as he thinks he is. Now you're going to lose more than just an inch or two of your flesh. You have led these men to their deaths unnecessarily. Oh, what a loser you are. Priceless, whore. Hey. I really like the little one. Can I have his head after the vampire is through with it?"

I let out a loud wail and then while struggling with all my might I yelled in reply, "Shut up Florian. Shut up, shut up. I'm not afraid of you or the Elders that are coming. If I were you. I'd run away, you coward. The Elders have a whip, and they love to beat stupid Priceless Kings with it. Hurry, Florian. They are almost here. Do you hear me? Don't you come in here. Run for your life you stupid bastard. Before the elders get here. That is a directive, God damn it."

Byron halted his work of stripping off my clothing. He stood there staring at me with a humored look on his face. Then he chuckled low and spoke, "Feeling a little anxious, Mad Maxx? Ah, well that is to be expected given the circumstances, ja? I suppose if I was about to be flayed to the bone I might be hearing voices too. Tell me something little brother, what would you be willing to give to have just a bit of mercy right now? Hmmm?"

I glared at him hatefully as I replied, "You're an asshole, Byron. As you can clearly see. I've no time for games. If you are willing to provide a service that could help me to endure what I must, then state your price. I will consider it. Say nein and after that you can shut the fuck up too."

The brute began to laugh loudly. Then he leaned in close to my face and whispered, "Ah, you want to be a tough guy, do you? Well, we will see if the Elders are able to soften up your hard limits shortly, now, won't we? Tell you what, Mad Maxx. I'll withdraw my offer, for the moment. But, if they let you live. I'll be around if you change your mind. I'm more than willing to bet that you will."

Byron's attempts to seduce me into a renegotiation of an unbalanced, nasty contract with him were interrupted by the sounds of many boots approaching. I gulped in terror. The Elders were coming.

Friedrick whispered out in an anxious sounding tone, “Byron, you’d better stop dicking around. I’m not in the mood for a whipping. Hurry, we still have a few minutes before they get here. Get his majesty undressed and let’s clip him into the chains.”

Byron growled out in reply, “Be quiet you moron. I can hear them coming. Bring him here, hold him tight. If he manages to escape you while I fasten the locks, you’ll have a lot more than punishment from the Elders to fear.”

Friedrick began his trip towards the center of the room. Sweat broke out on my brow as we approached the rusty restraining devices that hung limply from the ceiling. I immediately began to struggle against Friedrick’s attempts to drag me towards the chains.

“Nein, I command you to let me go. You must obey me, fools. I’m your master, not the Elders.”

My battling was hopeless. Friedrick had no difficulty forcing my arms above my head and holding them there. Byron locked me into the chains with ease, despite my best attempts to offer at least a little resistance.

The Elders came into the room and fanned out around me. I hung helplessly in the chains, naked, trembling and feeling very small. The sight of these cruel men that had come to employ their torture caused me to close my eyes in fear.

I confess. At that moment, the reasons for this situation were truthfully unknown to me. I didn't know if somehow they'd found out about my escape attempt. It was also possible that my attacks against their voter Rolf and trafficker Sigrid had been discovered.

However, there were a few other dark deeds I'd committed as of late that could have called down their wrath. Maybe someone had witnessed that trip I took through the yard, ja? Or perhaps, there was a complaint about my tendency to burn down cottages. *Oh, Meine Liebe, I tell you there were too many rotten things I'd done to dare speak a word until they give me a clue as to which of these things they'd found out about.*

Byron and Friedrick had withdrawn to take up a spot leaning against the back wall. While the Elders stood there for several minutes glaring at me with menace. I did my best to quell the physical response to the terrible pain from earlier attacks, the bone chilling temperature, and of course, honest fear of them. No matter how deep I shrank into my subconscious, I couldn't calm that rising terror within.

It seemed like forever before at last, King Claus broke the silence. He cleared his throat loudly then said in an authoritative sounding tone, "So, Your Majesty. I do believe we are all aware why we are here. However, what we'd love to know is what the hell were you thinking? Did you really believe you'd get away with it? For that matter, are you the only one involved? Tell us the truth and I can assure you we are prepared to grant you mercy. Try to lie to us and trust me, Sire, we will make you sorry for it."

I shook my head slowly then replied, "I've no idea why the men I used to call my beloved masters have issue with me. It breaks my heart that the ones I love the most have dared to commit such brutal betrayal. However, I guess this is what I deserve. I was a fool to buy into the tale tales of those capable of anything but selfishness. So, go ahead. Do your worst. I've nothing more to say to anyone about anything."

The Fur King was about to respond to my statement when Jonas interrupted him. "Stop trying to play dumb, Christian. You may be crazier than the march hare, but we all know you're not stupid. You know damned well what is going on here. Give us the names of your co-conspirators right now or else."

I began to laugh wildly. "Or else what, Jonas? Maybe you're going to try to tickle me with those ancient whips full of rot? Or maybe torture me with more of your hairy kissing? I already told you, all of you. I'm innocent of whatever bullshit you've concocted in your hurry to satisfy your twisted desires. I know you really love to hear me scream. That is what this is really about, ja?"

I let out a loud scream. "There, are you satisfied?"

A huge smile broke across the vampire's face. All his pointy teeth were on display while he clapped and replied calmly, "Ah, how cute. But I think we can do better than that. Byron, fetch the whip off the wall. Since Christian has forgotten that bad things happen to pretty little boys that tease. That's okay because he's managed to get me in the mood to remind him."

Claus used a hand gesture to halt Byron from obeying Jonas's command. The Fur King then glared at the vampire. "As I was saying before being so rudely interrupted by my brother prince. Your Majesty, we don't desire to cause you more injury than you've already suffered in abundance not that long ago. I'm asking you politely to give us the names of those involved in this plot intended to disrupt our ability to meet the annual fees paid to our honorable Stasi leadership. Do that and our sentence for your part in the crime will be far more lenient. Don't be a fool, Sire. Take our wish to show compassion while you still can."

I rolled my eyes and replied with a snort. "Oh? Is that what this silly show of brotherly unity is all about? So, you fine gentlemen are pissed that I've ended the cruel practice of sacrificing children to perverts. Though, I admit, I'm not surprised that it gets under your skin to be denied the joy of such disgusting practices. However, that's just too bad for Maxximillian because I'm unable to lay the blame for this on anyone else. You got me dead to rights, Your Majesty. I freely confess that I'm the bastard that plugged up your pleasure hole for a fucking change."

Jonas rushed forward and backhanded the shit out of me. “You insolent little prick.”

I recoiled from his blow. The taste of blood filled my senses, but the emotion of hatred filled my soul. I recovered my stance of defiance quickly. Then I faced the vampire and spit the warm, crimson contents from my mouth at him while I yelled out angrily, “Lap it up, dog. There is your dinner. Oh, and Jonas, you’re eyes are going bad. If you weren’t such a blind old man you’d have noticed I’m far from being a little prick. In fact, if I ever get the chance. I’m going to bend you over and demonstrate what a big man I’ve become.”

The vampire struck me across the side of the face again. Then before I could recover, he grabbed me by the back of my head by my hair. Jonas forced me to face him while he leaned in close and said, “Unless the next words out of that nasty mouth of yours are the names of the ones that put you up to this bullshit, I suggest you shut the fuck up before I end your ability to say anything at all. I mean it, Christian.”

This time I wisely decided to remain silent. My head was starting to pound with a killer headache. Both from Jonas’s backhands and from the rising inner need for more of Byron’s addictive suppositories.

When the vampire couldn’t get me to do more than glare at him hatefully for several minutes. He released my mane from his claws. Jonas raised his arm, to violently strike me again, but King Claus shouted out,

"Enough of this Jonas. Leave the Mortar King be and get your ass back here with your brother princes. I believe you've forgotten your place. Last time I checked, it is I who sits on the golden throne. Not you."

Jonas turned his head to look back upon his Fur King. I chuckled low and then whispered, "Better do as you are told, pops, before your big daddy gives you what you have coming."

Jonas snorted then replied sourly, "You forget yourself, Christian. We will continue this conversation later. When there is no one around to stop me from properly correcting your bad behavior."

I watched the vampire return to his spot standing next to Leo. It was then I realized that each man was positioned in his place of status. King Claus took the lead, then first prince Jonas. After him came Leo in the second throne, and Malfred the third. Bringing up the rear, was the fourth prince Justus. The fifth throne was empty at that moment because their true fur monarch Cora was still languishing away in the pit.

Until Claus's illness sent him to the grave, she would remain there too. Hahaha. Without Cora there to approve it, no new Elder could be raised to take up the empty throne.

That lack of a fifth man standing there to judge me brought some comfort. It hadn't been long enough for the memory of that vicious coronation ceremony to fade. If indeed these men intended to re-enact that nightmarish attack, I was grateful for the small mercy any absence could grant me.

Claus returned his furious gaze back to my own, once he was certain Jonas wasn't going to thwart his authority any further. We stared at each other for a few moments, and then finally he spoke, "You do realize the gravity of this admission you've given us, ja? Sire, the punishment for this crime is death. Does knowing that change your answer I wonder?"

A chuckling erupted from my throat while I replied, "Don't I wish you would end my life. Ha! No way that's ever going to happen though, is it? Try again, Your Majesty. This time, if you really wanted to scare me into giving false narratives, perhaps say you will sentence me to life, a long, long one. Besides, as Jonas has already told you. I'm not stupid. There is no Haus law that forbids me from doing what I have done. However, I do believe there is one that states killing kinder is the severest of crimes. So, why is it that I hang in these chains with a bloody lip. While you kinder killing freaks walk around free?"

Claus's expression turned dark while he shook his head.

"There is a Haus law that claims doing anything that would result in the destruction of her property and people results in the culprit being sent to the hill to burn. There is no distinction between the lowest level collar nor monarch written in it either. You speak with ignorance both of the laws that govern this place and of the brutal facts of our continued survival. So, I ask one final time. Do you deny someone else has manipulated you into committing this crime? Before you speak, I want you to understand. We know you didn't come by this secret knowledge all by yourself. Lucus put you up to this, ja? Go ahead and tell us, Your Majesty, and I swear on my honor you'll be spared."

I glared at the Elders hatefully while I replied, "If I say Lucus was behind this and I'm aware of what will happen next. Sure, I get to see that gross bastard burning at the stake. But what good will it do me? The very next day, Gretta will claim I'm breaching the contract with her. Lucus holds my will in gold and that agreement isn't transferable. If it were, I there say one of you would have unlocked this damned thing by now. Well, so no more Lucus, and then it's off to the palace for me three months earlier than scheduled. And without the comfort of a tongue to argue about the deplorable way I'll be treated. Ah, but you would like that wouldn't you Claus? As would you Justus. I know that is your wet dream come true, Jonas. But what about you, Malfred? Hmm? Or you Leo. You of all these men, sicken me the worst. How could you know about this horrible practice and do nothing to stop it?"

The Elder Leo dropped his face to look at his boots while he replied, "You don't understand, Christian. This abominable practice isn't something that I've ever agreed with. However, I'm helpless to stop it without endangering every man, woman and child in this Haus. You may not want to hear this, but in this case, the casualties are few in comparison to what it could be. Over the years, we've tried everything to get the Stasi to relent their sentence on this Haus. We must pay them or they will destroy us all."

I let my head fall back to emit a loud guffaw. "Oh, have you really tried everything Leo? You must really believe me the mad man to buy that bullshit you are selling. Speaking of letting innocent lives be ripped apart so that the corrupt can keep on breathing. Let's discuss a more personal situation, ja? You were going to sit on your thumbs while these bastards executed Jakob and Jager. Goddammit Leo. Jakob is your best friend and mine. Who are you? I don't even know you anymore. Well, never mind. I won't listen to any excuses anyway. Listen to me, you so-called honorable Elders. I am the Lord and Master of this Haus. My words are Law. I find all of you guilty of crimes against humanity. My sentence is to be Collared. Byron, Friedrick, arrest these men and take them down the hall to find the headmaster. He shall be the one to select which man belongs to which color, ja? Hahaha. Oh, and Leo, since you no longer will be needing your fortune I hereby confiscate it for use to pay the fucking Stasi's fines. I have spoken. Now cut me down from these fucking chains, you idiot brutes."

The eyes of every man, including my palace guardsmen went wide in expressions of disbelief. They obviously didn't expect that I would wield my mortar powers against them. That is the problem with holding too much power for too long, Meine Liebe. One can become complacent in the idea that no one could possibly ever possess more, or in this case, could side swipe it.

It's true that contract Lucus made with Gretta behind my back had neutered the most impressive of my powers. However, as Rolf had only recently found out, she had missed an important one. I could raise anyone I wished to the highest throne, but I could also lay them lower than the dirt beneath the Mortar Palace.

All I had to do, is say the words 'you are collared or you are king' and poof, they were obligated to obey. This was totally legal and beyond any rights they held to ignore it.

Byron recovered his wits before any of the elderly men did. He rushed forward to do as I commanded. I watched him in exhilarated thrill while he fumbled the keys to the locks that would set me free.

Claus put up his hand in the motion intended to halt Byron from his actions. I glared angrily at the Ex-monarch and yelled, "How dare you attempt to interrupt the proceedings of your betters, worm. I will have you whipped for such insolent behaviors. Friedrick, haul that bag of shit out of here. Nein, wait, take that ugly one with all the hair first. His face gives me the creeps. Byron, hurry up God dammit. I'll happily assist you in rounding up these other nothings. Ha."

King Claus growled out, "You forget yourself, Your Majesty. The Mortar King has no power without the approval of his regent. Friedrick, go to the pit and retrieve the stupid bastard that started this mess. Hurry up. We need him here to sort this all out. In the meantime, Byron, I believe it would be wise of you to consider your future. Perhaps there is something we may do for you in return for something you can do for us, ja? For this bargaining, my first prince is the best suited. Jonas? Would you be a dear and speak with this fine gentleman?"

Byron stopped his attempts to unlock me from the chains. He snuck a glance back towards Claus, then returned his gaze to my own. I glared at him feeling the fires of hell rising within me as I said angrily, "Don't you even consider it, Byron. These men no longer have any power to make promises of any kind to anyone. I'm your king, God dammit. Do as I command or I assure you the punishment will make what I've done to those less offensive to me seem like a mercy."

Jonas laughed loudly as he said in a menacing tone, "Byron my old friend, why do you bother listening to the words coming from the mouth of a boy that believes himself to be a king? Nein, he isn't even a child playing fantasy games. This so-called monarch that hangs in the chains is an insane creature wracked with delusions of grandeur. His only honest worth is as a sexual plaything that offers a challenge while you enjoy the pleasures of submitting him to your lust. The truth is that nothing he says makes any sense. Therefore, it couldn't possibly be advantageous to you to even hear his words of empty threats. Come over here and speak with a real man. I'm the one that holds the keys to your good fortune. I promise you, the things I'm prepared to grant are worth your consideration."

Byron grimaced then leaned in close to my face and whispered, "I've no choice but to do as Jonas asks of me, Maxx. They've sent for Lucus. Before you say a fucking word, listen to me. I know their plans. They are going to torture that whiny, weakling that calls himself your champion until he gives in to their demands. Then after that stupid bitch bows to their will and I've refused to even act as if I'm willing to negotiate. Well, trust me, my goose is cooked right along with his and yours. I hope you realize that my hands are tied in this delicate matter."

I growled low in my throat while I snarled out, "You're as blind as Jonas, Byron. It is my hands that are bound, you fool. You can do whatever the fuck you wish to do after you cut me loose from these motherfucking chains."

To my horror the brute completely ignored my command. He simply shrugged while turning around to walk over to speak with the vampire. I couldn't believe Byron would there to betray me like this. I'd wrongly assumed that he'd be eager to try and regain my trust after that rotten attack he'd pulled the day before.

After all he knew me better than most did at that time. I would be far more likely to overlook his transgression if he'd demonstrate a willingness to follow my lead.

However, my lack of insight into my growing addiction to his pain medications had blinded me to the reasons for his lack of loyalty. I honestly hadn't realized yet that I needed him far worse than he needed me. He was in control and I was already set up to become a bitch on his leash.

The Elders stood there silently glaring at me while Jonas engaged Byron in conversation. The two of them were whispering so softly even my keen ears were unable to pick up the gist of the promises being made to my dungeon master.

However, I could tell that Byron was thrilled by whatever Jonas was offering to get my brute brother to comply with the Elders' attempt to block my sentencing of them.

I was just about to set off into an explosion of curses over these assholes illegally withholding my rights when Friedrick returned with Lucus in tow. Though I heard the Elders order him to the pit last I'd seen him. He didn't seem to demonstrate any signs that any violence had been used on him. Not yet anyway.

In fact, he was trailing Friedrick, without indication of coercion or restraint. I sucked in my air in hopes that somehow, I could exhibit the same stoicism Lucus was displaying in abundance.

'But was his behavior all show and no substance? Would he be this tough once the Elders brought out their whips,' I thought to myself.

Well, Meine Liebe, this situation was a good, damned example of how the definition of torture is more personal than most people ever realize.

Lucus's gaze fell upon me hanging there in the center of the room in chains. His expression turned anxious almost immediately. I could see beads of sweat starting to form up on his brow, while he slowed his brisk pace to a crawl.

He licked his lips nervously then said, "How dare you treat your Mortar King so poorly. I demand you release him this minute. You've no right to punish him. That is my role, I do believe."

I had to hand it to him. Lucus may be a nasty, pervert in his sexual tastes, but he definitely was willing to pay me back for the displeasure of it. At least on the surface it appeared that way.

Claus snorted while looking down his nose.

Then he loudly said, "It is your role indeed, Lucus. We have every intention to make sure that you fulfill it too. Now, if I were you I'd start flexing that tongue of yours. Your Lord and Master have a few things to say to us. Of course, we can't hear him without his interpreter, ja? But before we begin this little chat I think it safer to make sure you don't overwork your mouth while his majesty delivers his messages to you. Byron, get that ball gag over there on the table. You know what to do with it, ja?"

Byron chuckled under his breath while he rushed to do as King Claus had ordered. I shot an anxious glance at the equally appearing frightened Lucus.

Then I yelled out wildly, "Nein, what you are doing is illegal and unfair. Lucus, listen to me."

Suddenly, my son Maxximillian shoved me from the wheel. He took a deep breath then said,

"I have sentenced all the Fur Thrones to be bound by collar. I've also confiscated Elder Leo's fortune. It's to be used exclusively to pay the Stasi fines. Hurry Lucus before they stop you from speaking my commands."

Lucus nodded in understanding and was about to repeat my words. Before he could get the first word out of his mouth. Justus flew at him and sucker punched him in the gut. Lucus reeled from the blow. He fell to his knees gasping for air while clutching his abdomen.

I rushed over and used one of my huge hooves to kick my handsome son away from the wheel.

He hadn't been expecting my attack. Maxximillian flew across the wheel room and smashed into the boy's mind. The flashing of a brainstorm strobed across the screen, just as a loud cracking ripped through the air.

Die Brutale yelled out from the back of the wheel room wall, "Hush, quiet boys. Don't you hear it? It's the shattering coming. Felicity, you must find Der Hund. These idiots aren't qualified to handle the vortex of madness."

Felicity bleated back in an anxious sounding tone, "Baaaaaaah. Baaaaah. Baaaaah."

I shouted back at the mother lamb, "I can't understand a fucking thing you are saying mother. God dammit."

Taube wailed out in reply, "How dare you speak to the mother lamb like that? If you wish to say something to Felicity. You must speak with me first. I will relay the messages, assholes."

In response I wailed back, "We don't trust you mother lamb fucker. We need Der Hund. Where the fuck is he?"

Maxximillian interrupted our argument by saying, while chuckling loudly, "Uhm, who left the speakers on?"

I halted my inner discussion with my brothers upon realizing everyone in the room was staring at me with humored expressions on their faces. Well except for Leo, Malfred, Friedrick and Lucus. Those men were glancing at the others anxiously.

Malfred raised his arm to alert King Claus that he desired to speak. Claus nodded his approval.

Then the third prince said in a soft voice, "I don't believe this stress is good for his majesty's mental health. Listen to me, Sire. Just tell these men you take back everything you've said since this interrogation began. And I'm certain we can all sit down like adults and work out something that everyone can agree on, ja?"

Jonas snorted loudly then yelled out, "Stop acting like a pussy Malfred. This boy was cracked long before this moment. If he hadn't been, we'd all be warm in our beds tonight instead of down here in this rat hole. Christian, retract everything you've ordered this minute. I command you to obey me, damn you. If you don't, I can arrange to send you right back to the white cell, at least until you turn eighteen. After that, there isn't any damage you can do while rotting away in this soundproof dungeon, oops, I mean your lovely Mortar Palace."

I shook my head nein. "I never take any of it back, Jonas. Go ahead and send me back to the nuthouse. I don't give a fuck anymore. What is one prison versus another?"

His wicked smile spread across his hairy face, as he said, "There are some very distinct differences, my pretty boy. I'm thinking soon enough you will be able to distinguish between all of them. Claus, I am tired of trying to reason with the illogical. Can we move on to the fun part of this council meeting?"

The Fur King nodded his approval, for whatever deviltry the Elders had planned for me and Lucus. Jonas motioned for Byron to fetch the whip off the wall.While he waited for that instrument of pain, he leaned in close to my face and said, "Because of your status as a monarch, no matter how silly it is that you are one. No man here, not even the honorable Claus can lay a finger on your flesh. That is why the Mortar Monarch is forced to assign personal dungeon masters to attend his royal person. However, I'm both your legal guardian and your blood bonded husband. That means, I'm capable of doing anything that Byron and Friedrick can do to you and so much more. Hahaha. For the moment, I think I'm going to just stand back and observe the Mortar Palace servants in action. When Byron and Friedrick have worn out their arms I'll happily led them a hand. So? Let's get this party started shall we. Oh, that is, unless you've decided to rethink your position of acting like a royal brat."

I snuck an anxious glance at Lucus. Friedrick was forcing the ball gag on the still winded Dominant. Lucus couldn't put up much of a fight even if Justus hadn't struck him down. The brute dungeon master was huge in comparison to his slight frame.

I whimpered softly but again shook my head, "I'm not going to relent, Jonas. No matter what you do to me. I can take a beating no problem. None of you can break me. I've endured far worse from all of you for years already."

Jonas smiled and said, "It's not your words that must be recanted nor you that we must soften up. It's your chosen Regent. Friedrick, make sure that Lucus has an unobstructed view of this show. Don't let him close his eyes nor cover his ears. I want him to hear every single word his Lord and Master have to say from this moment on. Byron, you may proceed."

Byron cracked the dust off the whip. Then without hesitation he used that ancient leather to cut into me.

My brute brother didn't hold back his strength. He lashed me relentlessly without caring for my safety. This wasn't just the typical whipping dished out to Haus residents that had earned punishment. Nein.

The Elders were demonstrating they were willing to beat me to death if necessary to get me to reverse my verdict. The flesh of my back, buttocks, and thighs was burning like hellfire. I could feel blood running in rivers down my legs. All the wounds the Stasi men had inflicted had only recently healed. Each of them seemed to have been reopened by the cruelty of the whip. It only took a few moments enduring Byron's brutal strikes before I'd begun screaming and begging him to stop.

While motioning Byron to halt his swing, Jonas walked over and investigated my sweating, panting face. "Well? Do you wish to say something other than please stop? You know what we want to hear, Christian. Say it, and we will end this torture."

I panted and gasped out, "Go to hell, Jonas. I told you already. I'll never take back my decree. Kill me if you wish. Just fucking hurry up and do it already, motherfuckers."

He rolled his eyes and nodded to Byron.

"Alright, Christian. As I've said, you always insist on learning everything the hard way. Byron. Put your back into it. I believe all you've managed to do so far is tickle, his majesty. Let's see if you can make him really scream."

Byron cracked the whip and then with all his might he let loose his strike. It caught me across the shoulder blades with viciousness beyond comprehension. The pain was so excruciating I nearly lost consciousness.

However, Jonas got his wish. There was no denying the sound that came out of my throat was a scream so loud, it echoed off the stoney walls for several moments.

Well, Meine Liebe, for a change I was more than willing to comply with Jonas's desires. Scream, I did, loudly, and constantly.

This brutal whipping went on for what seemed like hours before finally, Byron's swing began to soften. It wasn't that I noticed his strikes had become less fierce. My brute brother was the one that complained of his arm being strained.

I'd like to believe that Byron feigned his fatigue. He must have been aware that if he continued this cruel behavior I wasn't going to survive much longer, ja? But with that brute, who knows if he even cared if I lived or died.

Once Byron whined to Jonas about his weakened abilities, Jonas didn't hesitate to pull out the big guns. I was barely able to hold up my head, but I still heard him tell King Claus he had brought his cutter tools with him. The mentioning of pinwheels and rakes sent me into fresh spasms of terror. I used all the will power I had left to struggle in the chains.

I groaned and moaned while I pleaded with Jonas, "Please don't. Stop this madness someone. What is wrong with you, people? Just fucking stab me, or hell, light me on fire. But please don't cut me. I can't take that. Anything but that."

Then suddenly, Leo spoke. He sounded frightened and desperate as he said, "Claus, make him stop. He's killing him."

I watched the frantic Elder take a few steps in my direction. Leo appeared unwilling to wait for King Claus to take his statements seriously. His demands that my attackers relent their assault led to my becoming more frantic in my pleas for mercy.

I struggled wildly in the chains while I screamed out, “Let me go dammit. You have no right to do this. Leo, please help me. Someone please help me. Don’t let Jonas use the cutters.”

Justus and Malfred rushed forward to restrain Leo from his attempts to interfere with the brutal scene unfolding.

Jonas laughed out loud over Leo’s rescue attempt being foiled. He then returned his attention to me as he said, “Ah, so at last we have hit upon something that can catch your attention, Your Majesty. I wondered if anything could be heard above all the voices you’re hearing inside that empty head of yours. Well, my boy. Before we unleash your true tongue, I think it’s for the best that we first make damned sure Lucus understands the foley in speaking things we don’t wish to hear, ja? Byron, come here and hold this beast tightly, please. I wouldn’t desire to have him flinch too much. I might accidently nip a vein deeply enough to cause permanent and deadly consequences.”

Byron did as Jonas commanded. There was nothing I could do as Jonas ran his cruel pinwheel with unusually brutal force down my right thigh. I wailed in pain and terror as the vampire carved on me like a fresh Christmas ham for several minutes.

At last, the vampire seemed satisfied that my upper leg had been amply butchered. He motioned for Byron to ready my left one so that he could continue his ruthless actions.

However, before he restarted this bloody task he halted and turned towards Lucus. The perverted Dominant's cheeks were soaked with the fluids that had been running non-stop from his eyes.

It was a surprise to me that being forced to witness these men beating me to a pulp seemed to bother Lucus to tears. *As I told you earlier, Meine Liebe. Torture can be a very personal matter.* It all depends upon the definition of pain or trauma for the person being subjected to it, ja?

The Elders could've used the whip and cutters on Lucus and likely he would have relented under the stress of it. but it was just as likely this physically weak man would have died from the injuries outright or perhaps the infection from them later.

It was during this terrible situation that I finally understood none of the Elders desired to kill Lucus. The reasons for that were the same as my own. I could've named Lucus as the one that gave me the map that led to my discovering their dirty secret. I didn't because of that blasted contract Lucus held with the Silk Queen, ja?

Well, it turns out the Elders weren't in a hurry to see me sent below early and without a champion either. They wanted me to choose another regent, that was pretty obvious. However, they weren't interested in allowing the Mortar Throne to become the possession of the silk one.

You see, the founders of the Haus viewed the Mortar King as their companion to the Fur throne, not the Silk. But, if for any reason, I ended up without a regent. The Voters would gain my powers by default.

Ah, ja. I see that light of understanding in your eyes, Meine Liebe. You realize now why Gretta was in a hurry to illegally coronate me as King and send me to the palace, ja?

She took advantage of my ignorance of the rules about the mortar throne and since I'd broken Lucus's jaw. He wasn't around to fight for my rights. Cora relented the fur thrones legal claim to Gretta because those two harpies work together for the interests of the other, and not for what's proper or traditional. There is no telling the kind of favors Gretta promised Cora to gain compliance with that nasty trick they played on me.

Anyway, in the end Lucus was able to gain the votes from the Elders to overrule those greedy queens shady attempts to usurp their truthful place as co-rulers of the mortar throne. That of course, didn't stop Gretta from trying to assassinate me once she realized she couldn't gain possession of my powers. But let's not go over that horror again. You remember Henner, the Stasi night, need I go on with that disgusting list?

Well it turns out that though Lucus had lied to me on multiple occasions in his efforts to manipulate my powers into his hands, the one thing he was being truthful about was his feelings for me. Like it or not, he honestly was in love with me. Yikes and yuck.

The Elders figured this out long before I did. His love and desire for my good welfare was the weakness they exploited in those early morning hours. Lucus also made it clear on more than one occasion he despised the numerous scars I wear upon my flesh. He didn't desire I add any new ones any more than I did.

With their knowledge that I could take a harsh beating and Lucus unable to stand to see me damaged or in unnecessary pain, the Elders were able to force my Regent to negotiate with them without laying a single finger on him.

Jonas smiled knowingly while he directed Friedrick to dislodge the ball gag from Lucus's mouth.

The regent to be, spit and gasped for a moment before he said sourly, "What will it take to end your attacks on my Lord and Master, King Claus?"

Claus narrowed his brows, then replied, "You will not sentence the Elders to collaring. You will return Elder Leo's fortune to him, and you will restrain your ward from further interference with the Haus collections of money for the annal Stasi fines."

I gasped and panted as I yelled out, "Nein. Refuse that offer Lucus. Don't relent."

Lucus glanced at me for a moment, then he dropped his gaze to the floor and replied softly, "I won't endorse the Mortar King's sentencing of the Elders to the collar. However, I also won't relent regarding the abominable practice of collecting fine fees. Elder Leo is wealthy enough to pay those fines without seriously damaging his income. However, I believe it is unfair for him to cover the entire cost. The leadership of this Haus has become rich off the backs of its many warring factions contained within her. I dare say you spend a minor fortune annually to obtain the finest flesh to clad in silver. Then use wasteful practices such as tossing them to be devoured by Russian dogs once they are fully trained but barely touched. The power of this Haus sucks out all the change from the lowly residents and puts it into their own pockets. There is more than enough to pay the Stasi. There would be even more to go around if the laws regarding circuiting were enforced properly. That alone would cut down the need for obtaining so many expensive fresh silvers, now wouldn't it."

King Claus glared hatefully at Lucus while he said angerly, "How dare you make such criminal accusations regarding the leadership of this Haus, Lucus. I do believe any man that takes advantage of a clearly feeble-minded boy has no right to be pointing fingers at anyone else."

Lucus chuckled. "Oh? I seem to recall that poor boy you are referring to has a weekly appointment to endure your unwanted affection. This happens because of a contract he made with you so that he was able to walk around without being forced to wear the silver collar of the Elders, ja? Look, I don't intend to insult but if that is the way you choose to hear my wise words, who am I to complain? However, that doesn't change the verdict I'm endorsing as the representative of the Lord and Master of this Haus. The leadership shall find a way to pay the Stasi fines from the common coffers and the honorable Leo will cover the shortfall. The list of war criminals must be shortened as well. The Mortar King will continue to discover ingenious ways to subtract the names until the Stasi are convinced every man, woman and child from that role is dead. Once that happens, hopefully, they will end their demands for the annual fines."

The Fur King shook his head then replied in a hateful tone, "Shows how much you know, Lucus. The Stasi have become accustomed to the extra cash they extort from us. They aren't going to stop coming for the payments as long as even one person is still breathing in this Haus, even if the person was only born yesterday long after the wars."

Lucus shrugged. "Well, I guess we will find out if that is true or not. Because that is my final offer. Take it or go ahead and kill both of us. I would rather die with my hands clean than with the blood of innocents on them. I happen to know that is an opinion my king also shares. So? Do we have an agreement or nein? This is a fair deal, Your Majesty and you know it."

Claus glanced at his brother Elders, well except Jonas. That dirty bat was still standing there with his blood drenched cutter in his claws positioned to return to his torture. I kept one eye on his tool of pain while watching as the fur princes all nodded in approval to Lucus's proposal.

Once his fur prince brethren, including to my surprise Jonas, indicated they agreed. Claus sighed loudly, then said, "The vote among the Elders is unanimous. We will arrange to have a proper contract drawn up and expect you and his majesty will sign it without attempting further manipulation. However, I must warn you Lucus. This you say about the Mortar King crossing names off the list of war criminals is a dangerous proposition. Both for his majesty and for any one of us that are recorded as survivors. I wish to add that any name that holds a throne of power is immune to honest sentencing of death, collaring, banishment or entombment in the dungeon. If his highness wishes to erase the names of Elders or Voters, he must do it on paper only. Otherwise Jonas can continue his actions, ja?"

Lucus glanced at me as he said softly, "Do you agree to the arrangement as spoken, Sire?"

I groaned out in pain, then replied, "I can make it work as long as the babies are safe. What do I care if a few old men that will be dead soon enough find the grave by my hands or by natural causes. I will do what I must to nullify that list even if I can't touch the ones that honestly belong on it."

Lucus smiled bitterly at Claus. "There you have it, Your Majesty. Now, please release the Mortar King. He's in desperate need of medical treatment and rest, ja? I wish to take him to visit with Doctor Attila immediately, unless there are further issues we need to be discussing?"

Claus shook his head slowly as he motioned his brother princes to start their journey back to the sixth floor. "Nein. We are more than happy to leave. However, you will be coming with us to the Hall of Records. I don't trust you or his majesty won't change your minds the moment he's released from those chains. I know his temper all too well. Friedrick will accompany us to assure you don't pull any funny business. Byron, you will remain behind with his majesty. He is to remain here and tethered until Friedrick returns to indicate the deal is safely recorded. The two of you will then escort the Mortar King for a much-needed visit with his doctor. Okay, Lucus. Get your scrawny ass moving. It's almost breakfast time, and I'm an old man. All this excitement has riled up my appetite. Oh, and Your Majesty, I will be in touch with you soon to arrange a time for that bath service you promised me. Come on fellas. Let's go. I'm starving."

I whimpered while watching the men briskly filing out of the room. It was then I noticed Leo was lingering behind the others.

He waited for the last of his brothers, Justus had disappeared into the tunnel. Only Byron and I were left to hear anything the Elder had to say to me. He walked over towards me and reached into his jacket to pull out a large envelope.

He dropped it on the ground next to me and said in a sad sounding tone, "I know you don't believe I care, Maxximillian, but I honestly do. Here are the things you've requested. I've obtained them with the shame of realizing I should have thought of this myself. However, you were right about one thing. I'd become so self-absorbed with my own problems, I had failed to notice the serious danger the ones I love were truly in. I hope that this act and the intentions that go with it will one day cool your temper and reheat your opinion of me. If so, just remember that my door is always open if you wish to talk about this or well, anything at all. I do love you Maxx with all my heart. Please if you believe nothing else is sincere about me do know that is the truth. I will be waiting for you, forever if need be. Oh, and Der Makellose sends his greetings and gratitude for the generous gift of the buddy you've sent to him."

I snuck a curious glance at the brown sleeve of paper as I replied angrily, "Trust me Leo, you will be seeing me very soon. Now go away and leave me the hell alone before I realize it was stupid to ever fall for your lies."

Leo nodded then replied, "As you wish Sire. I hope to see you soon. Byron, take his majesty to visit with Doctor Attila with haste please."

Then without another moment's hesitation, he left quietly to join his brother princes in the Hall of Records.

I was left all alone with Byron, and helplessly still cuffed in the chains. I'd just told the only person that stood between me and that rapist brute to leave. I must have been out of my freaking mind.

Byron watched Leo shrink into the darkness of the tunnel for a few minutes. Then he turned his attention to me. I felt my heart sink as the brute began to slowly undo the buttons of his breeches while chuckling low under his breath.

My voice was barely audible due to the terror freezing it in my throat as I said in a soft whimper, "Please don't. Byron, not now. Look, we can work something out later when I'm in better shape to tolerate servicing you, ja?"

Byron shook his head and an evil grin erupted on his face while he replied in a whisper, "Nein, little brother. I'm all hot and bothered already. You left me wanting the last time and I'm not willing to endure that again. We are going to finish what was so rudely interrupted. No one is around to stop me this time."

Byron quickly rushed to take a spot behind me. I struggled with renewed strength against my restraints, but that was useless. I couldn't do anything to prevent my brute brother, or for that matter anyone, from doing anything to me that they wanted.

He put his arms around my chest holding me still for his penetration, as he whispered into my ear, "You know the Elders were very afraid of the possibility of becoming little sluts like you. Jonas was happy to promise me anything I desired just to keep that pretty mouth of yours shut. Do you know what I asked them for?"

Byron thrust himself into me with ruthlessness and a lack of lubrication before I could answer him. I let out a long, loud wail of pain. Once my cries of agony quieted a bit, he resumed his torturing of my mind as he said.

"Though I was unable to regain my status as a silk prince, Jonas has agreed that I can keep my apartment on the fifth floor. Luckily, no matter what you do, you can't withdraw my place as your dungeon master, Mad Maxx. But even better than that, I arranged to have Rolf become my personal mercenary and to make sure he is loyal to me. I've obtained a way to offer him vengeance against the man that tore his power from him. When you choose a queen we will be counted as the Voters for her collar selection. Oh, as will Friedrick. We are going to tear her apart Maxx just like I intend to do to you right now."

I let out another scream of pain driven terror upon hearing his statement. He laughed with joyful evil, reveling in his power over me, and one day my bride. Believing he had completely crushed my soul he began his brutal thrusting in one of the most vicious and drawn-out sexual assaults he'd pulled on me up to that day.

When finally, he finished using me as his plaything, he retrieved the keys to the cuffs. He released me from the chains, and I fell to the floor with a thud, unable to find the strength to stand. I was hurting so badly, even the teeth I don't have seemed to be aching. I just laid there on the cold stone, weeping and praying for a death that was never coming. Byron stood above me for a few moments, appearing to enjoy the fact that he'd broken my spirit.

Then with suddenness he jumped on me and rolled me to my face. I screamed and struggled against his weight, assuming he was going for a second helping of my dignity.

However, it wasn't his manhood that he shoved into me this time. I recoiled in a weird mix of disgust and relief as I realized he was using his finger to push in one of his suppositories. It took a full five minutes for the merciful numbness to quench the fires caused by his cruel injuries to my most personal areas.

However, that wasn't the only surprise Byron had in store for me, well other than that rape.

After the calming effects of his pain killer worked its magic, he rolled me to my back. I watched in eager and grateful anticipation while he knocked the bubbles from one of his needles full of his special curative.

I didn't even flinch when he roughly pushed the sharp into my naked hip. He smiled at me and I closed my eyes to await the rapture of feeling completely healed. I wasn't aware at that time what was in those needles of his, but no matter how damaged I was, it could fix me up good as new. At least until its effects wore off.

Then I would need more of it if I wished to forget I'd just endured one of the worst beatings I'd taken in my young life. The Stasi of course was the worst.

Anyway, so while I lay there enjoying the sensations of being mostly pain free, Byron had taken interest in the large brown folder Leo had left behind. He picked it up and examined the contents. A look of extreme thrill came across his expression, and I noticed he was trembling slightly. His actions of excitement brought me back from my cloud of grateful relief to that of cold, stark reality.

Byron snatched the two passports from the folder and held them before my eyes as he yelled out happily, "Maxx, look here, our tickets out of this hell hole. Oh, my God. Everything we need is included in this envelope to set us free of this God damned country. Hurry up and get dressed. Our plane is leaving in a few hours. We must get moving or we will miss it. How the hell did you manage to get Leo to give these to you?"

I shook my head as I replied with sadness in my tone, "Leo didn't do this for me or for you, Byron. Those tickets and passports are for Jacob and Jager. Put them back where you found them. We will have to escape the Haus some other way."

Byron's smile melted to an expression of disbelief as he said in a low growl, "Fuck Jacob and Jager, Maxx. Leo gave these to you, not them. I saw it with my own eyes. This is the only way we can ever get out of here, fool."

I replied calmly with a sigh, "We can get out using a hole in the tunnels, Byron. You were there yesterday. The secret escape routes are not rumors. They exist, ja?"

Byron's eyes went wide for a moment and then he began to chuckle as he said sourly, "You didn't learn a damned thing tonight, did you? Brother, I've always known about that hole Snot showed you. I've also always known that isn't an escape from this Haus. I would think after trying to get out last night, and finding it sealed you'd have figured that out too."

I sucked in my air with startle as I blurted in response, "Wait, how did you know it was sealed, Byron. You are the dirty rat that squealed, ja?"

He shook his head as he replied flatly, “Nein, I overheard Ivan reporting to Claus that the Stasi had called about an attempted breakout. Ivan told the old bastard that the description he was given matched up with a certain Mortar King. I saw Claus hail down Jonas in the hallway. I knew right then and there what was going to happen next. I did my best to stop you from getting caught trying to escape from a hole that was at best sealed and at worst a trap set for you. But you managed to overcome that fast acting sedative of mine. Just goes to show that you are a greedier slut than I could have guessed.”

I glared at him hatefully while I replied, “Well, turns out the Elders had bigger issues to settle with me than a fruitless escape attempt, ja? Byron, give me that folder, and get the fuck off me right this minute.”

He shook his head and bared his teeth. “I’ll do whatever I want with you for as long as I like. We are using this unexpected gift to escape. After we are free, you will do as I tell you or I will chain you down for good. There is nothing you can do to stop me either, you little slut.”

I kept my eyes glued to his own, while secretly watching the huge Noah slipping upon the brute. The headmaster moved with speed and stealth until he was within striking distance. Noah smacked him in the back of his head with Mercy’s flashlight. Byron fell into an unconscious heap without uttering a single peep of protest on his way down.

A sigh of relief escaped my throat as I gazed at the prone body of my subduer.

I didn't pull my attention from Byron as I spoke in a whisper to the headmaster and Mercy, "I'm grateful you two heard my warning about the troubles. I'm forever at your feet for arriving just in time to prevent far worse from happening than already has. However, there is no time right at this moment to properly reward you both for your loyalty. Lucus, or worse, will be coming back soon expecting to take me into their possession. Noah, help me get redressed. Mercy, grab those passports. Put them back into that folder over there on the floor. Once I'm presentable, Noah, escort Mercy up to the fourth floor. Go to the honorable Jacob's apartment and deliver it to him. Tell him to take only what he and Jager can carry and get the hell out of here while they still can. After you've done that, high tail it up to your fifth floor apartment and take Mercy with you. Boys, get some rest. I'll come retrieve you soon enough. We've still got a lot of work left to do."

Noah reached out his hand to offer me aid off the floor while he said in a nervous tone, "Mad Maxx, are you sure it wouldn't be wiser to escort you to the doctor's clinic? If I'm with Mercy on the fourth floor, I can't protect you from anyone that believes you're an easy target. I mean no offense, but you don't look very well."

A groan escaped me while I took his hand to pull myself up. I shook my head then said calmly, "I'm alright, Noah. The damage isn't as bad as it appears. Mostly just bruises."

Mercy sucked in his air with an expression of disbelief coming over his face as he said, "Sire, I must beg your punishment for daring to dispute your statement of good health, but bruises don't bleed. You're in need of some stitching and no doubt some tender loving care. We were hiding deep in the tunnels but from time to time we could hear your screams. That beating the Elders gave you wasn't a gentle one. As your advisor I suggest it is wise to allow Noah to go with you to see Doctor Attila."

I snorted then motioned Noah to begin aiding me in my dressing. "Your advice is noted, and request for punishment denied, my pet. You two will do as I said, and I won't entertain any further discussion about it. I will wait until a few minutes after you've cleared the palace door and follow you out at a safe distance to keep any witnesses from wagging their tongues. I can get to the doctor's office without the need of anyone holding my hand."

Noah nodded then said softly while sneaking a glance at the unconscious Byron, "Mad Maxx, what do you want me to do with this scum bag? I will happily beat him to death for you, if you wish."

I chuckled and petted the side of his handsome face as I replied in a humored tone, "If anyone is going to take that trash out, it will be me my beloved. Now hurry up and do as I told you to do. If he wakes up before we can get out of here. We may have to kill him. You're wasting time we don't have, ja?"

The headmaster didn't have to be told to follow my orders twice. Within only moments the terrible sight of the torture I had endured was camouflaged by yards of dark cloth. Only my face with numerous bruises and severely busted lips indicated I'd suffered some serious violence.

Byron still hadn't moved an inch by the time Noah and Mercy took off in haste and headed for the palace exit. I loitered behind in the coronation room, keeping a baleful eye on my felled older brother. For a few moments, I considered various ways I could cut those blasted chains from the ceiling.

I was deep in thought of ways to severe them when the tiny voice of Taube called out from my jacket pocket. "Mad Maxx, Felicity says this crime Byron committed against you isn't something you can leave unpunished. She says if you don't teach him a lesson about messing with us. He will return and do worse the next time. There is no valid contract between you two. He has stolen what isn't his to take."

With a trembling running through me, I glanced at Byron then said in a whisper, "Does Felicity want me to injure him while he is helpless? Surely, she knows when he awakens his wrath will be terrible. Other than killing him, what would she have me do? I would happily end his life, but if I did that the Elders would know it was me that did it. They aren't going to send me to the hill, but they will send me to the palace. We don't want that and neither does she."

Taube snorted loudly then jumped from my pocket onto the floor. I watched in terror as the ram approached the violent man and stood there staring at him for several minutes. Then to my utter shock, Taube hiked his hind leg and let loose his bladder. Byron didn't stir as the ram urinated buckets of piss all over him from head to toe.

Once Taube had drained out all his water, he turned around and kicked the dust over the sleeping dungeon master. I couldn't believe the balls on that ram. He was well aware of how much Byron hated him.

If the man had awakened to find Taube there and doing what he was doing, oh, Meine Liebe, I can't even imagine the horrible outcome. But Byron didn't wake up. Taube returned and stomped his hooves demanding that I return him to the pocket with his Frau Felicity. I picked him up and rolled my eyes at him as I said in a whisper, "If he asks, I'm telling him you did that, not me."

Taube snorted. "Go ahead and tell him. I'm not afraid of that blow hard. He's afraid of little things. Like me and Mercy, ja? Now get going, Mad Maxx, before that beast wakes up or Lucus comes creeping back looking for loving."

No doubt the dirty ram was right to give me that warning about Lucus. I knew the pervert would be in a hurry to rush back down to the palace to collect what he believed was his. Without any further hesitation I hauled serious ass down that narrow path headed for the rot infested wooden door. I cracked it open slightly and listened for a few moments. The sound of silence greeted my ears. I'd managed to escape the palace without any obvious witnesses and traveled up the dungeon steps before I caught sight of Lucus. He was practically running over the mass of residents that were packed in the hallways, all headed for their breakfast in the Great Hall.

He didn't appear to have spotted me spotting him yet. But I didn't stick around to give him that chance either. I took off at a brisk pace down the side hallway that only the day before I'd traveled with Sigrid. All I could do was hope that Lucus hadn't managed to catch sight of me ducking into this mostly abandoned pathway.

That closet from hell was just ahead of me when all at once I heard a voice call out that I recognized immediately. I halted my tracks and turned around with startled speed. The voice of the DJ appeared to have come from behind a pillar just to my left.

I cleared my throat and tried to sound stern as I said, "Stop following me, weirdo. Don't you have anything better to do?"

He peeked out from around the corner and called out to me in a whisper, “You look like shit, Robin. Did the Joker get you? Ah, that’s where you’ve been right? Battling with the villains of Gotham City? Why didn’t you call me? I’m Superman. I can leap banisters in a single bond. Hey, did you ever get that mouse I asked you for? Why do you keep bothering me? I said to leave me alone, dammit. Stop crowding me.”

I glared at him unable to understand what the hell this guy’s problem was as I replied hatefully, “I’m on my way to see the doctor, Superman. I wasn’t bothering you. You are bothering me. And nein, I didn’t get that fucking mouse. As you can see, I’ve been a bit distracted by more important things. Now, unless you have something important to say. I suggest you move on before I move you.”

The DJ’s hairy face fell as he replied, “But I came here to offer a friendly warning, Robin. The Vampires are coming. They are flying around the halls looking for sweets to eat. Do you want to be dinner for the fiends? Didn’t your buddy Batman tell you they are hot for your blood? They are jealous of that fancy car he drives, you know.”

I shook my head and snorted. “I never understand a damned thing you say, Superman. Listen, I know we have a deal about the special services. While I’m kind of not in shape to provide them to you at the moment, is it possible that you can trust I’m a man of my word? I found one of the holes that leads out of the Haus, but they sealed it. I assumed that was the one you were using. However, here you are. So, you must be using another one. If I take you to the tunnels, will you show me the one you use? I promise after that, I'll give you anything you want, anything."

He shook his head wildly as he smiled and yelled out, "Really? Can we go there now? Oh, nein. Wait, come with me first. I want to show you my lair, Robin. Lately, the view has gotten less interesting but that's all going to change now that you have found a way to escape from Gotham. Before we go, can I swing by and say goodbye to Lady Ada? Oh. I forgot. Do you have enough room to carry the partridge and its pear tree too? If not, then I'm not going. Hey, watch out. The vampires are here."

He suddenly took off running down the hallway. Then, like the vapor of a mist the DJ shrank back behind the corner of the wall and seemed to disappear into it.

I stood there staring at the spot he'd melted into until suddenly a chocolate donut rolled by me across the hallway floor. It had been over twenty-four hours since I'd eaten, so believe me when I say it was very difficult to ignore that sweet treat.

However, I'd already been attacked twice by that sneaky DJ after he'd used that trick of feeding me drugged chocolate. I wasn't going to be his fool for a third time. With a sigh of disappointment, I strolled past the delectable donut and resumed my trek towards Doctor Attila's office.

I'd managed to pass the closet from hell without incident and was nearing the exit that led to the good doctor's clinic. It was there that I saw the huge Lenius heading in my direction. His expression wasn't friendly and I was in no shape for a physical confrontation with anyone.

Without skipping a beat I turned tail to start heading back the way I'd come. I didn't get very far before Lenius called out to me, "Your Majesty, hey. Hold up, Sire. I know you don't owe me any favors but if I could beg your forgiveness could I ask you to do something for me?"

I didn't even turn around as I yelled back in reply, "Ja, you're correct, I don't owe you any favors and nein. You can't ask me for any nor receive my forgiveness Lenius. You'll leave me alone if you know what is good for you."

Truth is, I was afraid of Lenius. It wasn't that I hadn't grown large enough to hold my own if it came down to a battle with him. That day, however, I knew I wasn't in any condition to be getting into unnecessary fights. My hands were still bandaged and though Byron's magical curatives were working well. I knew they were nothing but a superficial and temporary fix for serious injuries.

I needed to visit with Doctor Attila as quickly as possible. Only the doctor possessed a more permanent solution to my ailing. But I wasn't willing to cross Lenius to do it.

So, I retreated down that abandoned hallway, headed right back toward the closet from hell. As it came into my sight, I slowed my brisk pace to a crawl. I wasn't in a hurry to tempt the fates by crossing its path twice in the same day. There were just too many bad memories of incidents that'd occurred there during my many moments of weakness in the past, ja?

I stopped my journey inches from its door and turned around to make sure Lenius hadn't decided to follow me. A sigh of relief escaped me upon the discovery he had thought better of it if he'd been planning any ambushes.

I glanced down at the opposite end of the hall and saw the beautiful Anna approaching with a smile on her face. She called out to me, sounding full of thrill upon finding me standing there all alone.

"Well, looks like it is Anna's lucky day. Good morning, Sire. Are you a busy man or do you have a few moments to spare on one of your most loyal subjects?" She giggled into her hand coyly.

Her sudden appearance startled me to silence. I just stood there staring at her like a dummkopf for several seconds. Then the sight of that discarded donut caught my eye. Intense hunger chewed at my stomach like a ravenous lion devours his dinner. I knew it was quite possibly drugged but the need to quench that aching need pushed me to reach down to retrieve it.

Killian's lovely sister had been patiently standing there only a few inches away waiting for my permission to speak. Anna watched me clumsily trying to pick the sweet off the floor.

She let out a small gasp then said, "Oh, my goodness. Don't eat that, Your Majesty. You've no idea the gross things people throw onto the floor around here. Where the hell is the black collar maid? She is such a lazy bitch, ja?"

I halted my actions and glanced at the beauty as I growled in reply, "Why are you here bothering me, Anna? Shouldn't you be off somewhere with your boyfriend instead of harassing busy monarchs?"

She spat out angrily with a sour look on her face, "He left me for a younger woman, Your Majesty. Isn't that just like a man? He steals a woman's best years then leaves her out to dry the moment she starts to season properly. Oh, do I hate that sonofabitch. Let's not discuss him, though. I've noticed that you are also without proper company, Sire. I was wondering, that is, if you aren't seeing anyone, might I apply for the position of your consort?

I let out a gasp of surprise and abandoned my attempts to pick up the chocolate covered dough. "Huh? Did I hear you correctly or am I hallucinating? Are you really offering your bid to become my queen to be?"

Anna grinned at me happily while nodding an undeniable ja to my question.

I snorted loudly then replied angrily, "I've no time for your foolish games, woman. There is no doubt that you are attempting to pull some nasty trick because I know you hate me, just as much as I hate you. Be on your way. I've better things to do than listen to your false offers of promises you never intend to keep."

With quickness I turned my back on her and began to limp back towards the clinic.

Anna appeared anxious as she blurted out, "Wait, don't leave just yet Your Majesty. You need not give me an answer right away. Let's discuss the possibilities over breakfast, ja?"

I stopped my journey and turned to face her as I shouted, "Are you deaf, Anna? I told you to go away and leave me alone. Besides, I'm not hungry, and even if I were. You'd be the last person I'd share my breakfast with."

My stomach growled loudly.

Instead of appearing upset over what I said, she giggled happily then offered her arm. "You say you're not hungry but that growling in your tummy disputes your claims. Please take pity on this unworthy woman and escort me to breakfast. I wish for everyone in the Haus to turn green with jealousy over your new lover, especially Lenius, that two timing bastard. Oh, won't he be sorry he dumped me like I never meant a thing to him. Well, as it turns out, it was my lucky break, ja? I've traded up. Ah, the wonderful, sexy things I'm going show you, Your Majesty. I can barely wait. Nein, let's not wait. How about we slip into this closet, and I will give you a demonstration, ja?"

She rushed to the closet door and opened it wide. I watched in pure shock as the pretty woman flipped on the light switch, then looked inside to assure herself it was unoccupied. I stood there unsure if I should stick to my initial belief that this was a rouse. Or give into my desperate urges to engage in a sex with the gender of my preference.

Before I could make either decision a sudden and powerful vertigo overtook me. I swooned so severely I had to lean into the wall to stay on my boots. Anna saw my near fainting spell and came running over to help keep me from falling face first onto the hallway carpet.

Her tiny hands certainly felt wonderful, gripping my upper arms, while I tried to steady my wavering balance. I shot her a sly glance then said with an embarrassed chuckle, "Oh, danke Anna for your assistance but I think I'm fine now. I don't know what came over me. Give me a moment and I'm sure this dizziness will pass, ja?"

Anna pursued her lips and then a smile broke across her pretty face while she reached into the pocket of her wool jacket.

"I bet you're having a sugar crash, Sire. Here, eat this. Hurry, it will help calm that dizziness."

She handed me a small piece of chocolate. I couldn't believe my luck to be offered such a delicious treat by a beautiful woman. I tried to take the candy from her hand, but my worthless fingers couldn't grip it. She noticed my lack of dexterity and without a word, reached out and pushed the chocolate into my mouth. The pleasure that chocolate always grants me filled my senses while I chewed its gooey goodness and swallowed it.

Once I'd cleared my mouth I returned my attention to Anna. I was about to thank the pretty mistress, but that strange vertigo came over me once again. This time it was much stronger than before. The image of her face became fuzzy in my vision as she said in an echoing tone, "You really don't look well, Your Majesty. I think you'd better sit down before you fall and injure yourself. Wait right here. I'll go fetch Doctor Attila."

I nodded and replied groggily, "Okay, Anna, I'll just wait here till you get back. I'm in need of a quick nap anyway."

For the next hour or so, I have no memory of what happened. I believe I enjoyed dreams of that beautiful woman seducing me with her pretty hands, but I'm not sure that's not just wishful thinking. The reality that even I couldn't deny is that Anna Altergott would rather have fucked a pig than spend a single moment in my arms.

After that long moment of nothingness, I opened my eyes to the vision of a disheveled man peering down into my face. He seemed concerned as he said in a whisper, "Robin, I think you're going to turn into a vampire soon. Let me tell you something, false Mortar King. I'm not letting you drink my blood. I've told you a million times already. Stop following me. I'm not your friends and I'm sure as hell not your lover. Go away. I mean it. Next time we meet I will bend you like a piece of steel. Because I'm the man of steel, ja? Hey, can you fly yet?"

I groaned out feeling quite irritated as I replied, "Superman? Did you manage to drug me again? Oh, my God, you did, didn't you. And you've raped me too. Don't try to lie because I can tell you did. God dammit. You must stop taking without asking, asshole. You're going to injure me beyond repair."

The DJ looked away from my face, appearing suddenly fearful as he whispered out, "Pop, Pop, goes the weasel. Get up, Robin. These walls are the only safe place for a superhero. I'll see you in the fortress of solitude. Fly away, ah."

He took off running down the hallway, once again seeming to vaporize into thin air, just as he rounded the corner.

I sat up and moaned out from the mild pain that was radiating from my, uhm, ravaged areas. I cursed the DJ under my breath while I used the wall to help me to return to standing. Clumsily I attempted to take a few steps back in the direction of Doctor Attila when I suddenly realized I had been laid out right in front of that damned closet door.

The sight of that horrible place had distracted me to the point of not noticing I was no longer alone in that hallway. A familiar pop rang out and then a voice that always had brought me joy called out to me, "There you are, Mad Maxx. We've been looking all over this dump for you. Don't you even try to run you bad boy. You're Auntie has a few words, she'd like to say to you, and you are going to listen to them, like it or not."

I stood there staring in dumbfounded confusion while the queen Jacob and his lover Jager approached me with furious expressions on their faces. A frog of fear had taken residence in my throat and was strangling my voice box. I wanted to run away before my best friend in the whole world had a chance to tongue lash me for the cruelty I'd demonstrated to him and Jager.

But I seemed frozen to the spot, unable to do anything but wait for him to unleash his fury. The truth is, Meine Liebe, I wanted to remember only good experiences with this wonderful man. My terror at hearing his complaints that he had the right to lodge at me were from a place of total selfishness on my part. I just didn't want it to end between us with hurt feelings, ja. Okay obviously the feelings I didn't want injured were my own. Otherwise Jacob wouldn't be seeking me out to raise hell, ja?

Well, Jacob and Jager arrived too quickly for me to rethink my plan to escape them. Jager glared at me and Jacob crossed his skinny arms encased in a sweater in his pink signature color. I dropped my head to stare at my boots while Jacob tapped the toe of his pink, chunky, heeled, frau shoes as if he were pissed.

Finally, Jacob popped his tongue and said, "I wish to say some things, Maxx, but I desire to do this privately. Jager, baby. Maxx and I are going to hold a meeting in this frightful closet. Would you be a dear and guard the door? I don't wish to be interrupted, nor is what I have to say for ears other than his."

He frowned then glanced at Jacob as he said, "Are you sure you will be alright, honey? You already know I don't try to tell you what to do. However, if you do this, remember to make it short. We leave in less than thirty minutes."

Jacob replied as he nodded and put his hand on his hip while popping his tongue, "Oh, you bet your sweet ass this kitty can handle this little mouse. I'll be right back Jager. Don't you fret over it. Maxx, after you. And don't you even try to give me any shit about it. You know damned well you have this coming over what you've done to us."

I kept my gaze to the floor while I nodded slightly. Then without further hesitation I opened the closet door and motioned him to follow me inside. Jacob closed it behind us and then let out his breath while running his eyes up and down my flesh. Then he said, "Honey, I've spent hours trying to think of what I wish to say to you. But when it comes to you, my beloved. I'm never able to find words strong enough…to…to." Jacob's voice broke and he began to weep so badly he couldn't speak.

I immediately rushed toward him and took him into my arms. He reached his arms around my waist and held me tightly in his grip while he sobbed for several minutes.

Then softly I whispered into his ear, "Danke, Jacob for always being there for me. It breaks my heart to know that when you needed the favor returned, you didn't seek me out for it. Luckily, I discovered the secret you were hiding before it was too late. I'm a cursed man with many nightmares to torment me day and night. But the one terror I'll never had to endure is watching helplessly while the only man I have ever truly loved burned at the stake for being the angel he truly is."

Jacob sniffled loudly then whispered back, "Christian, I didn't tell you because I thought there was nothing you could do about it. Baby, please believe me when I say the only thing that I will miss about this Haus is seeing you. The only thing I fear is that I'll never see you again. And the only thing I regret is that I will never be able to pay you back for the amazing gift of life that you've given to me and Jager."

I pulled back slightly from our hug and looked deep into Jacob's eyes. "Once a long time ago, you gave me the same gift my love. If not for you, I'd never have been able to break my bat collar. Oh, beloved, you paid me back already and so many times since then you have been there trying to protect me."

Jacob shook his head nein. "Honey, I didn't save you. Look at your face. They beat you, torture you, and rape you and there was never a God damned thing I could do to stop them. You have no idea how many nights I've laid awake crying. I've been useless to prevent the evil these monsters do to you. Now, I must leave you behind. Oh, my God, who will protect you? I just can't go and leave you here to suffer all alone."

I replied with a bitter chuckle, "Auntie, listen to me. Your sacrifice brought me the chance to live a life of choice, but it was never a guarantee that I could live that life the way I wanted to live it. I've arranged for you and Jager to escape this hellish place, but what happens after you land in Tahiti isn't something I can control. Maybe you two will be able to find happiness that I could not or maybe like me you will fail. There is absolutely nothing I can do about it, nor can I protect you out there in the big world. See, the exchange of favors between us is equal. All I can do, like you, is hope that fate is kind and that one day we will be reunited, but not in this life, I'm afraid."

Jacob said with a loud sob, "Don't say that, Christian. I won't listen to it. I can't let you go. I just can't."

I leaned down and lightly kissed his pink glossed lips. Then I said softly, "You must go, beloved. Jacob Wagner is dead. He was a good man with a beautiful heart and clean soul. That means, he went to Heaven. In that beautiful place, the skies are always blue, and the weather always warm. Gorgeous men run naked in the white sands and Jacob sips pink drinks while sunning next to his Mann Jager, ja? He will never suffer the ravages of age and will remain perfect, unblemished. He will always be forever young in my memory. Did I ever tell you that I loved Jacob more than I could ever tell him? But now that he is free of this hell he finally knows the depth of my heart."

Jacob gasped softly and closed his tear drenched eyes. The he replied, "Jacob did know it, Christian. And he will never forget you nor stop loving you no matter how long he must wait for you to join him in Heaven. Please, before Jager comes in here to take me away. We met for the first time in this awful closet. It's fate that this is where we say farewell. I want to remember this moment with you for the rest of my life, the second most perfect date of my life. Would you dance with me? Oh, how I wish it were to the sound of music, I want so badly to sway with this beautiful man in my arms one last time."

I said while nodding. "There is an old radio behind you on the shelf. We can try to find a station playing something worth dancing to."

Jacob popped his tongue and broke from my hold to retrieve the dusty machine. He placed it on the table that I endured too many assaults to count and turned it on.

As fate would have it, the song Nights in White Satin began to echo through the air. Jacob gasped then looked at me as he said, "Ah, this is the song that Leo loves so much. I've never understood anything the man is saying but the tune is beautiful. Leo says it's a love song. This is perfect, ja? Wait, would it be wrong to have my last request granted to the sounds of this music that honestly belongs to you and Leo?"

I took Jacob back into my arms and began to slow dance with him while I replied sourly, "I don't love Leo anymore, Auntie. He was going to let you and Jager burn, and he did nothing to end the kinder killings. That man is not any better than Jonas, or Peter, or Lucus or me."

The queen Jacob halted his swaying and glared at me for a moment before he said softly, "Christian, what you've just said is wrong in so many ways that I've not got the time left to explain it. I know you wouldn't listen to me anyway. So, before it's too late, I beg you to grant me one final favor and I will give you a promise in return. This is how it is done around here, ja?"

I replied with a nod, "Ja, that is the correct protocol. Name your prize and price, beloved, and I'll do my best to see it done."

Jacob said while he gazed into my eyes with tender affection, "Once I'm gone, go to Leo. Hear him out. Do this with an open heart for me. Christian, Leo is a good man. This Haus is the problem, not him. If you will do this for me, I promise when you have married, I will come to meet your beautiful frau."

I replied with a snort, "Ah, but that promise isn't fair, Jacob. You know damned well no woman would ever have me, even if Lucus permitted me to woo one. But, because I don't want to say goodbye with irritation between us, I will accept your favor exchange. If only to keep the hope alive that one they I will see you again."

Jacob's eyes filled with fresh rain as he said, "There is one more request I wish to make. Is Felicity with you? I want to say goodbye to her properly."

I felt the mother lamb struggling in my pocket. She was bleating with anxiousness over the fear that she would lose this chance to gaze upon her hero one more time. I reached into my pocket and handed Felicity to Jacob.

He put her up to his face and smiled sweetly at her while he said softly, "You've always been my favorite because you brought this gorgeous man into my life. Danke, Felicity for everything. My gift to you is the taste of my lip gloss that you've loved so much."

Jacob kissed Felicity and rubbed her on his wet cheek gently. The music wafted through the air while Jacob cuddled me and Felicity in his arms for several more minutes. Silence fell between us, but the unspoken understanding of our connection strengthened our bond for the last time.

Then at last, the door opened. Jager came into the closet nodding to Jacob that our time was up. They needed to leave in a hurry or they would miss their only chance to escape.

Jacob wept silently while he leaned in and kissed me. I felt his hand press something into mine just before he broke from our lip lock. I watched him walk towards Jager, slowly, and without his usual bouncy step. His melancholy at having to leave me behind was more than a little obvious.

Jager approached me and held out his hand in the gesture to shake mine as he said softly, "Thank you for everything, Your Majesty. Try not to worry. I promise I'll take good care of him for the rest of our lives however long or short that may be. For what it's worth, I'll always think of you fondly and as my true friend. Take care of yourself. And if you manage to escape this hell hole. Come visit us in Tahiti. We will always have a place set at our table for you in the hope that one day you'll join us."

I replied while nodding, "I'll sleep better at night knowing Jacob has you to lean on. Maybe one day I will find my way to your home. Good luck to you both. Write if you can. Hopefully Lucus will allow me to have the letters."

Jacob wailed out while sobbing, "I'll send you a letter every day, Christian. You'll know he's hiding them because your Auntie has never told you lies."

I chuckled and said, "I know. I'll be looking forward to the mail from this day forward. Goodbye Auntie. God speed and I hope Heaven is everything you always dreamed it would be."

Jager put his arm around Jacob. He had to drag him out of the closet. I could hear Jacob's sounds of sorrow for several minutes echoing down the hallway.

While I listened to his cries, I glanced down into the palm of my hand, curious to see what Jacob had placed there. A gasp of true agony escaped my throat. It was a tube of Jacob's favorite lip gloss. On it he'd written: For Felicity.

I fell to my knees and covered my face with my bandaged hands and wept harder than I'd ever cried before.

I'd had rather suffered a thousand whippings, cutters and rapes than have let Jacob go. He was the light in my darkness. The joy in my despair. The color in my ugly, drab world.

Now that he was gone forever, I didn't think I could go on. And oh, Meine Liebe, the price I had to pay to set him free was horrific but I've never regretted it. Knowing that the Haus could never hurt Jacob was worth it, all of it and more.

So, I cried like a baby there on that closet floor unable to find a reason to get up and try to save myself from infection by visiting the doctor. But, like always, the reason came looking for me. The door was slightly ajar and it was easy to see me laying there bawling.

Not long after Jacob and Jager had left, Byron discovered my hiding place. He yelled out while flinging the door open wide, "Lucus, he's here. Hurry up dammit."

I gasped in terror while I did my best to back away from the towering frame of my brute brother.

He chuckled low, "I'd be blubbering too if I had the ass kicking you've got coming for daring to piss on me, Maxx."

I replied in a whimper while shaking my head, "I didn't do it, Byron. Taube did it."

He snorted loudly, "Crazy mother fucker. Well, no matter. I told you I'd have you like a dog on my leash, ja? Well, puppers, here comes daddy with that restraining device just as I promised."

Lucus rushed into the room, and I noticed immediately he was holding that God damned leash in his hands. I attempted to rise to my boots, but Byron came at me too fast to escape him. He held me to the spot while Lucus attached the golden chain to my collar and locked it in place.

Once he had me securely fastened, he said in a relieved sounding tone while he wiped the sweat from his brow, "Danke for the help finding him, Byron. If you'd be so kind, would you mind traveling with us while I return his majesty to our apartment?"

Byron smile widened. "It's my honored duty to guard his majesty's royal person. Lead the way honorable Lucus. I'll be right behind you."

I whimpered in fear but was helpless to stop Lucus from dragging me behind him without inciting further violence from Byron.

That didn't stop me from arguing my case. "Wait, please, Lucus, I need to visit Doctor Attila. Besides, our contract states you have no authority over me until nine tonight."

Lucus replied while chuckling and taking the slack from his rein, "I've already contacted the doctor. He'll be by in a few hours to attend your wounds. In the meantime, I believe you've forgotten that our contract has changed substantially since we renegotiated it. Jacob and Jager are off to Tahiti and your false visit with Jonas last night is over. I've agreed to welcome Mercy into our home. So that means my side of our bargain is complete, ja? So, time to pay up what you owe, my little lamb. Come along politely or Byron will make sure you comply in a way I doubt you'll appreciate."

I snuck a glance at Byron and saw that he was itching to have a reason to pound on me some more. I wisely decided not to start a fight with Lucus about this, at least not right at that moment.

As the three of us traveled through the hallways of the Haus, I noticed many of the residents were practically running past us in a hurry. I was unaware of the cause of such exciting commotion. Byron and Lucus appeared to be oblivious to this odd behavior or they didn't seem to care.

When we arrived at the foot of the main staircase, I turned my attention to the growing crowd gathering around the front door guards.

It was then I saw the Haus exit wide open. For a moment, the bright sunlight flooded into the entry of that perpetually dark place. The blue skies were a stark contrast to the ancient brown wood of the doors. Everyone in the gathered mass started shouting wishes for safe travel and offering bids of good luck.

My heart broke in half as I saw the image of Jacob and Jager walking out the door into the light where they seemed to shine briefly and then disappear off to Heaven.

I dropped my tear foggy gaze to the floor and followed the leash up the staircase behind Lucus. Byron held up the rear, ready to make damned sure that I paid the price for daring to set decent men free.

To be continued in book five entitled
"Mortar Combat" of
The Most Brutal Man in Europe Series

About the Author: Alexandria May Ausman

Alexandria May Ausman in her 16th year was diagnosed with Schizophrenia. She was quickly abandoned by her foster parents. While still only a teen, she was forced to battle this devastating illness alone.

Alexandria has struggled with lack of a support system, numerous psychotic episodes, exploitation, homelessness, and an uncaring mental health system.

Alexandria raised two healthy children. After obtaining her bachelor's degree in psychology she worked as a child abuse investigator and became a diagnostic psychologist while acquiring her Master's in psychology. Alexandria never forgot the experience of 'slipping through the cracks.' Her life's goal is to help people suffering abuse and/or mental illness have access to necessary services. By accident, she became a model of 'gothic attire' and the World Goth Queen.

She began writing a fictionalized account of her life experiences after a catastrophic return of psychotic symptoms. Today, Alexandria is retired, and homebound due to crippling symptoms of Schizophrenia. She currently lives in Tallahassee, Florida, with her loving husband and a loyal support dog.

www.ingramcontent.com/pod-product-compliance
Lightning Source LLC
LaVergne TN
LVHW020651110826
845149LV00012B/1962

9781963335606